PRAISE FOR KRISTOPHER RUFTY

Bigfoot Beach

KRISTOPHER RUFTY

Bigfoot Beach
Paperback Edition
Copyright © 2015 by Kristopher Rufty
Cover Art Copyright © 2015

For my son and daughter—your boundless imaginations inspire my own.

PROLOGUE

They'd only been walking for fifteen minutes and Ethan was ready to wrap up this late night beach stroll. With a crisp wind coming from the ocean, it felt as if someone was dumping invisible buckets of ice water on his bare back.

Mackenzie, walking beside him and smiling, had a slight bounce in her gait. The cool night didn't seem to bother her, so he'd pretend to be fine as well, ignoring the stiffening of his skin as goosebumps rose.

"Such a *gorgeous* night, huh?" she said, gazing at the softly lapping waves to their right.

Ethan tried to see what she was talking about. All he could distinguish were oily black crashes that fizzed like spilled soda across his feet. Maybe at sunset it would have been gorgeous. Right now, it was a waste of time, unless she'd brought him out here to screw around.

Fat chance.

She hadn't even hinted of being interested in him in that way and he'd spent almost the whole day with her. Maybe now she would. Why else would she have asked him to come along?

Might just want to walk and didn't want to be alone.

Knowing his luck, Ethan figured that was probably it.

"Yes," he lied. "My favorite kind of night."

Mackenzie's arm brushed his. She had moved closer to him, so much so that whenever their arms swayed, they bumped.

1

She wouldn't do that unless she wanted me to put my arm around her.

He gave it a try and was surprised to feel her snuggling closer.

Smiling, Mackenzie leaned her head on his shoulder. Her body radiated the scent of suntan lotion from a full day of being caked in it. Her curly hair was even bigger and springier from the salty air. Her skin looked painted in butter, except for the pale triangles over her breasts and the wedge at the crotch and rump from her bikini.

Still hesitant of trying anything, he figured it might be best to wait until he knew without any doubt she wouldn't reject him. She was still teetering on the friendship ledge, but if it looked like she was going to slip, he would catch her by shoving his tongue in her mouth.

Just play it cool.

"I've always loved the beach," she said. "And night swims are the best."

"Night swims?"

"Yes! Don't you just *love* swimming at night?"

"Uh..." Maybe in a swimming pool, he did, even the lake. Not the ocean. Although he was starting college in the fall, he was in no way an expert in oceanography. But he'd learned plenty from his parents and the *Jaws* series.

You never swim close to the piers and you definitely don't swim at night. Sharks feed at night.

He was about to share this information with Mackenzie, but it slipped away from him when she pulled his arm down, gripped his hand.

"Yes," he lied again. "Night swims are the *best!*"

"Yay!" She jumped up and down, her breasts bouncing behind the hardly existent top. "I knew you were my kind of guy!"

"I am?"

She squeezed his hand. "You're surprised?"

"Well..." He shrugged his shoulders. "Yeah, honestly."

"I bet so. You totally weren't picking up any of my signals today."

If her signals were the complete avoidance of him most of the day, then he completely missed it. He'd quickly become privy to Glen's matchmaking attempts before they'd even left for the beach yesterday. Glen, his best friend since freshman year, had invited him to his dad's beach house. Ethan had politely declined the offer, not wanting to be the third wheel to Glen and Jackie's weeklong bonefest. After Glen's pleading hadn't worked, he'd finally fessed up and told the truth. Jackie was bringing her cousin, Mackenzie, and they thought Ethan would be the perfect guy for her.

Ethan wasn't looking for flings. Even with school coming, he wanted a girlfriend. Jackie told him Mackenzie was going to be attending college in their hometown, the same college Ethan would be attending. And she would be staying with Jackie until she could afford her own place. Such an idea had enthralled Ethan. A girl with her *own* place. The possibilities were unlimited. Finally, he'd agreed to go.

Since arriving late yesterday, Mackenzie had barely acknowledged he was on this trip. Their longest exchange was during dinner tonight at Krispy Krust Pizza. She'd started talking about her detestation for Quentin Tarantino movies, and he'd quickly jumped on that rant with her.

He'd thought a bond was formed, but he wasn't willing to put any wagers on it.

But now…?

Have to see how things go.

"I guess I'm not good at noticing signals, signs, hints…"

"So, I have to be pretty blunt then?" she asked.

"With me, yeah."

"I'll keep that in mind. Don't want you to miss what I'm trying to say."

"The best way to ensure that doesn't happen is by *saying* what you're trying to say."

Laughing, Mackenzie stopped walking. She raised his hand to her mouth. "How's this?" She formed her lips around the tip of his finger, gently pulling it into her mouth. Then she slowly bobbed her head, flicking the underside of his finger with her tongue.

Ethan felt stirring behind the netting of his swimming trunks. He didn't have the room to expand down there, nor did he want to move so he could adjust. He liked this too much.

After several long seconds of sucking, Mackenzie pulled her head back, unveiling a slobber-drenched finger, and lowered his hand. In the blue hue of the moonlight, he could see the teasing expression on her face—the arched eyebrow, the smirking.

Knowing there was no need for anymore hints, he reached behind her head, slipping his fingers into its curly thickness. He pulled her to him and kissed her. She raised a leg around his, running her foot down the back of his calf. He slid his hand behind her thigh, and squeezed. The skin under his fingers was slick and smooth, almost too slippery to hold.

Then his hands invaded her. Groping and pawing, there wasn't a section of her exposed skin he didn't touch. She felt so slick, so warm. His hands glided across her.

"Um…" Mackenzie tried to talk through the kisses.

"Yeah…?"

Their lips wouldn't stop smacking.

"Slow down," she said.

"Wha…?"

"Slow down. Not so fast."

Ethan stopped kissing her and looked down. He found one of his hands had snuck under the padding of her bikini top and was cupping a breast. His thumb was frozen on her rigid nipple. The other hand was down the back of her bottoms, gripping a buttock.

"Whoa," he said, carefully removing his hands. "I am *so* sorry…."

Mackenzie laughed softly. "It's okay."

"I didn't even mean to…" He shrugged. "I don't know what to say. I feel like an ass."

"It's *fine*." She stepped back, adjusting her top so it covered the pale mound of exposed breast, the dark dot of her nipple. "We have all week for that. I don't want to ruin anything by moving *too* fast."

"My God, me either. I just sort of *went* there."

"I saw that."

"Force of habit, I guess."

As soon as the words had left his mouth, he regretted having said them.

"Habit?" she said.

"Not that I mean…well…what I'm saying is…" Sweating, he had no clue how to fix this.

Mackenzie smiled, but gone was the cute playfulness, the eagerness. "I know what you meant."

Ethan's arms dropped by his sides. He sighed.

No you don't. I don't even know what I mean.

4

"Still up for that swim?" she asked.

"No thanks…"

"What? Why not?"

"I've done enough damage tonight. Think I'll head back to the house and let you enjoy your night."

"Are you sulking?"

"Sulk…?"

Mackenzie shook her head. "Sorry. Are you pouting?"

"No!" As he crossed his arms and turned away from her, he realized that was *exactly* what he was doing.

Mackenzie laughed behind him. "You're so damn cute."

Glancing back at her from over his shoulder, he raised his eyebrows. "Yeah?"

"Yeah."

"I think the dark is just playing tricks on your eyes."

"Maybe. Still, you're cute."

"You're not so bad yourself."

"Well, thank you, kind sir." She spun around on the sand, putting her back to him.

"What are you doing?"

Walking toward the sloshing blackness, she glanced back. "Getting in the water."

"Don't you think…it's a little dangerous?"

"What?"

"You know. Sharks."

"Oh please. There aren't any sharks here. Area's too populated for that."

That's a load of bull…

As he looked around and confirmed there was no population other than two in the area at the moment, he heard the splashes of waves being trampled. He looked at the ocean. Mackenzie vanished in the murky water up to her knees. Once it reached her hips, she put her hands together in front of her and dived.

Damn.

A few seconds later, the dim smudge of Mackenzie's head thrashed to the surface. Screaming, she slapped at the water. "It's got me!"

"Oh, shit!"

5

Ethan ran for the water as Mackenzie's wails carried on in agonizing descants. He kicked off his sandals before his feet met the water. "What's wrong?!"

"It huurrrrrts!"

I knew it! I fucking knew it!

A shark. He knew they fed at night. It wasn't something he'd fabricated in his mind. He'd *learned* it. From where, he couldn't remember.

The water was cold as it wrapped around his shins. The ocean climbed his body, and he quickly overcame its chilly shock. Then he launched himself forward, knifing through the water, paddling wildly as Mackenzie started to sink. His arms broke the water, whirled, then slapped down again. Stinging splashes hit his eyes.

Finally he reached Mackenzie. Head barely above the water, she moaned. He hugged his arms around her waist. As he started to pull, she wrapped her arms around his neck and brushed her lips against his. He felt her tongue fighting its way into his mouth.

"Wait…" he said.

She was all over him, kissing, groping, squeezing. He tried to pull away from her hold. He couldn't. His feet found purchase in the soft sand, and he stood up straight. The water dropped down to his chest, making little drippy sounds as more cascaded down his shoulders and chest.

He felt Mackenzie's legs wrap around his waist, her crotch pushing tightly against his.

A trick.

Mackenzie's smile poked through the darkness in a block of white. "My hero."

"What the *hell*, Mackenzie?"

"If that didn't get you in the water…"

"That wasn't funny. I thought you were in trouble."

"I could've been, and you still rushed out here to save me."

"Dammit!"

"Don't get angry. You showed me that you're brave enough to fight a shark for me. That takes a certain kind of man, in my opinion."

Ethan wanted to be mad, but several things kept him from successfully pulling it off. For one, Mackenzie's wet body was pressed against his. All that separated them from each other were his thin trunks and the wispy material of her bikini. Another reason was she was too damn cute and charming to *stay* mad at. "Oh yeah?"

"Big time. My man came to save me." She shook her head.

Her man.

He liked how that sounded. But at the back of his mind, there was doubt that Mackenzie was emotionally stable where it mattered. Before he could say anything else, she was kissing him again. Her hands released their grip from his neck. They delved into the water. He felt her fingers pushing at the elastic band of his trunks. Finally, she shoved them down, unleashing his penis. It bobbed in the water, stiff and ready.

Now would be the time a jellyfish would swim by.

Ethan stopped that thought. That was something he didn't need, paranoid thoughts ruining this moment.

Mackenzie's hands moved away from his trunks. He could feel them bumping his stomach as she rose slightly, digging at something. She pulled to the side. Wondering what she was doing, it made sense when she lowered back down, impaling herself. She'd pulled her bikini bottoms to the side, out of the way. The lower she came, the higher he pushed into her.

Mackenzie leaned her head back, moaning. "Damn. So much for waiting."

"We suck."

Laughing, Mackenzie raised her head. "Yep—oh shit!" She tensed up. He felt the heat in her skin wash away with the gentle ocean waves.

"Wha…what's wrong?"

"Someone's watching us," she said in a harsh whisper.

Ethan laughed. He didn't attempt to lower his voice. "Nice try." He attempted to thrust, but the constrictive grip of her thighs prevented him from moving.

"Seriously," she said. She wasn't looking at him. Her eyes were focused over his left shoulder, wide and scared in the moonlight.

"Look," he said, "if you don't want to do anything, we don't have to."

"I'm not playing a goddamn joke on you. *Look!*" She slapped the back of his neck.

Trying not to show her how bad the smack had stung, he turned his body, moving her with him so he could look. At first, he didn't notice anything wrong. He could see the pale slopes of the dunes in the distance, the weeds sticking through like shady noodles. The moon washed the area in a dim smolder, making the darks even darker, and the sand like white flaky carpet. Once his eyes adjusted to the change in light, he began to make out a shape at the shoreline. A *big* shape. Looked like he was wearing heavy tattered clothes. Long hair fluttered in the breeze.

"See him?" Mackenzie asked.

"Yeah…"

"Who do you think it is? Think it's a cop?"

"Doubt it. Looks like a bum."

"Why do you say that?"

"How he's dressed."

"You can see that far in the dark?"

"Well…no, not really. I mean, he's wearing way too much heavy clothing to be someone out on a stroll."

"Then why's he just standing there?"

"Probably heard you screaming earlier."

"Me and my stupid ideas."

"What happened to me being the hero?"

"Oh, shut up."

Ethan tried not to let that comment bother him, but it did. "Anyway, don't worry. I doubt he can see us."

"The hell you say. It's not *that* dark out here. I bet he can see plenty."

Ethan supposed she was right. Where the moon was positioned behind the man, it darkened him into a black cutout, but threw a glowing curtain of ripples onto the water. "What do you want me to do?"

"Make him leave."

"I'm kind of…" He gave his hips a little thrust. "In the middle of something."

Mackenzie tensed at his prodding. Her fingers dug into his back. "As much as I *like* you being in the middle of something, I am *not* comfortable putting on a show."

Ethan heaved a sigh. "Me either."

"So make him leave."

"All right." He started to pull out, but stopped when Mackenzie squeezed him. "What?"

"Don't leave me out here!"

"Well, dammit, Mackenzie, you're not giving me very many options."

"Hey, asshole!"

Ethan flinched at her sudden shout. For a moment he thought it'd been directed at him, but realized it was meant for their spectator. Looking back to the shoreline, he saw the large head tilt slightly.

"He heard you," said Ethan.

"How could he not?"

Ethan cleared his throat, and smiled nervously. "You can go on now, sir. We were just fooling around, you know. No one's in any trouble."

The man continued to stand there.

"What's his fucking *deal?*" Mackenzie asked.

"I don't know…" Ethan couldn't ignore the twinge of fear in his stomach. He felt himself starting to withdraw from Mackenzie, shrinking. "Maybe we should leave."

"Good idea. We can take a shower when we get back to the house."

"Together?"

Mackenzie gave him a little pinch on the arm. "You know it."

That perked his spirits a tad, though not much. He pulled away from Mackenzie, reached into the water, and tugged his trunks up. Mackenzie stooped in the water to her chin, shoulders swaying as she worked to fix her briefs.

"Ready?" he asked.

She nodded once. "Ready."

Something brushed Ethan's hand. He gritted his teeth to hold in the scream. When he felt Mackenzie's fingers slipping between his, he relaxed.

Would've looked like an idiot.

"Why don't we just make our way over there?" said Mackenzie, referencing toward the left. "Walk down a little ways."

"Away from him?"

"Exactly."

"Sounds good to me." Then he remembered their shoes on the shore.

Forget them. The tide will carry them away.

9

They worked against the current, moving to the left. Waves tapped Ethan's side, sprinkling cool water across his chest. Sand shifted under his feet, making him dip and stumble.

"Son of a bitch," gasped Mackenzie.

Ethan didn't need to ask what had her upset. He looked toward the shore and saw the large shape was moving with them. He walked slightly leaning forward, shoulders slouching as long arms dangled by his knees.

My God...his hands...

The fingers were elongated chubby digits the size of humorous cigars from a gag shop. Balls of knuckles jutted up, gnarling the fingers into deformed slices.

"He's following us," said Mackenzie

"Uh-huh..." He tugged her arm. "Come on."

"I'm trying."

A stronger wave knocked into them, shoving Mackenzie against Ethan. Both of them dipped into the water. Salt water deluged his eyes, burning and blinding. "Damn!" He rubbed his eyes with his forearm, only achieving to spread even more water into his eyes.

His eyes felt sore and strained as he blinked the water away. Finally, he could somewhat see again. As if looking through a blurred camera lens, he scanned the shoreline.

The figure was gone.

"Mackenzie?"

"Huh?"

"Is he gone?"

He felt Mackenzie turn. "I don't see him."

"Are you sure? I got water in my eyes and can hardly see shit."

A moment of silence, then, "No. He's not there."

"Good."

"Let's go," she said, tugging him forward, towards the shore.

"Where do you think he went?"

"I don't care, so long as he's gone."

The ground under their feet felt like soggy oatmeal as they trampled over it, pulling Ethan down to his ankle. He yanked on his leg to extricate himself.

Finally, the water level started to drop. Subtly at first, the water sank to his abdomen. It went away to his crotch. Another couple steps and he was exposed to his knees. Then he could only feel the retracting fluxes under his feet as the tide pulled the water back into the ocean.

Bending at the waist, Ethan put his hands on his knees and breathed. He was more winded than he wanted to be, proving to himself how much he'd neglected exercise this year. Water dribbled down from his body, leaving shallow dots in the sand.

A breeze drifted across his wet skin, feeling like cold tongues licking.

He felt Mackenzie's hand on his back. Her nails poked him.

"Ouch! You've got some sharp nails."

Then he noticed Mackenzie standing off to his left, retying the knot of her bikini strap at her hip. She glanced at him. "What were you saying…?" Her words petered out as her lips started to quiver. Eyes rounding, she raised her arm, pointing.

A horrible odor like a dead fish soaked in skunk spray wafted through the salty air. It brought tears to Ethan's eyes, gagging him.

What the hell's behind me?

Ethan slowly turned around. His eyes landed on a hairy chest with thick pectoral muscles bulging like two furry boulders.

Ethan slowly looked up.

He opened his mouth to scream.

Giant hands clamped each side of his face, wrenching his head around in one quick spin of splintery cracks. Ethan could see Mackenzie again, stumbling backward. Her feet became entangled and she tripped, landing hard on her rump.

Ethan knew his head had been twisted around. But other than the first quick burst of popping bone, there was no pain. His legs folded, dropping forward, but to Ethan it felt as if he was falling backward.

The massive thing stepped around him, heading for Mackenzie. Its feet made heavy punching sounds in the wet sand. As the thing scooped up Mackenzie and tossed her over its shoulder, Ethan dropped onto his side.

It ran down the shoreline. Mackenzie, screaming for Ethan to help, pounded the undulating hairy back with her fists. Then the shadows swallowed them. Mackenzie's shrieks slowly faded.

The last image his brain processed was the giant, humanoid footprint in the sand.

CHAPTER 1

"There's not going to be any girls there if everybody's gone home already," Gunner said.

Paul Thompson looked at his son in the rearview mirror. The kid was a duplication of himself at seventeen, save their hairstyles. The teenaged Paul had worn his hair shaggy around the ears and front, slightly long in the back—not quite a mullet, but close. Though Gunner's hair was a tad lengthy, he kept it mostly neat, which Paul was thankful for.

"There's going to be *local* girls," said Paul. "Those are much better."

"What makes them better, Daddy?" asked Natalie from her booster seat. She was on the right of the 4Runner's backseat, and had been gazing at the undulant waves of the ocean beyond the sandy fields for the last several miles.

Giving his eight-year-old daughter a glance in the mirror, Paul felt that familiar lump in his throat. She was such a pretty little girl, who'd grow up to become beautiful. Boys already threw themselves at her feet, volunteering to do whatever she wanted. Sometimes she used her natural gift to her benefit if someone had a snack she wanted, or if a Mom had sent chocolate milk with lunch or pudding for dessert. Her hair was the longest it ever had been, hanging well past her shoulders in golden waves. If Alisha was here, she'd find the next stylist on the way and make them stop.

Alisha.

Paul released a ragged sigh. He couldn't let his mind drift to Alisha, and his worries of how she's holding up, already.

"Daddyyy?" The impatient tone in her voice was followed by the smack of a tiny hand on her knee.

"Well…Gunner will tell you."

Natalie looked at Gunner, her eyes widening as the eager smile curled her mouth.

Shaking his head, Gunner said, "I can't if I don't even know the answer."

Paul laughed. "Fine. Local girls are here to stay. So they're not pretending to be someone else for a few days during their fantasy getaway. You know what kind of girl you're getting without all the games."

Gunner was quiet as Natalie snickered. Paul waited for Gunner's response, but after a couple minutes, he understood he wasn't getting one. Gunner had finally said something after two hours of silence only to shut up again after two comments.

Better than nothing.

Paul turned on the radio. He pushed the seek button and waited for the receiver to pick up something. A song by the Beach Boys came on. "Awesome!" Snapping his fingers, Paul glanced into the backseat. "Sing along!"

Grimacing, Gunner shook his head. Natalie laughed, clapping with the beat. Though she was off-rhythm, Paul was glad to have her in the band.

Paul butchered the words to "Surfin' U.S.A.", but Natalie didn't notice. If Gunner did, he gave no mention of it, for that would call for him to stop staring out the window. Paul detected the sadness and regret forcing the frown on his son's face, because he felt the same way.

Up ahead on the right, Paul spotted the town sign. A giant seashell welcomed them in, the town's name displayed between wooden palm trees.

"We're here!" he called.

"Yay!" said Natalie, clapping.

The announcement pulled Gunner from the window. Lowering his head to see through the windshield, his frown seemed to dip lower.

"What's wrong?" asked Paul.

14

"I thought you were joking when you said the name of the town we're moving to was Seashell Cove."

"Nope. I'm not *that* funny."

"Wow." Sighing, Gunner collapsed against the seat. "Wonderful."

"Come on, Gunner. What's wrong with the name?"

"What isn't? Sounds gay—goofy." He glanced at his sister, slightly worried.

"No, it doesn't. And watch your mouth."

"Bigfoot Beach," said Natalie. "Daddy, what's that mean?"

"Bigfoot what?" he asked.

"Bigfoot Beach. That's what it said on that big sign back there." Gunner laughed.

Confused, Paul looked in the rearview mirror, as if he might be able to see the sign himself. Of course, he couldn't now that he'd left it behind. "What sign, baby?"

"It was a big yellow sign back there."

"Hmm. Interesting."

He wondered what it actually had said for his daughter to have misinterpreted it so badly.

"Red light," said Gunner.

"Huh?"

"Red light."

Paul faced the front and saw the stoplight. The top circle blazed red. "Shit!" He stomped the brake. The tires screeched as they bounced to a halt. Thankfully there were no cars in front of him, or he'd have rear-ended them for sure. The tangy stink of burning rubber wafted inside the cab.

"Not even residents for a full minute and you almost perform a traffic violation?" asked Gunner. "Terrible first impression for the soon-to-be deputy."

Paul's heart pounded. Hands gripping the steering wheel so fiercely, his knuckles were white. "Not now, Gunner."

"Just pointing out…"

"I don't think you need to point it out. We all saw what happened."

"Your nearly running a red light?"

Because Paul was happy to have his son finally talking, he ignored his snarky tone. "Well, I don't claim to be the most attentive driver, but—"

A giant furry head crashed onto the hood of the car, eclipsing most of the windshield.

The abrupt landing cut off Paul's words, making him jump in his seat and throw both arms out as if to shield his children behind him. The lifeless gray eyes inside the massive head seemed to stare through him. Its face was almost human-like, with an ape's nose, and dingy black hair stirring in the breeze. The crooked mouth was full of dull teeth, and a bloated tongue canted to the side.

Natalie screamed first, Gunner followed. Then Paul joined them. With the Thompsons screaming in three different timbres, Paul barely heard the car honking from behind to alert him the light had changed.

A hand knocking on the passenger window caught Paul's attention. His scream ebbed to a soft whine in the back of his throat. An old man leaned down, gazing into the car through the glass. He wore a wide-brimmed khaki hat, the kind a gardener might have on to keep the sun off his neck. His eyes were squinted blue streaks on a heavily tanned face rutted with wrinkles. Teeth so perfect they had to be dentures showed behind a pleasant smile.

"Hello there," he said, waving.

Paul cautiously raised his hand, offering a single stroke back.

"Gave you quite a start, huh?" His voice was muffled through the glass.

So was the blaring horn behind them.

"Um…" Paul looked in the rearview mirror, seeing the front of a car at his backside. Though there was a glare on the windshield, it wasn't so bright to block out the middle finger being thrust in his direction.

The old man gestured the car, signaling for them to go around. "Pull off to the side here, so I can take care of the mishap for you, if you don't mind. These damn tourists get a little impatient, especially when they want to pack up and leave."

A BMW pulled up beside him. The horn blared one last time, then the car sped off.

"Why's he so mean, Daddy?" asked Natalie.

"Probably needs to change his meds," Paul said.

16

Natalie wrinkled her nose. Clearly she didn't understand Paul's bland humor.

"Must not be enjoying his stay very much," said Gunner. "Can't say I blame him."

"Not now, Gunner."

Stepping away from the car, the old man motioned Paul over. He pointed at an empty parking spot in front of a row of buildings. Written in colorful paint on the window of the nearest one was an advertisement for discounted hermit crabs.

Paul cranked the wheel as far to the right it would go. He eased his foot down on the gas and slowly rolled into the parking space. He straightened out. When the tires bumped the curb, he put the gear in park. He started to shut off the engine, but decided to leave it on so the kids would have the A/C. "Stay in the car, guys."

"Come on, Dad," said Gunner, annoyed.

Paul sighed, nodding. "Fine. Hop on out. Natalie, sit tight, I'll come back there and—"

Natalie unfastened her seatbelt without any difficulty. It bothered Paul how easily she could do it on her own. Hopefully, she wouldn't do something dumb and unbuckle while he was driving.

"Gunner, help her out of the car."

"I am, Dad."

"Thanks."

Paul killed the engine, snatching the keys from the ignition. He climbed out, dropping the keys in a pocket of his cargo shorts. Gunner hopped out, reached back into the car, and assisted Natalie. They joined him on his side and, together, walked around to the front.

The old man was waiting for them on the sidewalk. He held his hand out to Paul. "I'm Quint Lingle."

"Paul Thompson."

The man nodded. "Thought you was. You look just like your brother."

"He's got a reputation as being good-looking, too?"

Quint laughed. "Never heard any complaints from the women."

Paul glanced at Gunner, expecting to see a beam of pride on his son's face. Instead, he got a grimace of slight nausea.

"Sorry about that," said Quint, pointing at the hood of the car. "Mind if I check the hood for damage?"

"No, not at all. If there's any damage, I'll trust you to handle it. We don't need to get any insurance companies involved."

Quint gave Paul a weird look on his way to the 4Runner. "I'm talking about the head," he said. "Took me a long time to put it together. Hopefully your gas-guzzler didn't damage it."

"Right," said Paul. "When it fell on my truck…"

Ignoring Paul, he approached the vehicle with a slight crouch. He started examining the fuzzy head.

"What is that thing?" asked Gunner.

"Oh, it's something I whipped up on the fly before the summer. It lasted longer than I thought it would. Noticed the head was starting to slouch a bit, and when I was up there trying to fix it, the damn thing just fell off."

Just as she usually did when someone cussed, Natalie gasped.

"Trying to fix what?" asked Gunner, a hint of eagerness in his voice.

Quint looked up and laughed. "Where's *my* head at?" Then he glanced at the monstrous head that was probably denting the hood, and laughed harder. "This head," patting the top of his hat, "not this one." Then he slapped the top of the other head.

Paul made himself laugh to be polite.

"I own the pawn shop right there," he said, pointing to the small shop to the left of the discounted hermit crabs window. "I put this up to attract tourists. It's supposed to be the head to that." He pointed over Paul's shoulder.

Tracing the path of Quint's finger, he saw the light post. Attached to the top of it was a large headless torso that resembled an ape. Its burly arms were extended out, hands gripping the post as if holding on. Its legs curled around the thick pole lower down.

"Is that the Bigfoot?" asked Natalie.

Quint laughed. "You've heard of it, too, huh?"

Natalie gave him a single nod. "I saw the sign back there."

"Ah, the sign. The Mayor's idea. You must be a very smart little girl if you can read such big words like that."

Natalie snorted. "I *am* eight, you know."

"Whoa, eight? You're almost in college!"

Giggling, Natalie's cheeks turned red.

Paul was about to ask, but Gunner beat him to it. "What do you mean by 'you've heard of it, too'?"

18

"Heard of our Bigfoot, our local celebrity. It's brought the tourists in like flies on shi—dookie." He made a strained face that was part wince and part panic.

Natalie cupped her hand over her mouth and made quacking sounds of laughter behind her palm.

"Big—what?" Paul shook his head. Surely he'd misunderstood what Quint said.

"Big—*foot.*"

Paul had heard him just fine. "Right."

Turning, Quint pointed at the building behind him, to a poster taped to the window. Reward was printed above a sketch of a humanoid character, smooth cheekbones and brow, hair covering the rest that hung down to its shoulders and neck. Quint looked back at Paul, his smile threatening to envelop his whole head. "See?"

"You've got to be kidding me."

"No, sir," said Quint, humorously. "Surprised your brother never told you about it. Aren't you our new deputy?"

"I am," said Paul.

"Maybe he thought it would have scared you off?"

Paul was about to say something else when the double chirp of a siren fired behind him. Looking to the road, he saw a sheriff's Suburban parking next to the 4Runner. He knew who it was even before the tall, lean man slipped out of the car and put his dark brown campaign hat on.

"Quint," called the sheriff, "you're not trying to sell my brother something from your shop are you?"

Laughing, Quint put both hands on his belly. "No, sir, Sheriff. Though, now that you mention it, I might have some video games this little princess here would be interested in."

"Uncle Howie!" squealed Natalie. Running over to the sheriff, she jumped into his arms and was scooped up. "I missed you!"

Uncle Howie, or as the residents of Seashell Cove knew him, Sheriff Thompson spun in a circle. Natalie's legs flew out behind her like a cape. "My goodness, girl, you've grown a foot since Christmas!"

"Nuh-uh!"

Paul tried not to feel the teeth of jealousy nipping at his insides, but it was hard to avoid them whenever it came to Howie. He was five years older than Paul, their parents' obvious favorite. He'd done better in school, had plenty of luck with women, but picked the right one in college and had been married to her ever since. They had three kids with only two years separating each. The youngest had just left for college, and the other two were living on their own. Plus, he was better looking, though Paul would never openly admit it. And his hair showed no hint of grey, while Paul's was growing more and more every day. When stubble appeared on his face, some of it was nearly white.

"Hey, Uncle Howard," said Gunner. Paul noticed the change in expression when Howie arrived, almost an admiring gleam.

But he couldn't allow those routine feelings to manifest, especially since it was Howie who'd arranged for them to come here.

"Hey, Gunner. Been working out?"

"A little."

That wasn't true, unless countless hours of playing Minecraft on his smart phone was exercise.

Howie nodded as he put Natalie down. "I can tell, getting leaner."

"Ha!" said Paul.

Heads turned to him, all looking upset, so he quickly acted as if he was struggling with a sneeze. "Sorry," said Paul. "Not used to the air here. Getting my allergies going."

"I've got some allergy pills in the shop for four bucks a box," offered Quint.

"Thanks, but I'll be okay, I'm sure."

"Well, if you change your mind."

Howie noticed the 4Runner and put his hands on his holster belt, slipping his thumbs behind the buckle. "What's this, Quint?"

"Oh, that's Big E's head. Damn thing fell off."

"Uh-huh. I told you it wouldn't hold up, didn't I?"

"Well, yeah, but I thought it would."

"It didn't."

"No, I guess not."

"Why don't we get it off my brother's truck?"

"Sounds good, Sheriff."

"I can help," said Paul.

Howie waved his hand. "No need. We've got this."

"I'll help, Uncle Howie," volunteered Gunner.

Paul was about to repeat Howie's riposte but Howie said, "Sure, Gunner. That's the kind of help we *definitely* need."

"Cool." Gunner joined them at the hood, taking the middle as Howie and Quint slid the head towards him.

I can't even get him to bathe regularly.

Paul sighed. When he saw his daughter watching them, hands clutched together against her cheek like someone in love, he wanted to scream.

It took no effort for the three superheroes to lift the head and carry it over to the light post. Paul walked over to his car and surveyed the damage. There wasn't any. Not even a dent. He'd hoped for something to be wrong, but wasn't sure why.

"How is it?" asked Howie.

"It's fine," said Paul.

"Sure?"

"Let me double-check." He stared at it a moment longer. "Still fine."

"Good."

"Sorry, again, about the mishap," said Quint.

"No worries on my end," said Paul.

"So," said Howie, clapping his hands together. "Just getting in?"

"Yep. Haven't been beyond this point yet."

"Ah, so you still haven't seen the house."

"Nope. Other than the pictures, we have no idea what the place looks like."

"Are you going by GPS?"

"No, just the roadmap. I think I can find it without the GPS."

"Well, just keep in mind when you come to Peanut Lane, you have to stay to the left when it forks. Your place is the last one."

In the dead end, Paul remembered.

"And it's not on the beach?" asked Gunner.

"Not on it, but not far away at all. You can walk to it in twenty minutes." He glanced up at the bikes mounted to the rack on the roof. "Quicker with one of those. Just go out the back door, down the path, and it'll lead you right there."

"Want us just to follow you?" asked Paul.

"Huh?"

"Aren't you heading out there, too?"

21

"No, not right now. I'm going to help Quint here get his blasted eyesore put back together."

"It's a town treasure!" said Quint.

"It's something all right."

"All right, well we're going to get moving," said Paul.

"Good deal. I'll swing by after five, when I'm off duty, and see how you like it."

"Sounds great," said Paul, turning for the 4Runner. Behind him he heard Natalie and Gunner say their byes as if Paul was taking them to be executed.

The tiny clap of Natalie's sandals on the sidewalk rushed to Paul. He felt his daughter's tiny hand slide into his. He was happy to have it there, and gave it a gentle squeeze. Looking down, he saw Natalie's enormous eyes gazing up at him, loving and full of delight. "Do you think Uncle Howie's ever shot anybody?"

Paul's mouth dropped open. He could hear Gunner laughing as he got into the back.

"What kind of talk is that?" asked Paul.

"D'you see that gun? It was huge!"

"Little girls shouldn't want to know such things."

"Well, I do, mister!"

"Get in the car you little booger before I knock you one!" He opened the door for her.

Laughing, Natalie climbed in. Gunner reached over and buckled the safety harness across her booster seat. Once she was settled, Paul shut the door.

"See you later," Howie yelled.

Walking around the front of his vehicle, Paul waved. "Looking forward to it."

"I'll bring Trish, and some pizza."

Nodding, Paul extended his thumb. "Awesome."

He opened his door, then glanced at his brother. Quint was halfway up the ladder while Howie stood below, holding the head in one arm like an infant.

Sighing, he got into the car.

CHAPTER 2

Paul found the house just fine. On his second try. The first attempt, he'd neglected Howie's instructions, keeping right instead of merging left. But it wasn't his fault. Left turned into gravel, so he'd mistaken it for a driveway. Had Howie told him just to go left where the road became gravel all would've been fine.

The house looked better than the pictures Howie had sent him. A one level nautical-themed structure erected on stilts, the cottage was on a private lot with two sets of stairs leading to a sundeck. A two-car carport had been built underneath. Clusters of grass sprouted from the sand. Bushes so green and healthy they could have been artificial bordered the property. To Paul, it was like the perfect vacation house, but it had been someone's actual *home* before Howie won it at an auction.

Now it's our home.

And his older brother was now his landlord.

And his boss.

God, how'd I get here?

Standing in the compact kitchen, his back against the counter, he stared through the sliding glass doors at the sparkling smear of the ocean far in the distance. It would be impossible for any other person to be sad with such gorgeous scenery all around, but the view deepened Paul's depression. Putting his back to it, he walked to the island in the middle of the kitchen floor. On top were boxes of dishes that needed to be unpacked, washed, and put away.

Paul groaned.

Though a dishwasher had been installed under the counter, there wasn't any detergent. He had some dish soap for the sink, and thought he could probably use it in the washer, but he didn't know how much to add. Knowing his luck, he'd put in too much and flood the kitchen with soap suds. So that meant washing the dishes by hand.

And he was not in the mood for it.

Maybe get the kids to do it?

He listened, trying to hear them. A couple faint thumps came through the walls. They were in their rooms, moving around. Gunner had seemed okay with his, although his approval of the room wasn't accompanied by tears like Natalie's had been. She'd twirled circles through the empty space, singing an improvised song on how much she loved it.

Standing in the doorway of his, Gunner had offered a single nod with an additional, "Cool."

Howie had let the movers in yesterday and supervised as they'd separated the boxes to the appropriate rooms. It had been his idea to have them come ahead of Paul and the kids so the stress of waiting for their belongings to arrive would be avoided. Not a bad idea and Paul was glad Howie had suggested it. If only he would've thought to throw in a couple hundred bucks and have them unpack everything.

Right. With what money?

Paul had enough in the bank to hold them over until his first day as a Seashell Cove deputy. Any extra expenses would be pushing his luck.

He looked at the box of dishes again. He exhaled a heavy breath, puffing out his cheeks. They weren't going to put themselves away.

Paul got to work. He let himself become absorbed with the chore of unpacking, washing, drying, and putting away. Soon he was moving as if he was a robot programmed to do this. His mind was clear, yet focused.

The doorbell chimed, startling Paul. It was his first time hearing its clamor and he cringed at its bluntness. Sounded more like someone had dropped a stack of pans than a cadence of bells. He checked the clock on the microwave, surprised it was after five.

Drying his dishwater-pruned hands, he stepped out of the kitchen, catching Natalie as she skipped around towers of boxes on her way to the door. "Be careful," he pointlessly warned. She had the reflexes and balance of a cat.

"I will," she said, then vanished on the other side of the foyer wall. The clacking of the door knob being turned followed. "Uncle Howie!"

Paul had assumed as much. He tossed the towel behind him, waiting for it to land. When it was snagged by the sprayer on the kitchen sink, he headed into the living room.

Howie, still in uniform, entered the living room, effortlessly balancing three enormous pizza boxes on his left arm. Trish, Howie's wife, followed. It was hard for Paul to see her due to his daughter wrapped around her body as if she'd crashed partway through her midriff. Laughing, Trish leaned her head back, giving Paul a good view of her gorgeous face.

He felt the same nervous flutter in his stomach that always came when Trish was around. Not that he would ever try anything with her, but there was something about her that made him jittery and talk way too much and *too loud*. Paul understood it was his way of trying to show Howie he didn't look at Trish the way every other guy certainly did. But he also understood it made him look like he was trying to hide something.

Gunner entered from the hallway at the far corner of the living room. "Pizza, all right!"

"The best," said Howie. "I swear it."

"We have a Krispy Krust in Granite Falls," said Gunner.

"Not like this one you don't. The only thing in common is the name."

"Hi Gunner," said Trish, trying to delicately peel Natalie off her body.

"Hey, Aunt Trish."

"Look at you," she said. "You're almost a man."

Blushing, Gunner looked at the floor. "Nahhhh."

Seeing the trouble Trish was having, Paul said, "Come on Natalie, you look like a bug on a windshield."

Natalie laughed. "I do not!"

Trish winked at Paul, causing that flutter to turn to a surge. He felt himself sweating and had to strain not to call attention to it by

25

wiping his forehead. Maybe Howie would think it was from the work he'd been doing. Then he had an idea.

"Let me help you with those," he said to Howie, reaching for the pizzas.

"Thanks."

Paul took two from the top and hadn't expected them to weigh so much. "What's in here? Wet towels?"

"That's the extra cheese. It's as thick as a wet towel."

"Ah."

"Got any plates?"

"Just finished washing them."

"Great. Anything to drink?"

"Got some bottles of water. That's about it. Haven't even been to the store to get milk or anything."

"That's all right. I brought some. Picked up a few groceries for you too. Take this other pizza and I'll go get them."

"Did you pick up a case of Husky's?"

"Why wouldn't I?"

Smiling, Paul said, "That's a good man."

"I'll never understand how the two of you can drink that," Trish said through a grimace.

"It's good stuff," said Howie.

"Tastes like old apple juice to me."

Howie shook his head as he slid the other pizza box on top of the two already cradled in Paul's arms. "Women just don't understand quality beer, do they?"

"Nope."

"I'll be right back." He turned away from Paul. "Gunner, come help an old man carry some things."

"Howie," said Paul. "How much stuff is there to carry in?"

His older brother glanced over his shoulder. "Not too much." Then he was walking again. Gunner hurried to catch up.

Trish managed to get Natalie's feet on the floor. "I'm going to warn you—he went a bit overboard."

Sighing, Paul shook his head. "I was afraid of that. He always does."

Paul walked into kitchen. As he was putting the boxes on the small dining table, Trish entered with Natalie at her heels.

"He also bought you some towels and other little things for the house," said Trish. "It's because he's excited."

Turning his head, Paul frowned. "Oh?" He headed for the sink where the clean dishes were drying in the rack.

"You wouldn't believe how much."

"You're right. I wouldn't."

"Come on, Paul, you have to know he cares. Look what he did just to get you out here."

Paul felt a tight pressure in his chest. Not bothering to count plates, he took a stack from the rack, and turned around. "I know he cares. I've never doubted that. I just feel bad that he had to go through so much trouble."

"He didn't have to. He wanted to. It's not like we're well off or anything, so please, don't let pride be an issue."

Glancing at Natalie, he saw how she was transfixed on the pizza boxes. Her eyes didn't blink, her mouth frozen in a valuing grin. He doubted she was hearing any of what was being said. "I won't."

"Good. He's actually scared of doing anything to help, because he's afraid of making you feel how you already are."

"I see what you're saying, and he's right. It's hard for me, you know. Things were okay until the first of the year."

"And they'll be fine again."

Paul's throat felt tight, hard to swallow. Was he about to cry? In front of Trish? Quickly, he turned around and started setting out the pizza boxes. Hopefully, it wasn't obvious to Trish that he was trying to hide from her. Opening all three boxes, he smiled at the familiarity in Howie's ordering. Just like Dad. One cheese and two sausages. Judging the size of the pies, Paul guessed they were extra-large.

He heard Trish taking the preparatory breath as she was about to say something else, but the bump of the front door stopped her. So, in one quick gust she said, "Don't tell him I said anything."

"No problem there."

Trish smiled, then rustled Natalie's hair. His little girl jumped, as if she'd forgotten where she was.

CHAPTER 3

Though he was stuffed, Paul grabbed another slice of sausage pizza. He couldn't make himself stop eating. Hopefully it wouldn't clog him up for days, but he thought it might be worth it. He held the slice up to his mouth. The cheese had cooled, but was still gooey. Biting down on the tip, the sauce burst in his mouth. He chewed. Though only slightly warm, it tasted fantastic. Howie was right—this was the best pizza, way better than the Krispy Krust back home.

This is our home now.

Paul wondered if it ever would truly feel like it.

Trish entered the room from the hallway. "She's asleep now."

"Good," said Paul. "I was beginning to think you might have to wear her home."

Laughing, Trish sat down beside Howie on the couch. She sank in the soft cushions. The position angled her hips up, so when she crossed her legs, her smooth, tanned skin looked very bare. They gleamed as if she'd just rubbed them in lotion.

Howie patted her dusky thigh. Trish looked at him and smiled.

"Thanks for lying with her until she dozed off," Paul said. "I'm sure she loved it."

"It was my pleasure. After so many years with boys, I needed some little girl time." She raised her leg, slowly brushing her fingers across it.

Paul quickly looked away, pretending he was trying to see down the hall toward Gunner's room. His son had eaten a few slices of pizza, then withdrew to his room a while ago. He wondered what

Gunner was doing to keep himself busy. Couldn't be watching TV because the cable wasn't going to be hooked up until Wednesday.

Maybe he was on the phone. Paul listened, not hearing the deep tone of Gunner's voice.

Probably texting a friend about how much he hates it here. And how much he hates his dad for bringing him here.

Paul decided he didn't want to feel sorry for himself right now, so he chose to assume Gunner had fallen asleep. It had been a long day, and if he was half as tired as Paul, he'd probably conked out.

Leaning back in the chair, he let the cushions hold him. It really was a comfortable place to sit. Howie and Trish seemed to be enjoying the couch. He'd probably sleep there tonight since his bed hadn't been put together yet.

He watched Howie's hand stroke Trish's thigh. There was nothing sexual in his actions, just a tender gesture that showed he was there for her. Paul smiled. He used to do things like that with Alisha. Just a soft, skin on skin connection, as a sign of affection. Sometimes it led to other things, others it did not. Either way, it was good knowing someone cared enough about you just to touch you.

Looking up, he saw Howie was watching him. Heat rushed through Paul. He prayed Howie didn't think he was gawking at his wife's smooth legs, so glossy they seemed to reflect the light in the room like a mirror.

"You look tired, baby brother."

Paul nearly puffed out a relieved breath, but nodded instead. "I am."

"Want us to skedaddle?

Shaking his head, Paul waved a hand. "Nah. You're fine. Unless you *want* to go." When they'd first shown up, he'd hoped to rush through the visit so he could have some time alone, a chance to become acquainted with the new house. Now, he didn't want them to leave, dreading even a moment of solitude. He'd had fun catching up with his older brother.

"I don't think we're in any hurry," said Howie, looking at Trish.

"Nope. You're the one who has to get up in the morning, not me."

"Not working at the hospital tomorrow?"

"Nope. They cut some of our hours back since things have slowed down around here."

"Slowed down...?"

"Wow. That sounded bad, didn't it?" Trish shook her head, laughing. "Did I sound like I want things to be chaotic?"

Howie sat up. "No, not at all, you tragedy-addicted madwoman."

Trish playfully swatted his arm. "I don't want to hear that!"

"I take it since all the vacationers are leaving, the ER business isn't booming?" Paul said.

"Exactly," she said, shaking her head. "We don't have any more people accidentally shooting themselves in the leg, or shooting each other."

"What?" Paul gaped at her, confused.

Trish's mouth slowly dropped as if she was starting to catch on to a joke. Looking at Howie, she pointed at Paul. "You didn't tell him about it, did you?"

Leaned back on the couch, Howie shrugged. "It never came up."

"What never came up?" asked Paul.

There was a beep followed by a blast of popping static. "Sheriff Thompson, this is Junior, come in, over."

"Shit," said Howie, sitting up with a groan. "Should've cut the damn thing off."

"He'd just call you on your cell," said Trish.

"Yeah, yeah." Howie reached for his belt. Attached to the side was a radio. How Paul hadn't noticed it jutting from Howie's hip before, he had no idea. Unclipping the radio, Howie raised it to his mouth, and squeezed the button on the side. "Yeah, Junior, what's up?"

"Got a break-in at Walt's Drugstore."

"And? Radio Schneider and tell him to get his ass over there."

"He's patrolling the beaches, it's his night."

"What about Lillard?"

"He's investigating a domestic disturbance. Plus, ol' Walt is at the drugstore himself, and is demanding you to come out there. I can go, if you can either send someone to watch my post, or maybe I can call in somebody."

"No, Junior, don't bother. I'll be there in ten minutes."

"Great, Sheriff. I really appreciate it. I'll let Walt know."

"Okay, thanks."

Groaning, he returned the radio to the clip on his belt. "Well, there goes our night."

"It's all right," said Trish. "There'll be other nights."

31

Howie nodded, though his frustration still showed. "So, looks like we get to have a date night. Nice romantic evening listening to crotchety Walt."

"I don't want to go. Can't you drop me off on the way?"

"Trish, that'll tack on another eight minutes. I won't get to the drugstore for twenty minutes then."

"Is that so bad?"

"Why doesn't she just stay here?" The question had left Paul's mouth before he'd realized it was going to. When both heads turned in his direction, he quickly added, "I'll go with Howie and she can stay here and keep an eye on things. That way, I'll get a quick training session and you can pick her up when you drop me off."

Howie's eyebrows curled upward. "Wanting to go check out a B and E on your first night in town?"

Paul made a face. "Sounds like a blast."

"I'll stay and watch the kids," said Trish. "I don't mind."

"That's fine," said Howie. "It's better than going on this run. I'd babysit instead, too."

Trish laughed, then hugged him. She kissed him, quick and sweet. "Hurry back."

"As fast as I can," he said, standing.

Paul also stood, already wishing he hadn't suggested going along. He could have stayed here with Trish, most likely, but he was too worried about Howie thinking he had hidden motives in mind. He wanted to stop stressing himself about it, but for whatever reason, he couldn't stop.

"Thanks for going with him," said Trish.

"No problem. Just don't have any boys over while I'm not in the house."

Trish mocked a gasp, putting her fingers to her mouth. "How could you accuse me of such things?"

"It's that Howie Thompson you run around with, he's a bad influence." Paul shook his finger at her.

Laughing, Howie started for the door. "It didn't stop her back then and it doesn't stop her now."

Trish laughed. "I know. What's wrong with me?"

"You love the excitement that being married to a small town sheriff brings you."

"She must be thrilled easily," said Paul.

"Whoa, below the belt," said Howie, laughing. "Ouch."

"Don't forget about the break-in," said Trish.

"Right," said Paul. "The men must go out and protect the village."

Howie shook his head. "Maybe he should stay here with the other kids."

Paul waited at the door while Howie hugged Trish and snuck another kiss. Again, Paul smiled watching them. They were still in love, after so many years together. He wondered what their secret was. He might ask Howie about it sometime.

The air outside was crisp, slightly cool with a mild breeze. If it was this cool in August, Paul was curious what the nights in September might be like.

Howie's cruiser was parked halfway down the driveway. Paul got into the passenger side as Howie climbed behind the wheel. A locked pump-action shotgun separated their seats. The wood stock was clicked into place in the floor and the barrel had been fit into a groove in the ceiling. A small laptop was on a tray, attached to an arm that led to the dashboard.

His eyes returned to the shotgun. It was larger than any he'd used himself. Seemed a little intense for such a small beach community.

"Is this a required accessory for us Seashell Cove bluecoats?"

"Became mandatory in the spring."

"Why?"

"Safety precaution."

"Precaution from what?" Paul remembered what Trish had said earlier, and how she hadn't gotten to finish telling him about it. "Does this have to do with what Trish was talking about?"

"It does." Howie cranked the car, pulling the lever behind the wheel down to R.

"Planning on telling me about it?"

"I'm surprised you haven't already heard."

"I guess I am, too, if it's such common knowledge."

"Well, baby brother. Seashell Cove has become quite the popular place to visit."

"I take it this isn't a good thing?"

Howie backed down the driveway, using the side mirror to see. "Helps the economy."

"But it causes you to keep a riot gun wedged between the seats?"

The car rocked as the tires bounced over the shallow gully between the driveway and gravel road.

"It's not the tourism," Howie said.

"So, then it's…?"

"The Bigfoot."

Paul recalled the giant fake head on the hood of his 4Runner. He'd laughed at the old man's explanation.

Bigfoot Beach.

Howie stepped down on the gas. As the car shot forward, the siren wailed, red light pirouetting outside the windows. Paul stared at his brother, waiting on him to laugh, or to show some kind of suggestion that what he'd just told him was a joke.

Howie remained silent.

CHAPTER 4

Nights like this made Deputy Perry Butler despise his job. As a kid, all he'd ever wanted was to be a cop. Watching cool shows like Miami Vice had given him the impression that not only did being a cop help people—it was cool. Now at thirty-eight, plodding along the beach with concrete feet strapped to the bottoms of his shoes, he understood just how damn naïve the kid version of himself was. If he could go back in time and confront the adolescent sitting cross-legged on the floor in front of the TV while Sunny Crocket snuck into a drug dealer's house, holding the gun in that awesome pose of his. "Find a different dream!" he'd scream, grabbing the slightly drooling kid by the shoulders and shaking him.

As much as he hated his work, there wasn't much else he was qualified for. Not in Seashell Cove, anyway. He could always move in with his parents and take some online courses for some certifications if he really wanted to try something different.

No thanks.

Just thinking about being back under the same roof as his mother again was enough to keep him here on the beach, lugging these muscle-straining blocks under his feet.

It wasn't so bad, really. He only had to do it two nights a week, sometimes only one. It was Mayor Caine's idea. Leaving some footprints at night for the tourists to find in the morning kept them coming, which in return kept revenues up for the local business. Also, it ensured nice bonuses flowed into the police department. And together, it all made sure Barefoot Beach and its mollycoddling town, Seashell Cove, didn't wither away like so many small beach towns had in the last few years.

Get out there and leave those Sasquant prints...

Rarely would the mayor call the cryptid by its appropriate name.

Don't leave them everywhere, though, he'd continued. *Walk for a little bit, making a nice spread as if the stupid thing doesn't know where it's going. Then take them off and carry them to another location and leave some more there. It'll screw with the people, make them wonder how it can go from here to there. It might even make them think there's more than one!*

Lack of monster education aside, Perry thought the mayor's ideas were pretty good. Even Sheriff Thompson agreed, though he didn't approve of the methods that pulled it all together.

It's for the town's survival.

Since the murder of Ethan Wilson and the disappearance of Mackenzie Dalton, rumors of a Bigfoot in Seashell Cove had run rampant. It was the footprint that started it. And the countless sightings and animal mutilations since have kept the legend alive. Whenever things quieted down, Mayor Caine sent them out to leave the tracks.

Nothing like an Abominable Foot to pull in some tourism, he'd say.

And tomorrow Perry's lower back would feel like it had been stretched on a rack. That was all right, though, he was off duty, so he could just lie on the couch all day. At least Sheriff Thompson never had them doing these stunts when they had to work the next day. He might really quit if that was the deal.

Probably not.

Perry strained to raise his foot, letting the weight of the concrete shoe pull it back down. It hit the sand with a crunchy thump. As he was about to bring the other foot around, he noticed a pair of prints in front of him matching the ones he'd already made.

He froze. Standing with one foot out and one behind him, he studied the prints. Frowning, he removed his flashlight. He clicked it on. A narrow pipe of light parted the darkness, and threw a disc of light down on the mysterious prints.

He saw two more a few inches in front of his shoe. He followed their path with the light. The tracks continued forward.

Did I already do this section?

Looking behind him, he tried to retrace his steps in his mind. He'd started down there by the fence. Shining the light, its reach couldn't touch the tilting pickets, or the netting that ran alongside it. He'd come a long way, he knew, but couldn't pinpoint the areas he'd already covered. There was a point where he'd circled back to make it look as if the creature might go into the ocean. That was farther back, wasn't it?

He had no idea.

Damn. I should really start marking my path.

This had to be his prints.

What if it isn't?

A prickle of fear tightened his bowels. He suddenly felt as if he might have to visit the toilet.

It's my prints. There's no other explanation for it.

He put the light back on the trail. Though he knew he must've been the one to make them, he wanted to see where they went. Maybe one of the other officers assigned to the beach patrols had done them.

Wouldn't someone have found them by now?

Maybe, maybe not.

Perry started moving, struggling with the damn concrete platforms. He should take them off, but he wanted to leave another trail heading off. Plus, two sets like this would really throw people for a loop. Maybe people would start thinking there was a Bigfoot herd!

He continued to slog his way along the ocean, listening to the soft crashes of the waves when they met the shore. At least the ambiance was nice. Made the job somewhat easier, listening to such a relaxing soundtrack provided by the ocean.

A few minutes later Perry was cussing the ambiance. Focusing on the waves helped keep his mind off the work, but it also made him have to pee. He'd hold it a little while longer, until he could take off the concrete feet. His knees felt so tight, he feared the ligaments were bowing like a slingshot and might propel his kneecaps through his skin.

Enough was enough. He stopped walking. He stood there, hands on his hips, head leaned back and panting as if he'd sprinted for miles. Looking behind him, he guessed he'd barely made any headway from where he'd first noticed the peculiar tracks.

Taking his flashlight, he aimed it ahead. The prints continued a little ways, suddenly veering off to the right. The jittery splash of the light ignited large depressions in the sand curving back, heading in the direction Perry had been coming from. Looked as if they'd given up on this direction and turned back.

The light continued to follow the foreign patterns, and Perry turned to keep his eyes on them. As he threw his leg around so he could turn completely around, the light landed on a solid furry mass.

"Oh-shit!"

Perry pointed the light up as he pulled back.

The disc climbed a large body, brownish dingy hair, bald in spots because of puss-oozing scabs. It lighted a face, causing it to flinch, throwing an arm over its eyes. In the brief moment Perry saw the eyes, he noted their tiny size and yellow-brown color. The skin around them was bare and bulging. It had a flat nose, puffy lips swelling through a heavy beard and moustache. It looked almost like an ape, but more evolved, and much bigger.

"You're…real…"

Before Perry had noticed it had raised an arm, he felt its hand smack against his. The flashlight flew from his grasp, throwing his hand back with a snap like breaking celery. The pain was tremendous, exploding through his arm. When he raised his arm to caress his wrist, he felt jagged pricks of bone through the skin. Blood dribbled on down his fingers.

Perry screamed.

The Bigfoot roared back, drowning out Perry's cries. The force of its rancid breath blew the hat off his head, ruffled his hair. His cheeks flapped. The fetid odor singed his eyes, and filled them with water.

A beefy hand punched into his mouth. He felt the enormous girth snaking down his throat, bulging his neck as if he was swallowing a tree trunk. The wiggling fingers gripped his esophagus and tore shreds away as it dug deeper. He felt it shove its way into his stomach, the massive hand curling into a fist as it crushed his stomach into a juicy wad. He could hear the moist crunches, could *see* the skin of his abdomen rippling like boiling water.

The arm wrenched back.

Perry was hoisted into the air with a double pop of splattering crunches. The arm, wedged through his gullet and holding his innards, carried Perry away. In his shaky vision, he spotted the denticulate tips of his legs from the knees down still planted in the sand.

The concrete shoes kept them up.

CHAPTER 5

"See the window?" asked Walt, pointing at the giant hole in the big display window.

"I see it," said Howie.

"I think that's where they got in."

"I agree," said Howie.

Paul was impressed by his brother's unruffled response. If it had been Paul, his response probably would've been mordant. Where else could the perpetrator have entered?

They'd arrived at Walt's Drugstore a couple minutes ago, and Walt had been waiting for them on the sidewalk in front of the store with his arms crossed. Wearing plaid golf pants and a pink polo shirt, he looked to be approaching ninety, but still had a head full of coal-black hair, resolutely held in place with oil. One eye was squinted, the iris rolling loosely behind the lids, suggesting it was actually made of glass.

When they'd stepped onto the sidewalk, Howie gave quick introductions. Paul offered his hand, only being met with a quick thrust of Walt's chin. Then he'd shown them the window.

Howie peered through the busted glass. "I see a trash can on the floor in there." He looked to his right, up the sidewalk. Nodded. "Yep. Looks like they took the trash can from right there and threw it through the glass."

Walt joined Howie, his hands not lowering from his hips. "How the hell did it wind up all the way over there?"

"Maybe it rolled."

"Chief, come on. That far?"

"What are you suggesting? They threw it so hard that it not only broke the glass but landed that far inside the store?"

Now Paul was intrigued. Walking to the window, he stood next to his brother and looked in. It took him a moment to locate the trash can. When he spotted it, he was surprised at the distance it had traveled. On its side, it lay easily halfway through the store at the end of a path of debris.

"So why didn't an alarm sound?" asked Howie.

"Don't have one."

"You know it's county law that all businesses have alarms."

"Guess I missed that meeting."

"Then how'd you know there was a break-in?"

"I saw the window when I was driving past. Went to Glory Doughnuts."

"Is that so?"

"You can check the backseat of my car if you don't believe me, Chief. Got plenty more if you want any."

Paul hoped Howie checked. Doughnuts sounded great right now.

"Maybe later." Howie walked over to the door, gripped the handle, and gave it a tug. The door rattled in the frame but stayed closed. "Well, they didn't bust the lock. Why don't you let us in, Walt, so we can look around?"

Inside the store, Paul stayed close to Howie, hoping to avoid Walt's wrath. The old man looked as if any moment he might break into a fit of rage. Face reddening more and more as he surveyed the damage. Walt let out a grunt every so often.

The interior was small and old-fashioned, cramped with aisles of merchandise. It looked less like a drugstore and more like a general store that supplied a little of everything.

They checked the cash register first, though Walt told them he kept the cash in a safe in the back. The drawer hadn't been busted. It appeared untouched.

"Strange," said Howie.

"So they didn't want my money," said Walt. "Must be the drugs. Let's head to the back."

"In due time," said Howie. "We'll get there. Let's do a walk-through first, compile a list of what's missing. And for Christ's sake, be careful, they might still be in here somewhere."

"Should I wait outside?" asked Walt.

"Might be a good idea." He turned to Paul. "You can too, if you want, you're not on the payroll just yet."

Although the thought of being ambushed by a fiending junkie terrified Paul, the idea of being alone with Walt somehow seemed even scarier. "I'll stick around."

Howie nodded. "We'll be out in a few, Walt."

"Fine."

They waited until Walt was outside before they started moving again. Howie kept his pace slow and cautious, gazing down each aisle on their way to the pharmacy in the back. Wherever there was a spot someone could be hiding, Howie checked. Other than cardboard displays, a bouncy ball pen, countless endcaps of greeting cards, they found no one.

When they reached the pharmacy window, they noticed the aluminum shield used to block the window right away. It had been pried open. Paul thought it looked as if someone had punched something through it, something large. About the size of a beach ball, serrated lappets of tin dangled around the gap.

"Guess Walt was right," said Paul.

"Yep. Went for the drugs."

Approaching the pharmacy window, Howie lowered his hand to his gun. He used his thumb to flip back the safety strap. Paul saw his brother's hand settle on the gun's grip, ready to draw it if he needed to.

"Is anyone in there?" Howie called.

The sudden shout made Paul flinch. "Do you really think they'll answer you and say 'As a matter of fact, there is'?"

"Shut up, Paul." Howie pointed at the door. "Try the knob."

Paul stepped behind the counter, heading for the pharmacy door. As he reached for the doorknob the image of someone from the other side suddenly opening fire came to mind. He pictured bullets ripping through the door, punching holes into his stomach. His hand froze in place, hovering an inch from the knob. Looking over his shoulder to where his big brother waited on the other side of the counter, he said, "Are you sure this is a good idea?" He was reminded of being kids and Howie daring him to poke a dead snake with a stick. Like a dummy, Paul had taken the dare, only to get bitten on the hand by a sleeping King snake.

"I've got you covered."

"You could at least take the gun out of your holster, couldn't you?"

"I never pull my gun, unless I absolutely need to."

Noble.

And completely stupid.

By the time he realizes he needs it, I'll be dead.

Sighing, Paul gently put his fingers to the knob. The metal was cool and smooth in his hand. He gave it a couple quick turns. The knob stopped whenever he tried turning it either way. It was locked, and he told Howie so.

"All right," said Howie, frowning.

"What's got you bothered?"

"I don't know yet."

Instead of walking through the small breach in the counter, he planted his hand on top and swung his legs over to the other side. His feet landed with two soft clicks, then he walked to the window.

To Howie, the hole was at shoulder level. He needed to bend slightly to look inside. Keeping to the left, he peeped through the aperture like a pervert trying to see through a keyhole. Eyes squinting, he sucked his bottom lip under his teeth. It was something he'd picked up from Dad, and Paul was caught off guard by how much Howie looked like their father at this moment.

"Anything?" he asked.

Howie shook his head. "I see some things have been thrown around, the floor's covered in bottles, but there's nobody in there."

"You sure?"

"Yeah. It's a small room. I can see all the shelves, looks like they're attached to the wall, so there's no way anyone can hide behind them."

"What do we do now?"

"I can't fit through this hole, and I'm sure you can't, either."

"Calling me fat?"

Howie smiled. "I'm calling us both slightly above average. Only someone very skinny, or a kid, could squeeze through here." Howie faced him. "Let's get Walt back in here to let us in, so we can survey the damage, make a list of what was taken."

They turned around.

A gorgeous woman stood in the space between the counters. She shoved a gun at them. "What's going on?"

Paul took an involuntary step back, ducking behind his big brother.

"Becky, what the hell are you doing here?"

"I was driving by."

"Damn, is everyone going to Glory Doughnuts tonight?"

"No," she said. "The movies. I saw your car on the way back. Stopped to ask questions."

"And you decided to let yourself in?"

"No. Walt let me in."

Paul wondered how Howie could talk so calmly to this lovely woman while she aimed a gun at him. He looked at the weapon clutched in her hand, realizing it wasn't a pistol after all.

It was a voice recorder.

"Is he the perp?" she asked.

"Close," said Paul. "I'm his brother."

"No way."

"Afraid it's true," said Howie. "Paul, meet Becky Aniston."

"I'm truly honored," she said.

Paul's cheeks warmed with a blush.

"Honored to break the story that Sheriff Thompson's *brother* broke into the pharmacy. That will sell a few papers."

Howie shook his head, sighing. "One, my brother didn't break into the pharmacy, he came here with me. And another thing, you don't sell papers. People read the news on—"

"Don't say it," she said, cutting him off.

Howie smirked. "The in-ter-net."

"You're so cruel."

Reporter.

She looked like one of those reporters from a movie—sexy and firm in the right places, curved hips, pleasant breasts that pushed against her red T-shirt, wavy brown hair that swathed her shoulders, and tight dark pants that accentuated her toned legs. He imagined her butt was packed into the seat of those pants, tight and curvaceous. No way was she any ordinary small town correspondent. Paul gathered right away that she'd settled here, coming from bigger dreams that had been crushed to lick her wounds.

And she'd never left because she woke up one morning and realized she'd become rooted here.

He already pitied her.

Howie stepped to the counter. Becky moved back to give him room to pass, which he did. He didn't stop, continuing toward the front. Paul wondered if he should follow him.

Becky spun around, facing him. "So if you're not robbing the place, what *are* you doing here?"

"Nothing too exciting, I guess. Just sort of tagged along."

"Tag along on a lot of patrols?"

Paul laughed. "Not if I can help it. Usually I'm the one *on* patrol. I start working on the force soon."

"Uh-huh." She clucked her tongue, already tired of listening to him. "Well…this was a waste."

He sensed the disappointment in her posture, and knew no matter how hard he tried, she wouldn't be swooned tonight. But he didn't want to stop talking to her. She would leave, and he wouldn't learn anything about her. "So…lived here long?"

"Too long."

"Is it that bad?"

"It's really not so bad…at least it didn't use to be."

"What happened?"

"I'm sure you've heard."

"Ah, sure. The uh…the Bigfoot?"

Becky made a face as if she smelled something foul. "Yeah."

"What *is* all this Bigfoot nonsense? My brother said something about it but wouldn't elaborate."

"Of course not. The authorities just go along as if no one has Bigfoot fever, as long as it keeps people coming here, spending their money. In the process, they're littering, polluting, and vandalizing."

"Really?"

"Well," she shrugged. "I made up the last part, but it's pretty damn close to vandalism."

"Why would anyone believe in Bigfoot, not to mention, think that one could live at the beach?"

"Who knows?"

"Maybe he's on vacation."

46

"Needed a change in environment?"

"That's probably it."

"Maybe he'll get a house out here, spend his winters in the warmer climate. It would be an interesting change from the snowy mountains."

Laughing, Paul nodded. "He's a real estate genius. That would be the perfect time to rent at the beach. During the summer, he probably rents out the house to college kids."

Their laughter was interrupted by the banging of the door. He looked to the front. Howie was rushing toward him, a frantic look in his eyes. For a fleeting moment, Paul was worried something had happened to the kids.

"What's wrong?" Becky asked.

Not acknowledging her, Howie said, "Paul, we've got to go."

Paul's usual temptation to say something snarky wasn't there. It was his brother's expression that concerned him, the ashen tone to his face. He looked almost scared.

Nodding, Paul stepped out from behind the counter. To Becky he said, "I hope we can talk again soon."

"Sooner than you think," she said, walking with him.

"No," said Howie, pointing at her. "You stay here."

"Something's happened," she said, convinced.

"I'm not saying that. But I am saying you're not coming along."

"I didn't ask. And I'm saying that you can't keep me away. It's my right, Sheriff. Freedom of the press, you know?"

"I can't keep you from following, but I can keep you off the scene."

"Scene?" she asked. "Crime scene? Murder scene? Give me *something* to work with."

Howie looked at Paul. "Let's go."

"You know she's just going to follow you."

"Nothing I can do about it."

"Might as well give her a ride. Am I right?"

Becky opened her mouth to argue, but looked at Paul. A slight grin started to form on her face. "Asking me out, Mr. Thompson?"

"Maybe."

"I'll ride along with you."

"Let's go."

Howie groaned. "Paul, did you forget who the damn sheriff is here?"

CHAPTER 6

Other than calling Trish to tell her he would be late, Howie said very little on the way. Paul decided to not pester Howie for any kind of information. He knew his brother, and could tell when something really bothered him. In the swash of green light coming from the instrument panel, his big brother looked even more like their dad. It was how Paul remembered Dad, even though he looked nothing like this now. Whenever he thought of Dad, he automatically got the image of how he looked when Paul wasn't completely a teenager yet. Why this reflection had been cemented into his mind, he had no idea.

If Howie looked this much like their dad, then Paul must have gotten their mom's characteristics. Which gave him a fairly good idea what he'd look like when he got older.

"So, Thompson, are you going to share where we're going?" asked Becky from the back.

"The beach," he said grimly.

Becky was quiet after that. They arrived at a small parking area. Paul felt a cold sensation inside when he noticed the two police cruisers already there.

Howie was out first. Paul followed, opening the back door of the Suburban so Becky could climb out. As he walked with her around the side of the car, Howie held up his hand like a traffic guard. "Stay out of my way. Both of you."

Paul was shocked by Howie's bluntness. "Jeez, Howie—"

"I mean it. Keep your distance. She'll only get in the way and your paperwork hasn't even been processed yet. Until I can officially start paying you, you're still a civilian."

Paul and Becky shared the same expression as kids who'd just been publicly scolded by their parents. They followed Howie, walking several feet behind him. Passing a small surf shack, Paul saw Bigfoot Beach T-shirts with *You know what they say about big feet?* printed across the chest area hanging in the windows. Women's shirts, he figured. Beside those were boogie boards shaped like Sasquatch feet and countless other Bigfoot-themed souvenirs and surf stuff. Posterboards, covered with a bold scrawl, were tacked to the outside walls and trembled in the wind coming from the ocean.

It felt ten degrees cooler when the asphalt vanished from his feet and sand took its place. The wind was heavier here also, fluttering his shirt, throwing it against his body. He looked at Becky. Her hair danced wildly behind her head as if she were the model in an '80s hair band video.

Howie stopped, removed his Mag-lite, and fired three quick clicks to his left. In the distance, a series of blinks responded. Nodding, Howie lowered his light, aiming the beam onto the sand. "Come on."

Again, they kept to Howie's rear as they walked. Grits of sand got into Paul's shoes, making his feet itchy through his socks. The uneven surf caused him to stumble a couple times. Becky seemed to have an even harder time walking in her shoes. They weren't high heels, but some kind of open-toed footwear with a small heel.

Noticing Paul watching her, she said, "I should take my shoes off, but I'm afraid I might step on a jellyfish or something sharp that washed up."

"Good idea," said Paul. "I read an article once where a Killer Whale that had been attacked by a shark washed up on shore. Turns out it was a giant Great White and it terrorized this beach community for several days."

"Really?"

"Yeah, if I remember it correctly."

"Are you sure about that?"

Paul feigned thinking it over. "It was either an article or *Jaws 2*."

Becky laughed. Paul thought it was one of the greatest sounds he'd ever heard. How could he ask her if she was seeing someone?

Probably by asking her if she was.

Nice, Paul. You've only been divorced from Alisha for a couple months and already have her replaced?

Now he felt lousy. It wasn't fair to think like that, he knew, but he couldn't stop himself. Besides, he hadn't asked a woman out in twenty years, so he was a little out of practice. And he felt as if he was betraying Alisha.

How would she know? She doesn't know much at all anymore.

He felt crummy for thinking such things, even though they were true. His last visit with Alisha was back in the spring, and it would probably remain his last unless one of the kids wanted him to chaperone them. Seeing her in the room, sitting in a chair facing the window at the mental facility, oblivious to what was around her had been awful. But when she finally started talking, he wished she'd remained comatose. She'd hurled insults and expletives, making fun of his manhood, calling him a loser. She'd even called Natalie a *Spoiled Daddy's-little-bitch.* Thankfully, he'd left Natalie with one of her friends, and she'd missed her mother's adverse opinions of her. But Gunner had been there to witness all of her invasive admonishments.

Dr. Guilford swore it was the illness talking, but to Paul—and probably Gunner—it didn't matter. Words were words, and they hurt even if the person saying them didn't mean them.

"Watch out, Sheriff," called a man's voice. "You're about to trample over the prints."

"Shit," said Howie, pausing with a foot in the air. He slowly brought it back down.

Paul wondered how far they'd walked while he was lost in his painful thoughts. He looked over to Becky and found her watching him with a tilted frown. "Are you okay?" she asked.

"Yeah, I'm fine. Just sort of dazed out there."

"Must be some pretty emotional stuff."

"Why do you say that?"

"You have tears in your eyes."

Reaching up, Paul wiped an eye with his finger. He rubbed his thumb across the tip and felt moisture.

Damn.

"Maybe it's the salt in the air, making my eyes water."

Becky's face was a pale smear as she nodded. "Or maybe it's none of my business," she said.

Paul shrugged. He looked for Howie, not finding him right away. When he did spot him, he saw he'd moved off to the right and was a couple yards away. Becky hurried after him. Following, Paul walked slower as he lifted the neck of his shirt over his mouth. Pinching a section, he used the fabric to dry his eyes.

Nearing Becky, he noticed she'd stopped walking. He stepped beside her and could see why. A block had been made of the area with yellow caution tape. Two uniformed officers stood inside the yellow square, waiting for Howie as he stepped under the tape.

"You guys like working in the dark?" Howie asked them.

"We were waiting on you, Sheriff. Didn't want to do much until you got here."

"Or draw attention to us," said another voice.

"Good call," said Howie. "Sorry for being an ass about it."

"I understand. Want me to throw on some flares?"

"Please."

Paul noticed two pale objects on the ground, smudged with darkness. The two officers stood to one side of them, and Howie's bulk threw another towel of black on top of them. They looked like tomato stakes, broken at the top.

A snapping crack, followed by a flush of pinkish light pushed the dark back, unveiling two severed legs protruding from the sand. The cuffs of dark slacks belled around the ankles of dark boots. Two lines of straps ran over them.

"Jesus," said Howie.

Becky gasped.

Paul felt the cloying pinch in his stomach as it tried to push the pizza up. Those spikes were legs. And judging by the pants that matched Howie's and the other officers, they belonged to a cop.

"What happened here?" asked Becky.

The shorter of the two officers, a rotund man with a moustache and a crop of hair lining his bald dome said, "We're not sure."

"Hey," said Howie. "Don't talk to the press. Not yet."

"Sorry, Sheriff."

"No worries."

"Is that your brother?" said the younger officer. He was lanky and tall, super thin arms and bulging elbows that gave him the semblance of Shaggy from Scooby Doo. Slightly leaning forward, he tipped his hat and squinted as if doing so would answer his question.

"Yeah," said Howie. He pointed to Officer Shaggy. "Paul, meet Deputy Lillard. He's going to show you the ropes when you start." His finger moved to the portly man. "And Deputy Blake, who'll probably be sheriff one day."

Paul gave them a single wave.

"So, give me the rundown," said Howie.

Blake took a deep breath before starting. "Butler failed to check in. When Junior tried radioing him, he got no response. So he radioed us and asked if we'd come check on him. And that's when we found *this*." Even in the guttering pink hues, Blake looked green.

"Those are his shoes, aren't they?" asked Lillard.

"Looks like it," said Howie.

"What do you think happened?" asked Becky.

"I'm not doing interviews," said Howie.

"Jesus, Howie," said Paul. "What's up your ass?"

Becky put her hand on Paul's arm to hush him, but she kept her eyes focused on Howie. "I'm not asking for a quote, asshole, I'm asking because Perry was my friend."

Howie exhaled heavily through his nostrils. "Right. I forgot you know his sister." His nose hissed with another deep gust.

"And what the hell are those things strapped to his feet?" she added.

"*That* is none of your concern."

Becky started for the cordoned area.

"Sheriff Thompson?" called another voice.

Stopping, Becky looked over her left shoulder. Paul followed her line of sight to two approaching figures. One was a white man, probably in his fifties with tight curly hair. He had on a red satin robe over khaki pants and a T-shirt that had *Bigfoot stomped my heart* splashed across the front.

The gigantic black man with him wore a raven black suit and Paul could clearly see the coiled wire in his ear. An earpiece. This man was a bodyguard.

"Caine," said Howie. "What brings you out here?"

Paul looked at Becky. She stepped over to him, leaning close. "Mayor of Seashell Cove," she said.

"No shit?"

Becky shook her head. "Must be really serious to get him out of his mansion."

Mayor Caine's hands moved frantically as he talked. "Bubba here monitors the radio chatter for me, listening out for sightings and whatnot. He heard the call and woke me immediately."

"Wonderful," said Howie. He looked as if he was in pain, and Paul couldn't help but to feel sorry for him.

"It was *It*, wasn't it?" asked Mayor Caine.

"You have to be kidding," said Howie. "If you think I'm going to name Bigfoot as our prime suspect, you're insane."

"What else could it be? Look at all the damn prints everywhere? It's gotta be the Sasquant."

"Sas-*quatch*."

"Exactly."

"The prints are probably Perry's."

"All of them? Did you see all the ones over there?" Mayor Caine pointed to a trail of giant footprints that seemed to be going in another direction.

"I haven't even had a chance to examine the scene yet."

Becky turned to face the mayor. "Since our dear sheriff won't tell me, maybe you will. What are those things on the bottom of Perry's feet?"

Mayor Caine looked at the feet, unbothered by the gory scene. "Those are the Bigfoot sandals."

"Caine," said Howie. "I thought we weren't telling anyone."

"What's the point?" said Mayor Caine. "We won't need them anymore since…" He stopped talking when Howie whipped his head around. Paul doubted the politician had even realized how cold-hearted and inconsiderate his words were.

Throwing his hands up as if surrendering, Howie turned to Officer Lillard. "Take Ms. Aniston back to her car at Walt's Drugstore and get a statement from him regarding what was taken. Then take my brother home and pick up my wife. You can take her home as well, then get your ass back here."

"Yes, Sheriff."

As Lillard ducked under the tape, Becky walked to the yellow line. "You can't send me away from here. This is the news, pal. I have a right to be here."

"Not right now you don't," said Howie. "I've just marked the entire beach as a crime scene. Civilians aren't allowed on site."

"Howie," said Paul. "Come on, man. That's a little harsh, don't you think?"

Howie stared at Paul a long moment before he said, "I'll catch up to you later."

"So you're Sheriff Thompson's little brother?" said Mayor Caine. "I hear you're quite the superstar back home."

Paul felt his face twist into a grimace. "That's what they say."

The white of Caine's teeth glowed in the dark when he smiled. "It's a pleasure to meet you. I just wish it was under different circumstances."

The mayor held out his hand. As Paul went to shake it, his arm was intercepted by Becky. Holding him with both hands, she tugged him away from the mayor.

"Whoa!" he called, pedaling his feet to keep up.

"Let's go, Paul," she said. Nose aimed high, she stomped through the sand.

Officer Lillard trotted up next to them. "Sorry about this, Becky."

"Can't you tell me anything?" she asked, releasing Paul's arm.

Paul massaged his forearm. It felt sore and burned slightly from her hold.

Lillard shook his head. "I would if I knew something."

"At least tell me what those things on Perry's feet are."

Lillard groaned. "I *can't* tell you that."

"You owe me that much, Tony."

"Off the record."

"Come on."

"Damn it, Becky, it's off the record or nothing. This is my job."

Becky nodded. "Okay."

Paul gave a quick glance behind him. The crime scene was a dim glow in the distance. He saw the quivering flash of another flare being fired.

"Mayor Caine's cousin works in the special effects business. He contacted him to make some shoe plates that would look like Bigfoot tracks in the sand."

"What the hell, Tony?"

"It wasn't my idea."

"But you went along with it?"

"We all had to. What else could we have done?"

"Said no."

Lillard laughed. "Yeah, right. Sure."

"So it was Perry's job to play Bigfoot?"

They reached the parking lot. Paul was glad to be on level ground again, but still felt a little off-balanced as he walked. He wondered if his equilibrium was off from the rutted sand, or from what he was hearing.

"No, we take turns," Lillard said.

"The sheriff? Was he in on it?"

Lillard gave a careful, hesitant glance at Paul.

"I kind of want to know also," said Paul.

"Yes," sighed Lillard. "He didn't have to put on the plates, but he knew. He wasn't happy about it. But just like us, his hands were tied."

"So it was a publicity stunt? All those tracks that I took pictures of and wrote stories about were fake?"

Lillard shrugged. "Not all of them were ours. But, the majority, yes."

"Son of a bitch, Tony. Why didn't you or Perry ever tell me about this?"

"We were sworn to secrecy. It was our jobs if we talked. That's why you can't tell anyone anything."

"I feel sick to my stomach," said Becky.

Paul felt the same. He couldn't believe Howie had allowed himself to be pushed into something so ridiculously deceiving.

Did he expect me to strap those things on and walk around in the dark, too?

Paul felt bad for worrying about that when a man had been killed.

"So they did this to attract interest?" asked Becky.

"Tourism. You know as well as the rest of us, Seashell Cove is drowning." He opened the back door of his squad car.

56

Becky harrumphed, then got in. Paul walked over to the car. He was about to get in but Lillard stopped him.

"You live out off Eastman, right?"

"Huh? Yeah-I think so."

"I'll drive him home," said Becky. "Just leave us at my car."

Paul felt a nervous sizzle in his gut.

.

CHAPTER 7

"Sorry, the A/C's busted. You might want to roll down your window."

In the passenger seat of Becky's tiny Volkswagen, Paul searched for a button on the panel. Not finding one, he patted around the door until his fingers brushed the crank handle.

"Yeah, it's an older model," she said. "Sorry."

"No problem," he said, rolling it down. Cool briny air gusted into the car, stirring his hair. It smelled vaguely of fish and rain, though it hadn't rained all day. "Aren't you going to roll yours down?"

Steering with one hand, she patted her door with the other. "The cord snapped. I've got half of a two-by-four wedged in the door to keep it up."

"Ah."

"Yeah." She sighed. "I know. My car's a piece of shit."

Paul laughed.

"Still waiting on that story to land me a job at a bigger paper, for a better salary."

"Then you'll get a new car?"

"First I'll get a new TV. The car will follow."

"What kind of TV do you have now?"

"It's a thirty-two inch Sony. One of those big tube monstrosities."

"Wow."

"I know. They said that cable wouldn't work on them anymore because of going digital, but they lied. I can still watch just fine. I rarely use it, so I'm good."

Paul tried to move his arm, but his elbow had somehow become wedged between his side and the door handle. He couldn't stretch out in the tight space. "So, did that cop tell you anything about what was taken from the pharmacy?"

"Yeah. Laaame. I probably wouldn't even cover it, but it's still local news."

"Drugs?"

"No drugs, other than a couple boxes of Tylenol that Walt found torn open on a shelf. Tony said some bandages, antibiotic creams, and the Tylenol was taken from the store. But, from the pharmacy they got away with Triamcinolone, Retinoid, and Topical Treatments."

"What are those?"

"Skin creams and ointments. Usually for Eczema and serious skin rashes and irritations or STDs."

"That's it?"

"That's it."

"Weird."

"And lame." Becky shook her head. "I'm tempted to head back to the beach and check things out."

"They'll make you leave again."

"Not if I'm hiding."

"Where would you hide at there? Not many places you won't be seen."

She seemed to consider this a moment. "True. But I hate not being there."

"Want to give it a shot?"

Her head turned toward him. An eyebrow was raised. "Feeling naughty?"

Paul felt a flutter in his stomach that burst with warmth before turning cold. "Well…"

"Your brother would kill you. Besides…Lillard's on his way to your house. If you didn't show up, Howie would know."

Paul had completely forgotten about Trish being at his house. He wondered how she would react to Lillard's showing up to take her home. Gunner could watch Natalie, but Paul hated to think what his son would think if he awoke in the middle of the night and found everybody had left. Probably think something bad had happened.

And he'd be right.

Paul sighed. "Yeah. Bad idea. Scratch it off the list."

"Oh, well," she said. "We'll have to be naughty another night."

Paul snorted. "Right. Yes. Another night."

He felt Becky's lingering gaze, but when he turned, she quickly faced the road again. He studied her as she drove: both hands low on the wheel, sitting slightly forward, her head leaning back as if she had trouble seeing over the wheel. Somehow she made just driving a car seem adorable.

"Are you going to write about what the officer told you?"

"You mean about Perry Butler?"

"Yeah."

"I wish I could, but no. Not yet, anyway. I have too much loyalty to Tony not to make a fuss about it yet, but also a loyalty to Perry to tell the world. One day."

"Are they old boyfriends?"

Becky laughed. "Hell no! I knew Perry's sister back in the day. Perry was her older brother, and I always thought he might be gay, though he never came out or anything. And Tony is my cousin."

"Ah."

"But I have no loyalty to Thompson. We clash. He lives in the clouds most of the time and I'm stuck in reality."

"Wow. He must've really pissed you off sometime."

Becky wrinkled her nose, baring some teeth. "Damn. If I'd quit forgetting he's your brother, I might stop shoving my foot in my mouth."

"So what happened?"

Becky shrugged. "We just don't like each other."

"Seems more to it than that."

"We didn't have an affair or anything, if that's what you're getting at."

"Not at all. My brother's a lot of things, but he's not a cheater. He's loyal."

"Then why do you keep asking me about it?"

"I don't know—I mean, I'm not used to someone other than me not thinking he's perfect."

Becky glanced at him, lips pursed. "Ohhhh, okay. Yeah, I see what you're getting at. And this town is no different. They eat him up, and that's fine, because he's really a good sheriff, but I just don't like him. Maybe it's because he stole my sister's house right out from under me."

Paul flinched. House? Did she mean...?

"Can you believe he would do something like that?"

"What house? His house?"

"It's his now. I heard he's going to rent it out. Her husband walked out on her, and she couldn't make the payments, so the bank foreclosed on it. She'd just gotten a better job and moved in with our parents to save up for a deposit to get it back, but the bank sold it at a private auction. I researched it and found it was Thompson who bought it. He knew she was trying to get the money to make a good faith payment so the bank would hold onto it, but..." She shrugged. "Asshole bought it anyway."

Paul's mouth felt dry and cottony. "Where did you say she lived?"

"I didn't. Off Eastman, which is the main road that runs through here, a little lane called Peanut? Don't you live near...?" Her eyes widened. "No."

"Uh..."

"Are you renting a house from your brother?"

"Well...you see..." He sighed, lowering his head. "Yes."

"Sonofabitch!"

Stamping the brakes, the tires shrieked. Paul felt himself being pulled against his door. He prayed it wouldn't suddenly spring open and pluck him from the car.

When the car came to a halt at an angle on the verge of the road, Becky slammed the gear into park. "Get out."

"Wh-what?"

"Get out!"

"But I'm not sure where I am!"

"You're not real far, so you'll be fine. Now get the hell out of my car."

"I didn't know it was your sister's house."

"Save it. I don't want to hear any bullshit. Now, get out of my car before I use my pepper spray on you."

Paul threw the seatbelt off, hurling himself from the car. Before his hand had even released the door, Becky took off. The door was stolen from his fingers, banging shut, as the car sped away from him. He watched the red glimmers of taillights shrink until he could no longer see them.

He waited a few more minutes, expecting any moment to spot the headlights of Becky's car coming in his direction. Surely she'd realize what she'd done and come to her senses. No way would she just leave him out here. Alone.

A few minutes later, Paul understood she wasn't coming back.

Standing in the road, Paul looked behind him, then back to the front. Nobody was coming from either direction. The only sounds he detected were the insect life, the very faint slurping rush of the ocean, and his own heavy breaths.

Can't believe she just left me here.

Actually, he could understand just fine. He was lucky it was all she did.

Sighing, Paul started walking, following the route Becky had retreated in. He stuffed his hands into his shorts' pockets, keeping his head down as wind buffeted his face in spurts.

After a while, mailboxes appeared on his left. Narrow paths bordered by trees led to hidden houses on his right. No lights seemed to be on anywhere.

Everyone's asleep.

He wished he was.

Should've just stayed home.

Wouldn't have met Becky if he'd stayed home.

A lot of good it's done me. Now I'm walking home!

And he would have been spared the grisly sight of those legs on the beach. They'd once carried a human being around, but now the human belonging to them was nowhere around. Where was he at? No one seemed to care once the mayor showed up.

But if he wouldn't have gone with Howie tonight, how long would it have been before he was educated on the mayor's secret missions? Would Howie have asked him to wear the Bigfoot plates?

Paul couldn't shake the feeling that something was definitely strange here, and this was more than just the new kid on the block jitters. He'd felt it from the moment the giant Bigfoot head had nearly smashed the hood of his 4Runner.

What is *all this Bigfoot business?*

Keeping his head down, Paul walked against the breeze. He must have gotten closer to the ocean since the wind was heavier and more frequent. Felt as if he'd walked an hour before he spotted something that was familiar. Another bout of walking brought him to where the road forked.

As he approached home, he wouldn't have been surprised to find Becky in the act of rolling the house in toilet paper.

The house was fine. All he found was Officer Lillard standing on the front porch with a concerned Trish.

"What happened to you?" she asked.

"My ride ditched me."

Lillard nodded. "Guess she found out you're living in her sister's place?"

"Yep."

"Sucks."

"Yeah. Thanks for the warning about that, by the way."

"None of my business."

"You could've saved me a lot of trouble had you made it your business. You're her cousin, right?" Before Lillard could confirm, Paul was talking again. "You could've told her at the drugstore and then taken me home yourself. I hope you're a better cop than that."

Lillard looked fed up with Paul and was opening his mouth to say something when Trish intervened. "Let's not let tempers flare here. You made it home in one piece, so that's what matters."

"Tell that to my knees." Paul wasn't sure what that was supposed to mean or even why he said it. His knees didn't even really hurt.

He told Trish good night, ignored Lillard's farewell, and went inside. The house seemed uneasily quiet. It felt as if the walls were holding their breath and would suddenly shout *Boo* at any moment.

Tiptoeing down the hall, he stopped at Natalie's room. He peeked inside. She had her nightlight plugged in and he could see her tiny form sleeping in the dim spill, head on the pillow and a smile on her face. So peaceful. He hoped he never disappointed her, and that her unyielding love for her daddy never faltered.

He moved down the hall to Gunner's room. There was no nightlight in here, but the iPad on the pillow illuminated his features. A thin wire ran from the side of the device and split at his son's chin before going to his ears. He was sleeping just as Natalie, though void a smile. His eyes were pinched tight, and his mouth was a tense line. Even in his sleep he appeared to be annoyed.

I really failed with this one.

Sure, he got along pretty well with his son and they shared the same sense of humor, but he worried he'd already missed his opportunities for categorization as a good father. It was all the years of working so much, missing out on the family trips they would take with their mom and mother-in-law, not being home when it was time for homework, sometimes missing dinner. When it became that he was home all the time, Paul feared it was too late. He felt like more of a nuisance to his family than a provider or leader or protector.

Paul's throat felt tight, eyes misting. He walked away from his son's room and entered his own. It took him a couple minutes to locate the bag with his shampoo, soap, and toiletries. Taking the bag, he headed for the bathroom, about to take his first shower in their new house.

The new house and endless possibilities.

CHAPTER 8

Gunner coasted downhill on his ten-speed, feeling the wind in his face, ruffling his hair. It felt good just to cruise, free and invigorating, almost like flying. He was tempted to take his arms off the handle bars and hold them out, letting the air flow all over, but he knew it would be a stupid thing to do. He'd crash.

Just like the last time he'd tried.

He was glad Dad let him take his bike out and explore. When he'd first asked, Dad had seemed a tad hesitant to allow it, but after a few minutes, he'd finally agreed. The wheels whirred and the tires made scratching sounds over patches of sand on the road. Gunner had no idea what he was going to do, but whatever it was, it would be on the beach. With it so close to the house, he planned to spend as much time as he could near the ocean.

It was a hazy morning, hot and humid, though the sun was blocked by steel-colored clouds. His white T-shirt was plastered to his body, already darkening with sweat. The dirt under the bike's tires turned into sand. The wheels spun in place, unable to carry him any further. So he climbed off the bike, pushing it the rest of the way to the beach.

He stood at the edge of an embankment, staring down at the flat plane of sand. Waves crashed on the shore, thinning out into fizzy streams. The crowd was scarce, though more than he'd expected were spread along the shoreline. The closest was a woman in a lawn chair, wearing a one-piece bathing suit and shorts, a hardback book propped on her large gut. Gunner couldn't tell if she was pregnant or just overweight.

A volleyball net had been set up several yards down the beach. From where Gunner was, he could count the number of people playing: two. They seemed young, but he had no idea if they were around his age or not. He wasn't going to intrude on their game to find out. For all he knew, they could be older assholes that didn't want to be bothered and wouldn't mind showing him how much.

Sighing, Gunner started downhill. The bike kept trying to tip over as he descended, and he needed to work harder to keep it upright. He wasn't going to go through this all day. Finding a cluster of weeds to his left, he walked the bike into the center and let it drop. Hopefully it would be all right there while he walked around.

He made his way to where the water reached, kicked off his sandals, and crouched to pick them up. Then he stepped into the waves. The water crashed onto the shore, dispersing around his shins. Tiny bubbles tapped his feet like little fingers. It felt great. A tad cool, but not cold. By the time he'd finished walking around, it would feel great to jump in.

Not knowing which way to go, he picked right and started walking, holding his sandals by his side. He walked behind the woman reading. She didn't look up at him as he passed by.

The sand was warm, growing hotter as he walked. Clumps squished between his toes, powdering them with tan sprinkles. He went on for a long time, finding no one his own age. A little bit further, he still found nothing of interest, and started back.

Several minutes later he reached the woman reading once again. This time he walked in front of her, seeing the cover of the book. It was written by an author named Heather Graham. He wondered if it was the actress or someone who just happened to share the name. This close to the woman, he also saw that she was not overweight. Her legs were thick and toned, her arms thin and muscular. The belly was obviously housing a baby inside. Her skin looked glossy, as if it was painted in clear coat.

He noticed her eyes appear above the top of the book. Blocked by sunglasses, he could tell they were aimed right at him. He quickly looked away, picking up his speed in case she shouted at him for staring.

No shouts came.

Why did he always assume someone was mad at him? He smirked. If he really thought about it, he'd know the reason. But doing that would require his thinking about Mom, and reliving her mental collapse step-by-step in his head. He was enjoying his time alone on the beach too much to think about her.

Gunner hadn't even noticed he'd neared the volleyball game until hearing, "Look out!" A moment later a white ball plopped in front him, the sand catching it.

"Sorry about that!" called one of the two. Gunner had been right about his original notion that the guy was young. He looked close enough to Gunner's age, with spikey blond hair and a chiseled body. "Did I hit you?"

"No," said Gunner. "It's cool."

"Will you toss it back?" asked the other guy. He, too, looked Gunner's age and could have been made from the same factory the first guy was developed in.

"Yeah," said Gunner, leaning over and grabbing the ball. "Who do I throw it to?"

"Me," said the first one. "I was the idiot who hit it wild and almost nailed you."

Hardly nailed, thought Gunner as he threw it like a basketball to the first guy.

"Thanks," he said.

"No problem. See you." Gunner started to walk away.

"Hey, man."

Gunner stopped, looking back. "Yeah?"

"You play?" asked the guy with the ball, rolling it from hand to hand.

"Volleyball?"

"No, table tennis," said the other.

Gunner felt like an idiot for asking. "Well, I haven't played in a while."

"But you know how to?"

"Sure. I guess."

"Want to join us?"

"Um..."

"I mean-if you don't want to, it's cool."

"No, I'm not saying that. But wouldn't it make things a little uneven if I join? I mean, there're only three of us."

69

"No there's not. There're four."

He pointed to his left, to the beautiful girl lying on her stomach on top of a beach blanket behind them. Her bare legs were bent behind her, feet crossed at the ankles and toes nearly touching her shoulders. Somehow Gunner hadn't noticed her before now. "Our sister needs a partner."

Gunner suddenly forgot how to speak. He nodded, hoping they understood he wanted to be her partner.

"Great," said the first guy. "Megan? We found you a partner."

Megan looked up, pulling her sunglasses down her nose to see him better. Her eyes scanned him up, then down, and back up once more. She nodded once, approving. "Good. So, I get to play now?"

"Looks that way."

"Awesome." She rose to her knees, rubbing her arms. They glowed under the sunlight, blazing like two torches from the sleeves of her T-shirt. Her long yellow hair was pulled into a ponytail behind her head. She stood up. The seams of the shirt reached partway down her thighs and somehow it made her even more appealing that a lot of her was covered, though he had plenty of hints that what was underneath was beyond words.

Then she gripped the bottom of the shirt and pulled it over her head. The world seemed to slow as she did this, and Gunner could see every movement, every dimple of tanned skin that wasn't covered by the skimpy white bikini. The gentle bounce of her breasts that were firm and round behind the triangle patches of her bikini top. Though Gunner didn't think she'd been swimming, her skin appeared slightly damp and sleek.

Gunner ceased a gulp.

"Kick ass," said the second guy. He ducked under the net, joining his doppelganger. "We serve first."

"Cool," said the other.

"Shouldn't we flip a coin?" asked Megan, making her way to the other side.

"Do you have a coin to flip?"

"No."

"Then age has it and we're older."

"Barely."

"We're still older."

Megan shook her head. She looked at Gunner and he felt his breath snag in his chest. "You coming over here or what?"

"Oh, sorry." He walked over to the side she was on.

"What's your name?" she asked.

"Gunner."

"I'm Megan, and those two douches over there are my brothers. That's Malcolm." She pointed to the first one who was trying to spin the volleyball on his finger. "And that's Max."

Gunner waved. "Nice to meet you all."

"They always like to point out how they came out first. Asses."

Now Gunner understood why the two guys looked so much alike. He'd assumed they were brothers, but now he realized they were twins. "So, you're all...?"

"Triplets," said Megan. "Yep."

"Wow."

"Ever met triplets before?"

"Nope."

"Well, scratch it off your list."

"What are we playing to?" asked Max.

"Twenty-one. Like always."

"All right."

"You from around here?" asked Megan.

"No. Just moved in yesterday."

"Oh. So, you're here to stay? Not just visiting?"

"As far as I know, we're staying."

"Awesome," she said, then moved to the front of him. She glanced at him over her shoulder, arching an eyebrow before bending over. She jutted her firm rump high in the air as she braced her hands on her knees. The seat of her bikini was a small white crescent that seemed to be failing its job of covering her entirely. The round gradients of her buttocks squeezed the fabric into a narrow patch.

Holy shit on me damn...

Gunner averted his eyes, not wanting her much buffer brothers to catch him staring.

"All right, wimps," said Malcolm. "Zero-to-zero. Serve's up!"

He tossed the ball into the air. It seemed to hang there, spinning many times before coming back down. He smacked it with his fist.

CHAPTER 9

In her confined, stuffy office, Becky leaned back in her chair, feet propped on her desk. The window unit strained to blow cool air into the room. She felt its cool breaths on her bare feet and wiggled her toes. She had her phone to her ear. The cord was stretched as far as it would go. The base trembled slightly as if it might launch at her face any moment.

Tony Lillard answered on the fourth ring. "What?" he said, his voice almost a whisper.

"You said you would give me an update at ten, it's almost one."

"I've been busy."

"Doing what?"

"Dealing with this thing with Perry."

"Well, that's what I'm calling about."

"We don't know much yet. It's still way too early."

"Well, it's only the day after, so I didn't expect things to be wrapped up already."

"Again, you can*not* print this."

"I won't," she said, crossing her fingers. She had no cruel intentions in mind, but if it was something that the public should know, it would be on page one tomorrow morning. "Tell me."

"They found some strange hairs on the scene."

"Perry's killer?"

"Possibly. Could just be a dog. We're waiting on the reports to come back."

"Thompson thinks a damn dog killed Perry?"

"He's not ruling anything out."

Becky held the phone away from her, stared at the ceiling. *Why me?* Then she brought the phone back to her ear. "You better have more for me than that."

"Well..."

"Come on, Tony. Tell me."

Static crackled in her ear from his sigh. "It's the prints."

"What about them?"

"Not all of them are Perry's."

"Well-duh, how many people were tromping around out there last night, plus throughout the day?"

"You don't understand."

"Make me understand."

"The *big* footprints. The tide washed most of them away, but we pulled some casts of what were left, around six I believe. The first two are dead ringers for Perry's, but the other four, well...they're different."

Becky felt squirmy inside. "Please elaborate, Tony, and stop being so damn ominous."

"There's no way those other big prints belong to the concrete plates Perry had on. Those other prints were from something completely different."

"And what do you suppose they belong to?"

Tony was quiet for a moment. "I think it's real."

"Oh, Tony, come on."

"Call me crazy..."

"You're crazy."

Another pop of static from an exasperated sigh. "Maybe I am, but I still think those prints might be from a *real* Bigfoot."

"They could be fakes as well."

"If so, they didn't come from us. We only have the one set and we take turns with it."

"Maybe Mayor Caine has other people out there when you're not. You know, to keep you guys wondering too."

"Then explain how Perry's body was snapped off his legs like that. They weren't cut off. Doc Summerset said they'd been *broken* off. Takes a hell of a lot of strength to do something like that. *Inhuman* strength."

74

"Tony…"

"I might be labeled the village idiot if I say so in public, but between you and me, I think there's really something out there."

"And do your peers share your theory?"

"What do you think?"

If they had half an ounce of common sense, then she would say no. But she knew better. It was probably a hushed theory flowing through the department. Maybe Thompson didn't believe it, but she supposed the others did.

"Thanks, Tony." Before he could say anything more, she sat forward, and dropped the phone into its cradle. She stared ahead for a few moments, her eyes locked on her door. "Bigfoot. Yeah, sure."

Shaking her head, she spun her chair around to face the laptop at the corner of her desk. It was the only spot clear enough she could put it. The rest of her desk was buried under clutter: old papers, folders, unopened mail, and books, some for research, but mostly trashy paperbacks filled with even raunchier sex. She thought there was also half a peanut butter and jelly sandwich somewhere under the rubble as well. She'd brought it with her last week, and had only taken a couple bites when it vanished.

Microsoft Word was opened to a blank page, the cursor blinking in front of her. She had no idea what to type. She couldn't make herself even peck the letters necessary to spell Bigfoot. Instead, she typed something else that seemed to flow from her fingertips: *Tony is an idiot.*

That wasn't news because the town was already well aware of that statement.

"Shit," she sighed.

Becky leaned back, running her hands through her long hair. Adjusting her reading glasses, she sat forward once again. Though she loved her laptop, she hated the touchpad and had installed a cordless mouse to use with the computer. She put her hand on it, moving the arrow to the minus tab in the corner and minimized the Word document. Her research was waiting underneath where she'd left off.

It was a newspaper article from the Granite Gazette, a weekly circulation for the small town of Granite Falls.

Paul's hometown.

As angry as she was, and how much she loathed the idea of him living in her sister's house, she hadn't been able to stop thinking about Paul Thompson. So much so, she'd decided to do a little bit of background checking on him. This was nothing his actions had triggered. She did this kind of thing to every guy she became interested in.

Hardly interested. Curious, maybe, but definitely not interested.

Typing his name in the search bar, she had been shocked to find several links to various articles about him from multiple sources. All of them had similar headlines, usually featuring Paul's name with hero following shortly after.

Scrolling down the page, the links seemed to carry on and on. A video link popped up for a local news station somewhere close to where Paul used to live. She clicked on it. As she waited for the opening advertisement to finish playing, she read the description underneath the video block.

Local cop, Paul Thompson, saves life of Senator's daughter.

The date showed the video was almost two years old.

Finally the car insurance ad faded to black. A bumper of edited clips of news anchors and field reporters flashed across the screen, trying desperately to make the small time players seem more intense than what they truly were. When it was over, the camera cut to a blonde woman with way too much makeup sitting next to a much older male co-host.

"Good evening, welcome to Your News Fix on Channel Six, and I'm Mary McDonald. Our top story comes from the small town of Granite Falls, where local cop, Paul Thompson resides. On his way home from a grueling day on the force, Mr. Thompson drove onto a scene that didn't sit quite right with him. Let's go to field reporter, Tawna Briarson, for the story. Tawna?"

The video cut to the front of a large brick house. Camera slowly panning down to give the viewer a clear shot of just how lovely of a home it was. The shot stabilized on Paul Thompson. Though the date declared this video hadn't been recorded even two years ago, Paul looked five years younger. His hair was darker and fuller, less stress lines around the eyes and the dents leading down from his nose on each side of his mouth weren't nearly as deep. A woman who looked barely legal stood beside him, gripping a microphone. Her red hair was not her natural shade, Becky could tell, just from glimpsing its intense smoldering hue.

There was a pause before Tawna spoke. "Thank you, Mary. I'm standing here with Paul Thompson in front of the mayor's home where he and his family have been invited. He's granted us at Channel Six his very first interview after the ordeal from two nights ago." She turned to Paul, thrusting the microphone at his mouth.

He cleared his throat. "Huh-hello there."

"Mr. Thompson, I want to thank you for talking with us today."

"My pleasure." Smile.

"Please, tell us exactly what happened when you left work two nights ago."

Paul took a deep breath. "Well, I was working the midshift, like I usually do on Thursdays. But because a cattle truck overturned on the highway, I had to assist with traffic and it was actually closer to one in the morning when I was able to end my shift."

"Lucky for Miss Blaylock."

Paul politely laughed. "I guess so, but maybe not so much for those cows. Anyway, I was driving my personal car along Bender Road. It's a private road, very scenic and woodsy."

"Right," said Tawna.

"Usually I don't even see any cars on that road at night, so when I saw a man and woman walking alongside the road, I was surprised. I was rounding a curve when they suddenly appeared and I veered to the left to avoid hitting them. I was passing by when I noticed the young lady's face."

"What was wrong with her face?"

"Nothing was wrong with it. She's a very lovely girl."

Becky smiled. Paul just had to include that, didn't he?

"What had me concerned was the fact that she'd obviously been crying. That caught my attention—her red eyes, tears coming down her cheeks. As my headlights swiped across them, I noticed, very subtly, that she mouthed something."

"Like saying something to you without speaking?"

Paul paused. "Right."

Becky sighed. "You're a moron, Tawna."

"What did she say?" asked Tawna, her voice hardening with tension.

"Help me."

77

"Oh, shit," said Becky, getting into the video. She leaned even closer to the screen. A fingernail slipped between her teeth and she started to chew.

"So what'd you do?"

Paul took a deep breath, puffing out his cheeks when he exhaled. "I drove up a little ways, going no faster than ten miles an hour. I had decided that I was going to turn around and head back. As I was taking out my phone to call it into the station, I noticed some tire marks on the road."

"Skidmarks?" asked Tawna.

"Exactly. They went off to the side. And that was where the car was. The passenger wheels had become lodged in the ditch, so the car wasn't going anywhere."

"What'd you think had happened?"

"In a quick glance of the scene, I became convinced the young woman had been abducted and she'd struggled with her captor, making him crash the car."

"You knew this just by looking?"

"Yes. It was a gut feeling. Maybe it was the look in her eyes, but I knew she was in some serious trouble."

"Then what happened?"

"I turned around."

"And went after them?"

"That's right, after I called it in."

"And you caught up to them."

"I did. They were still walking. I had no idea where they were heading. But once I got close enough, I hit the brakes. When my car stopped, I hopped out and attacked the guy. I was on him before he even knew I was coming. I told the woman to get into my car."

"Did she?"

"Not at first. She helped me...incapacitate the man. I put cuffs on him, and helped her into the car. Then we waited for my backup to arrive."

"Incredible." Tawna shook her head. "And it turned out the man had kidnapped Miss Blaylock for a ransom, correct?"

"That's what I learned, yes."

"And did you know at the time that the young woman was Katrina Blaylock, the daughter of our state senator?"

Becky remembered hearing about this incident two years ago. They'd only done a reprint from a larger paper and Becky had hardly given the story a glance when she'd added it to the spread. No wonder Mayor Caine acted as if he wanted to make out with Paul last night. A *hero* had moved to Seashell Cove. She wished she would've known sooner or she might have run an article about it. Now that she thought about it, how had she not known Thompson's brother was a celebrity?

Becky considered it. Maybe she should run that story: *Hero comes to Bigfoot Beach, ready to tackle a monster!*

Smirking, Becky returned her focus to the computer.

"Such an amazing story, Mr. Thompson," said Tawna from the streaming video.

"Nah. I just did what anyone else would've done. Plus, it's my job."

"Yeah, right," said Tawna. "Most would've kept driving. I wouldn't put it past any off-duty cop to shrug off their walking as taking a late night stroll."

"Maybe, maybe not. I try to have more faith in people, but you might be right."

"Thank you, again, Mr. Thompson. I understand that you and your lovely family will be eating dinner tonight, here at the Mayor's mansion."

"He's been kind enough to invite us, yes."

"I hope you're ready for the change, Mr. Thompson."

"Change?"

"Yes. Your life will never be the same again."

The video ended. Becky sat there a moment, digesting what she'd just watched. She hated to agree with such a twit like Tawna Briarson, but it really was an incredible story. Paul just happened to be in the right place at the right time and had acted fearlessly. Becky wasn't one to admit when she was wrong, but she had definitely misjudged Paul. An apology was in order.

Intrigued, she started to dig a little deeper. For months, Paul's popularity seemed only to expand. There were talk show appearances, public speaking appearances, and he even got to tell the gentlemen to start their engines in several Nascar races. Then, as with most cases, the stories came less often. Then they ceased to

79

exist entirely. There wasn't another article about Paul until several months ago that read: *Hero Cop loses his job in budget cuts.*

"Damn," she said.

Another article followed a few weeks later. When she read its headline, she felt sick inside and couldn't read the story that followed.

Hero Cop's wife suffers nervous breakdown, attacks him with a knife.

CHAPTER 10

Derek squirted a pearly line of suntan lotion onto the small of Marcie's back. She arched from the cold stream, releasing a quiet squeal, but relaxed when he started smoothing it across her tawny skin. Her flesh absorbed the white goop, turning her skin velvety and slick under his fingertips. Fingers sliding across, he massaged her as he worked.

She lay on a towel, arms folded under the side of her head, a cheek on her forearms. Moaning, Marcie said, "It's nice out here, isn't it?"

"Yeah," he said. He squirted another quarter-sized puddle between her shoulder blades.

"Hang on." She reached back and pulled the strap of her bikini where it was knotted at the center of her back. The strings unraveled, falling like soggy noodles on each side of her. "Get it all, rub it in *gooood*." Laying her head back down, she wiggled with excitement.

Derek squirmed, fidgeting with the rising pressure inside his swimming trunks. He'd been dating Marcie for over a year now and he still had these reactions whenever he touched her bare skin. The supplementary lotion and rubbing, and now that she'd unhooked her straps, made it even worse. He had to restrain to keep from pouncing her.

"I'm about to admit something, and that isn't easy for me," she said.

"You *do* want to have some beach sex? I knew it." He got to his knees and was tugging down his trunks when she started laughing. He paused. "Oh…that's not it?"

Laughing, Marcie shook her head. "You're so silly."

Disappointed, Derek plopped back down, taking the lotion bottle in his hand. "That's me. Silly as can be."

"What I'm about to admit is that I was wrong."

Derek stared at the back of her head, the reddish hair tangled from sweat and humidity. "Wrong? About what?"

"You were right. This is the perfect time to come to the beach. Being so close to the end of summer we have it all. The hot weather, the ocean and sand, and we can enjoy every bit without the crowds."

Derek's mouth dropped open. She had argued with him all summer about their vacation plans. If she'd had her way, they would've been out here Fourth of July weekend. With the mobs, the ocean would've been like a public swimming pool. He'd claimed the *end* of summer would also mean the end of the tourist spike, so the heavy hordes would be gone. He hated crowds, especially when he was on vacation. How could he be expected to relax and have a great time with strangers smothering him?

"Glad to see you admit the error of your ways," he said, giving her a light pop on the rump.

Marcie squealed, laughing as she shook her butt for another, which he obliged.

"You're something else," she said. "And this spot, wow, it's great! Like something from an old romance movie, with the rocks and everything."

"Wow, two in one day?"

"I don't know what's gotten into me."

"Neither do I, but I like it. I get some credit. Maybe I should rub lotion on your back more often. It weakens your defense systems and you admit I'm right."

"I can still get off this towel and dropkick you," she said.

"With your top being untied, that might just be worth it."

Marcie laughed even harder. "Get to rubbing, lotion-boy."

"Yeah, yeah."

He started on her legs, rubbing the backs of her thighs. They were perfectly shaped, tapering down to her knees and arching back out at her muscular calves. Derek was very relieved to hear her say she liked the spot. He'd worried she would never forgive him for making her cross over the rocks along the shore as they were lashed by the heavy waves. It was a small section of surf, heavily shaded underneath a large rock jutting from a huddle of even larger boulders. There was probably a cave somewhere farther up the incline, but he had no desire to hike up there to find out for sure.

No, it was much better down here, sliding his hands across Marcie's backside. Maybe if he was lucky, she'd let him do her front.

Should he do it now? Should he ask her? He'd been planning it all summer. The engagement ring had waited at the jewelry store for him to rescue it from layaway since Valentine's Day. Yesterday before driving to pick up Marcie, he'd made the final payment and now the ring was in his bag.

He looked at the bag sitting on top of his towel. Now would be a good time. Maybe he could sneak it out of the bag and start rubbing it across her back. He imagined her face scrunching with confusion.

"What's that?" she'd ask.

"What?"

"That sharp thing? Do you have a hangnail or something?"

"I don't think so. Maybe you should check."

Even more puzzled, she'd roll over and grab his hand. When she pulled it open, the ring would be sitting there, its small diamond twinkling. A tear would bud in the corner of her eye, breaking free and sliding down her cheek.

He was tearing up thinking about it.

Derek reached for the bag.

And saw a shadow flutter across Marcie's back. Something large plunged in front of him. A rock the size of a bowling ball smashed into Marcie's back, imbedding itself deep into her skin. There was a horrible crunching of her spine snapping.

Marcie tensed. Her legs lifted, feet arched, toes extended. Her arms stretched out ahead of her as if groping the air in a skydiving adventure. Eyes and mouth wide, she squeaked underneath her breathy groans.

"Mar-Marcie?"

What felt like endless hours of dumbstruck watching passed, but in reality Derek knew it was only a couple seconds. He shook his head, unable to comprehend what he was seeing. The rock was buried in the soft skin his hands had just been massaging, the soft skin that had wrapped around his body during sex. All the showers they'd taken together, the baths, and the skinny dips.

Now a hefty rock extended from a spread of pulpy gore.

Her face was frozen in a combination of surprise and agony as she tried to peer over her shoulder. Her eyes seemed to be searching for him.

Crawling around beside her, he got on his knees and leaned down. "Marcie, my God, are you okay?!"

Groan, squeaky shrills.

"My God, what happened?"

He doubted she could even answer, but he would never know. Another rock struck the back of her head, exploding through her face. Hot streaks of blood and prickling bits of skull splattered across his face and chest. Her stiff arms and legs dropped to the sand, limp and still.

Derek's screams broke off. Holding out his hands as if to ask what happened, he slowly shook his head from one side to the other. He felt his lips moving though he had no words to give them. Looking up, he saw the darkened shape of a large man on an angled ledge above him. He looked ragged, long nappy hair flapping in the wind. His arms were coated in dark hair that matched what was on his head. The longer Derek studied him, the more he realized it couldn't really be a man. Not that big and hairy, no way.

Then he remembered the stories the locals had told him. Sighting of a monster on the beach. It had killed one person already, was still on the loose.

Derek screamed.

The thing hoisted another large rock above his head and shook it with both hands. And roared.

Derek wet himself. The warm streams of urine filled the netting inside his trunks, spilling through the folds of his legs. There was no way any ordinary man could roar like that.

He glimpsed the rock coming down at him fast.

And he only felt the punching shock of pain from the mini boulder colliding with his face for a moment before blackness took him.

CHAPTER 11

Gunner bit down on the hot dog. Chili and mustard dribbled down his chin. Quickly, he grabbed a napkin and wiped his mouth. He looked across the table to where Megan was forming her lips around the end of a corn dog blotted in ketchup. Suddenly his stomach began to feel as if he'd swallowed a cell phone set on vibrate. It was how her lips tightened around the corn bread, wrinkling slightly and puckering out. Even though she'd taste like a carnival, he wanted to kiss her.

Noticing him staring, she winked.

And that simple gesture sapped the rest of his appetite. He was too nervous to eat. Looking down at his plate, he had two and a half chili dogs left. How was he going to do this?

Malcolm arrived, putting his Styrofoam cup of soda down first, then he swung one leg over the bench and sat down, straddling it like a motorcycle seat. "How is it?" he asked Gunner.

"The food?"

"What else?"

"It's good." And it really had been until his nerves ruined his hunger. He took another bite and its juicy warmth reminded him he wanted to eat. "Really good."

"Told you so. Quigley has the best hot dogs." He set his plate beside the cup. On top were five aluminum-wrapped tubes.

"Damn, Malcolm," said Megan. "Did you leave any for anyone else?"

"Doubtful," he said, taking one from the plate. He unfurled the aluminum wrapping. The dog was fully loaded, with onions and slaw smothering the chili.

Quigley's was located on the beach at the end of a pier that charged five dollars a person for its view. The food was expensive, but Malcolm had demanded he be allowed to pay. Gunner was grateful for the offer, for it kept more money in his wallet, but he also felt like a moocher for allowing it. When the cashier saw it was Malcolm, she'd given them the food for free, so the offer had only been for amusement.

"How'd you manage that?" Gunner had asked.

"You get free shit when your father's the king."

"Your dad's Quigley?"

Laughing, Malcolm shook his head. "Quigley is an old kook that can't piss without someone's help. Nope. Our dad's the mayor and he bought the place from Quigley's family when the old fart went senile."

Gunner resisted his initial reaction which would have been shock. Instead, he nodded coolly, making his way down the buffet line, telling the people behind the counter what he wanted on his dogs. Just like a Subway restaurant, they prepared his meal to his liking.

Now, taking another bite, he was convinced his appetite was no longer in jeopardy.

Max sat down beside Megan. He had a small mound of hot dogs and a basket of fries tittering on top. How he'd managed to carry the overstocked plate plus the giant cup to their table was a feat worthy of accolades.

Several minutes of silence passed as the small group sated their bellies with greasy hot dogs, soda, and fries. In between bites, Gunner looked around. It really was a neat restaurant. There was no glass for the windows, just gaps like a horse's stall in the wood and screens. The breeze from the ocean was incessant, a mild brush on his cheek that gently stirred his hair. Traditional booths lined the wall next to the long gap of windows. But where they sat in the center, instead of tables and chairs were picnic tables and benches. To Gunner it was like being at a cookout with the cool kids. He was certain these guys were considered the cool kids.

Hopefully, they'd never realize he wasn't one.

"So what do you do for fun?" asked Max, his mouth stuffed with bread and meat.

Gunner had his lips pressed around the straw, sucking up Cherry Coke. He lowered the cup. "Um…well, I board."

"Skateboard?" asked Megan.

Nodding, Gunner put his hands together on his lap. "Yeah."

"There're a few skaters around here," said Malcolm. "Cool guys. I wish I could do that shit. I'm too clumsy."

Gunner wondered if he was trying to pull a trick on him. Either he was, or he was fishing for compliments. He'd seemed nowhere close to inept back on the beach.

Malcolm continued. "I'll introduce you to them. I think there's some place around here they go to and spend the weekends skating their asses off."

"Cool," said Gunner, but on the inside he was elated. Malcolm must be talking about a skate park. There weren't any in Granite Falls, and the only one that had been within driving distance was still two hours away. "I'd love to check it out."

"I can take you there one day this week."

Gunner's gasp snagged in his throat. Malcolm hadn't been the one to volunteer such a kind service. It was Megan. Sitting across from him, she smiled innocuously behind her cup. She raised the straw to her lips, and puckered down. The drink made squelching sounds as she sucked it through the straw.

"That sounds…" Gunner swallowed. "Fun." He could feel the blush on his face and hoped they couldn't see it. Maybe they'd mistake it for too much sun.

Shaking his head, Max groaned. "Jeez, Megan. Make it obvious."

"Shut up!" She slapped Max across his boulder-like bicep.

If Gunner's cheeks became any warmer, they might ignite.

Megan snapped her fingers at Malcolm. "Ask him."

"Ask him what?" said Malcolm, his voice sounding like he was choking on cotton from the surfeit amount of food he was chewing.

"What we discussed earlier." Teeth clenched, she'd virtually growled her last words.

Malcolm held her intense stare another moment as he finished chewing. Then he said, "There's a get-together on the beach tonight. You should come."

Gunner couldn't stop his head from jerking toward Malcolm. "A party?"

"Whoa, who said that?" asked Malcolm, holding out his hand. He leaned closer, gave a quick look around as if to make sure it was safe to talk, and shook his head. "We're not allowed to have *parties* on the beach. But…get-togethers haven't been banned yet. Just an annual end of summer hangout with a few people. Really, we don't invite that many because it draws too much attention from the sheriff's department. But we like to have a good time before school starts after Labor Day."

Max snickered. And Gunner couldn't help but to feel he was being either put on or set up for something.

As if sensing his hesitance, Megan reached across the table, putting her hand on his. His flinch was refined but he was sure she'd noticed. "Relax, Gunner. I'm sure it sounds like some kind of new kid initiation, but it's not. I promise. No, it's just a couple of my friends having some fun now that the tourists are gone. I mean— they'll come back Labor Day weekend, and school starts right after that, so it's really our only shot at having the beach to ourselves before going back to school."

Though he felt a tad better, he wasn't fully convinced. "And *you're* going to be there?"

"Of course," she said, smiling. "It's my idea."

Gunner ignored Malcolm's and Max's giggling and nodded. "Sure. I'd be up for that."

"I'll text you the directions," she said. "It's easy to find."

Text?

That meant she'd want his number. And he'd have hers.

He suddenly felt very anxious.

Megan wiggled her eyebrows. "It's going to be *fuuun.*"

CHAPTER 12

Gunner wasn't having fun.

It was a chilly night and the campfire did very little to warm him from the persistent wind carrying from the ocean. Using an inverted bucket as a stool, he sat next to Megan and across the fire from the others.

Troy performed with his acoustic guitar and Gunner hoped he'd managed to hide his revulsion. Though the wood popped and crackled inside the trembling flames, it wasn't loud enough to drown out the god-awful music. The chord patterns were nearly as terrible as Troy's whiny off-key vocals about the soul of the ocean pumping essence into the aquatic life that swam in it. Wearing an afghan beanie on his head, long hair curled down either side of his face and hung down to his shoulders. A hemp pullover draped his plaid shorts. With his eyes closed, his lips poked out as he either tried to make a melody or howl, Gunner wasn't sure which.

Jon, shirtless and lacking any kind of body tone, held out a joint and Troy stopped playing to accept. Jon seemed to be the cleaner cut of the two, but shared Troy's asinine behavior. Though Gunner wasn't a smoker, he was glad Jon had fired one up if it meant an end to Troy's maladroit concert.

Gunner glanced at Megan. She looked ill. Her golden hair seemed to float around her face and curled out around her neck. Her purple T-shirt was cut in V and left her chest open down just below the juts of her breasts. He could see the tight valley between their glossy humps. Her shorts were white and very short, showing a lot of her tanned legs. Shadows danced on their tawny smoothness. Just the sight of her made him feel slightly better. When she noticed him looking, she lifted a shoulder and gave him a look that was equally apologetic and nauseated.

Ellen, who was introduced as Megan's *bestie*, sat between the two goofballs, laughing at something Gunner had missed. Her dark hair was pulled into lengthy pigtails that hung over each shoulder. She had long toned legs flowing from her denim cut-offs that suggested she was a cheerleader or some kind of athlete. Though she was very pretty, she couldn't compare to Megan. Ellen hadn't said much to Gunner after finding out Megan had invited him. From what he could gather, Ellen had assumed they were on a double date with Troy and Jon. And his presence was a monkey wrench in her plans.

When he'd shown up, it was only the four of them hanging out around the fire. A painful hour later, they were now only a group of five, with Gunner being that extra wheel. He wondered if that was the only reason he'd been invited. To act as a buffer between Megan and Jon.

Lucky me.

He'd felt lucky until he'd gotten here. All afternoon, he'd looked forward to hanging out with Megan. With any luck, the evening might've led to something more. What, he didn't know exactly, but anything was better than what he was used to.

Even this?

Gunner sighed. He'd only been to a couple parties, but he was sure this one was the worst.

Ellen puffed on the joint and gritted her teeth as she held in the smoke. She leaned forward, holding out the damp tip of the joint out to Gunner. He shook his head. Ellen leaned back on her upturned bucket, making a face as she exhaled a thick plume of smoke.

"Really?" she said. "You don't *smoke*?"

"Sorry," he said. "My dad's a cop."

"So?" said Jon.

"And his uncle's the sheriff," added Megan.

Troy made farting sounds with his lips. "Big deal."

Ellen, rolling her eyes, looked at Megan. "Who *is* this guy?"

"My date," said Megan.

Gunner hardly felt anything hearing her say it. Sure, he was her *date*, but it didn't mean much if he was being used to diffract a guy she wasn't into.

"Sounds like a winner," said Troy. He made quaking sounds that Gunner supposed was laughter. "A *wiener*."

Now Jon and Ellen joined him.

Gunner sighed again. "Wow."

Troy pinched the joint between his fingers and tightened his lips around it. He sucked in, making the cherry end glow brightly. When he took it away from his mouth, the spark dimmed. Then he passed it back to Jon. "We should go boogie-boarding," he said in a strained voice. Smoke puffed with each word. Finally he let it all out in a gray cloud that hung around his face. His eyes looked bloodshot in the carroty flicker of the campfire.

"Hell yeah," said Jon, raising the joint to his lips.

"No," said Ellen. "The water'll be cold and I don't have my suit."

"Go naked," said Troy. "I am."

"Are you nuts?" she asked.

"I have some. You'll see them if you go boarding."

"Shrunken versions," said Jon. "Cold water makes you shrink."

"Oh, yeah. Forget it, then."

Jon pointed at Troy's crotch. "Cold water will make those pebbles invisible!" He loosed a hyena-like cackle.

"Up yours," said Troy. "Been peeking on me in the shower again?"

Jon's laughter died. "Suck it, Troy. Not funny. I told you I didn't know you were in there that one time."

Gunner stared at the ground, unable to believe what he was hearing. But somehow he knew one of the stoners would probably screw Ellen before the night was over. Guys like that always got the girl.

He looked at Megan. Maybe not all of them. Obviously, she's not interested.

Or she's already had her taste.

Maybe she'd dated Jon in the past and wanted to show him she'd moved on. That was why Gunner was here.

Or maybe she just wanted you to come along. Did you ever think about that?

91

At first. But not now. He was just an idiot-deflector tonight.

But he supposed it was a smidge worth it to be near Megan. Better than sitting at home.

"Hey, new kid," said Jon.

"Gunner," corrected Megan.

"Whatever. You said your uncle's the sheriff?"

"Yeah," said Gunner.

"What's this business I heard my dad talking about?"

Gunner waited on him to elaborate, but when Jon began to raise the joint to his mouth, he realized he wasn't going to. Troy quietly plucked guitar strings with his thumb and forefinger, apparently holding out on the vocals to hear Gunner's answer.

"What business?" asked Gunner.

"I heard my dad telling my mom something about a cop being killed last night."

"What?" said Ellen. "Last night? Where?"

"I think on the beach."

Ellen looked pained. Her eyes roamed the dark surf around them. "Near here?"

"How the hell should I know?" asked Jon. "Ask Gunner, his family is cops."

Ellen looked at him. Her eyes were round with worry. "Was it?"

"I have no idea," said Gunner. "This is the first I heard about it."

He wasn't sure Dad would've told him one way or the other. But it might explain why Dad kept asking if they were going to be on the beach tonight. Gunner felt bad for lying to him when he said they'd be at Quigley's. Now he kind of wished he'd been honest.

Dad wouldn't have let me come.

Maybe that would have been a blessing.

"Bet it's true," said Troy, plucking away on the strings. "Wouldn't be the first time."

"It wouldn't?" asked Gunner, hating that he'd been baited. By the look on Troy's face, he could tell the doofus had wanted him to ask.

"That's right," said Troy. "You're new, so obviously you haven't heard."

"About the Bigfoot?" asked Gunner.

Troy looked surprised for a moment before he shook it off and returned to his faux ominous expression. "So maybe you have."

92

"It's posted all over the damn town," said Gunner.

Troy smacked the base of the acoustic, making it ring out. "But you don't know the legend. Am I right?"

Gunner held up his hands, patting the air. "No. I suppose I don't."

Megan groaned. "Troy, I'm not in the mood."

"From what I hear, you never are."

Jon smacked Troy's shoulder. The long-haired stoner spun around on his bucket and slugged Jon's arm. Both guys leaned forward, moaning, rubbing where they were hit.

Ellen shook her head. "Troy thinks he saw Bigfoot one night."

Through his wincing, Troy nodded. "I *did* see it. It was around the Fourth of July."

"Whatever," said Ellen. She looked around. "Where's the marshmallows?" She looked behind her. "Never mind. Found them." When she faced forward, a bag of marshmallows hung from her fingers. She reached in, removed a fluffy sphere and impaled it on a skewer. Then she dropped the bag and reached out, holding the marshmallow above the flames.

Troy leaned forward, letting his arm hang over the guitar. "I was out here one night with a girl."

"That's how I know this is a lie," said Jon. "No girl around here would come with you to the beach."

"Dude, shut up," said Troy. "I told you she was out here with her folks on vacation. Anyway, we're on my blanket and making out. Couldn't keep the bitch—*girl*...the girl off me. I heard these noises at the water. Kind of like..." He paused. Staring at the fire, his nose wrinkled as if he couldn't find the words he wanted to say. "I guess kind of like caveman. Yeah...noises like a caveman. You know what I mean?"

Ellen laughed. "Like this?" She bent her arm and patted her stomach with a fist, making noises that reminded Gunner of gorillas in a zoo. Her breasts were smaller than Megan's, but Gunner could see the jiggling impressions they made inside her tank top.

Troy smiled. "Damn you're sexy when you go all *ooga-booga.*"

Laughing, Ellen held out her hands and did a little bow. "Thank you."

"But no," he said. "Not quite like that. Close, though." He took a deep a breath and let it out, puffing his cheeks. "Anyway, I didn't want to stop making out with her, but I did want to see what the noise was, so I got her to lay down and I crawled on top of her..."

Megan held up her hand. "T.M.I." She shuddered. "I don't want to hear the details of your taking advantage of vacationers. Just tell us what you saw."

"Fine." Troy took what was left of the joint from Jon and winced when the hot nub burned his finger. He had to pucker his lips to get anything off it. "It was hard to see much, but it was huge. And hairy. It was in the water, taking handfuls and splashing it all over its body. It would make those *hooting* sounds whenever it splashed itself."

"Didn't you say you were on acid that day?" asked Jon.

"Yeah, earlier. But it'd worn off by then."

"You were still tripping, man. Getting with the girl got you all riled up and made you have a flashback. Were you telling the girl all about the Bigfoot before you started banging her?"

"Of course," said Troy. "It's all they want to talk about."

"There you have it," said Jon. "You imagined it. You were still feeling the lingering effects of the acid and you're tripping brain created the image. End of story."

Troy looked lost in thought as he processed this. "Huh." Then his dazed expression turned into a frown. "Maybe that would explain why I thought I saw a woman in the water with it."

"What?" Jon laughed. "A woman?"

"Yeah. The girl I was with said she thought Bigfoot was sexy. Maybe it made me imagine the woman in the beach too."

"Was she hot?" asked Jon.

"Which one?"

"The one with Bigfoot? Does he have good taste? I already know yours isn't worth a shit."

"Looked like she had a smoking bod on her."

"All right!"

Jon and Troy smacked their hands together in a clumsy high-five.

"I'd say that's a big yes that you were high," said Ellen. She picked off a gooey clump of marshmallow and sucked it from her fingers.

"Oh well," said Troy. "Guess it was a hallucination after all."

"You know what helps with that," said Jon.

94

"What?"

"More weed."

"Damn right."

Troy leaned back his head and began to sing at the star-dotted sky. His hand strummed the guitar so vigorously the strings rattled on the neck.

With a groan, Gunner looked down at the sand again. He scratched his head. What did Megan find entertaining about hanging around these people?

"Want to get out of here?" Megan whispered in his ear.

Gunner turned. Their faces were so close they nearly touched. If he moved a fraction of an inch, their lips would join. "If you want to," he said.

Her breath was warm on his face when she said, "I do."

When Megan made the announcement they were leaving, nobody seemed to care. Ellen acted a little bummed, but after a quick glance at the two goofballs, she smiled, realizing she would have them all to herself.

Megan took Gunner's hand and led him away from the campfire. She didn't let go as they hiked up the large mounds of sand. Weeds brushed Gunner's legs, making them itch where his shorts didn't cover. Sand sloughed between his toes. It was hard to keep his flip-flops on as he walked up the hill, the ground shifting under each step.

Finally, they reached the top. It was much cooler up here. And darker. The campfire had destroyed Gunner's night vision. Whenever he blinked, he saw phantom flashes of flames.

Megan paused and looked down. Gunner followed her stare to the bottom of the dune. Ellen had an arm around each guy, swaying as Troy played. Jon was either trying to light another joint or a cigarette.

He felt Megan squeeze his hand. "I'm so sorry about that," she said.

"For what?"

Holding hands, they started walking toward the parking area. It was much easier on somewhat level ground.

"Those doofuses," she said. "They can be a little..." She let the words trail off.

"Yeah. I see."

95

"We were supposed to have more show up, but Dad told me the beach was on a silent lockdown, whatever that means. That's why we moved the party way the hell out here. It's not as cool as the rocks where we usually meet up, but I still thought more would come out. Maybe their parents heard the rumors too and wouldn't let them. Who knows?"

"Think it's true?" he asked.

"About the murder?" Gunner nodded. "I don't know. So many stories like that start up around here, usually they're just bullshit. You just don't know what to believe. How were you able to come tonight?"

"I told my dad we were meeting at Quigley's."

"Oh? Good idea. Malcolm had to work tonight, which was why he couldn't come. I'll get him to cover for you, in case your dad asks around."

"He works there?"

"We all do. But he's a supervisor. He likes you, so he wouldn't mind."

"That's cool. Thanks."

"No problem." She smiled. "Do you like them?"

"Sure. Your brothers seem all right."

"Not them," she said, laughing. "I could tell you like *them*. I meant my friends."

Gunner took a deep breath. "Want me to lie?"

"No."

"I can do without them."

Megan laughed. Keeping hold of his hand, she swung out her hip, bumping him. Their legs touched. He could feel warmth where her smooth skin had rubbed across his. "Yeah, I don't really like my friends, either. But they're all I have, really. For now."

"For now?"

"Yeah. I'll be going to college after high school and they're going to stay here and work for their parents."

"Ah."

"Yeah. Troy's dad is going to manage the putt-putt place for my dad, so I'm sure that's what he'll be doing, prowling helpless teenage tourists in the process."

Gunner laughed. "I can see that."

"And Ellen, well, we've known each other for a long time, but I don't know if we've ever really *liked* each other. Her parents were friends with mine, so we just kind of hung out, you know? Her family owns two shops in town. And Jon, well, who knows what Jon will do? His mom is a waitress at the Pancake Palace, so they don't have a lot of money. Out of those three, he seems to have his head on the tightest, but it's only held there by chewing gum."

Smiling, Gunner shook his head. He wanted to ask if she'd ever dated Jon, but decided not to bring it up. It was an answer he probably already knew.

"Will your college be far away?" he asked.

"Not real far," she said. "Asheville."

"From the beach to the mountains, now that'll be an experience."

Laughing, Megan said, "That's what I'm counting on. So what about you?"

"Me?"

"Got your head on tight?"

"Yep. Just replaced the bolts."

"Like Frankenstein?"

"Pretty close."

Megan grinned. Her fingers wriggled between his. "Got plans after you graduate?"

Gunner thought about it. Did he? Maybe back at home there were things he wanted to do. Here? He had no clue. "I don't know, really. I just got here. I haven't even thought about tomorrow yet."

"I bet it's all so confusing, huh?"

"That's putting it mildly."

"No doubt." Megan's nose wrinkled. "New guy in a new town. About to start a new school his senior year. You hardly know anybody. Must be terrifying."

"Well, it is now!"

Megan tilted her head, stuck out her tongue. "Oh, stop it!"

Laughing, Gunner said, "Now I'm scared to death."

"Did you apply to any colleges?"

"A couple."

"And?"

"I was accepted to all of them."

The pale block of her teeth appeared through her huge smile. "That's *great!*"

"Yeah. When I applied, I wanted to get as far away from home as possible. So, I applied in Maryland, Florida, and Wisconsin."

"Oh," said Megan. Her peppy tone had diminished noticeably. "That's great, though."

"I did it, really, to piss off my dad. I don't want to go to any of those colleges."

"Have you looked into any others?"

"Not in a while. I figured I'd do the community college thing for a year or so, then transfer out. Hopefully by then I'll know what I want to do with my life."

"I bet you will," she said.

"I'm glad you think so," he told her.

The dark shapes of cars appeared. Three of them. The closest was white and glowed in the dark, the lot's safety lights glinting off the pricey rims. Megan's, he'd figured when he first got here. He spotted his bike on its side, partway on the sand, the front wheel pointing up. It had been upright when he left it. The wind probably knocked it over. As if to confess, a heavy gust buffeted them. Sand pelted his shins, stinging slightly. His clothes trembled.

Megan pulled out her keys, thumbed a button. Headlights flashed on. Their bright beams assaulted Gunner's eyes, making him squint.

"Sorry," she said. "Bright bastards, aren't they?"

"Yeah. I think I'm blind."

He heard her laugh, the shuffle of sand as she hurried ahead of him. Her body cut black shapes inside the blaring shine when she flitted across. She pulled open her door and the headlights faded to a dim smolder before clicking off.

"Better?" she asked.

"Much." Now when he blinked, he saw flashes.

Megan turned around and leaned against her car. She folded her arms under her breasts, lifting them higher. They looked about to flop out of the low-cut shirt. "Seriously, though. I'm proud of you."

Gunner tried to recall what they were talking about.

Colleges.

That was it. She was congratulating him.

"Thanks," he said.

"You'll figure it all out in time. You're already miles ahead of people like Troy and Jon."

"Thank God for that," he said. "Although, I don't share Troy's musical abilities."

Megan released a laugh that echoed around them. It was a contagious guffaw that brought one out of Gunner as well.

Wiping a tear from her eye, Megan said, "Can I give you a ride home or is that sad thing there yours?"

He saw her head look down. He followed her gaze to his pathetic bike. "I'd love a ride, but yes, this hog is mine."

"Around here, it's all you'll need. She must've noticed Gunner's quick glance at her car. She laughed. "I know what you're thinking. 'How can she say that when she drives that overpriced bitch?'"

"Not really what I was thinking," he said. Not in those exact words, anyway.

"My dad's idea." She shook her head. "I mean—I'd be lying if I said I didn't like the car, but I do think it's a little much. But you should see my brothers' cars. *Those* are ridiculous. For a town this small, you can walk, jog, or ride a bike to get where you need to go. I've barely put any miles on this car, unless I go out of town, which is rare."

"I'll trade you," he said.

Megan swatted at him. "Forget it!" She laughed. "I didn't say I *wouldn't* drive it. Just that I don't need to."

"Ah. Now it makes sense."

Megan stared at him, the smile not leaving her face. Silence spread over them. The ocean crashed in the background, swilling with the hushed sounds of flowing water. Somewhere in the distance, a seagull cawed.

Gunner wondered if she wanted him to kiss her.

Try it and find out.

Sure. Like he'd do that. Last time he worked up the nerve to try was last year, and the girl had swiveled her head to avoid his lips. If Megan did that, he thought he might actually cry in front of her.

But what if she wants me to and I don't do it?

She'd probably be disappointed. She'd think he wasn't as charming as he'd somehow led her to believe. But Gunner would never know. When he looked at her again, she was no longer smiling.

"Guess I better get home," she said.

I blew it. Blew it!

"Yeah," he said, trying to stay upbeat. He failed. "Same here."

Megan climbed into her expensive car. Reaching for the door, her shirt drooped low. He could see the pale slopes of her breasts hanging. She looked up at him. "Will I see you around?"

"Definitely," he said.

I hope so.

Smiling, Megan pulled the door. It bumped shut. The interior light stayed on, so he could see her as she fumbled with her keys. Her brow was slightly creased, as if the dim light hurt her eyes. She found the key she needed and slipped it in the ignition. She glanced at the window, smiled, and twisted the key. The light clicked off and she was slowly swallowed by the darkness inside. The car vroomed to life.

Gunner stepped back, watching the car back up. The headlights raked across him. He doubted she was looking, but he decided to give a short wave anyway. Taillights swathed the parking lot in red as she drove away.

And there she goes.

Gunner felt depressed. He should've kissed her. Nothing major, just a lengthy soft kiss.

He saw it in his mind, could feel those bowed lips warm and moist against his. He looked down at her and told her good night, then turned away, picked up his bike and pedaled off. She sucked in a gasp at the sharp jangle of his handlebar bell firing off two quick farewells in retreat.

Gunner laughed at how stupid his fantasy was.

You're an idiot.

He heard tires crunch and slide. Looking up, Gunner saw the red of her brake lights switch to yellow. The car started back, in reverse.

What's she doing?

The car approached and stopped. The trunk popped open. Megan's head hung out the window. "Put it in the trunk and hop in. I'll give you a lift."

Smiling, Gunner walked his bike to the back of Megan's car. He lifted the lid. The inside of her trunk was empty and smelled like a new car. He doubted anything had ever been put in here before now.

He felt lousy that his dirty, rusted bike would be first. But not bad enough that it prevented him from feeling bouncy inside.

She came back.

For me!

Gunner couldn't believe his luck. What a girl. He'd tried to convince himself she was like other girls he'd known when they were at the campfire. But she wasn't anywhere close to the snobby bitches back home. She was genuinely sweet and so, so beautiful. She made him laugh, and more importantly, he made *her* laugh. She seemed to like his jokes, not finding just his company a humorous punchline.

It took some effort, but he got his bike in the trunk and the lid closed without damaging anything. He walked to the passenger door. The door opened as he reached for the handle. He pulled it wide. Megan was leaned across his seat, her shirt so low on her breasts he could see the upper curves of her bra cups.

"Need a ride, hot stuff?"

A nervous flutter traveled through his bowels. "Uh...yes."

She laughed. "Then hop in."

Gunner climbed in, pulling the door behind him. The lights dimmed. It smelled like fruity lotion inside. Cool air blew from the vents. She had music playing, but it was so low he couldn't tell what kind. As long as it wasn't Troy, he'd be happy with it.

"All right, I'll drive, but you have to navigate."

Gunner nodded. "Deal." He leaned back and didn't bother trying to stop the smile spreading on his face.

Megan must've liked it, for she smiled too. She started driving. The smile drooped to a partial frown. "Huh?" Her eyes glanced from the rearview mirror to the windshield and back. "Odd."

"What?"

She shook her head. "Nothing, I guess. Thought I saw somebody standing back there."

"Really?"

"Yeah. I don't see anybody now."

Gunner checked the side mirror. All he saw in the red glow behind them was a thin sandy cloud the tires made.

CHAPTER 13

Ellen shivered. She hugged herself, rubbed her arms. She felt the rigid texture of goosebumps on her flesh.

"You know, Ellen," said Troy, "if you're cold, we could always use our body heat to warm you up."

Ellen rolled her eyes. "You wish, Troy."

Jon laughed. "He's been wishing since the fourth grade."

Nodding his agreement, Troy huffed on the joint. With his cheeks puffed out, he offered the joint to Ellen. She'd just had a hit and didn't want anymore. She was already hungry and the weed, combined with the wood smoke, was giving her a headache.

"No, thanks," she said.

Troy puckered his lips to the side and exhaled a long fluttering beam of smoke. "Great. Don't tell me you're getting like Megan's new guy."

Ellen snorted. "No way. What a drag he is."

"Who are you, Yoda?" asked Troy. He hitched up his shoulders, trembling. In a frog-like voice, he said, "A drag he is."

Laughter exploded from either side of her. Being alone with Troy and Jon made it easy to recognize just how loud they really were. "You guys are something else."

"Well, thank you very much," said Troy.

He leaned across Ellen's lap to give Jon the joint. As he sat up, she noticed how he made sure his hand rubbed her thigh. More goosebumps stippled her skin. "I don't even know why I hang out with you stupid-asses," she said.

Jon, the joint to his lips, said, "Our devastatingly good looks?"

"Charming personalities?" asked Troy.

"Not even close," said Ellen.

Troy played a few notes on his guitar. Or, at least, Ellen thought they were notes. There was so much string buzz where he didn't get his finger in the right place, it was hard to tell. She hated this. Her hunger was killing her high, making her have a lousy time. But she didn't want to risk smoking more and feeling worse.

Megan hadn't made things any easier. This was supposed to be their last night of having fun before school started in two weeks. The beach being put on lockdown had put a damper on the plans. But she'd ruined it by inviting the new kid. Sure, he was kind of hot in a plain sort of way, but this wasn't meant to be a gathering for strangers to crash. It was obvious he wasn't having fun. And that was most likely why Megan left so soon.

I could've gotten to know him. Maybe he'd stayed longer.

Instead, she was a bitch to him most of the time. It might be a good idea to have somebody with such close ties to the police as a friend. They might be willing to help her out of some sticky issues in the future.

Screw that. I have Megan. Her dad's the mayor!

Couldn't go any higher than that in this town.

Ellen turned on her bucket. Behind her was her water bottle. She wished they had beer, but since Chad couldn't come tonight, that meant they didn't have his fake I.D. to buy any. Oh well, she'd make do without it. She grabbed her water, turned on her stool, and unscrewed the cap. She guzzled down a few heavy gulps and noticed the tug in her bladder.

She needed to pee.

Fantastic.

Where the hell was she going to pee out here?

Looking around, she scanned the area around them. Dark concealed everything three feet past the orange tent of light the fire provided. Her eyes landed on the shadowy undulations of the ocean. From here, it looked like breathing shadows. Plenty of places to pee out there.

No thanks. Don't want to get soaked.

If she only went out a little ways, she could squat and just let it go.

With these guys watching?

She turned to her right and saw Jon had his eyes closed and head back. He swayed as Troy on her left did a horrible rendition of Sugar Ray's "Fly". The need to empty her bladder intensified, becoming a hot clenched fist in her lower back.

Ellen stood up. She'd just walk a ways down the beach. Make sure there was plenty of darkness to hide her. She put a foot forward, but her hand was grabbed. She stopped and looked down. Jon was staring up at her with those green eyes of his. She felt a tingle in her chest. Something about his eyes always made her heart do a little tizzy.

"Where're you going?" he asked.

"Just taking a quick walk. Stretch my legs. I'll be right back."

He shook his head. "Shouldn't go anywhere alone."

"Yeah," said Troy. "Bigfoot's watching."

She could've smacked Troy. She gave him a look that he seemed to interpret as an order to shut his mouth. Wincing, he looked down and strummed away on his ratty guitar.

"I'll be fine," she told Jon when she turned back.

Jon was already starting to stand. "It's okay. I don't mind tagging along."

But I do.

But not really. She kind of liked the idea of him walking with her.

"Okay," she said. "Suit yourself."

"I do," he said. "Every day."

"We going for a walk?" asked Troy. He was about to put his guitar down when Jon stopped him.

"No," said Jon. "We'll be right back."

Troy looked annoyed. "Fine. Leave me here. I thought you said nobody could be left alone."

"You're a big boy," Jon said. "Sit tight."

"Whatever."

Jon turned to Ellen. "Ready?"

She smiled. "All set."

"Let's walk."

Together, they left Troy, a melodic song playing behind them. It almost sounded good until Troy obviously played the wrong chord, making the song go suddenly flat. Jon and Ellen shared a look and laughed.

"Damn," said Jon. "He just plays and plays and never gets any better."

Ellen laughed. "That's mean."

"It's true. He's been at that level since eighth grade."

"All that weed, he probably just forgets what he learns."

They laughed at Troy's expense again. Ellen almost jumped when she felt Jon's arm curve around her back. His hand settled low on her hip. Her shorts were so short, the white pouch of her pockets hung out from the ragged fringe of denim. His fingers tapped her through the wispy fabric.

What's he doing?

She wasn't surprised that she didn't mind. She'd always had a thing for Jon. But she'd never put much thought into it because of Megan. They'd dated off and on last year, but Megan made it clear at the beginning of the summer she wasn't interested.

Now I can have a turn.

She started to smile when another thought struck her. Why the sudden show of affection toward her? Megan blew him off and now he thinks he can just snuggle up to her? What did he think she was? Easy?

Ellen leaned against him, not caring what he thought. She was glad to have the attention. "So," she said. "You're over Megan?"

"What does that mean?"

Ellen bit her lip. Terrible way to phrase the question. "Sorry. Didn't mean it like that."

"I don't think Megan and I were ever really a thing to begin with. Kind of hard to get over something you never had."

"You had her."

"Hardly. She messed my head up pretty bad."

"Bad enough to put your arm around her best friend?"

Jon softly laughed. "I guess so."

"Well, I'll take it." She turned to look over his shoulder.

She could see the guttering glow of the campfire off in the distance. Troy sat with his back to them, still strumming. Though she could still hear him, it wasn't as loud. They'd probably gone far enough.

Ellen stopped walking. Jon paused beside her. He faced her, putting a hand on each of her hips. In the moonlight, his face was veiled in shadow, but his bright green eyes twinkled like glass. She knew he was about to kiss her. Knew what that kiss would lead to. And she was ready for it. But there was a slight issue.

"I hate to ruin this moment," she said.

"What? Don't want me to...?"

"Not that. I *do*. Really bad. But I came out here because...well...I had to..."

Just tell him.

"Let me guess," he said. "You needed to use the facilities."

Ellen laughed. "You're so smart."

"But I feel so stupid," he said.

"Why?"

"I really thought your *walk* was your way of getting me out here, away from Troy."

"It wasn't at first, but now..." She nodded. "I suppose it is."

"No problem," he said. "I'll uh—I'll head over here."

"Not too far. But turn around. We're not that far in our relationship yet that I don't mind you watching me pee."

Jon laughed. "Jeez..."

She felt a small pull of loss when he moved his hands away. He turned around and walked a few steps away. "That's good," she said.

"I won't go anywhere."

"Good."

Ellen kicked off her sandals. She heard one smack something.

"Ow!" cried Jon.

"Sorry!"

"It's all right. Was that your shoe?"

"Yeah. My bad."

She watched the dark shape of his head shake from side to side. Laughing, she turned toward the ocean. The moon reflected off the water in sparkling ripples as shadows curled and flattened with each crashing wave. Thin streams of cold tickled the tips of her toes, fizzing between them.

She was about to step in when she realized Troy's music had stopped.

A scream tore through the night, carrying over the swooshing sounds of the ocean. Her bladder nearly released, but she squeezed her legs together as her back felt like an icy hand was trying to tug her spine through her anus.

"What the hell?" Jon said.

Ellen turned. The black shape of Jon ran toward her. He stepped partway in the moonlight, revealing himself down to his bare stomach.

"Did you hear that?" he asked.

"Sounded like Troy."

"Yeah," he said.

Ellen peered at the camp. She saw the fire, but Troy no longer sat on the bucket. She couldn't see him at all.

"Think he's fucking with us?" Jon asked.

It would make sense, she realized. That was Troy's sense of humor. But that scream…it had sounded so awful. He was in pain.

"I don't think so," she said.

"I'm going to check on him," said Jon.

"Don't leave me here."

No longer caring if Jon watched, she unbuttoned her shorts. She bent over and slid them over her rump and down her thighs. Squatting, she gripped her shorts in the folds of her legs. Before she started, Jon turned away. It took her a moment to will her muscles to relax enough to let the pee out. The waves covered any sounds she made.

Finished, she quickly pulled her shorts up. On her way to Jon, she buttoned them. "Let's go."

Jon grabbed her hand and pulled. They started running. Ellen kept slipping in the sand, staggering. More than once, she almost fell. Jon was moving so fast, it was hard to match him, but he didn't let go of her hand. The conception that she'd forgotten her shoes hardly registered.

The campfire seemed to grow. Invisible heat drifted through the air, warming as they got closer.

Reaching the camp, Jon let go of her hand and made a wide dash to another point of the area. He jerked rigid. "Jesus Christ," said Jon through his wheezes. His shoulders rose and dropped with each breath. He stared at the ground.

"What?" She wasn't quite as winded. Cheerleading kept her in pretty decent shape. But all the weed they'd smoked tonight had left her lungs feeling like they were two sizes smaller.

"The…footprint." He pointed to the ground ahead of him.

Ellen saw it right away. It looked about the size of a pizza box, though shaped like a human's foot—a gargantuan footprint. And there wasn't just one. A trail of them led around the campfire, vanishing on the other side.

"Dear God," she muttered.

She stepped toward Jon and noticed that her outward foot was a tad higher than the other. Looking down, her planted foot was inside a wide hollow. She saw five more circular dints above it.

I'm standing in one!

Squealing, Ellen ran toward Jon. She slammed against him, hugging him from the side. "Let's get out of here! It's been here! It's real!"

"We have to find Troy…"

"Fuck Troy! Let's go!"

He pulled away from her and shot her a disgusted look. "He's our friend!"

"He's your friend!"

"I can't believe you," he said. Walking backwards, he shook his head. "Selfish bitch!"

Ellen wasn't shocked by the slur because she knew he was right. But she couldn't believe Jon was leaving her. "Don't go!"

"You're such a selfish, egotistical bi…" His head whipped to his left. In the dancing shadows on Jon's skin, it was easy to see the color drain from his face. "Holy shit!"

He was leaving. She couldn't let him abandon her. Not out here. Ellen ran to him. Tried to squeeze into his arms, but they wouldn't move. Wouldn't embrace her. They just hung limply by his sides. His eyes gazed beyond her, lower.

Ellen turned around and suddenly had to pee again. Her stomach felt as if it was pulled inward, crinkling like a beach ball losing air. Her eyes pulled the image in, but her brain had trouble processing it.

Troy, lying on his stomach, had his rump jutted in the air. The body of his acoustic guitar protruded from between his buttocks as if it was a dialogue balloon in a comic strip and his ass had something to say. Torn fabric flapped in the breeze as blood seeped down, dripping into a blob on the ground that the sand quickly absorbed.

Ellen wasn't sure how long they stared at Troy's dead body. But it took Jon's pulling to make her move again. He spun her around, grabbed her arms, and leaned close. He put his face to hers.

"Do you have your phone?"

Ellen couldn't remember if she even owned one.

Jon jerked her close. Shook her. "Ellen? Do you have your phone? Mine's in the car!"

She was about to answer him when she saw the subtle movement in the shadows beyond the glow of the fire. Something large lurked just outside the carroty spread. The moonlight behind it cast a dim glow that outlined its form. Nappy hair fluttered, curling out and trembling like snakes on Medusa's head.

"Oh…no…" she gasped.

Jon stopped talking, slowly turned around. She saw him jerk.

A large beast tore through the darkness as if being birthed from a nightmare. Its roar shook the ground. Ellen felt the tremors under her feet, inside her body, moving like a rushing current through her bowels. The fillings in her teeth vibrated.

Beefy hands slapped together on either side of Jon's head. He was hoisted off the ground. His feet dangled at the creature's hairy knees. A stench like a skunk smeared in fish blood drifted into Ellen's nose. It froze her, paralyzed her with fear. Her legs were locked, feet rooted to the sand.

Screaming for help, Jon pounded the long hairy arms with his fists. Scabby bald spots were spread across its biceps, shoulder, and side. Its mouth opened impossibly wide and loosed another bone-jarring roar. Jon's hanging feet kicked uselessly, not connecting with anything but air.

Ellen watched as the creature's arms flexed. Through the hair, a boulder-like bicep curled. Its hands pushed together. Jon's head crumpled between its wide palms into an avalanche of blood and skull. His eyes were launched outward, fired off like two orb missiles that shot past the creature's huge head. Jon's arms dropped, hanging flaccid like dead vines. His legs stopped kicking. Then he was tossed aside, landing in an awkward pile a few feet away.

None of this made Ellen move. She only stood, her eyes glued to the creature. It stepped forward. Snarling, its huge teeth reminded her of a horse her mother used to ride on the weekends. Something had been wrong with its mouth, so its lips couldn't quite cover the big white blocks. These teeth looked similar, but instead of white they were piss yellow and tarnished with dark stains.

The flaring of its nostrils suggested it was sniffing.

"Stay away from me," she managed to squeeze out.

It didn't.

Hands shoved her. Her back pounded the ground and jarred her back into reality. She felt the cold blanket of shock dissipating as the creature dropped down to its knees. Now she could *hear* it sniffing, snorting sounds deep in its sinuses. She kicked out, but her foot was easily swatted to the side.

Its hands gripped the waistband of her shorts and yanked down. The denim ripped wide, leaving the legs in place and a long fabric tongue hanging between her thighs. Her panties had been torn also and draped an inch over the shorts.

"No!"

She tried to get up. A hand slapped between her breasts. She crashed back down, the hand holding her down. She watched its large head dip down. She expected to feel a tongue, or at least a finger, penetrate her. Instead, she could only feel the tickling of heavy breaths. More snorting sounds came from down there as it sniffed the folds of her flesh. It kind of tickled, but mostly revolted her.

Not knowing what to do, she let it sniff her. She stared at the sky as its wet nose moved back and forth, brushing the lips of her vagina. The stars looked so peaceful, as if unaware of the sickening actions taking place on the beach.

The breaths went away.

Gazing down between the V of her legs, she watched as the creature's big furry head appeared between them. Its eyes were narrow yellow slits underneath a brick-shaped forehead. Thin hairs flapped around them. Pustule scabs dotted its face like bad acne. Furrows formed on its leathery skin as a low growl rattled inside its throat. Whatever it had smelled down there, it didn't like.

Did it smell my herpes?

How? She wasn't in the middle of a breakout.

The creature continued to rise. It braced itself on its muscular arms. The growl rose in volume and depth, vibrating her inside. She shook her head. The thing was getting angry again. Whatever it wanted from her, she wouldn't be able to provide.

"Stay away!"

It roared. The gust of its anger spun her pigtails like propellers. She turned away from the potent wave of its breath. Her eyes landed on the marshmallow bag. She saw what was beside it and patted the ground until her hands closed around the thin metal.

Sitting up with a cry, she punched the skewer into its right pectoral. The creature groaned, rising on its knees. The marshmallow skewer jutted out from its chest like a tiny silver diving board.

Ellen rolled onto her stomach, pushed herself up to all fours, and crawled. She'd only gotten a few feet when a hand clasped her ankle. Looking back, she saw the creature held her with one hand as it jerked the skewer from its chest with the other. A line of blood shot out behind it. Other than that, it hardly seemed to trickle.

The creature studied the instrument a moment before tossing it away. When it turned back to her, its face was twisted into a savage sneer.

Ellen couldn't hear her screams over the thunderous tune of the creature. She was jerked back. Her fingers left thin channels in the sand as she clawed for purchase. Flipped over, she gazed up at the massive creature.

It roared again.

The temperate ocean soundtrack filled with barbarity as Ellen was torn apart.

CHAPTER 14

Sheriff Howie Thompson stared down at the mangled corpse in silence. Counting to twenty in his mind over and over, he'd forced his heartbeat to slow down. Breathing in through his nose and out his mouth, his breaths were now under control. To anyone viewing him from the outside, he'd appear composed and calm. But on the inside, he was a detonated building crashing to the ground in a cloud of destruction.

He looked away and spotted Deputy Lillard approaching from the side, wiping the froth from his mouth with a napkin. A glimpse of the body had sent him running off to vomit in private. Howie understood. It was all he could do to keep himself from doing the same.

Being so early in the morning, the temperature had a slight chill hidden in the mugginess. The tide was still in, but seemed to be shrinking by the minute. Howie's shirt was clinging to his back from sweat. And he already noticed small dark patches around his armpits.

He checked his watch. It was getting closer to seven. He wondered when Butler was coming and had to remind himself he wasn't. Butler was dead. The DNA tests were a match for the legs they found. Butler had been a good guy and an extraordinary deputy.

Lillard stood on the other side of the corpse.

Howie frowned. "Going to be all right?"

"I think so," said Lillard, taking a deep breath. He kept his eyes on Howie, probably to avoid looking at the body. "I'm sorry about that."

Holding a hand out to stop the apology, Howie said, "Don't be. It happens."

"I'm just glad I did it before Blake and Caine showed up."

"Hopefully you got it all out of your system."

"I think so."

Lillard released a silent burp that Howie could smell over the fumes of the decomposing body. His stomach gurgled.

Lillard took another deep breath. "Until now, finding Butler's legs was the worst thing I'd ever seen."

Nodding, Howie squatted. He patted around his pockets for a pen but couldn't find one. "Let me borrow a pen," he said.

Lillard's skin was the color of milk. Sweat coated his face as if glazed. Without looking down, he reached into his chest pocket, pulled out a pen, and held it out. His eyes never moved.

"Thanks," said Howie.

He took the pen and started poking the body. The skin felt like rubber, dipping under the tip of the pen. The chest had been torn open, the ribcage broken in half. But he knew it was female because the jagged section of skin where the left breast should be matched the severed breast he'd also found. It stuck up from the sand like a small hillock topped with a nipple.

All over the cadaver were areas that showed bone inside the sinewy craters. Most of the face was masticated except for a piece of the brow. The hair was intact and styled into pigtails that were nappy from sand and mites. He found some congealed blood in the hair, a few dime-sized holes here and there in the scalp. Crabs could be blamed for that.

Howie turned his head away. He gazed at the cherry red blot of the sun as it began to rise above the ocean. It spread across the dark sky like spilled syrup.

"Who do you think it is?" Lillard asked.

Howie wanted everything around him to vanish, so he could be alone with such a beautiful sight. A sunrise seemed to make people forget all of their woes, even nasty ones like what he was crouched beside of. "I have a pretty good idea, but we're going to need dental records to prove it for sure."

"Ellen Chambers?"

Howie nodded.

Poor girl. What'd she get mixed up in?

114

Mayor Caine had already named Bigfoot as the culprit. Of course he would, though. The dope acted as if he *hoped* it really was. Howie was less likely to believe a fictional beast was responsible, but the brutal condition of the body didn't suggest a human had done it.

Keep it discreet, Caine had ordered before hanging up this morning. Howie had to call and report the discovery to him and he was glad the mayor wanted to play it quietly. At least for now. They needed more theories before presenting this to the girl's parents.

"Where do you suppose the boys are?" asked Lillard.

Howie stood up, groaning. "Don't know." He tossed Lillard's pen into the water and watched it bop on the bubbly surface. A wave swooshed over, making it vanish.

"Hey..." Lillard looked on the verge of tears.

"Did you really want it back?"

Lillard shook his head. "Not really."

"Didn't think so. I'll get you a new one."

Lillard nodded. "Maybe the boys had already left."

"You saw the cars, just like me. They didn't leave."

Jon Schaffer's mother had been the one to call it in. She was leaving to work the breakfast shift at Pancake Palace and discovered her car wasn't in the driveway. When she'd checked Jon's room, the bed was empty and showed no evidence it had been slept in. She told Junior on the phone that last she heard he was going out with Troy Basinger and Ellen Chambers.

A year ago they would've waited twenty-four hours before opening up an investigation. Things had changed since last summer.

Lillard's cell phone jangled from his pocket. He tugged it out, checked the screen, and nodded. "Styles just texted. The mayor's waiting up the hill."

Howie nodded. He turned around and looked up. The yellow tape was stretched across the top of the hill and made rattling sounds as it fluttered in the wind. A stinking notion crept up the back of his neck to whisper a message in his ear:

This was just a part of something that was going to get a hell of a lot worse.

CHAPTER 15

Through the lens, Becky watched the deputies move around the crime scene like ants over spilled bread crumbs. Each one carried something away from the cordoned area, and trudged up the hill to toss it in the back of an unmarked white van. Mayor Caine supervised as if he were a contractor making sure his crew completed the task in an exceptional manner. A small crowd had gathered atop the hill, but was being kept far back by Blake and the mayor's bodyguard.

Lowering the camera, Becky rubbed her eyes. They felt sore and achy as her fingers worked over the closed lids. She wasn't sure how long she'd been hiding out here, but it felt like weeks. She'd heard the reports on her scanner and decided a trip to the beach was in order. It was supposed to be a nice day and she could also work on her tan while there was still warm weather to enjoy. So she'd changed into her purple bikini and put on her beach robe. Then she'd filled her beach bag with her camera, voice recorder, a thin blanket, towel, water, and sunscreen. It was kind of exciting, almost like a day trip to the beach. It had been a long time since she'd just gone to the beach and relaxed under the sun or swam in the ocean.

But she hadn't been relaxing. She'd been taking pictures through her powerful lens all day.

Opening her eyes, everything seemed much brighter and made them hurt worse. She blinked a few times, then checked her phone.

Four hours.

She'd been lying on her stomach on this dune for four hours. The skin of her back felt tight from the sun. She'd lost count of how many bristle balls she'd plucked from her skin thanks to the shrubs in front of her.

Becky reached behind her back and retied the straps of her top. She felt drained. And hot. A headache was coming on. Plus she was hungry. Checking her beach bag, she saw she was out of water too.

Becky groaned.

At least nobody had spotted her. That was a plus. She'd be really annoyed if she'd spent this much time out here only to be busted.

"Get any good pictures?"

Becky jumped, let out a squeaky cry, and rolled over to her back.

Thompson stood over her, hands on his hips. With the sun behind him, he looked like a dark superhero.

"Damn it," she muttered.

Thompson laughed. "Want us all to gather around and pose for you?"

"Not funny, Thompson."

Thompson's grin reeked of arrogance. "You know, we had a poll going—how long would it take for you to realize we knew you were up here? I won. I said you *wouldn't* notice until I came up here to confiscate your camera equipment."

Becky's eyes flitted toward her camera. It lay on the blanket, the lens still aimed at the crime scene. She looked back at Thompson. "You can't do that."

"You're right. But I can take the memory card if I deem it necessary."

"The hell you can. I'm the press. I have the right to take pictures and post them if I want."

Thompson bent over, reaching for the camera. Becky dived for it, throwing her body over the SLR as if it were a grenade about to detonate and kill innocent bystanders. "Stay away from my camera, asshole!" she yelled.

Thompson jumped back, hands up. "Jesus, Aniston! What the hell?"

"You're not taking my pictures."

"Yes, I am. Don't make me call Lillard over here to slap some cuffs on you. I'll hold you overnight and still get the damn photos anyway."

"You have no right…"

Thompson exhaled heavily through his nose. His lips were pressed tight. "I don't want to do this, but my hands are tied." His voice had lost its snarky tenor for a more somber tone. "If your photos might tamper with the ongoing investigation and put information out there that we feel can jeopardize things, I can rightfully take the pictures. And I'm sure you were planning to run with the photos, make a huge spread on the cover. Am I right?"

"Nope." She shook her head, nose in the air. "Wrong."

"Don't lie to me."

Becky stomped her foot. She felt her breasts jiggle freely. "It's my job, Thompson. In case you've forgotten, I'm the damn press around here. And this is *news*." She pointed behind her at the clean-up taking place. "The people have a right to know what's happening on their beach."

Nodding, Thompson's face was almost a wince. "I agree with you. Believe me, I agree. But right now they don't have that right, apparently. We're in the same boat, you and me, and you'd make things a lot easier if you'd just give me the memory card. Keep the camera, so long as you promise not to sneak around and snap pictures every damn time we get a lead. Not right now, anyway. And keep your damn scanner shut off."

"Is this Caine's call?"

"What in this town isn't his call?"

Becky looked down. She sighed. Sure, she could fight Thompson until she was blue in the face. The end result wouldn't change. She'd have to give up her pictures. "Will I get my card back? With the pictures intact?"

"Yes. When we get the clear to release the information, you can write whatever the hell you want."

"You know, I could still write an article about *this*. Seashell Cove might find it interesting to know their sheriff is stopping the press from printing."

"It would be chalked up as tabloid nonsense and you know it. Caine would see to that."

Thompson was right, and she did know it. Nobody would take the story seriously without the photos. And Caine would just deny everything, so would Thompson. Her word against theirs and, in this town, their word was the gospel.

"Fine," she said.

Sitting up, Becky set the camera in her lap. A soft layer of sand was glued to her inner thighs from the sunscreen she kept spraying herself with. It looked as if she'd rolled around in cinnamon. She suddenly felt very exposed in her purple two-piece. Her breasts were glossy and slick behind the thin patches of her top. She looked up, expecting to find Thompson ogling her.

He wasn't. He kept his head turned, as if avoiding any glance of her.

She felt something like respect for Thompson faintly inside of her. Since she didn't like him much, she wouldn't allow it to be more than an indistinct notification. But she couldn't ignore how most men would've gawked at her body, drooling over every shape and curve. It'd happened more than she cared to recall.

Thompson had never been like that. And not just with her. He was a truly happily married man, devoted to his wife. And, so far as she knew, his wife was completely devoted to him.

Becky opened the small compartment on her camera and removed the memory card. She held it up. "Here."

"Thank you for making this easy," he said. He took the card, keeping his eyes on hers. They were Paul's eyes, soft yet piercing, nearly soothing in their gaze, and she was willing to bet their father had a matching pair.

"Easy for *you*, maybe," she said. "I'm getting fucked over."

Thompson stood up straight, slipping the memory card into the chest pocket of his shirt. He nodded. "You really are," he said. "And I'm sorry."

She shrugged. "What can you do, really?"

"Not much, I suppose. I'm just the damn sheriff here and I have no authority."

"Yeah," she muttered. She looked up at him. "Just tell me this much. Do they think it's real? First Butler and now whatever that was that you toted off in that body bag earlier. Do we have a creature running loose on the beach?"

"I'd like to believe that I have enough sense to think not," he said. "Maybe it's just a madman."

"But *do* you believe that?"

Thompson held her gaze. "Have a good day, Aniston."

She rolled her eyes. Should've known he wouldn't divulge anything extra. "Whatever."

Thompson turned away. He started down the dune but paused. He looked back at her from over his shoulder. "Heard that you kicked my brother out of your car the other night."

"So what?"

"He seems really sweet on you," said Thompson.

Becky felt cool prickles in her chest. She hid it from Thompson when she said, "And?"

"I don't know," he said. He shrugged. "Maybe an apology's in order? That's all I'm saying." He threw his hand up in a wave and started walking again. She watched the hill eat him up to the shoulders. Then his head vanished.

"Asshole," she whispered to herself.

Takes my damn memory card, then tries to play matchmaker? Who the hell does he think he is?

But it might be a good idea to apologize to Paul. Especially if she planned to do the hero cop comes to Seashell Cove story. He'd be more apt to cooperate if she cleared the air and said she was sorry. Besides, she just wanted to *tell him* sorry. Paul had done nothing to warrant the kind of treatment she'd given him. He was sweet, albeit a little goofy, which she found adorable.

Maybe ask him out?

Her stomach tightened at the idea. She hadn't asked anybody on a date in a couple years. Usually she was too busy declining them to try establishing one of her own.

What if he tells me to kiss his ass?

She'd deserve that kind of response after what she'd done. Two days ago she abandoned him on the side of the road and now she was going to ask him out? What kind of mind games would he think she was trying to pull?

Am I playing mind games?

Not intentionally. But she was definitely up to something. What, she had no idea.

And she knew she would tell him about her recent encounter with Thompson.

CHAPTER 16

Paul, standing in front of the dishwasher, dropped the detergent packet into the compartment. He raised the door, programmed its cycle, and heard streaming water sounds, as if a troll inside was peeing on the dishes.

He walked to the sink and washed the icky feeling off his hands.

He heard footsteps behind him. Looking over his shoulder, he spotted Gunner heading to the fridge. "Still hungry?" he asked.

Paul had made spaghetti and garlic bread for supper. There was nothing left afterward except the dirty dishes. A salad would've been a nice addition, but he didn't think about it until they were already eating.

"Not really," said Gunner. He opened the door, crouching in front of the shelves. He grabbed a pack of bologna and ham.

"Thank God you're not hungry, or you might eat all the food."

While Gunner hung around the house today, Paul and Natalie had ventured into town, taking in the sights. Though there wasn't much to see other than souvenir shops and Bigfoot paraphernalia, they'd had a good time. Natalie had enjoyed all the cool statues and displays of Seashell Cove's bestial mascot garbed in Hawaiian shirts, sunhats, and overly large sandals. One shop had its back wall covered in a mural that presented the giant monster on a surfboard with a shark swimming up from the depths ready to take a bite.

There were plenty of places for them to purchase something with Bigfoot's large hairy face plastered across the front. But whenever he asked, nobody seemed to know why the town was sick with Sasquatch fever.

On their way home, Paul remembered they had no food in the house other than what Howie and Trish had given them. So they'd stopped at Terri's Market and spent way more than he'd planned. But the market was a nice little place, just like something from an old family sitcom, owned by a jolly couple who couldn't stop smiling.

On their way back to the car, Paul noticed the sign for the Seashell Gazette above the door of a tiny space and had all but dragged Natalie past its window. Wanting to avoid any run-ins with Becky Aniston, he'd even shielded the side of his face with his hand until they were far away from the tiny building. He'd half expected them to run into her somewhere around town, but fortunately it didn't happen. Nor did he spot Howie. He'd figured he would've bumped into his brother at least once. Maybe he was busy.

Still rummaging through the fridge, Gunner stood with a groan. "I'm kind of hungry. Don't really know what I want."

Paul detected nervous energy that seemed to buzz from his son. "Everything okay?"

"Yeah. Of course."

He closed the fridge and headed over to the counter where the breadbox was with his arms full of sandwich accessories. He rolled the lid back and pulled out the loaf of bread.

Crossing his arms, Paul leaned his hip against the counter. He was starting to figure it out. The inability to stay still, making a sandwich only because he couldn't think of anything else to do, the slight jitter in his movements.

His son had a crush.

Smiling, Paul said, "Who is she?"

Gunner tensed, then went back to work on his sandwich. "Who's who?"

"The girl."

"What makes you think there's a girl?"

"I'm that good of a cop." Gunner made a *pffft* sound. Frowning, Paul said, "Plus, I just have a feeling. Father's intuition."

Gunner pulled a slice of ham from the pack and folded it onto the bread. Then he added the bologna and cheese. He was squirting mustard onto the sandwich roof when Paul started to understand he wasn't going to answer.

"Gunner, it's okay to talk to me about things," Paul said. "I promise."

Sighing, Gunner turned around. "She's just a girl."

"And is this girl the friend who invited you out last night?"

Gunner shrugged. "Maybe."

"Does she have a name? Or did her parents really curse her with *Just-a-girl* for a name?"

Sighing, Gunner pressed his sandwich together. "Her name's Megan Caine."

"Caine?" Gunner nodded. He took a large bite of his sandwich. "As in Mayor Caine?"

"Yep," he said between chewing. "His daughter. She has two brothers, too. Can you believe they're triplets? Isn't that weird?"

"Wow. How were the kids?"

"What do you mean?"

"What are they like?"

"Oh, well, they seem pretty cool. I only got to know the brothers for a little while, but Megan was..." He smiled. "She's nice."

"Well that sounds...something."

"I might introduce you to her sometime."

"I've met her dad..." Paul shook his head. "Hopefully she takes after her mother."

Gunner made a face. "You know, I don't think she ever mentioned her mother."

And Paul was willing to guess Gunner never mentioned his. "But let me ask you this: Does she seem to have common sense?"

Gunner laughed through a mouthful of food. He nodded. "A lot more than her friends, that's for sure."

The phone rang, startling them both. Gunner looked confused, as if he'd never heard such a sound before.

Shrugging, Paul said, "They must've connected the phone today. Want to answer it?"

"Sure." He walked over to the wall-mounted phone across the kitchen. He snatched it from the base, nestling it between his ear and shoulder. "Hello?" He looked at Paul. "Yeah, he's standing right here." Nod. "Sure, hang on." He took the phone with the hand that wasn't occupied by a sandwich, extending it out to Paul. The coiled cord straightened, pulling against the base. "For you. Someone named Becky."

Paul felt a tremor of excitement. "Becky Aniston?"

"That's what she said." Gunner smirked and for a moment he looked just like his mother. "Guess I'm not the only one who met a girl." He laughed.

"Hardy har-har. Give me that phone."

"It's all yours, stud."

Paul took the phone. "Want me to ground you?"

"Nope!" Gunner sprinted out of the kitchen, the heavy padding of his footsteps echoing as he hurried down the hall to his room. Paul could feel soft vibrations through the floor.

Shaking his head, Paul raised the phone to his ear. "Hello?"

"Hi, Paul."

The voice, though it was trying much too hard to sound courteous, was wonderful to his ears. "Is this who I think it is?"

"I'm sure it is."

"Well, Ms. Aniston, what do I owe the pleasure?"

"You sound like you're being sarcastic."

Paul immediately dropped the sardonic tone. "Sorry. I was trying to be clever."

"Well, keep working on it."

Paul winced. "So, how did you get my number? I wasn't aware it was even working yet."

"Come on, Paul. Give me some credit. I'm a reporter. It's my job to figure these things out."

"Called information?"

"Exactly."

"That's putting all that investigative knowledge to good use."

"Ouch. Was that paying me back for the clever putdown?"

"Possibly."

"I deserved it. And I also deserve much worse for throwing you out of my car the other night."

"Oh…that's what this is." Paul was disappointed this was just a courteous phone apology. "Listen, I understand you were upset…"

"No. Upset is so not the word for what I was. Furious. Enraged. Those are words for what I was. But I shouldn't have taken it out on you. It's like you said, you didn't know anything about it. How could you have? You don't seem like the kind of person who'd gladly move into a house knowing how it was acquired."

Maybe a couple years ago he would have been, back when he was smug and expected people to throw their coats over puddles so he could cross. The sad reality of the old Paul was one he wanted to forget. "No. And that was why Howie didn't tell me. But please understand, I doubt he had any devious motives for buying the house. I think he really just felt sorry for me and wanted to help."

There was a pregnant pause from the other end. A sigh followed. "You're probably right. It's hard for me not to blame him, though."

"I bet it is."

"So how about you let me make it up to you?"

"Make what up to me?"

Becky groaned. "Can't I ask you to dinner without you making me spell it out?"

"I'm not sure I understand."

Becky laughed, heavily distorting the cheap phone. "Forget I asked."

"Wait, I'm not saying no."

"Are you sure? It sure sounds like it."

"Wow, I really suck at being clever."

"I told you that you did."

Paul's heart drummed. He could feel sweat forming under his arms. "When would you like to schedule this dinner arrangement?"

"What are you doing now?"

"You mean *right* now?"

"No, later now."

Paul could sense her smile through the earpiece. "Nothing, but—"

"Great, it's settled. I'll come pick you up. Be ready in twenty minutes."

"But…"

"See you then."

He heard a click, and the phone went silent as if it died. Frowning, he walked back to the wall, the stretched cord winding back up. He hung the phone on the base. A quick glimpse of the clock told him it was nearing eight. Where on earth would they be going to eat this late? Besides, he wasn't even hungry. He'd tried to mention he'd already eaten. He should call her back and arrange something for tomorrow night.

Snatching the phone from the cradle, he raised his finger to the pad. Then he realized he had no idea what her number was.

Call information and get it like she did mine?

No. If he canceled or rearranged the plan, she might think he was trying to back out. And he did not want her to get the wrong impression.

He needed a shower. Fast. But before he did that, a quick stop in Gunner's room was in order. He needed to let his son know he would be babysitting tonight.

CHAPTER 17

Gunner basically had the house to himself again. Natalie was in the bathroom brushing her teeth and would be going to bed in a few minutes. All he had to do was read her a story. She'd probably be asleep before he was halfway through the book. After she was asleep, he could do whatever he wanted for a couple hours.

Plopping down on the couch, he remembered there was nothing to do. Today had dragged by and he'd found himself ready for his dad and sister to come home. Megan was working a stretch at Quigley's and had been texting him when she could. She'd be too tired to do anything when she got off work, so he wasn't going to bother inviting her over.

Dad wouldn't let her come over without him here anyway.

He might, since Natalie was here. If Gunner did anything out of line, she'd be quick to nark him out.

Don't try it. Give it some time. He might be more easygoing after we've been here for a few days.

It was hard to tell for sure, but Gunner thought his dad hated it here. Though he'd never come out and acted in such a way, he knew his father and knew what his behaviors represented. Since they'd only been here two days, he was certain Dad would grow to love it.

"All clean!" a squeaky voice announced from behind him.

Gunner jumped with a short gasp. Turning around, he gazed over the top of the couch. Natalie stood a few feet away in her gown and shorts. Her curly hair hung in bouncy waves past her shoulders. Smiling, he draped an arm over the couch. She really was cute, though she got on his nerves most of the time.

"Did you decide on what story yet?" he asked.

"Um…" Lowering her head, she put her hands behind her back, nudging at the floor with a toe. "I was thinking…"

"Yeah?" He had an idea where this was going. With The Rule Enforcer away from home, she was going to see what she could get away with.

"Can I watch TV instead?" Gunner was about to respond, but Natalie quickly added, "Just for a little while!"

Gunner sighed. The cable was working when they woke up this morning, even though it wasn't supposed to be turned on until next week. All evening, Natalie's face had been plastered to the TV. "Yeah, go 'head."

"Great! My favorite show's on!"

"Okay, but when it's over, TV's off."

"Awww, but there's two episodes in a row tonight!"

Gunner's lips tightened. "Okay. But no more after that. I don't care if it's an all-night marathon."

"Yay! I promise!" She spun around and bolted for her bedroom.

Gunner stared at the empty spot where she'd been standing and a felt a pang of sadness. He wasn't sure where the sudden woefulness had come from. Maybe he was grasping that she was getting older. Watching the Disney channel now, but before he knew it she'd be rushing off to gawp some kind of drama about relationships and teen pregnancies.

Ugh…I hope not.

Gunner turned around, propping his feet on the coffee table. He looked at his phone again. Nothing to do but wait for Megan to text him again.

His phone chimed. When he checked the screen, he saw his wait over.

****

Paul persuaded Becky to substitute dinner for ice cream, and she'd obliged. They'd gone to a place called Quigley's, where a sign hanging above the entrance guaranteed the best hot dogs in the state. He'd ordered a vanilla cone in a butterscotch shell, and for Becky, instead of butterscotch, she'd chosen chocolate.

Now, they walked along the beach. The sun was down and a mild breeze flittered along the shore, making Paul wish he'd brought a jacket. Becky seemed a little cool from the wind, but she didn't look as if she struggled to keep her teeth from chattering. He supposed she was used to the weather, even with ice cream. As Paul finished eating his cone he wished he had some coffee.

She'd asked him about working for his brother and he'd told her he would be one of the deputies. It was nothing major but Becky had reacted as if he'd told her he would be personal security for a king. He could tell she was just being overly supportive, but it still felt great hearing congratulatory praises, even if they were exaggerated.

"And if you don't mind my asking," he said, "what got you into writing for the paper?"

"Please. The Seashell Gazette is hardly what anyone would consider a viable source of news."

"Local news, though, right?"

"Barely. The extent of my journalistic skills is used for advertising. That's all I really do, if I want to be honest with myself. The paper is only a two-page spread, just a single front and back splash during the off season. And all I'm usually writing about are holidays, sales, or specials. Sometimes I'll review someone's local recipe for chili or something else utterly pointless. During our active months, I get six pages, and even then I'm just trying to sell our town to the tourists."

"Why do you keep doing it?"

"Building up the practice. It looks good on a resume. Someday I might be able to get a good job writing for a real paper." She shook her head. "Paper. Like those will even still be around then."

"Sounds like you're giving up."

"No. I'm too stubborn for that. But it wasn't until last summer that I actually got to write what I consider a real article for the Gazette."

"About Bigfoot?"

Smirking, Becky bit into the nub of her cone. From where Paul walked beside her, it looked as if she'd excavated the ice cream. "Yeah. Our Bigfoot." Her tone was like someone speaking about a scandal. "Big whoop."

Paul stuffed his hands into his jeans' pockets. He wondered if he should ask more about the Bigfoot stuff. She wasn't hollering at him, or abandoning him some foreign place, but he was afraid prying might bring her wrath upon him. But he was interested to know more about it. How could such a mythological creature even be considered real—and at the beach—was something he wanted to learn.

"How'd it start?" he asked.

"Depends on who you ask. And since you're asking me, I can say it actually started spring before last, with the boat crash."

"A boat crash? Interesting."

"Yeah. Pieces of a mysterious boat washed up on shore. It looked as if it had been blown apart. The wood was charred beyond recognition. Your brother sent out a search party and they scoured the ocean around the clock. But all they found were more strange boat fragments. At the end of the search was when they found the cage."

Paul resisted a shiver. "A cage?"

"That's right. The bars had been bent." She put her fists together and slowly pulled them apart to show him. "I saw the cage myself. Of course, I wasn't allowed to take any pictures of it, but I did see it."

"Wow. Was it big enough to hold a Bigfoot?"

"I suppose. It looked big enough to sustain an elephant, so a Bigfoot should have been no problem."

"But the bars suggested otherwise."

"That's right. But after a few weeks of finding no clues to where the boat came from or even how old it was, the case was put away and considered unsolved. They found nothing else. No bodies of crew members, nothing to indicate where the boat had come from. There were no logs or charters matching the boat's description. So I believe the authorities just wrote it off as a drug boat that sank during transport."

"Does that happen a lot?"

"Surprisingly, yes. So we were all okay with forgetting about it. Then along came the strange sightings on the beach. People on late night walks reported seeing someone big splashing around in the water. Whenever it would see people, it would run away. One person said he thought a gorilla was running around. Then there were some complaints about roaring that no one could label. The reports said it sounded almost human but not quite. And then there was the murder and disappearance."

"Whoa. Are you serious?"

Becky finished her cone, nodding as she chewed. "Yeah. A young couple out for a late night walk. The boyfriend was found with his head twisted completely around on his body and the girl still hasn't been found. That was shortly after the Fourth of July last year."

"Do you they think the girl could've killed the guy and fled?"

"No way in hell is that possible. I saw the body. It literally looked as if someone twisted his neck like unscrewing the cap on a bottle."

Paul's sphincter tightened. "Ouch."

"I still have bad dreams about it."

"Then what about the girl?"

"Nobody knows. The investigation is still ongoing. Her parents have been squeezing the mayor for results, but so far, he's been able to keep them calm. I imagine like the boy's family, they're probably getting a nice cut of all the Bigfoot-inspired profits."

"How does all this lead people to suspect a Bigfoot is responsible? That's what you're about to tell me, isn't it? That the mayor and countless others are convinced a Bigfoot has taken refuge in this small beachfront town?"

Becky smiled but it was without merit. "I honestly don't know if anyone believes there's really a Bigfoot, but it's sold a lot of merchandise and attracted a lot of tourism. There's even been talk of changing the name of the beach from Barefoot Beach to Bigfoot Beach."

"And the mayor doesn't think that'll bring the victim's parents out here demanding his head?"

"At this point, I seriously doubt it."

"But that still doesn't explain why Bigfoot."

"The footprints at the crime scene. Next to the boy's body were a pair of prints that the tide couldn't reach to wash away. And they looked almost human, except..."

"Except they were really big?"

"Right. And there were traces of hair on Ethan's skin that still hasn't been clarified what it belongs to. That was when the Bigfoot talk started, and it just sort of spread like wildfire. The people jumped on it."

133

Paul nodded. "I guess I can see it. Something so ridiculous it's almost harmless, you know? I mean, everyone knows a Bigfoot would not be in this environment, even if it was real. So it's a safe way to cash in on the tragedy of death and the missing girl without coming across as inconsiderate douchebags."

Becky laughed. "It's a way to cash in, but I think you have to be an inconsiderate douchebag to even try it."

"I see your point."

They walked in silence for the next couple minutes. Becky was the first to speak.

"So, without trying to sound like I'm snooping, what brought you to our Bigfoot-obsessed town? I mean, other than taking a job for your brother."

Paul had known the question would be asked sooner or later, but he'd hoped for *way* later. "Just came here to start over."

Becky nodded. "I see."

"Which reminds me. I haven't seen a church anywhere around."

"There isn't one."

"No church?"

Shaking her head, Becky said, "This is a small town, but it's still eminently built around tourism. And no one wants to go to church on vacation."

Hearing this depressed Paul. He'd hoped to start going back to church, hopefully in the process teaching his children there was more to life than the misery they'd been living with.

"So, you're a Jesus freak?" she asked. There was nothing derisive about her tone. She'd asked as if curious what his favorite color was.

"When I was a teenager, yeah. As an adult I became a success freak. I figured since I've come to a new place to be a new person, maybe I could start going to church. Who knows if it would last, but I still thought it'd be a good idea to try."

"I'm sure you can find some around, but you'll have to drive a ways to get there."

Nodding, Paul figured as much.

"Wow," said Becky.

"What?"

"You totally changed the subject on me."

It hadn't been his original intention, but after he'd asked the question, he'd hoped it would steer them to a conversation where he didn't have to talk about his past. "Did I?"

"Yes, you did. And I *almost* fell for it."

Paul snapped his fingers. "Dang. I should've tried harder."

"If you don't want to talk about it, it's fine."

"No, it's not that I *don't* want to talk about it. I just don't know where to begin."

"Give me the cliff notes," she said.

Laughing, Paul nodded. "Sure."

He hardly flinched when Becky held his hand. It felt good having her fingers slipped into the grooves between his. It helped him talk about memories he'd tried to block. He told her about his stint as a local hero. She'd reacted in a way that hinted she might have already known about it and he figured she probably did.

"So," said Becky. "It's just you and your kids out here?"

"Yep. My son starts his senior year in a couple weeks and my daughter will be in the second grade. Technically, she should be in the third, but because her birthday misses the deadline, she didn't get to start when I think she should have."

"But no wife, correct?"

Paul felt a sharp jab in his heart. "No. No…wife."

"I'm sorry, that sounded so awful. I didn't mean it like that."

"It's okay. Alisha suffered a damaging nervous breakdown last year and she was locked up permanently by her doctor. I signed the papers saying I agreed and now she hates me. She hates all of us, actually."

"I'm so sorry. How'd it happen?"

Becky rubbed her other hand down his arm. It was the first physical act of affection he'd received from anyone, other than Natalie, in almost two years. It felt nearly as wonderful as a hug, though he imagined that would be just short of exorbitant.

"It really began after Gunner was born. She suffered great bouts of depression throughout the years afterward. But she started to get better and her doctor suggested another child might just be what she really needed. So along comes Natalie and it did seem to help her a lot. After a couple years, we started fighting again. *A lot*. I think we were on the verge of divorce when she had her first real breakdown.

135

She went away for a few weeks and when she came home, she was better.

It didn't last, though. When the depression and anger came back, it was really bad. She resented me for most of our marriage, but she was starting to really hate me at this point. Then I came across that car and the mayor's daughter and suddenly I'm this big hero."

"Did she agree?"

"I don't think so, but she had a good time with the illusion. When the spotlight on our family finally dimmed, I was so grateful. I wanted our normal life back, but Alisha was happy with the farce spectacle it had become. I stopped doing the appearances—not because they weren't asking me to, I was just tired of them. I only kept doing them for as long as I did to keep Alisha happy. So they eventually did stop asking me. Before long, everyone forgot about Paul Thompson, Hero Cop."

"Not your wife, though, right?"

"Right. Now she had this other Paul to compare me to. And she did it whenever I messed up. Didn't matter if I was hanging a hook for a picture frame, she'd say something like: 'Wow, the mighty sure has fallen. Before you could save lives, now you can't even hang a picture.' And it only got worse. Soon she was saying things like that to the kids. It got to where I was scared of leaving them home alone with her."

"Did she abuse them?"

"Physically, no. Mentally, you have no idea. I took an extended leave from the force to spend more time with the kids. Alisha had her fourth and final breakdown during that time and was locked up again. With her gone, I figured I could go back to work, but when I told the higher-ups I was ready to come back, they told me the budget for my salary was no longer there. Times were hard for everyone. So we go visit Alisha with her parents and I tell her that I'm looking for new work and that sets her off. She starts screaming at everyone, including her parents. The nurses had to sedate her just to calm her down. We all decided that the institution was the best place for her: her doctor, her parents, and me. We *all* decided. I talked to Gunner about it and he agreed, too. I'm sure Natalie would have had we asked her."

"Was that the last time you saw her?"

"No. Like suckers for abuse, we went back to visit her again. It was bad. *Really* bad. That was the last time. Then Howie called a couple months later with an offer I couldn't refuse. He had a house lined up, a job, and a good family town for the kids."

"And a Bigfoot."

Paul laughed. The bouncing it caused helped loosen the pinch in his chest and swelling in his throat. He hadn't realized how close to crying he actually was.

"And me," she said. She stopped walking, turned to face him. "I'm glad you're here, Paul. I don't know why, but I feel so completely comfortable with you. I hate what you had to go through to get here, but I'm happy you finally made it."

He couldn't believe what he was hearing. This seemed like an appropriate opportunity to kiss her, but he still wasn't convinced he should try. Maybe it was just a confidence booster that his pitiful story had brought out of her. She could still be saying anything she might offer to a friend who obviously needed some encouraging support.

When she hugged her arms around his neck, he realized she wasn't just trying to perk him up.

Leaning down to meet her, his lips brushed hers.

Then a deep blood-curdling roar ripped through the night.

Paul and Becky jerked their heads toward the shuddersome grumble with a unified gasp.

Little pinpricks of coldness traveled up Paul's back. And he had to agree with Becky's prior description of the roar.

Almost human, but not quite.

CHAPTER 18

The ocean seemed to hold its breath. The only sounds Paul heard as he struggled to keep up with Becky were the squishes their feet made in the sand. Even the waves, when they burst onto the shore, somehow seemed muted. He hadn't given it much thought earlier, but now as they jogged along the sand, he wondered where the other night strollers were. The beach was deserted: no bonfires, couples walking together, joggers, nighttime parties, or even bums. He knew from experience bums liked to prowl around the piers, begging for spare change to those who happened to walk by.

The water looked like black oil with a swath of sparkling blue from the moon hovering above the ocean so low that it might be about to dip into the sea. So far away from the pier, they didn't have its lights to see by, but the grayish, crater-filled disc in the sky provided plenty.

"Where are we going?" asked Paul.

"You heard it!"

"Yes, and it looks like we're heading *towards* the noise."

"We are. And I think I know where it is. Earlier today, your brother was with Mayor Caine and they were covering up some kind of crime scene."

"What?" Paul couldn't believe what he was hearing. "What kind of cover-up?"

"I don't know," she said, her voice bouncing. "I took pictures, but Thompson made me hand over my memory card. Cops were everywhere. I think it's something about some missing teenagers, but I don't have any specifics."

Gunner was out with some teenagers last night.

Paul wondered how close his son had come to being among the missing.

"I bet it's over in that area," she said, huffing.

Paul wanted to pull her, kicking and screaming if he had to, back the other way. Instead, he ran with her.

The roar resounded another time, triggering a patter of cold taps up his back. Whatever it was sounded angry, and somehow sad.

And very close.

The flat stretch of beach continued onward endlessly. To their right were sandbanks, lining the edge of the shore like sandy hillocks with little grassy sprigs poking through the top. Bushes and shrubs ran across the top like shaggy green hair. Beyond that was a barrier of darkness the woods provided.

"Up there," she said, pointing to the top.

They started up. It took some exertion, feet sliding on the sand, stumbles, but they finally made it to the top. Bushy stalks slapped Paul's shoulders, bristly leaves scratching his forearms and cheeks as he sunk to a crouch. Keeping low, they peered over the top and stared down to the sand below. Though it was heavy with shadows on the far side of the sandbanks, Paul could see the white carpet of sand. Nothing was down there. No person, no animal, and no Bigfoot.

"This was where it came from, right?" asked Becky.

Paul waved his hand ahead of them. "I...well—yeah, it sounded like it."

"Right?"

"Yes, I think so."

"Then where is it now?"

"Not down there."

Becky squinted, leaning forward as if doing so would make whatever she was looking for suddenly appear. "See any footprints?"

Paul copied her stance, straining his eyes to see. "No."

"Me neither."

"It doesn't mean they're not there. We can go look."

"We will."

"Think someone's pulling something? Like with the fake feet casts?"

"I don't know—maybe." She rose to her knees, arms slack to either side of her, knuckles in the sand. "We would've seen it if it had run."

"It?"

"Yes. Him, it, whatever. Either direction, we would have seen it when we were approaching."

"But if it ran that way," said Paul, pointing into the darkness that was a like a thick black wall several feet ahead. "We wouldn't have seen it if they went there."

"I would've," she said. "I was staring this way the whole time."

"So it was on the other side of this bank, we're agreed on that."

"Right."

"And unless it turned to vapor and floated away, it should still be down there."

"Agreed."

"So why isn't it?" Becky threw her shoulders up in an exaggerated shrug like a pouting child. Paul sighed. "Maybe there're speakers hidden somewhere."

Becky looked at him. At first she was smirking but the simper expression broke away. "You might be onto something there."

Together, they stood up. Becky slowly turned her head one way and another. Her pose was tense and ready, hands clenched into fists, but by the time she had given two complete scans of the area, her posture slouched. "Nothing."

Then she seemed to drop two feet in height.

Arms flapping, Becky shrieked. "Help me, Paul!"

Staring in shock, Paul watched her sink into the dune. She was down to her thighs before he blinked. "What's wrong!?!"

"Something's pulling me!" She dunked down to her belly, eyes getting bigger with each tug. *Help!*

Paul dove, landing hard on his stomach. The compacted sand punched the wind out of him, but he still grabbed her hands. Getting to his feet, he remained crouched in a squat as he pulled. He felt her climb, saw her become dislodged down to her hips. Then she was yanked back down, yanking Paul down to his front again.

He kept his grip, though he could feel her fingers starting to slip through his sweaty hold. Becky's screams hammered his ears like spikey jabs. He turned his head, trying to muffle her cries as he got to his knees. Then he leaped over her head, releasing her hands long enough to slip his arms under hers and pull with all he had. His feet sank into the sand down to his ankles.

He expected something to grab his feet as he pulled. Nothing did, and Becky kept rising. Once her knees appeared, she started moving them as if running. She didn't go anywhere, just jogged in place while fighting to break her legs free.

Finally, they burst from the sand. She toppled over the side, bringing Paul with her. They tumbled down the incline, crashing through bushes and hitting the flat turf. They rolled to a stop. Paul jumped to his hands and knees and crawled to Becky. He helped her to her knees.

"What was that?" he shouted.

"Its hands were so *big*!"

Getting to his feet, Paul leaned over, pulling at her. "Come on! We have to get out of here before—"

The sandbank's wall exploded in a gritty cloud that engulfed Paul, filling his eyes with granular bits, blinding him. He staggered back, digging at the sand with his fingers. Blinking only made it worse, like trying to stare through an hourglass of sand-filled water. Feet tangling, he dropped onto his ass.

"Paul!"

"Becky!"

"Oh my God—he's *real*!"

Paul viciously dug at his eyes, pulling out little grits of sand. It helped to unclog his vision, but it was still wet and blurry. He could see something large and coated in fur moving toward them.

It roared.

The powerful din shook Paul's insides.

Thunk. Thunk.

Paul recognized the heavy punches as footsteps.

Coming toward them.

"Becky! Come my way!"

Becky screamed.

Through the flooded goggles that were his eyes, he saw the beast approaching Becky, holding out a long, thickset arm. Its giant hand was fully extended as if wanting to give her a high five.

It grunted, softly and curious.

142

"Stay back!" she shouted.

A whining whimper, almost like a coo, followed. To Paul it sounded like the thing was trying to be sweet. It gripped the bottom of her shirt, twisting the fabric in his hand.

"Get the hell away from her!" Paul shouted.

The beast stepped back, ripping her shirt. A tidbit of fabric dangled from its fingers as it gave another bone-shaking roar, holding out its massive arms like someone ready to hug. Paul understood if something that size hugged him, he would be crushed during the embrace.

The beast charged.

Paul saw it quickly narrowing the distance between them.

A click resonated behind Paul, followed by a whistling pop that loudened as orange light started to brighten a dome around them. A sparkling ball punched into the dune wall, bursting into crackling flashes. In the orange smolder, Paul glimpsed the beast's face. Even through tear-soaked eyes, he could see it.

Not quite humanoid, but close enough with its bulging proboscis flaring out to two caverned nostrils. Infected scabs were spread across its bulky brow. Yellow eyes were set deep into a projecting face, the forehead a furrowed block above them. When it opened its mouth to roar, Paul saw its teeth were mostly humanlike, except for the canines which came to two narrow points. Not quite fangs, thicker and rounder on the ends.

Another spangled ball struck the sandbank beside the other that continued to pop and sparkle wildly. The combination of the sizzling orbs threw down writhing shadows across the sand.

Paul remained in his spot as if planted, unable to move. The beast scurried in reverse, holding its arms in front of itself like a shield. It roared at the sparklers, then stomped at one. Paul assumed it burned itself from how fast it snatched its foot back and hopped around in an irate tantrum.

Then the beast spun around and sprinted off into the dark.

Paul dropped forward, bracing himself up on his hands. Panting, he looked at Becky. She lay on her side, head turned away, gaping at the vicinity the beast had fled. He could see her flat stomach through her tattered shirt, her navel a wink on flesh. Sweat beaded across her smooth skin.

"Are you all right?" asked Paul. His voice sounded like he was hearing it through headphones.

Becky turned to him. Opening her mouth to respond, her face quickly stretched into a cry.

Paul spun around.

Approaching was a man, holding a gun that looked more like a cannon from the Civil War. He was dressed in fatigues: navy green cargo pants tucked into knee-high army boots. He had a vest stocked with a large Bowie knife and grenades over a dark T-shirt that stretched over his muscular torso. Arms lined with thick roots of veins and boulder-like biceps hung by his sides. On his head was a military beret with graying neatly cut hair waving out from underneath. A brush of stubble for a beard was divided by a deep scar on his cheek reaching down from his right eye.

As the man lowered the gun Paul realized it wasn't actually a real gun at all. *A flare gun.* As the flares he'd fired sizzled to glowing slivers, the man reached Paul. "Everybody all right?" His voice was deep, nearly slurred in its thickness.

Becky rolled onto her stomach as Paul dropped back, resting on his elbows. He felt drained and imagined Becky did as well.

Becky looked up at him. Her hair had fallen into her face, thick twiglets of golden brown hanging in her eyes. "Was that a Bigfoot?"

The man was silent for a moment. Then he said, "As a matter of fact, it was."

Becky and Paul shared a look of disbelief, but hidden in it was a not so subtle look that suggested conviction.

"Freeze!"

Paul jumped at the sudden barking demand. Looking past the soldier, Paul saw somebody approaching, pointing his handgun in front of him with both hands. As he neared, Deputy Lillard's lanky form became decipherable. Giving Becky and Paul a couple fleeting glances, he made his way to the solider.

"Are you two okay?" Lillard asked.

"I was just asking them the same," said the soldier.

"Shut up! And drop your goddamn weapon. *Now!*"

"Hardly a weapon, Deputy Fife."

"Do it, now!"

"Fine." He tossed the flare gun in front of him. It landed by Paul's hand in a clinking thump. "Should I get on my knees?"

"I'm the damn cop here."

"Absolutely."

"Get on your knees!"

The soldier sank to his knees. "My hands?"

"What?"

"Where should I put my hands? Behind my head?" My back? I suppose you'd like to cuff them?"

Paul would have laughed had he been watching this on television. But since it was in the here and now, he couldn't find any humor in the peculiar scene before him.

"Who are you?" asked Becky, pushing herself back to her knees.

"Call me Striker."

"Your name's Striker? Really?" asked Becky, skepticism heavy in her voice.

He stared at Becky long and hard. "My name can be whatever you want it to be."

"Whatever it is," said Officer Lillard, his gun still leveled on Striker, "you can sign it on the dotted line at the station. You're under arrest."

"On what grounds?" asked Striker.

"Weapons on the beach."

"Did you see what just happened here?" asked Becky. "We were almost killed…"

"I'm not sure what I saw," said Lillard, removing the cuffs from his belt.

Heavy treads of feet stomping through sand made all of them jump and cry out, except for Striker, who stayed unmoving like a handsomely toned statue arrayed in survival gear.

He must have known it wasn't the creature, Paul realized, as Lillard's heavyset partner arrived. Leaning over, he panted through his chubby red cheeks. Paul couldn't remember his name, but he wondered if the man might need medical attention.

"You got them?" he asked.

Lillard nodded. "Cuff this one." He tossed the handcuffs to his partner. "We're taking *him* under custody, but all of them are coming to the station."

"You got it."

The rotund cop walked over to Striker, still winded, and began pulling his arms behind his back. Striker didn't resist, though if he wanted to, he could obviously make this arrest very difficult for the bumbling deputies.

Paul stood up, held out his hand, and assisted Becky to her feet.

Turning to face Lillard, she slapped her hands on her hips. "You can't be seriously arresting him. He saved our asses."

Lillard held up his hand. "Not now, Becky. I'm not in the mood. I'm sure we all have questions and this guy probably can answer them."

Striker shrugged, smiling like a kid who knew a devilish secret.

CHAPTER 19

Howie's office was heavy with uncomfortable silence, save the ticking from the wall-mounted clock. Paul and Becky had been ordered to sit in the pair of chairs in front of Howie's desk until he arrived and neither had spoken since Lillard left them in here. On the way to the station, Lillard had radioed in and ordered Junior to patch him through to Howie's home. Evidently, Howie had been awakened by the phone and was none too pleased to be disturbed. Paul had listened as Lillard briefly described the ordeal on the beach, leaving out all mentions of the Bigfoot. The only mention the beast had gotten was in a murmured *'Possible sighting'* from Lillard.

Paul fidgeted with his fingers, tapping the tips together, making funny shapes with them. A few times he'd made a church and opened it up to show the people. None of his hand games seemed to help make time go by any faster.

Leaning back in his chair, Paul sighed, and returned to looking around. He saw the pictures of his nephews again in a tripod photo frame. All of them were muscular and attractive, a perfect snapshot of success-in-the-making. There was another frame with a family photo taken somewhere in the mountains with the five of them standing abreast in front of a gorgeous waterfall.

Paul scanned plaques, awards, diplomas, and a bronzed pair of handcuffs on a plaque stating Howie was the world's best sheriff.

The rest of the office was plain. Dull paint and a bland strip of law enforcement brown wallpaper went around the entire room. It gave the overall impression of discomfort, like a principal's office, and that was how Paul felt, as if he was waiting on his punishment to be administered.

He jumped when the door swung open, banging against the wall and rattling the drab décor hanging from the walls.

"What the hell is going on here?" shouted Howie. Entering, he grabbed the door and flung it behind him. The door slammed. "Can you please explain to me why the hell I was dragged away from my beautiful wife to come here?"

"Um…" Paul didn't know how to answer.

"Oh, and don't worry, I woke Trish up as well and sent her to your place to sit with your kids."

"How'd she get in?"

"I have a—"

"Key. Right."

Howie stepped around his desk, jerking the chair back as if he was about to assault the comfy-looking seat. He had on his uniform, but the shirt hadn't been tucked in and hung unbuttoned over a white, wife-beater tank top. Paul noticed the muscle bulging against the wispy white shirt and felt a pang of envy.

Howie dropped down in the chair. Leaning over his desk, the chair popped with protest. The look on his brother's face once again reminded Paul of their father. It also made him immediately feel as if he'd been caught doing something wrong. He recalled the time Dad had come into his room after discovering Paul had been skipping school.

Scowling, Howie held out his hands. "So what the hell?"

Paul looked to Becky for help. She shrugged. Sighing, Paul turned back to his brother to find his face had darkened with another flush of anger. The bags under his eyes were puffy half-moons.

"*Well?*" said Howie.

Clearing his throat, Paul leaned forward. "It's real."

"It's…real." Howie repeated, slowly.

"Yes."

"What is?"

"The Bigfoot."

Howie held his glower a moment longer before it broke away to laughter and a wide smile. "The Bigfoot's real, he says."

"It is."

Howie laughed again. "So you're telling me that a mythical creature believed to rove the mountains in states far from ours is real?"

"Um—well..."

"And it's now on our beach?" Howie asked.

"Yeah...that's what I'm saying."

Howie tipped back his head and unleashed a booming guffaw. When he raised his head, tears were trickling down from his eyes. The laughter was contagious, spreading to Paul and carrying over to Becky who joined in, apprehensively at first, but before long, the once dead calm room was a hullabaloo of laughter.

Then Howie slammed his fists down on the desk, killing it. "Do you think I'm an idiotic buffoon!?!"

"We saw it," said Becky. "It attacked us."

"That's not possible."

"It is," said Paul. "It damn near got Becky."

"He's right," she said, leaning back. She swung her legs up, dropping her feet on the corner of Howie's desk. Her pants were torn around the ankles. She pulled them apart, showing a patch of tanned skin that was ruddy around the scrapes. "This is where it grabbed me."

Howie looked at her injuries, frowning. "Put your legs down, Becky." She did. "And this...Striker guy *saved* you?"

"That's right."

"That's a load of shit, is what that is."

"But my legs," started Becky.

Howie silenced her with a wave of his hand. "Probably did that yourself, shaving."

"Shaving?" Becky's mouth dropped, coughing noises coming from her throat. "*Shaving?*"

"You have to believe me, Howie. Why would I make something like that up?"

Howie relaxed some, but not much. "I'm not saying you made it up. I'm saying you didn't see what you think you did."

"There's no way it wasn't what I think it is."

"Or what *I* think it is." Becky added. She thrust her hands down at her legs. "Or what I *know* caused this. And it wasn't my goddamn razor!"

"And the two of you think it's a Bigfoot." It wasn't a question, but a statement, almost an accusation.

Paul frowned. "Unfortunately."

Groaning, Howie leaned back in the chair, entwining his fingers and putting them on top of his head. "Tell me what happened."

Paul told him everything, including the scabs, bald spots, and infected rashes spread along the Sasquatch's body.

"And we would have been killed for sure if that Striker guy wouldn't have shown up," said Paul, ending his recapping.

Howie poked out his bottom lip, looking as if he might be considering the story. "And you don't find that odd?"

Paul narrowed his eyes. "What do you mean?"

"This creature attacks you and this guy just happens to be there toting a weapon that scares it off?"

Paul hadn't considered how unlikely those odds were until now. There was no way Striker would have known, unless he already knew the creature would be there.

Or if he'd staged the whole thing.

Turning to Becky, he saw the look on her face suggested she might agree.

"And you said he didn't shoot the thing, right?" asked Howie.

"No. He fired off to the side. Like warning shots or something."

"See my point?"

"Yeah," sighed Paul. "I know what you're going to say next. That it was all some kind of stunt."

"Exactly."

"There's a good chance you're absolutely right."

"I know I am," said Howie, convinced.

"But you didn't see the Bigfoot, Howie. That was not a guy in a suit."

Becky shook her head. "Nope. And it was strong. Damn strong."

"Couldn't have been too strong if Paul was able to pull you from its grip."

Maybe sand got in its eyes, too.

He was about to tell Howie that, but the door swung open again. "Is it true?" somebody asked.

Paul recognized the voice. Mayor Caine. Paul turned around in the seat, seeing the mayor entering, dressed in silk pajamas with a matching robe thrown over it.

Does this guy always wear pajamas?

He cut between Paul and Becky to reach Howie's desk. "Is it?"

"Are you kidding me?" said Howie. "No. There's no Bigfoot. And turn off your damn scanner. I'm tired of telling you people this."

"Is it true you have a man in custody? Someone who stumbled onto the scene and scared it off?"

"Hardly stumbled. Just as I was starting to explain to my brother and his facts-twisting girlfriend here, there is no way someone wanders up on a scene like that and happens to be equipped to handle it."

Bubba stepped into the doorway, filling it with his bulky mass. Hands crossed at his stomach, he stood there quietly. Paul studied his shape and briefly pondered the idea of him dressed in a Bigfoot suit.

No way. This guy isn't anywhere close to being as lean.

Paul scooted his chair over so Caine wasn't standing right on top of him.

"Where's the man?" asked Caine.

"In a holding cell."

"And what are you going to do about it?" Caine put a hand on his hip, jutting out his side.

"Well," said Howie, leaning back in his chair. He put both hands down on his desk nonchalantly. "I'm going to let him go."

"What!?!" shouted Caine. His face soured, cheeks darkening red.

"The only thing I have him on is for having weapons on the beach, which weren't concealed, by the way. The grenades are okay since he's military and has the proper licenses. The flare gun isn't illegal, so all I can do is fine him the maximum of a thousand dollars and tell him not to do it again."

"I'm overruling your call on that one."

"On what authority?"

"Mine. The town's. Take your pick, I don't care."

"You'll have to submit your so-called superseding decision in writing to the board and it could take up to a week for them to vote. Have you lost your mind?"

"Not at all. My mind is fresh, crisp." He snapped his fingers. "Quick like a mousetrap."

Paul could not grasp how this guy had become mayor.

And Gunner has the hots for his daughter? Is she a loon like this imbecile?

"Listen to me, Sheriff," said Caine. "Let's go down to the pen and talk to this guy. Hear him out."

"What for?"

"Humor me, Sheriff."

Howie sighed, dipping his head. Paul recognized defeat when he saw it. He imagined Howie wanted to dispute this further, but probably figured it was pointless. "All right, Caine. We'll head down there."

"Not without me," said Becky.

"Of course not," said Caine. "The press should hear this too."

"Absolutely," said Howie. "Wouldn't be a party without her, right?"

CHAPTER 20

"I've been waiting on this meeting," said Striker. "I knew sooner or later you'd come down here, wanting to talk." He sat on the bench in his cell, a lone prisoner in a kennel of single cells. Leaning slightly forward, elbows resting on his knees, he looked at them through the bars.

Paul was amazed by Striker's bodybuilder size. His biceps looked to be as big as Paul's head.

"Arnold Striker?" asked Howie.

Striker looked down at himself. "I better be. I'm wearing his underwear."

Becky snickered, a soft quacking sound in her throat.

Howie leered at the buff man, not amused. "Making jokes?"

"The only joke here is your judicial system."

"You can rot in there, pal." Howie started to turn around, but Caine's grip on his forearm stopped him. The hard look he gave the finicky mayor sent a cold shiver even through Paul. "Want to let go of my arm?"

"Don't be pigheaded, Sheriff. We came here to talk. He's only sizing you up to see if you're a threat."

"And I'm sure he knows that I am."

"Howard," said Caine with a bit more hardness. "I do insist."

"Fine, if *you* want to talk to him, then talk."

"Thank you." Caine released Howie's arm and approached the cell. "Mr. Striker, I'm Mayor Caine..."

"I know who you are."

"Oh, you do?"

"I know who all of you are except for that guy over there on the right who looks like he's a guest at a party he doesn't want to be at."

Everybody turned to stare at Paul.

"Wow," said Paul. "You nailed that."

Striker nodded with a wink. "So, who are you?"

"Paul Thompson."

"Any relation to my kind host here."

"Brother."

"Uh-huh. Thought so. You guys look alike."

"Should I give you guys a moment alone?" asked Howie. "I mean—you're bonding so well already. Paul, you could take him home, you have a car with two seats, right?"

"Sheriff Thompson," said Caine. "Another comment like that and I'll be forced to ask you to leave. Please don't make me do that."

"Then ask him your goddamn questions and quit this polite bullshit."

"I'll ignore your harshness, Sheriff, and get on with it." Caine turned to Striker once again. "How do you know us?"

"I researched the town. I know who you are. And that burly guy who's always with you is your bodyguard, but the rumor is you're lovers."

Caine gasped. Bubba's mouth dropped soundlessly open.

Becky repeated her quacking neigh of concealed laughter. Even Howie's tightly pressed mouth arched a little in the corner.

"And the lovely lady is Rebecca Aniston, town reporter with aspirations of being a well-respected probing journalist for a much bigger gazette in a *much* bigger city."

Becky's eyes widened. Her cheeks dotted with red flushes. She looked around as if wanting to apologize for his being right.

"And my new best friend is Sheriff Howard—*Howie*—Thompson. Moved here years ago with his wife, Patricia, whose family owned a house out here. The paperwork claims you purchased the property from her parents, but I'd bet my favorite automatic rifle that it was a wedding gift."

Howie fumed, looking like he might reach through the bars and squeeze Striker's throat.

"Okay," said Caine. "I see you did your homework, though you're obviously wrong about my relationship with my associate. So why are you here?"

"You know why I'm here."

"Please, just share it with me. I'd rather hear it from your mouth."

"I'm here to get back my Bigfoot."

Paul felt a squirmy sensation in his stomach.

Caine smiled. "*The* Bigfoot?"

"*My* Bigfoot. The one you've turned into your poster boy. I've seen residents parading around for the tourists dressed in costumes, selling merchandise and clothing and trinkets with its face plastered across like some kind of goddamn mascot. If only you knew the kind of feral danger you're promoting, you wouldn't be doing it."

"Feral danger? Why don't you explain to us this feral danger, and why do you call the Bigfeet monster yours?"

"Bigfeet?"

"Sausfoot…whatever."

"He doesn't say the name right sometimes," said Howie. "He's an idiot."

"For the first time tonight, you and I are in total agreement."

"Fine," said Caine, waving his hand. "I will be the punchline to your joke if it will get you talking to me."

Striker smiled. "Fair enough. It's my Bigfoot because I have already captured it twice. And both times it's managed to elude me. I've hunted it since I was a teenager, through the deep mountains of Colorado and Utah. It's always managed to get the upper hand. We caught up to it once when I was nineteen, cornered it in some caves in Utah. We pumped elephant tranquilizers in it, enough to put a full-sized elephant out for a week. We had the beast chained up in the back of our cargo truck and were heading back down the mountain when it woke up. It snapped the chains as easily as someone breaking a carrot. Its strength is immeasurable.

"After it broke his chains, it ripped the back of the truck open and snatched my Papa right out. It tore Papa limb from limb. I tried to regain control of the truck but it was already careening over the edge of the ridge and down we went. When I came to I was being airlifted to the nearest hospital. The Bigfoot was gone and my Papa was dead." Striker sighed. "And all I have to show for it is this." He pointed at the long wavy scar on his cheek.

155

"Was that…?" Caine's voice petered out. He cleared his throat and tried again. "Was that the first time you caught it?"

"No. That was the *last* time my Papa caught it. The first time *I* caught it was fifteen years ago. It had snuck back into Colorado and I'd tracked it for six weeks in the wilderness. It wasn't easy, but I led the bastard into a trap. This time, I'd thought ahead. We had a cell erected from solid steel and after we had it incapacitated, we put it inside. Then we airlifted it out of the mountains. Wasn't two hours before it busted through the top and climbed up the chain and into the chopper. Killed my entire team, and the chopper went down in the mountains of North Carolina, near Wildcat Landing. And the only two survivors were it and me."

As Striker's story progressed, his voice had become more intense and whispery. Paul felt like he was in an old Rambo movie, listening to John Rambo convey a story about an old battle that had gone horribly wrong.

"The second time was a few months back. I'd assembled a new team of mercenaries, the best of the best they'd said. We caught back up to it outside of Seven Devil Ridge. Again, we laid a trap, and again we seized the beast. It had almost seemed too easy, but I thought maybe it was getting old and predictable. I was wrong."

"The pieces that washed up on our shores," said Howie, "was from your boat, wasn't it?"

"Yes. We had chartered a private boat, and for an additional hefty sum, the captain kept it off the charts. I'd hired a trap-maker to design a cage for the Bigfoot, something that he could not break. And he put together this unique cage. We tested its durability with a bulldozer. The bars broke the teeth off its blade. But as you can see it still wasn't enough to contain the Bigfoot."

"How in the hell can something be so strong?" asked Caine. "How?"

Striker shrugged. "Guess it got all the goods in evolution, and we got what was left."

"Do you really believe that?" asked Caine.

"What does it matter what I believe at this point? All I know is the bastard's real and very deadly."

Nobody disputed Striker's claim. A dark calm had spread through them all.

Becky was the one to break it. "What happened on the boat?" she asked, sounding fully like a reporter at a press conference.

"It got loose."

The group waited for him to continue, but he never did.

"*After* it got loose," said Becky. "What'd it do then?"

"Killed everyone on board. Captain included. The boat deviated abruptly off course and crashed into the rocks and shattered on impact. What didn't break sank. I went down with the ship, and so did the Bigfoot. Clinging to a floating piece of debris, I washed on shore. I thought the creature might have drowned, but I stuck close by just in case. When I heard about the sightings, I figured it was the Bigfoot. When that boy was killed, I knew for certain it was."

"Why didn't you come forward sooner?" said Howie.

"Sure. Right. That would've been a good idea."

"We probably would've believed you, especially after finding the footprint."

"You'd have thought I somehow caused it. Like I'm sure you were thinking when you walked in here. No. I had to let it show itself before I made my move. I waited and waited and it never did. I think it stayed out of sight because of the heavy amount of people you had here this summer. Maybe it was scared or just being extra cautious."

"Why do you think it's out now?" asked Howie. "It's killed one of my men, a teenage girl and possibly two other teenage boys. Maybe more for all we know."

Striker's eyebrows lifted, lips pointed out. "Looking for food? Exploring? It's what it does."

"And what about the missing girl?" asked Becky.

"What about her?"

"Should we assume she's dead, too?

"A year ago, I'd say there's a good chance that she is."

"What if she's not?" asked Becky.

"Then it's keeping her."

"Why would he do that?" asked Paul.

"It's lonely being such a rare species. It wants a female companion. You can imagine the rest."

"Jesus," Becky muttered.

Striker shrugged. "You asked."

"Well, that's a pretty amazing story," said Caine.

"Right," said Howie. "And what do you suggest we do about it?"

"The obvious thing," said Caine.

To Paul, the obvious thing would be stopping this Bigfoot parade the town had become. But something told him Caine wasn't thinking logically.

And he proved Paul right when he said, "Capture it ourselves. With Mr. Striker's help, of course."

"You've lost your mind," said Howie.

Striker laughed. "With my help. Is that what you think? Believe me when I tell you this is no longer a seek-and-capture mission. It's now seek-and-destroy."

"Fine," said Caine, waving his hand as if annoyed by a fly buzzing around his face. "Just as long as we get a picture of it. A good one like the kind they take when someone catches a giant shark or something. We can have it strung up, with me in the foreground clutching a giant rifle." His eyes as round as ping pong balls, he wiped his hand in the air from one side to the other. "Mayor saves his own town from Bigfoot menace. What do you think of that Ms. Aniston? Would that sell some papers or what?"

Becky seemed too shocked to reply, but she managed to mutter, "Sh-sure."

Striker stood up and walked over to the bars. He gripped them so tightly his knuckles strained white. "Did you not hear anything I just said? I've lost count of how many people this son of a bitch has killed—civilians *and* soldiers. This thing does not deserve to be celebrated in your town, Mayor. It deserves to have its head impaled on a stake."

Mayor Caine winced as if he'd just bit into a sour pickle. "So I take it you're in?"

Striker's upper lip twitched into an almost snarl, baring teeth. "I'm in. But not on your terms. On *mine*."

Caine clapped his hands together. The loud smack reverberated all around. "Tomorrow morning then. We'll all meet here at eight. I'll bring Bubba, and Sheriff, you bring a couple men."

"I'm going," said Becky.

"Same here," said Paul, not realizing he was going to volunteer until hearing the words aloud.

Howie smirked. "No way. Both of you can forget it. Becky's a civilian and Paul, you're not in the books to start duty yet. Too much of a liability if one of you were to get hurt."

Before Paul couldn't dispute, Caine cut him off.

"Deputize them," said Caine.

"I beg your pardon?"

"Deputize them and put a weapon in their hands. We can't take the entire police force, Sheriff, and we can't call in reinforcements from the other cities. I want to keep this hush-hush until the Beastfoot is dead. Then we'll call a press conference, and Ms. Aniston here will get first dibs at all the questions, interviews, and stories. After that, we'll unveil the carcass for the town to see. We'll be indestructible. Our town will live on well after we're gone. We'll be the new Loch Ness! No more worries, Howard. Can you imagine what it would be like to not have to worry if the summer months are going to fund our falls, winters, and springs?"

Paul studied his brother. He recognized the inner turmoil, though his expressions and movements showed none of it. Howard wanted all those things, wanted the confidence in knowing their town would survive. But he also didn't want to earn it from what would have to be done.

How bad is it for them that they have to even entertain such an idea?

"I don't like it," said Howie. He shrugged. "But what choice do I have?"

"No choice," answered Caine. "None whatsoever."

Howie sighed. He looked at each person before walking away. Paul watched him leave the room.

"I believe I share your sheriff's concerns," said Striker. "If we do find him, I doubt any of you will be alive to reap the rewards."

Paul's intestines felt as if they were being squeezed with cold hands. Somehow, he knew Striker was right. He'd seen the beast. He knew more about what they were up against than Caine.

And I volunteered to tag along.

But when he looked at Becky and saw the evident fear in her eyes, he decided going with them was the right decision. Howie would also need someone on his side out there. He doubted anyone else would have Howie's back more than him.

An awkward bout of silence filled the room. Though nobody seemed to enjoy the stillness, nobody was quick to end it, including Becky. Eyes were aimed at the floor, the walls, anything to keep from making contact with somebody else.

A couple minutes later, Howie returned with a Bible and a pair of tiny badges. "All right," he said. "Let's get this bullshit over with." Holding out the Bible, he stopped in front of Becky first. "I'm going to swear you in." He turned to Paul. "Then you. We still have a lot of paperwork to do before you become a legitimate deputy, Paul."

Paul nodded.

Howie said, "I'm going to make myself absolutely transparent here. I do not like this. I do not endorse this. This is your last chance to change your mind. Once you're deputized, I will hold you accountable out there. Got me?"

Becky nodded. Howie looked back at Paul. He also nodded.

Howie took a deep breath. Letting it out, his cheeks puffed. "All right. Here we go."

CHAPTER 21

Howie dropped off Trish when he picked up Paul. He thanked her for once again hanging out with his kids. She acted as if she was glad to do it, but he could tell on the inside she resented him for it. And Paul hated himself for putting her in a position where she couldn't say no. Again.

Now, sitting in the passenger seat of Howie's Suburban, on their way to the station, Paul battled whether his decision was what was best for his family.

It's not.

He should be spending time reestablishing the bond he used to have with them before Alisha's mental state drove a spike through it. They'd been a tightknit group, banding together during the hardship. However, since Alisha was out of the picture for good, they'd drifted apart. Even Natalie no longer seemed as close to Paul as she once had been. Technically, she was still glad to be Daddy's little girl, but there was this distrust that he detected with her. It was as if she was waiting for him to turn on her like Mommy had.

Never. I would never turn on her or Gunner.

"Uniform looks like it fits all right," said Howie.

Paul glanced down at the tan and khaki colored shirt and pants. His gun belt was a glossy black bar that separated the lighter tone from the darker one. But it did feel uplifting to have his trusty Ruger back on his hip. The familiar weight against his side was like an affectionate tap from a loved one. "Thanks," he said.

"Looks a little loose, though. Lost some weight?"

There were periods, though rare, when depression really ate at Paul which in return made him not want to eat anything. He'd fake it in front of the kids with small bites and spreading his food across his plate to make it look bare. But after they'd left the table, he would dump what was left on his plate into the trash. What little he'd actually ingested would come out quickly because of his upset stomach.

Instead of admitting all of this to Howie, he said, "A little. Got to look my best." He offered a smile that felt strained on his face.

"You seem bothered by something," said Howie.

"Who me?" Paul didn't take his eyes from the window. He stared out at the private homes, built on stilts and lined up beyond the road. He could see the ocean through the gaps underneath the houses in the distance. This early in the morning the water looked teal under the faded blue of the sky. It was already hot and humid, and Paul could feel little itchy welts rising on his arms from mosquito bites.

"Want to back out?"

Paul nearly groaned. "No. I'm not backing out."

"I didn't mean for that to sound insulting, if it did."

"It didn't."

"I'm just saying you can change your mind. You don't have to go."

"I know I don't."

"Then why are you?"

"I have no idea."

And yet, here he was, running out with his brother to track down a Bigfoot.

How ridiculous is that?

Paul might have laughed at the absurdity of the situation, had it been funny. But he figured he knew the real reason he'd volunteered to go along. *Becky.* Deep down, he knew the only reason he'd agreed to go was he wanted to be near her.

Chasing a woman when I should be rebuilding my family.

"I can think of one," said Howie.

"I'm sure you can, but please don't."

"Not really the kind of first date you need."

"Stop."

Howie glanced at him, nodded. "Fine."

162

"Do you really think we're going to be able to stop this thing?"

"Do you want me to lie?"

"Please."

"Sure."

"Do you believe that it's real now?"

"I'm not sure what I believe. I believe you saw something. And I can tell Striker believes. He wasn't lying when he was telling us his story. I've always had a great bullshit detector, and he thinks his story is real. He truly believes there's a Bigfoot out there that he can't kill."

"But you're not entirely convinced."

"Who knows? Maybe I am."

"Maybe you're not."

"Does it really matter one way or another?"

"You could have told Caine to fuck himself."

Howie nodded. "Yeah. I could've also refused this search party. But it would have cost me my job."

"Can Caine really fire you?"

"Not on his own, no. But he has the pull to get me canned. It would only take one board meeting and then a town meeting afterward to get me out of here. Why put everyone through that when agreeing with Caine would make things so much simpler?"

"I guess I see your point."

"Are you trying to prove something to yourself by going with us?"

Paul's eyes popped open with a choked gasp. "Where'd that come from?"

"It's just a question. You don't have to answer it."

Paul scratched his head. His hair was damp from a light misting of sweat. Even in the air-conditioning, he still felt hot. It was Howie's blunt query that had caused it. "What would I be trying to prove?" As soon as he'd asked, he wished he hadn't. He knew Howie already had an answer waiting.

Proving Paul right, Howie said, "Because you're angry with yourself. You blame yourself for Alisha's problems."

"Come on, Howie, I was a major cause of her…stress."

"That's bullshit."

"It's bullshit for you to say it's bullshit. *I* screwed up. I could've kept playing the hero, could've tried harder to make her happy. I know budgets were cut and the force had to severe ties with people, and there was nothing I could do to stop that, but there are other places to go work. I sort of just stayed in idle after I lost my job. I could've done—I don't know—more, I guess."

Howie seemed not to have heard any of what Paul said. "Does it make you feel better?"

"Does what make me feel better?"

"Shouldering all the blame and guilt. I don't think your kids blame you at all, but I think they can tell that you do and are too scared to point it out."

"You asshole, leave my kids out of this."

"Out of what? I'm just pointing out—"

"I know what you're doing, so knock it off."

"Damn it, Paul. You need to snap out of this. Alisha's where she's at because of a chemical imbalance. It's nothing you did to make it happen. *She* didn't even do it. So stop making yourself out to be the bad guy here."

"I'm not doing that at all."

Howie pushed back into the seat as if the car was slowly pressing together. Paul could tell this talk was peeving him.

"Yes, you are," said Howie. "That's exactly what you're doing. You're putting all this liability on yourself because you feel like you've failed your children, so you are constantly trying to make it up to them when they don't blame you at all."

"Yes, they do. Deep down."

"Trust me. They don't. You're weakening yourself because you think it will make your relationship with them calmer, when the truth is, your relationship with them is just fine. Or it was before you started acting like the boyfriend who's relentlessly kissing his girlfriend's ass. Stop that shit right away before they start thinking you can't handle their problems. If they think that, they'll stop coming to you for help."

Howie's speech hit Paul like a brick to the skull. Everything he'd said made perfect sense. Worst of all, he feared they already had stopped seeking out his assistance in their personal affairs. Even Natalie wouldn't willingly come to him whenever she had an eight-year-old's dilemma. She'd go to Gunner first and if he couldn't help, then she'd go to Paul.

Howie sighed. "I'm out of line and I'm sorry."

"Stop it, man, seriously. I don't think right now is the time for us to talk about this."

"It's the perfect time. Who knows if we'll get the chance later…" Howie's voice trailed off and he made a regretful face, as if he'd accidentally divulged information he shouldn't have.

Paul understood where Howie had been going with his last comment. He was about to offer some kind of reassuring negation when the backside of the police station came into view. A small group was already assembled in the back parking lot. From this short distance, he recognized Striker right away in his mercenary gear. Becky's petite frame was also easy to spot.

"Talk about a welcome wagon," said Howie.

"Really."

Groaning, Howie situated himself in the seat. "This is going to be a *long* day." He opened his mouth, about to say something more, but stopped.

And Paul was grateful.

CHAPTER 22

Harold Williams walked along the mist-shrouded street, moving behind the empty rental houses. He held Bobo's leash, the tip wrapped around his hand as the black lab kept his nose to the ground, sniffing. Every few feet he stopped and cocked his leg to urinate on something that smelled strange to him. This was an every morning routine that had become much more enjoyable since the tourists had gone home. He could actually move about freely without the lines of cars behind the houses, or the abundance of people wandering to the beach at this hour to search for seashells. He understood the summer months were what kept his town striving, but it never took long before he was ready to see the tourists go home. This year had been the worst and most crowded he could remember.

A lot more college kids this time, too.

Those were what he despised the most. Adult brats coming here to spend Mommy and Daddy's money on booze while treating the locals like horse piss.

And we're supposed to kiss their smooth rich asses so they'll come back?

Harold spat.

Bah!

Harold Williams was sixty-seven, thin, and walked with slightly-stooped shoulders. He still had most of his hair, though this morning it was an out of control squirrel's nest on his head. He owned a convenience store in Seashell Cove. And being one of the few local businesses that stocked beer, all he saw were those college assholes. The women were nice to look at, coming in wearing their skimpy bikinis and dark tans. It never failed to surprise him how so many women would just walk around in public without covering up. He supposed they figured since it was the beach, then it didn't matter. But the signs around town clearly stated that you must be dressed to enter the stores. Maybe during all their expensive tuitions and long hours at the schools, they'd forgotten to learn how to read.

Spitting again, Harold paused to give Bobo time to urinate on a small bush. There was a used condom wrapped around the base, the extended sperm-catching tip clinging to a prickly leaf.

Well if that isn't just awful.

If they were going to screw in the streets, they could at least clean up after themselves. He'd stopped counting how much litter he'd come across during his morning walks this week. The condom was the foulest and most disrespectable of them all.

So far.

He figured a guy had been knocking a girl's socks off in the backseat of his car and just discarded the used rubber tube out the window. Harold was envious of those young full-of-cum bums. Back in the day, he could rut like the best of them. Wasn't a hole he couldn't plug. In fact, he became quite popularly known as the trunk snake.

Smiling, Harold gave Bobo's leash a couple quick tugs to get him moving before he put his nose against the condom. He didn't want whatever coated the slick exterior to adhere to his dog's nose. He'd have to give him a bath when they got home, and he didn't want to spend the rest of his morning before going into the store to check on his part-time clerk washing the damn mutt.

Might have been stuffed inside a man's butt for all I know.

Fags were another thing he'd seen a lot of this year. They'd come into his store multiple times, daily, buying beer and alcohol-tainted lemonades and teas. Some of them blended in quite well and if he hadn't seen the male pairs holding hands, he never would have known. Others, well, they seemed to want everyone to know they preferred stuffing a man's pooper instead of that sweet honey pot between a woman's legs. Even their voices told all he needed to know about them. Seemed to Harold that sometimes when a man decided to be gay, he felt he had to alter his voice to make the uncertainty plain and apparent.

Maybe some of the guys were just confused. After all, a lot of the guys out here looked like girls with their skinny bodies and long hair. He'd just talked about it with Walt the other day, how a lot of fags even smelled like women, too. Harold started to smell that coconut-fruit aroma blended with sweat and shook his head, hoping to jar it loose.

It was probably one of those pillow-biters broke into Walt's store the other night.

That scent returned, trying to nauseate Harold. He pinched his nose, rubbing his nostrils with his fingertips as if he could pull out the residue of the smell.

Then he bumped into Bobo's hindquarters, nearly stumbling over the stalled mutt. He hadn't noticed Bobo had stopped walking until colliding with him. Looking down, Harold expected to find his dog either sniffing the dirt path or his leg up with a drippy stream of urine spraying a patch of grass. Instead, his dog stood erect, legs stiff and unmoving, head tilted back as his wet nose slowly wiggled.

Sniffing.

"Whatcha smell there, buddy?" The dog didn't acknowledge Harold's voice. "You smell them homos, too?"

Maybe there're still some lingering around, out for a morning walk.

If that was the case, then Harold wanted to be walking *away* from them, not toward. If they saw Bobo, they'd want to stop and pet him. Might want to make meaningless conversation while they ruffled his dog's ears with their man-loving fingers.

Another stench overpowered the coconut smell. This one was worse, like a combination of old rotted fish and dead animals. It seemed to be entrapped in the mist's hazy fingers.

Harold noticed the small patch of hair starting to rise on Bobo's back.

"What's over there?"

Bobo jerked against the leash. The momentum yanked Harold forward a couple steps. Had he not wrapped the leash around his wrist, Bobo would have gotten free.

"What's the matter with you, boy?"

Something clamored—a deep hollow rattle. Harold recognized the sound even before he saw the aluminum trash can rolling slowly forward. It seemed to be coming to greet Harold but it suddenly veered to the left and went into the grass. It stopped rolling. There was nothing inside. No bags or loose trash. Just a dark emptiness.

Another softer rattle resounded from up ahead, followed by a crash. It was too foggy to see what was causing the noise, but Harold figured it was also a trash can, this time the lid had been snatched off and thrown.

An aggravated grunt soon followed. Then there was a quick whistling that dove into another bang. Another trash can rolled toward them.

Bobo hunkered down, jowls twitching with a snarl. Harold tugged on the leash, trying to lead him away, but the dog just couldn't be moved.

"Come on, boy," he whispered.

Something roared. The loud rumble reverberated off the houses, feeling like a train barreling through. It fluttered Harold's clothes, stirred his humidity-mussed hair.

Bobo suddenly spun around and lurched between Harold's legs. The dog's hasty departure and large size snapped Harold's arm down. His feet left the ground and he twirled in the air, landing on the sand-sprinkled road flat on his back. The leash unraveled from his wrist and he felt the dog go.

Pain pulsed through his body. The wind hadn't been knocked completely out of his lungs, but it felt as if he was trying to breathe through a pinched straw. Rolling onto his stomach, he looked up. All he could see of Bobo was his tail tucked between his legs and the red leash dragging the ground behind him. A moment later he vanished in the fog, on his way home.

Harold shook his fist. "You *traitor!*"

A piercing yelp filled the air, killing Harold's cries. Bobo was hurt.

"Bo...bo?"

He stared at the swirling wall of mist as an eerie calm spread throughout. Bobo was running home, Harold didn't doubt that. But what had been behind them to intercept his poor dog?

Another grunt and heavy thudding footsteps followed. Harold felt his scowl slowly drop away into a panicked mask of fear. The stench grew heavier, bringing tears to his eyes as if he was inhaling pure chlorine through his nostrils. It burned the back of his throat.

He rolled onto his back, wincing at the pain in his left hip.

170

He froze when he saw the large dark figure shambling through the mist. It came from the direction Bobo had been leading him to. Something in the front and something in the back.

Something back there got my Bobo.

Harold's heart sledged painfully, making his left arm feel tight and stiff.

The curling white vapors parted, as if even they were too frightened to touch the massive shuffling frame. Harold knew what loomed before him. The whole town talked about it as if it was no big deal. But he hadn't joined their harmless revelry.

And now he knew why. It was damn horrifying.

"Stay back! Go on, now!"

It didn't listen, creeping steadily closer.

Harold tried to maneuver his way backwards by dragging himself on his elbows. The pain in his hip prevented him from moving too far. He dropped down, unable to move any further. What little bit of gallantry he had was used up. His bladder released. As he felt the wet warmth sloshing through the crotch of his knee-length shorts, he realized he hadn't even known he had to pee.

The fog thinned enough for Harold to see it: A large beast, mostly hairy except for the small atolls of scabs and pus spread across its body. Its knees were pink scabby flesh, yellowing with dark dots. Its huge head was conical and rutted. The sour fragrance emanating from its stringy hair was so repugnant now Harold's sense of smell seemed to crash.

Crouching next to Harold, the beast studied him curiously, coned head tilting from side to side. Another curious grunt seemed to come from its throat, like a chicken clucking at feed time. Raising its arm, the beefy hand stretched apart, fingers long and thick like sausages. Then the arm slammed down on Harold's stomach, blasting the air from his pinched lungs. Wet tearing sounds overwhelming Harold's dry wheezes.

Head bobbing, Harold managed to look down at his stomach. And wished he hadn't. If only the blow would have killed him right away, he wouldn't have been able to lift his head at all. He could have died without seeing what was happening to him.

He could have been spared witnessing his entrails being pulled from the deep gulley in his abdomen.

Harold's last vision before passing out was a long, gummy rope of intestine being fed out, the beast's wrist twirling, innards twisting around in the same fashion he'd had Bobo's leash around his own wrist.

Bobo. Damn dog...left me to die...

CHAPTER 23

Bubba, Mayor Caine's bodyguard, and supposed lover, passed Striker a folded square of paper the size of a small magazine. Spreading it across the hood of Howie's car, Paul recognized the layout as a map.

"This is good," said Striker. "Thanks."

"I figured it would be best," said Caine.

"Surprisingly, you figured right. This map covers the whole beach?"

"Barefoot Beach and the surrounding secluded locations of the state park."

"Good."

Paul looked around at their crackpot assembly. There was Officer Lillard and his partner whose name he'd forgotten before but had been reminded this morning was Blake. The rotund cop fretfully sipped coffee from a cup inside a cardboard sleeve. When he brought the cup down, brown fluid seeped into his moustache. It looked pretty disgusting, like a diarrhea moustache, and Paul felt his stomach churn. He wished he hadn't thought of that.

Allie Styles, a female deputy, stood on the other side of Howie's cruiser. She was heavily bosomed with a thick torso and wide firm hips. The uniform clung to her, but it wasn't fat that made the clothes appear like they were about to explode from her body. She could give the Bigfoot a formidable fight without any backup.

"Okay," said Striker, uncapping a red marker. "Tell me where every sighting has occurred. Plus any attacks or any reports of pets disappearing, anything that doesn't seem like a big deal. Even the smallest detail could lead us to the creature."

Howie's eyes rose with a heavy inhale. "Well, there was the obvious killing last summer, which was right here." He tapped the map. The paper made flimsy rattling sounds.

"Okay." Striker drew an X where Howie's finger had poked with the marker. "Where else?"

"Possible sightings here, here, and here."

"Got it." Xs were added. "Tell me everything. Don't leave anything out, even if it doesn't fit, I'll mark it."

A few minutes passed as Howie shared the information with Striker. Paul was impressed by his brother's memory, how he seemed to have stored every bit of information that was ever reported to his station.

It wasn't long before Xs were marked across the paper, some clustered together in tight groups and others spread apart in great distances. Paul listened to Howie report stories about strange noises, sightings, the roars, and several dogs and cats mysteriously vanishing without a trace. It was astonishing how so many reports could have gone ignored. How could the authorities not have known something was awry from the large number of accounts?

Howie ended with Paul and Becky's run-in, which wasn't far from where the teenage girl's body had been found.

"That's where it got a piece of my shirt," Becky added.

Striker slowly put the cap back on the marker. "It did?"

She nodded. Her head turned slightly. "What?"

Striker shrugged. "You didn't mention this last night."

"Didn't think it was important. Is it?"

"It's probably nothing."

Becky's eyes widened. "Well, if it's not, can you tell me what that look was about?"

"Look?"

"Yeah, you looked...perturbed."

Striker smiled, but on his big blocky head it looked as if it had been stitched to his face by Dr. Frankenstein. "He might've just liked how it smelled."

"I'm sorry?" she said.

"He probably just took it back with him because he enjoyed the smell."

Becky's head canted as if a weight had been added to the right side. "And what are some other possibilities?"

"That he likes you and took it so he could have something of yours. A keepsake."

"Gross."

"It's quite an honor, really. I must say that it's quite possible our Bigfoot has a crush on you."

Paul watched the confidence drain from Becky's posture. "What will that mean if we come across him out there?"

Howie stepped forward, interrupting. "Enough of the Bigfoot High School gossip. Striker, what do you suggest we do from here? Where should we go?"

"I'm working on it," said Striker. Returning his attention to the map, he put his finger on the crinkled surface and ran it along the shapes and lines printed across. "What's this area right here, Sheriff?"

Paul leaned forward so he could see. Striker was poking a dark blot at the edge of the map. Not all of it was even on the page.

"The caverns," said Howie.

"Caverns?"

"Yeah. Used to be open for tours until a hurricane flooded the caves. Now it's too damn dangerous to trek through, so it was condemned."

"Hmm…"

"I know what you're thinking," said Howie, "and it's crossed my mind too. I thought he might be bunking out in the caves, but we went in and didn't find anything."

"Interesting," said Striker, stroking his cleft chin.

"What are you thinking?" asked Paul.

"My theory here is that with a lot of sightings being in this general area here, and the recent killings and the attack last night over here, I'm willing to guess he's somewhere in this vicinity." He drew a circle around the dark blotch. "It's a great place to start."

Howie nearly grimaced. "That's still a lot of ground to cover."

"Then we should get started. How far away are we?"

Howie shook his head. "Not very far. It's a private stretch owned by Mayor Caine."

"That's right," agreed Caine.

"Can the caves be accessed?"

175

Caine nodded. "Sure. The parking lot's still there from when we did the tours. We can leave the cars there and hike over. Have to do some climbing since the hurricane caused the hill to crumble. Now there're rocks everywhere. But it can be done."

"We'll have to," said Striker. "Just need to keep people away while we're out there."

Caine waved his hand, as if brushing off Striker's suggestion. "I doubt there'll be much trouble this time of the summer. Other than locals, there aren't many people here, and they know not to come out there."

"All right," said Striker. "Let's head out there."

Howie turned to Officer Lillard. "Gather us up some gear— lanterns, lots of rope, and plenty of flashlights. Go into the storage closet and raid the water, bring as many bottles you can carry. Plus bags that will be easy to tote around all this shit in."

Lillard nodded. "I'm on it." Then he headed for the backdoor to the station.

"Wow," said Caine. "Who would've thought that all this time the monster was living right underneath me, his biggest fan and supporter? Talk about irony."

"Shut up," said Striker. "This is a feral beast, not some kind of children's storybook character. It's killed people, possibly more although we don't know it yet, and you're singing its praises?"

"He's done great for our town."

Striker took a step toward Caine, who stepped back throwing up his hands in surrender. Bubba stepped in the path between them. The burly black man, clothed in his customary black suit, shook his head.

"Not now," said Howie. "You guys can beat the shit out of each other later for all I care. But until we find this thing, you're going to have to act like grown-ups."

Striker smirked. "Until that time comes." Holding out his hand, he used his thumb to crack his knuckles on his fingers in a quick series of hollow pops.

"Can't wait," said Bubba.

It was the first time Paul had heard the big guy speak, and he found Bubba's voice unusually high and feminine.

"Get the stuff out of the car," Caine told Bubba, then gave his back a few quick slaps.

Bubba kept his eyes focused on Striker another moment before turning away. He nodded once and started for the gleaming BMW.

"What stuff?" asked Howie.

"We're going to document this, of course," said Caine.

"Document?" Howie looked pained. He shook his head. "How are you...?"

A door bumped. Heads turned to watch Bubba reach into the backseat of Caine's BMW. When they came back out, they held some kind of harness. Bubba started slipping his hands through the holes.

"Video it," said Caine, answering everyone's question. "We'll need it if Ms. Aniston plans on doing her story."

Howie turned to Becky. "Did you know about this?"

"Well..." Becky looked down, shrugged. "Yeah." She reached into the pocket of her tight khaki shorts and brandished her voice recorder.

"Damn," said Howie.

"Sorry," she said.

Paul wanted to be angry but knew she was probably forced into the situation. Knowing how badly she wanted to do the story, Caine had approached her at some point to share his plan.

I ought to punch the asshole in the face.

Striker's laughter made them all turn around. He leaned against Howie's SUV, arms folded over his chest. "You're all a bunch of damn fools."

Becky turned to Paul, hurt showing on her face. Her mouth moved without words.

"Ignore him," said Caine. "Are you ready to shoot the opening segment?"

Becky closed her eyes, nodded.

"Great," said Caine. "Right here will be fine."

"I don't believe this," said Howie. Shaking his head, he walked over to Striker and dropped against the Suburban beside the hulky man. He mirrored Striker's stance.

Bubba, snapping a video camera to the stem extended from the center of the harness, approached Becky. He folded out the LCD screen and flipped a switch. There was a soft beep and the camera came on with the slow whirring of tape being pulled through the heads.

Styles stepped beside Paul, looking disgusted as she watched Becky fix her hair. Even Paul was a bit bothered by Becky's inappropriate spectacle of her appearance. Realizing what she was doing, Becky stopped and looked at her hand as if it had violated her somehow. She slowly lowered it to her side.

Caine stood behind Bubba, his eyes fixed on the LCD screen. "The camera loves you, Ms. Aniston. So gorgeous."

Ignoring his remark, she said, "Is it on?"

Bubba held up his finger, then lowered it to the camera's top. He pushed a button. Then he raised his hand and silently counted down from three with his fingers.

When he reached one, Becky nodded.

"I'm Becky Anniston and we're here at the Seashell Cove Sheriff's Department, about to embark on a very dangerous journey into the prohibited caverns that run underneath the city…"

Paul watched as Becky delivered an amazing performance of a rehearsed introduction. No doubt she'd stayed up all night making sure she got it just right. She laid out their plans and gave a brief account of the Bigfoot's actions over the past year. Her voice remained a constant professional tenor as she spoke without error.

When she finished, Becky waited for Bubba to give her the signal that he'd cut off the camera. Then she stepped out of the camera's view, looking like a girl who'd just given her virginity away to a guy who didn't deserve it.

"Wonderful," said Caine. "Ms. Aniston, this is going to make you a star."

Paul noted her expression. There was no pride anywhere on her lovely face, only a grim frown that made her look years older.

CHAPTER 24

Beach?

Gunner sat on the edge of his bed, gazing at his phone's display screen. He'd read and reread the one word message countless times, trying to decide how to respond. Megan had sent him the text a few minutes ago. He wasn't sure if she was asking him to go to the beach or if he was at the beach.

For all he knew, she was only curious to learn if he just likes the beach.

Don't be retarded. She wouldn't send a message wanting to know my opinion of the beach.

Still…he couldn't think of how to write back.

The phone buzzed in his hand, making him gasp.

One new message.

It was from Megan.

He swiped his thumb over the screen and pulled the message up.

Meet me in 30?

Gunner gulped. She wanted him to *meet* her. The message didn't say anything about *us*.

Me.

Did that mean her brothers wouldn't be there?

About to send back a yes, he remembered Trish was here. Though he doubted she would make him stay home, he'd feel bad if he left her alone with Natalie. His little sister could be a bit hard to handle at times.

She likes Trish, though. It should be fine.

Besides, he *really* wanted to meet Megan. He recalled how she'd looked in the white bikini the other day, her tawny skin glossy around the white patches, her lemon-colored hair that seemed to blaze brightly under the sun. Remembering how her body had curved with tight muscle, how her breasts shook when playing volleyball, how her nipples pushed tiny points into the silky fabric, made him ache to see her again.

Trish won't mind.

He'd ask her to be sure.

Entering the living room, he noticed the only sounds came from a game show on TV. He looked to the couch and saw the top of Trish's head poking up above the top, tilted to the side as if about to fall over. He moved to the left to walk around the couch. Her bare feet, propped on the coffee table and crossed at the ankles, came into view. Her toes curled slightly.

Gunner liked Trish's feet. Her toes were evenly shaped and seemed to slant down perfectly from the larger one. He didn't like when a foot had one stray long toe that seemed to want to curl around the one next to it. Trish's were perfect, toenails painted a shiny purple hue that looked almost like metal.

Her legs appeared as Gunner closed in. The light of the room glimmered across her tanned shins. He saw the jut of her slightly bent knee, the curve of a dark thigh that vanished under the fringe of ragged denim of her cut-offs. Her faded pink tank top had slipped back on her midriff, leaving a patch of skin by her hip exposed. The skin bowed out into a soft point, tanned as the rest of her. Next were the humps of her breasts. The shirt, twisted to the side, pulled against her left breast and showed a tawny slope. From this angle, Gunner could see right down the shirt to the cups of her bra that barely seemed to cover the front.

Feeling ashamed, Gunner averted his eyes. Her hair came into view, draping the side of her face and part of her arm that reached up to her head. A bright curtain blocked her eyes.

Natalie was on the floor, sitting cross-legged and watching the game show with complete fascination. She hadn't heard Gunner's approach.

Nor had Trish turned to acknowledge him.

Then he realized he was tiptoeing, keeping his steps silent. He had no idea why he was doing that.

Because I was getting a good view...

Again Gunner was struck by guilt. He shouldn't look at Trish like that. She was his uncle's wife. Though she wasn't a relative by blood, she was close enough.

He stepped around to the front of Trish and looked at her. From this direction, he could still see more of her than he should. But he could also see her eyes were shut. The slow rise of her stomach suggested she'd fallen asleep.

He didn't want to wake her up. She looked so beautiful on the couch, dozing, her brow slightly wrinkled as if concentrating on whatever she was dreaming about.

"Gunner! Watch the show!"

Natalie's voice boomed in the room, making Gunner jump.

Trish jerked awake. Her legs flew off the table and she sat up. Her breasts lurched behind the tank top. Looking around as if confused, Trish didn't say anything. Then she turned to Gunner and leaned back her head to see him. She smiled.

"Caught me napping on the job, huh?" she asked.

Gunner smiled. "It's okay."

"Sorry. A late night followed by an early morning." She yawned. "I'm beat."

"I bet so."

She looked to the side of Gunner and squinted at the TV. Her nose wrinkled. "When did this come on?"

"It's about to go *off*," said Natalie. "You missed all of it!"

Trish groaned. "I'll live."

Gunner laughed.

"What time is it?" asked Trish. She started to reach for her phone on the coffee table. Her shirt dipped low on her breasts, but she hardly seemed to notice.

Gunner looked at the TV.

"Wow, still early," he heard her say. "So, Gunner, what do you have planned for us to do today?"

Gunner turned to Trish. She was leaning forward, her arms folded on top of her thighs and chest pressed against them. The position seemed to shove her breasts higher as if to show Gunner how nice they were.

He cleared his throat. "Well…that's what I came to talk to you about."

"Oh?" An eyebrow arched. "Planned out a full day?"

Man. She thinks I want all of us to go do something.

He'd feel like a jerk if he told her he wanted to go to the beach by himself.

An image of Megan stretched out on the towel, resting on her elbows and head tilted back, her skin gleaming with suntan oil, popped in his mind.

"Care if I head to the beach?" he asked.

"The beach?" Trish puckered out her bottom lip. "Great idea. A day at the beach. You know, I've lived here so long that it's become a common thing to me. I forgot that it's still new to you."

"The beach! Yeah!" Natalie bounced on her rump. "I haven't got to see it yet!"

Great. There goes that.

He could still meet up with Megan at some point. Maybe excuse himself from Trish and Natalie so he can spend some time with Megan.

It'd be better, though, if I was alone.

But seeing her briefly was better than not at all.

He turned to Trish and saw she was frowning at him. "What?" he said.

"You have a look about you," she said.

"A look?"

"Yeah. Like I just told you we're going to spend the day doing math."

Gunner blushed, which caused Trish to laugh. "Jeez…"

"No big deal. I think you want to go to the beach for other reasons than to play in the sand."

Gunner's skin felt hot. "Hey, no it's…"

"A girl?" Gunner nodded. Natalie made a retching sound. "Say no more. How about you ride with us to the beach, then I'll take Natalie to the sand and you go meet your friend? I'll text you when we're about to leave and if you're not ready, you can stay. Just text me when you want me to come pick you up. So long as we're done by five. Howie said they're closing the beach early tonight."

Gunner nodded. "Wow, Trish! Thanks a lot!" Though he was relieved he could spend the time with Megan, he felt bad. He was ditching his family for a girl he hardly knew.

Trish understands, though. She might feel bad if I ditched Megan for her.

He pictured Trish in a bikini like the one Megan had on. A day with Trish on the beach might be as rewarding as a day with Megan.

No thanks. She didn't bring a bathing suit anyway.

Plus, he wouldn't have to suffer the guilt when ogling Megan in a bikini.

"Well, go get ready," said Trish. "Natalie and I will round up her bathing suit. She has one, right?"

"Yeah, but she hasn't worn it since last year."

Trish wrinkled her nose, a corner of her lip stuck up. "Might be too small for her. I'll buy her one from one of the shops."

"Hey, you don't have to do that. I'm sure Dad would…"

"No worries. Since the tourist season is over, the prices will be discounted."

She smiled. And won the argument. Gunner couldn't argue with such a beautiful face.

Back in his room, Gunner sent Megan a text that told her he'd be there. A few seconds later she responded with: *Yay!*

Reading the message, his chest felt weird, as if it was being tickled deep inside.

I'll have the whole day with her.

The eagerness was quickly invaded with dread. What would he say? Back home, he was never good at talking to girls. Especially girls as hot as Megan. But at his old school, there was never a need to worry since they all ignored him. All the time he'd had with Megan had either been short or surrounded by people. This would be the longest bout of one on one time he'd had with her.

He felt dizzy.

Don't blow it.

****

Gunner liked Trish's car. A newer model red convertible Mustang with a loud engine that seemed to rumble off the houses as they passed by in multicolored blurs. With the top down, the salty air knocked Gunner's hair all over. He enjoyed the feel of the heavy gusts on his face, but he hoped he wouldn't show up to meet Megan with a wild bush on his head.

Run into a bathroom and wet it down.

He looked at Trish from the passenger seat. She drove with one hand on the steering wheel and her other arm draped across the car door. Her bright hair danced around her sunglasses, flapping behind her like golden streamers. She had a slight smile on her face, as if she was listening to someone tell her a story that was about to make her laugh.

Though the ride might be hell on his hair, it beat riding his bike any day.

"Good thing you're not driving," she said.

"What do you mean?"

"You're not keeping your eyes on the road."

Heat filled Gunner's cheeks. He quickly faced forward. "Sorry."

Trish laughed. "It's okay. I know these sights are new to you, so take them all in. Natalie's doing it, too."

Gunner looked behind him. Natalie, in her booster seat, gazed at the flat expanse of the ocean. Her ponytail twirled behind her head like a propeller from the wind. Springs swirled around her face.

Unlike Natalie who was enjoying everything around them, Trish was the only sight Gunner had been taking in. His eyes looked down at Trish's legs. They were spread, one reaching to the gas pedal and the other angled away. It left a wide part at her groin. Gunner could see the lacey material of panties at the end of the short corridor between her inner thigh and denim. Through the translucent panties, he saw a bare patch of slightly arched skin.

Shit...

His throat felt too thick to swallow. He quickly looked away and focused on what was outside the car.

A parking lot.

The Mustang began slowing down as it reached the entrance. There were only a couple cars parked in the large space. Beyond the lot were strips of stores and to the left was the path to the ocean.

We're here already?

Gunner was thankful. He had to get out the car and away from Trish. Thoughts of Megan had his mind spinning and he was using his uncle's wife as an object to focus those thoughts on. He felt awful, as if he'd spied on her undressing. He imagined what he'd done was pretty close.

He'd seen her bra, part of her panties, and her...

She shaves it!

Though Gunner wasn't cold, he trembled as if a chilly wind had blown across him.

"You okay?"

Gunner turned and saw Trish watching him. An eyebrow curved above the sunglasses. Gunner saw the warped reflection of a pasty kid in the dark lens. "Huh?"

"You look pale."

His head felt awfully light. The shock of seeing Trish's shaved crotch had left him dizzy. But he shook his head and said, "I'm fine."

"Nervous?" A corner of her mouth curved up. "This girl you're meeting, has she got your stomach buzzing?"

"Something like that."

"I hope she's a good girl and doesn't get you into any trouble."

"I hardly know her. I'll be able to tell you if she is after today."

Trish tilted her head and puckered her lips as if fighting a grimace. "*You* better behave."

Gunner realized she'd taken what he'd said the wrong way. "I will! That didn't sound right."

"It sure didn't, buster."

Gunner shook his head. "I'm going to get out of here before I say something else stupid."

Laughing, Trish waved him away. "Okay. Just be careful."

"Have fun with that *girl*," said Natalie in an annoyed voice.

Trish laughed.

"I'll try," said Gunner.

"You could come with us," Natalie reminded him.

"Not this time. Next time."

"Okay. But you better behave!"

Natalie waved a finger at him, narrowing one eye. The look reminded Gunner of their mother. Though Trish laughed, Gunner couldn't even smile at it.

"I will, Natalie. Have fun with Trish."

It took him a couple more minutes to finally get away from Trish and Natalie. Heading to the sandy trail that curled around the restrooms, he made a slight detour into the men's room.

He checked himself in the mirror. Surprisingly, his hair wasn't in too bad of shape. It seemed somehow fuller and wavier. He used water from the sink to make some parts lay down, then splashed some on his face. The cold water helped diminish those images of Trish, but didn't wash them away completely. They were still there, like faded pictures that he couldn't quite see.

After drying his hands, he left the bathroom. The heat dropped down on his back. It felt heavy as he walked onto the beach. He took a heavy whiff of the fresh briny smell of the ocean. He listened to the heavy crashes of the waves when they hit the shore.

Sand got between his feet and flip-flops as he walked, making it hard to keep going. He paused long enough to take them off.

Carrying his flip-flops in one hand, he patted the pocket of his shorts with the other. He felt the bulge of his wallet. A condom was inside it behind his driver's license.

He felt a nervous sizzle in his gut.

You won't need it. This is just hanging out.

But it was there, just in case…

Shaking those thoughts away, he started walking. He pulled his cell phone out of the other pocket, scrolled to the last message from Megan and texted her to let her know he was here.

At the top of a dune, he gazed upon the beach. It was mostly bare, other than a few people scattered about here and there. He saw some kids playing in the water with their father. Way off in the distance a group of guys were surfing. Other than some random walkers and sunbathers, nobody was around.

Gunner started down the dune, walking slightly to the side so he wouldn't fall. As he reached the bottom, the phone vibrated in his hand.

Gunner read the message from Megan and gulped.

Come to my house. I'm alone. Big house on the east side of beach. Past the fence.

"Oh, boy…"

He'd told Trish he would be hanging out with Megan on the beach, not at her *house*. What if she found out?

186

I could tell her. Just call her real quick and tell her that the plans had been changed.

At the house before they'd left, Trish had gotten his number and given him hers. But if he told her where he was going, she'd want to know if adults were going to be there.

Megan said she was alone. No way would Trish let him go without any adults nearby. She knew Dad's rules. The beach was one thing, but being at her house without her parents being home was something different entirely.

Trish wouldn't let me.

Though he knew all this, he texted Megan back to tell her he was on his way. He walked a few feet and checked the markers at the top of dune. A white post with crossing planks rose from the swaying weeds. He saw which way was east and started walking on weak and heavy legs. His stomach felt like it was twisting into cold knots. His heart was sledging.

But it didn't matter.

Nothing was going to keep Gunner from being alone with Megan.

CHAPTER 25

The entrance to the cave wasn't as hard to maneuver as Paul had expected. Though the rocks were slippery going up, there were plenty of places to hold onto as they climbed toward the cavern's yawning ingress. It reminded Paul of mounting the hills behind his uncle's cabin in Tennessee during the winters. Though they weren't treacherous, the snow had made them hard to do.

There was no snow here, only rocks and slick patches of wet sand, waves crashing between them and throwing up salty wetness. The front of Paul's uniform was drenched, dark with ocean water that made him look as if he'd peed all over himself.

From where Paul was, he could see the walls of the cave. They looked slimy, as if coated in baby food. Stringy bits that looked like mossy hair dangled from the ceiling and nearly reached to the sand floor.

Striker had already entered and waited underneath the overhang of rock, under a sheaf of shade that looked wonderful to Paul. Howie stood at the top of the rocks, hands on his hips and peering down. The rest of their unit was coming up from other sides, just to cover all angles, as Howie had put it.

"Shit!"

Paul's heart lurched. His foot nearly slipped out from under him. He slapped his hand down on the jagged edge of a rock to catch himself.

Who shouted?

Sounded like Lillard.

He turned to Becky. She was leaned against a cluster of rocks, head tilted back to look behind her. Her mouth was a tight line. Sweat dotted her upper lip. Though she wore sunglasses, Paul could tell her eyes had narrowed from the wrinkles in her brow.

"See anything?" he asked.

Becky shook her head.

"What's wrong!?!" That was Howie.

"Found some human remains!"

Paul's skin tightened. Becky turned to him, mouth falling open.

"Male *and* female!" Now Paul definitely recognized the finicky voice as belonging to Lillard.

Howie stepped up to the ledge and cupped his hands around his mouth to amplify his voice. "We'll have to leave them for now! Mark the location and get your asses up here!"

"Yes, sir!" called Blake.

"Yeah…" said Lillard, his voice thin and weak.

Paul caught a glimpse of Mayor Caine rising from behind some rocks further up. He wore a windbreaker suit that was solid blue except for the bright orange stripes going up his sides. He brushed his hands together as if just finishing a task.

"Can you get over to it?" Caine asked.

From this angle, it looked like he was talking to a rock. Bubba's head appeared on the other side in a ball cap at a jaunty angle. He'd shed the suit for a pair of cargo pants and a white tank top that bulged around his massive pecks. The harness looked very small on his beefy torso.

"I'm not crawling over there," Becky shouted.

Bubba gave Becky a quick glance back, teeth very white through his smile. It looked as if he was relieved Becky wouldn't make him trek to the other side.

Caine looked down, cupped his hands around his mouth, and shouted, "We'll get you to do a voiceover later! But it'd be better if we got the footage going on to show what we saw."

Bubba looked back. Gone was his smile. Now his lips puckered out to show his frustration. Shaking his head, he turned and instead of going up, he now went to the right. Paul watched him vanish behind a constellation of large boulders.

"Wait on Bubba," shouted Howie. "Our prodigy mayor is sending him over."

"Fine," said Blake.

Paul turned and saw Becky's rump sticking up in front of him. She had gone a few feet up and left him behind.

Damn it.

Paul started climbing. Each time he looked up, he saw Becky's rump flexing and pulling as her legs pushed her higher. The shorts pulled taut against her buttocks, tightening in the crotch and hiking up. The lower cambers peeked out from the edges above a pair of thighs that tightened with muscle. Patches of sand adhered to the sweat-varnished gradients.

Paul felt a tad lousy for gawking at Becky's backside, but it was all he could see. He glanced up once again and saw her legs kicking as they vanished over the grassy lip of the ledge. Her hiking boots gave a little thrust and she was gone.

Thank God, we're almost there.

Paul's stomach twisted.

The cave.

No turning back now.

There was no way he could accurately prepare himself for what they were doing here.

Exploring condemned caves in search of Bigfoot.

At the beach.

So absurd. Paul couldn't even fathom how much he should be afraid.

Then he saw the beast tearing through the sand dune last night, its massive swinging arms, the awful stench, the intimidating height and big blocky face, and remembered just how much danger they were in.

Finally, he reached the top. Howie was there, crouching at the edge and offering his hand. "Thanks," said Paul.

"No problem, partner." Howie spoke in an exaggerated southern drawl like a gunslinger. "Ready for a monster hunt?"

Paul grabbed Howie's hand. The pressure of his brother's grip as he pulled Paul over was painful. "As ready as I'll ever be, I guess."

"You wanted to come."

Paul scrambled over the ledge. When he was far enough away from the edge, Howie let go. "I'm beginning to regret my decision."

"Too late, pal."

"Who knows, maybe it'll be an adventure," said Becky. She was holding her hand, flexing her fingers. Howie must have squeezed her hand too hard also.

"Understand this," said Striker, peeling the plastic off a cigar. "We are up against a creature that has defied time. Something that most people don't even believe exists. There is no game plan here, and we'll have to be quick to adapt to whatever situation we find ourselves in. We have to be very alert." He turned to Becky. "And *very* serious. This is *not* an adventure of any kind. We are not here to have fun. We are not here because it'll be promising for our careers. We're *fucking* here to kill a monster. Hopefully we'll survive while doing it. But I hate to say this—I doubt many of us will."

"Trying to encourage us?" asked Becky. "You're a shitty motivational speaker, you know that?"

"I'm just stating facts." He put the cigar in his mouth. Something *snicked* and Striker raised a Zippo lighter to the end of the cigar.

"Hey, jerk," said Becky, stepping toward Striker. She pointed at him. "Don't forget that I saw him up close last night. I experienced firsthand the kind of danger we're up against. And so what if I'm making jokes, deal with it. It's how I cope with this shit. I mean—I *could* be like you, a scowling asshole that's about to explode out of my shirt, but that's not me. I make jokes when I'm scared, okay? Maybe you should try it sometime. It might help you make a face other than that brooding leer you're probably well-known for."

Paul walked over to Becky and started to put his arm around her. He felt her pull away.

"Don't," she said.

Paul hooked his arm around her shoulder and pulled her against him. She resisted at first, but eased against him. Her arms dropped in front of her and she let him hold her.

Howie sighed. He looked at Striker, then back to Paul.

Striker took the cigar out of his mouth and held it by his face. He licked his lips. "But this is my normal face."

Paul felt Becky shaking against him. At first he thought she might be sobbing. She wasn't. She was laughing.

"And I'm not a funny guy," Striker added. "So being a brooding, leering asshole is all I know how to do."

A smile split Howie's face. Paul felt himself relax some.

"But remember," said Striker, killing the good humor. "It's your scent Bigfoot has. He'll be eager to see you and we'll use that in our favor."

Paul saw himself walking over to Striker and punching him in the face. But Paul knew if he tried, he'd only ruin their mission by getting his ass kicked in front of everyone.

Mayor Caine. Bending over, he slapped his hands on his knees. He was huffing, his tanned skin soaked in sweat. His spiral nest of hair looked wild and frizzy.

Bubba appeared from around the corner, walking up to them. The camera was braced on the short rod jutting from his chest and he held it steady with his hands. He turned in all directions, sweeping over each person, getting everything on video. He hardly seemed winded. When he pointed the camera at Striker, his eyes rose. He nodded at the cigar clamped between Striker's fingers. "Got another one of those?"

Striker reached into his vest pocket and removed another single-wrapped cigar. It was the length of a toothbrush and thick as a sausage. He tossed it to Bubba.

"Thanks," the buff man said.

"Need a light?" asked Striker.

Bubba shook his head. "Got one. Just left my stogies in the damn car."

"Did you get the footage?" asked Caine.

Peeling the plastic from the cigar, Bubba nodded.

"Great," said Caine. "We'll show it to Ms. Aniston and she can whip up some dialogue to put over it."

Paul noted how Becky looked a bit paler than before. It must be like working for the devil from her side of things.

As Bubba lighted his cigar, Styles appeared from the other side of the cave's natural opening. She'd shed her uniform shirt and had it wrapped around her waist. In a white tank top, large breasts seemed to be shoved upward from a bra that must be struggling to support such a heavy pair. Sweat had turned the white fabric translucent in a few places and Paul could see dusky skin through the thinness. Her arms were lined with muscle, and the left had a broken heart tattooed on the bicep. Her short hair was glued to her forehead.

Seeing how athletic she was, Paul wondered if she used to play sports. Maybe even entered some weight-lifting contests.

Howie saw her and nodded. She nodded back, then began fanning herself with a glove-covered hand. The tips of her fingers were bare and stuck out from the gloves.

All gossips about Bubba's sexual preferences were eliminated when Paul saw the hungry way he studied Styles's every movement.

"Now if Lillard and Blake would ever get their asses up here…" Howie shook his head, as if remembering what had delayed their arrival.

"Think the…creature killed those people?" Paul asked.

Howie shrugged.

Striker puffed on the cigar. "I'd say it's rather self-explanatory that he did. More than likely they got too close to the cave and he felt threatened."

"Really?" Paul shook his head. "A thing that big feels threatened by people our size?"

"A bear can be frightened by a child if the kid yells loud enough at it. The Bigfoot saw intruders coming near its habitat, it panicked, and…" He waved his hand as if shooing a fly.

"And killed them," said Caine, still breathless.

"Correct."

"And you want to honor this thing?" asked Howie, directing the question to Caine.

Ignoring Howie's question, Caine shook his head. "I put that fence up for a reason. To keep people off my property. They didn't listen…"

"So getting killed is a justifiable punishment for them?" asked Howie.

"I'm not saying that…" Caine, for the first time since Paul met him, sounded grim. "I don't know what I'm saying."

Lillard's lanky form appeared on the other side of a pair of rocks. His usual spiked hair had gone flat from sweat. He turned around and ushered with his hands as if urging someone to hurry up.

Blake.

Paul wondered how the rotund deputy was handling the climb.

A few minutes later they were gathered at the opening. Striker raised a large flashlight. A square battery was attached to the bottom of the bulb. He thumbed the button. From the blaring sunlight, the flashlight barely made a dent in the darkness before them.

"It's time," said Striker.

Howie faced the group. "I'm sure I don't need to remind you all we're going to be in some very tight corridors and surrounded by rock walls. So please don't fire your weapons unless you have a clean shot. We don't want bullets bouncing all over the place, do we?"

No one disagreed.

Striker started forward.

Caine and Bubba followed closely behind.

Howie was next with Paul and Becky behind him. Styles, walking on the other side of Becky, removed her own flashlight and clicked it on.

Paul heard the clicks of two more flashlights behind him from Lillard and Blake, taking the rear.

They entered the cave, and were swallowed by the darkness.

CHAPTER 26

Gunner stepped around the fencing and kept walking. He stole glances over his shoulder to make sure nobody had seen him. The beach behind him was empty. Nobody was around to see. He was alone this far down the surf.

In the distance, Gunner could see a hilly slope of jagged rock. He thought he spotted people moving around up there. Just dark shapes, flitting about, but they were quickly gone. He scanned the jagged peak a moment longer, then headed to the right.

He stepped around a large bank of sand and stopped when he spotted the house ahead. He couldn't believe the size of it. A house this big was out on the beach? The mayor's mansion, but to Gunner it looked more like the home of a rich slave owner in the south—a Victorian structure, easily three stories tall with a tower on one end where the roof narrowed to a point like a witch's hat. The wood siding was the color of the sky with overhanging eaves that threw heavy shadows down on the wraparound porch.

Surrounding the house was a black wrought iron fence with sharp points at the top that was probably meant to dissuade intruders from trying to climb over. Gunner pictured one of those points jabbing into him and felt a sharp pain in his rump.

He put his flip-flops back on as he approached a gate. It was left open a bit, probably by Megan so he could pass through. When he was on the other side of the fence, he didn't know if he should close the gate behind him. He left it open and headed for the house.

He passed a large in-ground pool shaped like a giant egg. A small jungle of plants and palm trees surrounded the deck that enclosed the water. A diving board extended over the water like a tongue, its shadow a rippling darkness on the water's bright surface.

Gunner climbed the tall set of stairs to the back porch and stepped into the shadows the awning provided.

Wow! This place is...

Intimidating.

It made Gunner's home feel like a shoebox—cramped and stuffy with no privacy.

How could Gunner relate to a girl used to such luxuries?

What did you expect? This is *the mayor's daughter.*

It did nothing to change how out of place he suddenly felt.

Swallowing the forming lump in his throat, he raised a finger to the doorbell. Before he could press it, the door swung inward.

Megan stepped into the doorway, smiling, jutting a knee forward with her toes on the floor and leg swinging. Her appearance melted away his discouraging feelings. She had on her white bikini top over her plump breasts, but instead of briefs, she wore a pair of white jean shorts that hugged her like panties. Her legs looked very bare and even darker compared to the white of her clothes. Her lemony hair shined and hung past her shoulders in thick waves.

"You're here," she said. There was disbelief in her voice.

"Wouldn't miss it," he said.

She sucked her bottom lip into her mouth, smiling over it. Her tongue swept over it, leaving the pink curve moist. "I wasn't sure you'd come or not. I mean—the text I sent..." She shook her head. "Didn't want you to think I'm always inviting guys over."

The thought hadn't crossed his mind yet, but it probably would have before much longer. Though she was trying to tell him it wasn't something she did often, he couldn't help wondering if he was one of many.

"I'm just happy to be invited," he said.

"Yeah?"

Gunner nodded. "Yeah."

"Then come on in." She stepped back, granting him entrance.

Gunner crossed the threshold. From the heat outside, the cool air felt wonderful, though it made his shirt feel cold and soggy on his back. He reached behind him and plucked the shirt off his skin.

He looked around. They were in a room that seemed to be connected to a kitchen big enough to feed a restaurant. To the right was a long table with empty silver candle holders spread across the top. High-back chairs were pushed against the edges all the way around, squished close together.

How does anybody have any room to eat?

"It's only for when Dad hosts dinner parties," he heard Megan say. The door *snicked* shut. "We never use it ourselves."

"Ah," he said.

"I usually eat outside or on the couch."

She stepped beside him. Her arm brushed his.

"Nice place," he said.

Megan laughed. "I would offer to give you a tour, but somehow I think it might cause you to go into shock or something."

Gunner felt himself blush. "It's cool. I think I can handle it."

"I know. It's like the car—this house is overkill, huh?"

"No, not at all, really. It's..." Megan's eyebrows lifted, mouth opened. "It's a dream house, you know?"

"A what?" She laughed.

"Really. If I was to sit down and fantasize about the kind of house I'd want to spend my life in, this is the house I would envision."

"Oh, really now?"

"Swear."

She hugged his arm, escorting him through the kitchen. "And what kind of woman do you see yourself sharing the house with?"

He felt a nervous flutter in his chest. "Um..."

Megan laughed. "Maybe a blonde?"

Gunner felt the soft brushes of her hair on his neck. A fruity shampoo scent drifted into his nose. He smiled. "Most definitely."

"With a good tan and big boobs?"

"And nice legs," Gunner added, and couldn't believe he'd said it.

Megan squeezed his arm. "Nice legs?"

Gunner nodded. "And the most beautiful eyes I've ever seen."

He gave Megan a glance and saw her cheeks suddenly change to pink, as if she'd been in the sun too long. She swallowed. "Wow..."

Gunner hoped he hadn't pushed things too far with the last compliment. He knew they were playing around while Megan was also trying to pick him for information on what he thought about her.

I talked too much. As always!

Whenever he was nervous, Gunner lost the ability to shut up. Words that he had no idea he was going to say would spew from his mouth in an endless progression.

Megan stopped walking. She looked at him, her eyes watery. With Gunner nearly a foot taller, she had to lean back her head to gaze at him. She gave him a feeble smile, as if she'd just heard something that was hard to understand. "Nobody's ever said anything like that to me before."

"Well…" Gunner shrugged. He felt dumb. All he'd really done was comment on her legs and eyes.

And agree that she had big tits.

Had he really done that?

Gunner poked out a lip and exhaled a heavy breath. He felt it stir his dangling bangs.

Megan smiled. "I think your dreams are about to come true, buddy."

Gunner laughed.

It was cut off by her lips pressing hard against his. He had trouble catching up to her quick pecking pace, but he managed to find her rhythm. Her lips were soft and warm as they smeared over his. He felt her tongue run across his bottom lip, felt her mouth suckle the same lip. She writhed against him, moaning. Her breasts pushed into his chest.

He didn't know what to do with his hands, so he put them on her bare back. Her skin was hot, slightly damp as if she'd showered recently. He rubbed paths through the moist sheen with his fingers.

Megan pulled away from his mouth with a final wet smack. The skin around her lips was ruddy.

"Wow," she panted. "That was…"

"Uh…"

She shook her head. "You make me crazy…in a good way."

"You don't even know me."

"I'm a good judge of character." She moved in, kissed him softer this time, then leaned back. "And I like you, Gunner. A lot."

"I like you, too."

"Want to see the game room?"

"You have a game room?"

"Yeah. It's pretty cool."

Taking his hand, she led him into an area that looked like a foyer. Shut doors were all around. A staircase to the right led to the upper level. They walked to a pair of closed glass doors up the hall and to the left of the front door. Dark was on the other side of the window pane blocks, so he couldn't see what was beyond the glass.

Megan pushed one open and pulled Gunner inside. Sounds of lasers, beeps, and old synthesizer music rushed at him with the warm smell of freshly popped popcorn.

Gunner's mouth dropped open. "Wow...this is so *cool!*"

"I love it in here."

The game room was set up like an old arcade. Heavy with dim lighting, rope lights ran the entire length of the walls like flashing stripes. Gunner saw a set of pinball machines, old Atari arcade machines, Street Fighter, and a Skeeball table next to an air hockey table. A popcorn machine in the corner dumped a fresh batch of puffed balls onto the mound that was already filling the inside behind the glass. A pool table was in the center of the room like a green island. A triangle of balls was on top, lined together, numbers facing out.

Gunner was impressed.

"This is my favorite room," she said. "I love these old games."

"Really?"

"You sound surprised."

"Well, I am, actually."

"Thought I was just a beach bunny?" She playfully elbowed his side. "I'm a nerd at heart. I love video games, especially the older ones. I have more fun playing these classics than the new ones. You know what I mean? These are actually *games*. You *win* things— points, coins, treasures, whatever. Forget RPG, or whatever the hell that shit is. That's not a *game*. You don't *win*. I'll take Mario Brothers over Halo any day."

She is *the woman of my dreams!*

Was this real? Or was Gunner really asleep and dreaming he was here with Megan. He suddenly felt as if he was in a strange universe that had been designed just for him.

This must be what true happiness felt like.

"My mom was a Space Invaders legend," she said, heading to the machine. On the screen, tiny specks jerked from side to side, shooting straight lines at little globs over a black backdrop. "She was a featured article in Gaming Gazette, a magazine from the '80s. Nobody could beat her, and nobody in the family has been able to top her score."

Megan pointed to a photo frame hanging on the wall beside the *Space Invaders* machine. It was an 8x10 clipping of a young woman who looked a lot like Megan, leaning her hip against a *Space Invaders* machine. Her arm was stretched across the panel, fingers curled around the joystick in a seductive hold. She wore a sundress that had thin straps looped behind her neck that showed a lot of cleavage and leg.

"She doesn't play anymore?" Gunner asked.

Her mouth attempted a bogus smile. "No. She passed away years ago."

"Oh, shit..." Gunner felt himself shrink inside. "I'm so sorry...I...damn it..."

"Hey, it's okay." Megan put her arm around his back, leaning her head against his arm. "I appreciate your apologies, but you shouldn't feel bad for asking a question."

"I feel like an ass."

"It's okay."

Gunner felt her hand at his side, squeezing him. It sent a trembling ruffle through his body.

"Dad built this room just for her, after she got sick. Something to help her feel better. He spent an entire winter in here, replacing the walls, the floor, making it look just like the arcade that used to be open in town." She smiled as if she could see her dad doing all the labor before her. "They met at that arcade..."

Megan's face crumpled. Her mouth twisted into a quivering line as she tried to fight back her sobs. Tears filled her eyes.

"Jeez," she said. She pulled her arm away from Gunner and rubbed the back of her hand across her eyes. "Good thing I don't wear makeup."

"You don't need to."

Megan laughed. "Look at you, giving me compliments." She dabbed a tiny droplet in the corner of her eye with a finger. "You're so sweet."

Though it was meant as a compliment back to him, Gunner cringed inside. He hated when people called him sweet. Friends were sweet, old people were sweet.

People with broken hearts were once sweet to somebody who took advantage of them.

"Did your mom get to...enjoy the room?"

Megan nodded. "She did. A lot. The doctors told Dad it probably gave her renewed strength and made her time with us even longer. Dad and my brothers haven't been in here since she...died. I don't think they've ever recovered from it. But I come in here *all* the time. Not just for the games, either. I feel like I'm still close to her when I'm in here. Corny, I know."

"It's not," said Gunner in a husky voice. He cleared his throat. "Not at all."

Megan smiled and stepped over to him. She leaned against him, hugging him. Gunner folded his arms over her back. Her skin was still warm, but no longer damp.

"What about you?" she asked.

"Me?"

"You said you moved here with your dad and sister. No mom? Are they divorced?"

Gunner had hoped she wouldn't ask, since he had no intentions of telling her about his mother.

"Pretty much," he said. "Mom's gone for good."

"I'm sorry. Was she awful?"

Gunner sighed. "The worst."

"But your dad's cool?"

Gunner thought about it. "Yeah, I guess he is. I mean, I've never really given it much thought, but...yeah. I can tell he thinks he's always screwing up, but he's really not."

"Have you told him that?"

"That he's *not* screwing up?"

"Yeah."

"Well...no."

"You should. Might make your dad's day if he heard you say that."

"Lecturing me, are you?"

Megan laughed, bouncing against him. "Maybe."

Gunner felt bad. Why hadn't he told his dad about it?

Because it would be awkward for the both of them. But Megan was right, Dad would probably feel a lot better if Gunner told him he was doing fine.

"I'll say something to him," said Gunner.

"Good," Megan said. "My dad's not the same person he used to be...I mean before Mom...you know. He changed. He became mayor and kind of turned into an appearance-obsessed prick. My brothers were easier to fall into line, but not me. I don't care what people think about me. At least, I didn't until recently."

Gunner's heart started beating faster.

She cares what I think about her?

"So you didn't move in here *after* he became mayor?" asked Gunner. "I thought this was like a mayor's mansion or something."

Megan stepped out of the hug and headed over to the pool table. Gunner followed her.

"No, we've always lived here. A town like this never had a mayor's *mansion.*" She chuckled. "Whoever is mayor just runs the town from their bedroom."

Gunner laughed.

"Want to play some pool?" she asked.

"Sure," he said. "I suck at it."

"It's okay, we won't play for money."

"Good. Because I don't have any."

Megan laughed. "I'll teach you how to play."

He watched her cross the room to where a rack of cues stood in a formation by height on the wall. Reaching up on the tips of her toes, she pulled down two cues. Gunner liked how her buttocks pulled her shorts taut, how small bumps of pale smooth skin slipped out from the bottoms of her shorts.

He looked away as she started to turn around. When he faced her again, she was heading forward, the pool cues against the slants of her breasts.

She handed him one. "Since you're kind of tall, I thought this one might suit you."

The back end of the stick was heavier and swayed forward when he took it. Mimicking Megan, he put the fat end on the floor, gripping it a few inches from the top.

"Chalk?" she asked, bending over. There was a cubby in the border of the table. A blue block was in a groove above a narrow opening. She took the cube, stood up straight, and began grinding it across the cue's tip.

"Sure," he said. He didn't know why he would need to smear that stuff all over the end of the stick. If she was doing it, he might as well.

"As you can see I already have the balls racked." She snickered as if what she'd said was naughty.

Smiling, Gunner nodded and took the chalk block when she offered it to him. He saw there was a concave in the center and figured he was supposed to put the tip of the cue inside it. As he started twisting the cube around the tip, Megan reached across the table and carefully lifted the triangle away from the balls. She sat it on the glass top of a pinball machine close by.

"I'll break them," she said.

"How do we know which balls to knock in?"

"Whoever knocks in one first, that's who she is."

"She?"

Megan winked. "I'm pretty good, so I'll probably sink one first. If it's stripes, I play that and you go for the solids."

"Got it."

Megan rolled the white ball to the corner. She leaned over the table, the cue extended in front of her. Right leg straight, the left was bent and angled inward with her foot flat on top of the other one. Her breasts squished against the lip of the table. He could see a pale slope behind the tiny bikini patch. She made a V with two fingers and slipped the blue-dusted tip through. Slowly, she eased the cue back and forth, gliding it between her fingers. Her hair draped her face and gathered on the plushy green surface.

From his viewpoint, he could see the side of her face. Her eye was scrunched, as if she was squinting to see through a rifle scope. Finally, she thrust her arm forward. The cue punched the white ball against the others and with a loud crack sent them rolling in all directions. Though several balls came close to dropping into a pocket, none actually did.

Megan stayed in her position, bent at the waist, rump jutting high, a smooth curve of buttock peeking out from her shorts. Looking over her shoulder, she smiled.

"Your turn," she said.

And winked.

CHAPTER 27

Natalie saw the ice cream sign in front of Quincy's and started running.

"Wait!" called Trish, dropping Natalie's sandals into the shopping bag. "Don't run!"

Natalie had on the new bathing suit and a pair of shorts over it. Her ponytail bounced behind her as she dashed toward the wooden ice cream cone. Trish knew if the little girl's foot came down on some loose sand, it would throw her legs out from under her. She didn't want Natalie to get hurt.

"I said *stop!*"

Natalie slowed to a stop and turned around. The look on her face was one of sadness and a little worry.

Good job, Trish. Yell at her. Hasn't her mother done that enough?

"Give me a second, okay?" said Trish.

Natalie nodded. The excitement had left her. She stood with her shoulders slouched, hands clasped in front of her, fingers fidgeting.

Trish felt awful for yelling. She'd heard the stories about Alisha's condition. How she would spend hours yelling at Paul and the kids, how she'd attacked Paul in front of Gunner and if the boy hadn't been there, Paul might've been stabbed to death. Natalie didn't need her aunt yelling at her, even if she wasn't listening. The poor child probably wouldn't be able to handle anyone raising their voice at her ever again.

Trish got Natalie's old clothes in the bag, then held it out like a punching bag and spun it around. Once a tail had coiled at the top of the bag, she folded it over and looped it through into a knot. Done with that, she headed for Natalie, letting the shopping bag knock against the side of her leg.

"Got ice cream on the brain?" said Trish.

Natalie smiled. She started to turn around, arm rising to point at the sign, then she jerked rigid.

And screamed.

A large hairy beast stepped out from behind the wooden sign. Its dark hair was blown by the breeze coming from the beach. Its blocky head turned to Natalie. Bending at the waist, its arms extended, palms out, toward Natalie.

Trish dropped the bags and rushed to Natalie who hadn't stopped screaming.

"Get away from her!" yelled Trish.

The beast stood up straight and grabbed its head and started to pull. The head plopped off and fell on the ground. This caused Trish to scream and Natalie to scream harder.

Then Trish noticed the human face, a youthful face. His hair was so blond it was almost white. Quite handsome, though drenched in sweat. He looked panicked.

Trish dropped down behind Natalie and pulled her close. She hugged the little girl and felt wetness on her shorts.

Poor Natalie…

Sobbing, Natalie pushed her face between Trish's breasts. Her whole body shook, legs trembling.

Trish looked up at the young man.

The young man in a costume.

Another young man rushed outside. His hair was the same bright blond and was just as handsome. Instead of a fur suit, he had on a white polo shirt and green shorts. An apron was tied around his waist.

"What happened?" he said, coming down the steps of the wraparound porch.

The one in the suit turned to the other. "I scared the little girl."

The other one sighed. "I knew this was bad idea."

"Me too! I didn't *want* to wear this stupid thing."

"Guys!" called Trish. "What is this?" She pointed at the fur suit.

The one wearing it groaned. "Our dad wants someone wearing it at all times. Said it'll bring us more business."

Now Trish recognized them. Malcolm and Max Caine. Mayor Caine's sons.

"You're Max?" she asked the one in the suit. He nodded. She turned to his brother. "That makes you Malcolm."

"Yeah," said Malcolm. "And I'm sorry. Is she going to be okay?"

Though Natalie had stopped screaming, she still trembled. She made sniffling sounds against Trish's chest.

"I think she will be eventually…"

Malcolm pursed his lips and huffed through his nose. He glanced down at Natalie and his eyes rose. When he turned away, he looked almost grim. "We have a bathroom inside if she needs…you know…"

Trish nodded. "Yeah, I know."

If Malcolm frowned any deeper, it might leave permanent creases in his skin. "Are you two hungry? How about a free meal and some ice cream?"

Natalie's head whipped around. She jerked from Trish's embrace. "Ice cream!"

Laughing, Malcolm nodded. "Yeah! All the ice cream you want, forever. You, young lady, never have to pay for ice cream from us ever again."

Trish smiled. "That's very sweet of you, but…"

Malcolm held up his hand. "It's the least I can do. Come on in, we're just getting opened up. You two have the place to yourselves." He leaned over, putting his hands on his knees to address Natalie. "You like hot dogs?"

"Yeah!"

"We have the best. And you may have as many as you want."

"Forever?"

Malcolm closed his eyes, smiled, and nodded. "For you? Anything."

Gazing at Malcolm with dreamy eyes, Natalie clutched her fists together and raised them to her cheek. "Wowwwwwww!"

Standing, Trish put her hand on Natalie's shoulder. "I think she's in love."

Malcolm laughed. "Well, I'm honored." He stood up straight, turned to Trish. "Please. Come inside. Relax."

Trish nodded. "Okay."

Malcolm turned to Max. "And throw that stupid thing in the trash."

Max smiled. "Gladly. Dad's going to be pi—er—mad."

"It's *not* best for business. He'll understand once I explain what happened."

Max didn't look convinced, but he didn't argue with Malcolm.

The restaurant seemed darker than normal when they entered. Trish realized they didn't have all the lights on yet. A couple of servers dressed in clothes that matched Malcolm's were walking around, checking the tables, restocking napkins and condiments, and putting down menus. The serving line was being stocked by two other guys—tubs were being filled with hot dogs, chili, onions, relish, tomatoes, lettuce, and plenty more. Trish thought anything other than the routine accessories for a hot dog was a bit too much.

Malcolm led them to a table on the far side. A screen wrapped around the entire restaurant, making it look as if they were on a screened-in back porch.

"Will this be an okay seat?" he asked.

"It's fine," she said. "Really, you don't have to..."

"The best view in the house." He pointed at the screen.

Trish had to bend over slightly to see. A wedge of ocean showed between two massive dunes. Sunlight glinted off its sparkly surface. Malcolm was right. The view was remarkable.

"It's nice," she said.

"Thanks," he said. "Have a seat, please."

Trish sat down on one side and Malcolm helped Natalie settle in the other. Her head just barely reached above the table's edge.

"Do you need a booster seat?" he asked Natalie.

She held up her fist, closing one eye. "I certainly do *not*!"

Malcolm, holding up his hands as if surrendering, stepped back. "I'm sorry. No booster seats allowed for my new friend."

"Natalie," said Trish.

"Natalie," he repeated. He turned to Trish. "And you're Trish Thompson, right?"

Trish blushed. "That's right."

"I thought that was you. I guess Dad's out with Sheriff Thompson, huh?"

"I know they're out doing something. I just don't know what."

"I don't either." He shook his head. "What can I start you two off with?"

"Can I get a sweet tea?" she asked.

"Absolutely. And for Natalie?"

"A root beer float!"

Malcolm laughed. "You got it. I'll be right back."

He hurried away from the table.

Moments later a waitress wearing a very tight tank-top with a Quincy's logo on the breast and shorts like Malcolm's came to the table. She gave Natalie a pack of crayons and some papers with pictures to color and puzzles to solve. Natalie was ecstatic as she got started.

Trish watched her for a bit, then looked around. She no longer saw Malcolm, but did spot Max talking to the waitress. He still had on the fur suit as he animatedly moved his hands while sharing a story with the pretty girl. Trish figured he was giving her an account of what happened outside. After a bit, the waitress walked behind Max and unzipped the suit. With a goofy grin, Max thanked her and walked away.

As soon as Max was gone, the waitress turned to another girl and started talking. Trish could tell she liked Max, and most likely, he liked her as well.

Both boys seem really nice. Not at all like their father.

She supposed Caine was nice enough underneath that smarmy exterior. If she got to know him, she might find him fun to be around.

Trish nearly gagged.

She doubted she could ever grow to enjoy being around Caine. Plus, Howie couldn't stand the guy. They'd butted heads more than once over the years.

And this Bigfoot business had added even deeper resentment from Howie. But until today, Trish had never given it much thought. She'd kind of enjoyed all the decorations and merchandise, though she didn't like what had started it all.

Trish looked across the table. Natalie, a tip of tongue poking out the corner of her mouth, worked on finding her way out of a maze.

211

She was humming to herself. Other than her eyes being a little puffy and red, she didn't look as if she'd had the hell scared out of her.

After Natalie's scare, Trish was inclined to agree with Howie. The Bigfoot business needed to go away. There was going to be a vote on changing the beach's name to Bigfoot Beach. She would definitely say no to that.

I'll have to tell Paul what happened to Natalie.

Hopefully he wouldn't be mad. She also hoped Howie wouldn't blow his lid. He always seemed to look for a reason to bust Caine's chops on something. This would be plenty of motivation to get him worked up again.

A Mason jar of sweet tea was set in front of her. She stifled a gasp. Looking up, she saw Malcolm. He smiled at her, then put down another jar in front of Natalie. Two fat rocks of vanilla ice cream bulged from a dark frothy pond. A spoon was stabbed into the top. He gave both of them straws.

"Want me to get you a menu?"

"Really, this is fine," said Trish.

"You're sure?"

Trish nodded. "Very."

"Tell you what. Enjoy these, but come back at lunch. It's on the house."

"Forever!" Natalie fired back.

Malcolm jumped, pretending to be startled. "That's right!"

"Thank you," said Trish. "But we might have one, possibly two more at lunch time."

Malcolm swept his hand through the air. "Bring them. The more the merrier. More kids?"

"Well...about your age. My nephew, Gunner."

Malcolm lightly smacked his forehead. "Duh. I should've guessed that. The 'possibly two' would be my sister."

Trish's mouth dropped. Gunner was with *her*? That girl looked like a model.

Why not? Gunner was just as gorgeous as the other Thompson men. Sure, he was much quieter, but after what he'd gone through the last couple of years, she couldn't blame him for not talking much.

"Megan is crushing on him pretty hard," added Malcolm. "Gunner seems cool, though. I bet he'll eat lunch with Megan, though. She plans to cook for him. And that's going to be a true test of his feelings for her, because she is a *horrible* cook."

Trish felt her features droop. A frown was forming. "Cook? On the beach?"

"No, they're at our house. Megan was running all over when I left to make sure everything looked tip-top." He laughed. "She's got it for him bad. I've never seen her act like that. Especially with somebody she just met."

Trish didn't know how she felt about Gunner being at their house. He'd lied to her. He'd told her he was going to meet a girl at the beach.

Maybe the plan changed.

If so, Gunner should have told her.

"Anything else?" asked Malcolm.

"No, this is plenty."

"My pleasure," he said. "Enjoy your tea and float. I'll see you at lunch time. I'll save this table for you."

He turned and hurried away.

"What's the matter?" asked Natalie.

Trish blinked. Natalie was spooning in a large mound of ice cream.

"Nothing," said Trish. She smiled. "Good?"

Natalie nodded. "Yep. Are you going to beat him?"

"No. I think he's more than made up for scaring you, right? Free ice cream for life? How can I beat him now?"

Natalie looked confused. "Are you going to beat Gunner? For fibbing."

Trish laughed. "Gunner's too old to be beaten."

"But he did fib, right?"

"Well...I don't know if he fibbed. Maybe he just didn't tell us everything."

"Daddy says if you keep things to yourself, it's the same as lying."

Trish nodded. "Your daddy is very smart."

"Does Uncle Howie think so?"

"Does he think what?"

"Think Daddy's smart..."

Trish's throat tightened. "Of course he does."

"Sometimes he doesn't act like he thinks so."

Again, Natalie was right. This little girl was very observant to what went on around her. Trish was impressed how much Natalie seemed to understand. But it also made her feel bad, since she was able to recognize tension between Howie and Paul. That was something Trish hoped no one could see.

If she could see it, Gunner could too.

"Uncle Howie loves your daddy. He's the older brother, you know that?"

Natalie nodded. "Yep. Daddy's second daddy."

Trish laughed. "That's right. Howie does sometimes act like a daddy to him, huh?"

"I think it pisses Daddy off."

Gasping, Trish reached across the table and lightly tapped Natalie's hand. "You shouldn't use language like that."

"I've heard Daddy say it when he's on the phone with Grandma."

Trish laughed some more. It felt good as it relaxed the tension in her muscles from Natalie's earlier comments.

"Let me try to explain," said Trish. "You know Gunner loves you, right?"

"Yep. He tells me every night before I go to bed."

"That's good that he does that. But does Gunner sometimes act like a daddy to you? You know, if he sees you about to do something you're not supposed to do, he stops you, right?"

"Yeah. And he makes me go to bed on time." She rolled her eyes. "He *never* lets me stay up late!"

Trish looked around. Heads were turning toward them. Without any music on, the staff could easily hear Natalie's carrying voice.

When she turned back to Natalie, she shushed the little girl. "Not so loud."

Natalie grimaced. "Sorry."

"It's okay. But you see what I'm saying? Gunner is older, so he looks at it as part of his responsibility to make sure you're okay. That's all Howie tries to do with your daddy. He just wants to help."

Natalie looked to the side, nodding as she sucked a dark glob from the spoon. "I guess so."

"Maybe Howie just needs to come up with a better way to show it."

"Probably. I think Daddy doesn't like Howie always doing stuff for us. I think it hurts his proud."

"Proud?"

"Yeah…" Her eyes narrowed as she thought about it. "Proud. His…" Frustration crumpled her sweet face. "Makes him feel dumb."

"Oh…his *pride*."

"Yeah." Natalie looked relieved. "Pride."

"Let me tell you something about pride. Pride gets people into trouble."

"How come?"

"Never let what others think about you control you. I know you're young, but I bet you understand what I mean by that."

Natalie nodded. "I do. Mama went crazy because of it."

"Oh, Natalie…"

Trish reached across the table and held Natalie's hand. Though she kept eating her float, she did so slower, as if it no longer tasted delicious. Trish knew nothing she could say would make Natalie's last comment not be true. Natalie was a very observant girl, probably left alone too much and that gave her nothing but time to think.

I'm going to show her not all women are basket cases.

But she also knew she had to do something about Gunner. She couldn't just leave him at the Caine house, knowing that Mayor Caine was off with Howie and Paul. She would have to go get him.

No. Don't do that. Gunner will hate me. Even though he's the one in the wrong, this will be my fault in his eyes.

Then what could she do?

She looked at the phone and contemplated texting him.

It'd put him in a position to lie even more.

She could tell him she knows where he is. Tell him to come back.

Would he listen?

Trish wasn't sure.

Maybe send one of the Caine brothers over there? Have them tell Gunner he has to leave.

And if they walk in on Gunner doing things *with their sister?*

Trish could see Malcolm's polite demeanor dropping away. If he caught them doing something, Malcolm would probably kick the crap out of Gunner. And once her nephew learned she was the one who asked Malcolm to go check on them, he would hate her.

Damned either way.

Sighing, Trish leaned back. She took her hand from Natalie and curled it around the sweet tea. The glass was moist under her fingers.

What to do?

"Are we going back to the beach?" asked Natalie.

Trish took a swallow of tea. It spread cold through her as it went down. She smiled. "In a little while…"

"What are we going to do next?"

Trish nearly groaned. "I guess we better go get your brother."

"He's in trouble, isn't he?"

"Not yet. But I bet he will be later."

Natalie didn't seem pleased. "Oh, boy."

"Yeah," said Trish. "Oh, boy."

CHAPTER 28

"Are you sure we haven't already been through here?" asked Paul.

Howie looked back at him from over his shoulder. "Positive."

"Okay," Paul muttered.

He didn't believe Howie was entirely committed to his own answer. All these caves looked the same, so it was very possible they'd been through here once already.

"We're not lost," said Striker from the front. "No Xs."

Striker had been marking their path with an orange paint marker. Paul was grateful the tracker had planned ahead since nobody else had even bothered to think about it.

"Hang on," said Bubba in that feminine lisp. "I've got to change tapesth…"

"You've used up a full tape already?" asked Caine.

"Yeah."

"How many did you bring along?"

"Three."

"Well, take it easy on the recording. We need to ration the stock. It's not like we can run back to the car and get more."

Though Bubba didn't say anything, Paul figured the big guy wanted to remind Caine that he'd been the one who wanted Bubba to record nearly every turn, dark space, and crevice. And every time he forced Bubba to click record, Caine demanded Becky to step in front of the camera's red glow to do an introduction. It was no wonder they'd blown through ninety minutes of tape.

Striker halted and turned around. The group gladly did the same.

"You've got thirty seconds," said Striker. "If you're not ready by then, we're moving without you."

"Can I have some light?" asked Bubba.

Howie threw his flashlight's beam onto the camera.

"Thanks," said Bubba. He poked a switch with his forefinger. The camera beeped. It sounded like a car horn in the cramped confines of the cave. A grinding sound followed that was made even more irritating as it bounced off the rocky walls.

"If he had no idea we were here before," said Striker, "surely he's heard that."

"Sorry," said Bubba.

"Jesus Christ it's loud," said Lillard.

As Bubba hurried to change the tape, Becky stepped close to Paul. "How long have we been walking?" she whispered.

"Too long," said Paul.

"Seems like we've been walking for days." She huffed. "My legs are killing me."

"When we're out of here, I'll rub them for you."

Becky glanced at him, smiling from the corner of her mouth. "Yeah?"

Paul nodded. "If you want."

The smile seemed to grow. "When we're out of here, you can rub me anywhere you want."

Paul felt a tremor of excitement. But Howie's groan killed it. He must have heard them talking. It wouldn't be hard to eavesdrop since the tunnels were so narrow.

Becky's coy expression was smudged by shadows, but Paul easily detected the frown that replaced it.

Even without Becky's offer, Paul was ready to get out of here. All they'd done was walked and pointed flashlights. Each crevice they came to, every nook they passed, they stopped long enough to thoroughly search it before moving on. And then they had to wait while Becky told the camera what they were doing. It had been more of a hassle than probably any of them had bargained for.

Becky and I can't be the only ones who are beat.

"Time's up," said Striker.

Bubba clamped the tape into the dock and the metal casing slowly lowered. Then he snapped the case shut. "Ready."

Striker turned and started walking. Everybody followed.

Some passages were narrower than others and they had to form a single line to pass between the rocky walls. Paul had bumped his head more than once on mud that seemed to have hardened into rock during the process of dripping. The floor was a combination of sand and mud and water, which made walking slippery and difficult. The walls seemed to glow as if painted in slime, and all around Paul could hear hollow drips and the faint sound of rushing water.

They had found no indication of Bigfoot using these caves as his home. They hadn't even found a footprint.

But where else would he go?

If not here, Paul couldn't think of any other place, other than the walking trails. But the woods there wasn't thick enough to conceal it. These caves were as close to a natural habitat a Bigfoot was going to find out here.

Shaking his head, Paul couldn't believe his ridiculous thoughts. A Bigfoot? But he was there last night. He'd seen it. He knew it was real.

Another long stretch of time passed and Paul found himself in a sort of trance as he walked. It was easier than focusing on their mission if he let his mind drift. He didn't know how long they'd gone before he bumped into Becky's back.

She gasped.

"What are we doing?"

Becky shushed him.

What's going on?

Looking up, he saw the group before him in the spread of his flashlight. They'd all stopped walking. Striker, holding up his hand, signaled them to halt. The tracker turned his head to the side, lifted his nose into the air. Paul saw Striker's nostrils flaring.

Paul sniffed. All through the caves, the air had smelled briny and damp, a little like mildew. Now he detected another scent. Though it was very faint, it seemed to suppress everything else.

"Smell that?" asked Striker.

Before anybody could respond, Paul said, "Smoke."

Striker smiled. "Wood smoke."

Paul's insides felt squirmy. They were close.

"Keep moving," said Striker. "And be alert."

"Wait," said Caine. "We have to get this on..."

"Piss off," said Striker. "We don't have the time now. Everybody move."

Again he started walking. And again, everyone followed him.

Paul saw the dark shape of Caine's head turn to Bubba. "Is it on?"

The camera chimed. "It is now."

"Knock it off," said Howie.

Becky paused long enough for Paul to catch up to her.

"This is it, huh?" she whispered.

Paul nodded, though he doubted she saw him in the bouncy radiance of their flashlights. "Seems so."

"Oh, God…"

Paul put his arm around her. It was harder to walk this way, but he liked having her against him. How she pressed tightly against him, he thought she liked it also.

Striker spun sideways and pointed. "There!"

Howie raised his rifle and thrust the barrel forward. Paul jerked his Ruger from the holster. A staccato of ratchet-like clicks resounded from all around as guns were cocked ready to fire.

Paul saw nothing but shadows.

Striker chuckled softly. "Don't be so antsy, damn."

"What is it?" asked Howie.

"Down there. See it?"

The crowd huddled at Striker's back. Paul guided Becky in front of him and pressed against her. He felt the heat of her body soak through his uniform. Her rump pushed against his crotch, but she didn't move away from him.

"I see it," said Howie.

Paul strained his eyes, trying to make them adjust to the even thicker darkness ahead. In the distance, he began to make out a dim orange guttering across the bulges of rock. From here it was like a single candle in a dark room.

The fire.

"Somebody's keeping warm down there," said Striker.

"Can he light a fire?" asked Becky. "Seems out of character…"

"Coming from somebody who didn't believe they existed until last night," said Striker. He snorted. "Yes, they can start fires. It's not hard for them. If your brush is dry enough, then rub two stones together to get the spark. Anybody can do it. They actually enjoy the

220

heat fires provide. Plus, it helps them see better at night. Their vision is like ours, so they like having more light in these dark caves."

"You're telling me he's scared of the dark?" asked Becky.

"Maybe," said Striker.

Incredible.

Paul had seen movies where people chased away Bigfoot monsters with torches. He'd never suspected they actually relished a campfire like anybody else.

Becky squealed as she was jerked away from Paul. Spinning with his gun pointed, he held his fire when he saw Caine all but dragging her in front of the camera.

"Tell them what we've found," said Caine.

"Damn it," she said, yanking her arms from his hold.

"Tell them. And make it *quick.*" He pointed at Striker as if giving him the credit for the additional directive.

Paul holstered his gun and stepped closer. Becky was brushing her shorts. He could see dark smudges across the khaki fabric.

"She doesn't want to be in front of the camera right now," said Paul.

"Nonsense. This is what she's always wanted." To Becky he said, "Fix your hair dear, it looks a dab disordered."

Paul saw his fist soaring for the side of Caine's face. The mayor turned. His eyes widened. Then Paul's fist smashed his nose. Blood burst from each nostril, coating Caine's mouth in a moustache of red. He staggered against Howie, who turned and let him fall.

Paul's arm throbbed with pain. Holding his hand out, he shook it. The hot prickles didn't ease up. Looking around, he saw everybody had their flashlights aimed at him. He shielded his eyes with his arm.

"Finally somebody did it," said Striker.

Bubba shut the camera off, without speaking, reached into the darkness below. When he stood up straight, he was holding Caine by the collar of his wind suit. Blood had spread across the lower half of the mayor's face.

"Why'd you do that?" asked Becky.

"I..." Paul shook his hand harder. "I don't know."

"You're going to be in a world of shit for that."

Caine wobbled and Bubba caught him before he could fall.

"He'd need witnesses," said Howie.

"Right," said Striker. "And I didn't see anything. I mean, these stalagmites can be dangerous. I've bumped my head on more than one today."

"Me too," said Howie. "Damn things."

Becky started to smile. "Now that you mention it...I knocked my head on one earlier."

"Same here," said Blake.

"Yep," said Lillard.

"I think I just hit my head again," said Styles.

Bubba turned around. One arm reached behind Caine's back, the other was flush against his chest. The camera jutted from his chest and pointed at the wall. "Things can be bitches if you're not careful."

Paul smiled. He lowered his hand. Nobody was going to support Caine's claim.

If it even comes to that. Might not even remember I hit him.

"Is he going to be able to walk?" asked Striker.

"He'll be fine," said Bubba.

"Fine," echoed Caine in a loopy voice. "Did Becky do the scene?"

"Yeah," said Bubba.

"Good..."

Striker started forward, ducking as he entered the passage. Once he stepped through the squat opening, he was swallowed by shadows. A moment later, his bulky dark shape appeared as if his shape had been cut out in the fire's soft flicker.

"I'll be okay," said Caine, pulling away from Bubba. "Just keep the camera rolling." He looked around, said "There it is," then picked up his flashlight.

Caine followed Striker into the passage with Bubba close behind. The red dot of the camera trailed Caine like a floating ember.

Howie angled his flashlight under his chin, throwing brightness on the lower side of his face. He was frowning. "Stay close to me," he said.

"Okay," said Becky.

Howie glanced at Paul, as if telling him he didn't mean her and he was actually talking to Paul.

Paul nodded. For the first time, he was grateful to have his big brother's protection. He valued it above Striker's.

Howie turned to the others. "Everyone ready?"

Nobody spoke.

Howie nodded. "Neither am I. If anything happens in there, I just want you all to know it has been honor serving alongside you. I consider all of you my family."

There were a few hushed mutters and Paul thought he heard somebody sniffle. He had never heard Howie speak in such a way. It was as if he knew...

No. Everything's going to be fine.

But as Paul followed his brother through the mouth of the tunnel, leaning forward so he wouldn't bonk his head on the jagged rim of rocky teeth, he wished they hadn't come down here.

He felt through the darkness and found Becky's hand. He felt it jerk when he slipped his fingers between hers. Then she gripped him tightly.

This is it. Shit, this is really it.

At the end of this cave was its lair. They were trespassing in its home. The Bigfoot would not be pleased by this.

CHAPTER 29

Paul tugged his Ruger from the holster. His leg bumped against the barrel as he lowered it by his side. When he tried to swallow, it felt like he was trying to suck down a stone.

They reached the end of the chasm, another tunnel veered to the left. Striker went first, the others following, until the walls began to expand around them. The guttering glow became brighter, dark shadows writhing across the lumpy rock walls of a chamber.

A stench like rotten seafood was heavy in here. Mixed with it was a dingy smell, as if a wet dog had rolled in a dead animal. But mixed with it was a fainter stench, like infection, a yeast-like smell that was foul and hard to handle.

Grimacing, Paul raised his wrist to his nose and pushed his nostrils against the hairs on his hand. His Ruger pointed up by his forehead.

Striker stopped walking. Caine and Bubba stepped around to his right side and paused. Howie took his left with Paul and Becky lining up next to him. Lillard, Blake, and Styles filed around Becky to form an arc of bodies.

Nobody spoke. All of them stared at the naked woman squatting before them. Her back, facing them, was smeared with soot. Thick stripes painted her from the juts of her shoulder blades down to the crack of her buttocks. There were bruises in the shapes of handprints on each cheek. Legs parted wide, her arms could be seen reaching down between them, working at some kind of meat that was on the ground between the small gap of her groin and the dirt floor. Her skin looked glazed, shiny under the firelight. Her dark brown hair hung on her back in a tangled mess. Bits of debris were trapped in the filthy tresses like bugs in a spider's web.

As she stabbed the meat with a jagged rock, she grunted with each thrust. Paul began to decipher the meat had black fur. A red collar was clamped around its crushed neck.

My God... It's a Black Lab...

Paul felt hot bubbly fluids rise in his throat. He struggled to swallow it back down.

Striker held up his hand, flat in front of him as if signaling everyone to hold back.

They listened.

Nobody wants to say anything.

And Paul couldn't blame them. If he opened his mouth right now, he might scream.

The woman tore a sheet of black fur away from the dog's carcass. The backside was painted in a gummy red like glue.

Becky put her arm up to her mouth and bit down on her wrist.

Shit!

Paul fought to keep his breathing measured and slow. It wasn't working. Air huffed through his nostrils. He felt them sputter against the back of his hand.

The woman stopped what she was doing. Head turned to the side, nose rising into the air. Two quick sniffs and she sprang around, landing in the same squatting position, but now facing them.

Paul took an involuntary step back, gasping. Becky was right beside him. After a quick glance, Paul saw that everyone except for Striker had moved back a full step.

The woman's eyes were wide, unblinking. Her face was streaked with black that seemed to start at her temples and work all the way down to her knees. Mouth snarling, the lips quivering around her bared teeth were chapped and flaky. She had fairly large breasts, but it was hard to tell exactly from the amount of bruising and what looked like bite marks. Her left nipple was gone, leaving only a ragged stump that had healed in a faded color.

And she held the rock like a knife, high above her head, the sloping blade toothed like a thick saw.

"Ma'am?" said Striker.

She flinched at his voice, blinking. She looked frightened and very confused.

"Where is it?"

Her breathing came out in shrill gasps. Blinking, she turned her head slightly away from him.

"Mackenzie Dalton," said Howie.

The woman acknowledged the name. She looked up at Howie. Her bottom lip quivered. "Yuh...yes," she said in a hoarse voice.

"My God," muttered Becky. "I thought so."

The missing girl?

Paul couldn't remember for sure, but he thought the girl who'd vanished last year's name was Mackenzie. Had she been down here all this time? Living with the Bigfoot?

"What's he done to you?" asked Becky.

Mackenzie looked down at herself. As if seeing the condition of her body for the first time, her arms went limp and dropped to each side. When she looked back up, her bottom lip was bowed out and tears had cut paths between the smudgy sections on her face.

"It brought me here..." she said. "I've had to do...*things* for him. I—I—I don't know...I just kept doing it..." Sobbing, Mackenzie's head sank forward. Her shoulders bopped, making her breasts jiggle.

Paul felt like a lech, watching her like this, so he turned his head.

And saw Howie was ushering for somebody to go forward. When he looked behind him, he saw Styles stepping away from the others. Untying the shirt around her waist, she held it out as she approached Mackenzie.

The busty deputy sunk to her knees in front of the frightened girl, carefully reaching out. Her hand brushed Mackenzie's shoulder. She jumped and flinched away.

"It's okay," said Styles. "I just want to give you this."

Mackenzie lifted her head. The tears and filth had turned her face into a dark smear. Turning to Styles, she smiled when she saw the shirt.

"Thank...thank you," said Mackenzie.

"It's my pleasure."

Styles opened the shirt for her. Mackenzie dropped the rock and held out her arm. Style slid it over one arm, then around her back and held it as Mackenzie put her other arm through. Then, like a mother dressing a child, Styles moved to the front and began buttoning the shirt.

Now that she was somewhat covered, the men moved forward. As if her nudity had kept them away.

"We've got to get her out of here," said Blake.

Mackenzie's head jerked up. Listening, her eyes darted back and forth.

"Yeah," said Howie. "Styles, you and Blake escort Ms. Dalton out of here. Get back to the cars and head to the hospital. Call her parents right away."

"Yes, sir," said Styles.

Howie smiled as he looked at Mackenzie. "You're going to go home."

Mackenzie looked at the ground. As her head lowered, Paul spotted something behind her on top of the tallest rock among a cluster of several other rocks. A bag had been flattened into a cover and sitting on top were several tubes with white caps. He counted six different kinds. Some had been rolled from the bottom and working upward like tooth paste tubes.

What is that?

Paul stepped away from the others and moved behind the rocks.

"Where are you going?" he heard Becky say.

"What?" Howie asked.

"Paul?"

He held out his hand. "Hold it a second."

Standing over the rocks, he peered down at the tubes. He recognized the Walt's Drugstore label stuck to the front.

It clicked.

Oh, shit!

"Howie, these are the missing creams!"

Howie frowned. "The what?"

"Walt's Drugstore? The break-in? *She* took the creams!" He pointed at Mackenzie.

Heads slowly turned to her. On her knees, Mackenzie's shoulders slowly rose as if she was trying to be bashful.

"What are you talking about?" said Striker.

Howie put his hands on his hips. "We had a break-in at Walt's Drugstore. All that was taken were some prescription skin ointments and topical antibiotics. Some pain relievers, bandages…"

Striker stepped forward. "I told you to tell me everything, Thompson! Even if it didn't seem important!" He turned to Mackenzie. "His skin is irritated, right? He can't handle these conditions and is getting skin infections. And *you*…you stole the medicine for him…you're taking *care* of him!"

Paul felt numb as he stared at Mackenzie. Her mouth trembled. It looked as if she was about to start bawling again. Instead, she loosed a wild cackle that made Paul shiver inside.

"I love him!" she screeched.

"*Love* him?" said Howie.

Paul saw her hand grab the rock. Before he could warn Styles, Mackenzie had jerked the thickset woman in front of her. Gripping Styles's short hair, Mackenzie yanked her head back and punched the jagged blade of the rock into her throat.

Coughing and gurgling, Styles held her arms stiffly in front of her. Hands twitching, body jerking, she spat out blood.

"Get them!" Mackenzie shrieked, twisting the rock blade inside Styles's neck.

Paul turned.

And saw the Bigfoot standing inside the cave, blocking the way they'd come in. He stood crouched over from the low ceiling. His chest was patterned with infected bald spots that oozed clumpy green. His bulging brow furrowed, hairy mouth parted.

"He's in here!" Paul shouted.

The Bigfoot's roar exploded in the small space, bouncing off the walls like thunder.

CHAPTER 30

Striker raised his rifle, the barrel falling on his shoulder. "It's a trap!"

Mackenzie's maniacal cackle mended with the Bigfoot's roars.

Mayor Caine squealed and staggered back, pointing at the Bigfoot. "Keep taping! Don't cut that camera off no matter what!"

The Bigfoot held its arms out and flexed with its roar. Its muscles undulated under the fur like rushing water.

Caine threw his arms in the air, let out a long cry, and turned to run. He tripped over Mackenzie, landing on the fire. Rolling sideways, he fell onto his stomach. Writhing flames quickly spread across his back, igniting the wind suit with a whispery *whoosh*. Screaming, he pounded and kicked the ground.

As Bubba ran over to help Caine, Striker pointed at the Bigfoot. "Gun it down!"

As if rehearsed, the group spun around in unison, guns lifting.

Before anybody could fire, the Bigfoot charged.

Lillard was in its way. With both arms, it swung down at Lillard's skull. The young deputy's head vanished between his shoulders with a deep crunch, like a nail being driven into a board. He dropped to the ground.

Becky screamed. "No!"

Howie pushed between Blake and Becky. "Go! Get out of here!" He shoved them forward.

Howie looked at Paul. "Go with them! Get her out of here!"

Paul shook his head. He wasn't leaving Howie here alone. "Not without you!"

"I'm right behind you!"

Mackenzie appeared behind Howie's shoulder. She seemed to be growing from the way her head kept raising behind Howie. Suddenly she dropped back down. Howie stumbled forward with a yelp of alarm. Then she latched onto his chest with one arm, her dirty naked legs bending around his hips and clamping together over his stomach. The other hand, clutching the blood-drenched rock, came down at Howie's chest.

Paul pointed his Ruger, already knowing the shot was too much a risk to attempt in haste.

Not Howie!

Howie got his arm up and blocked the strike. The tip of the rock stopped before punching his chest, hovering half an inch above his heart. Shrieking, Mackenzie jerked and bounced on his back, straining to get the knife lower. Her feet kicked on either side of Howie as he spun circles to throw her off.

Paul followed them between the sites of his Ruger.

"Paul!"

He glanced at Becky. She fought to pull away from Blake as he dragged her out of the cave.

"Go with Blake!" shouted Paul.

"Come with me!" she cried back. Tears flowed down her cheeks in freshets.

"Go!" Paul shouted.

Though she looked hesitant, she stopped fighting Blake. After one last cry, she turned and followed him out.

Paul trained the gun's sight on Mackenzie's forehead. His finger curled over the trigger.

He saw movement in the corner of his eye.

He turned and glimpsed Striker's body soaring toward him. The muscular man's bulk filled his vision. His first thought was Striker was running, but a quick glimpse that showed his feet weren't touching the ground proved he'd been thrown.

Paul felt the impact like a mule kick and was slammed to the ground. The gun flew from his hand.

He was trapped underneath Striker. Squirming, Paul jerked from side to side to get out from under him. His arms were pinned against his chest, legs spread with Striker's frame filling the space between them. All he could do was kick at the air.

The thick padding of Striker's vest pressed against Paul's face, blinding him. But he heard Howie grunting, Mackenzie growling, Caine sobbing, and Bubba screaming cusswords.

What's happening out there!?!

"Come on you son of a bitch!" Bubba's voice. "You want some of this, huh!?!"

Another roar and Bubba's screams rose in pitch.

Paul wriggled under Striker. He could feel the mercenary's breaths on his face, could feel the scratchy stubble of beard on his cheek. Though he was pleased to know Striker wasn't dead, he wanted the big man off him.

Digging his elbows into the dirt, Paul shoved upward with his lower back. For a moment, Striker didn't budge. Then he began to dip to the side. Paul angled to the right and thrust harder as if performing some kind of intense workout routine. And to Paul, it felt like one. Working with his hips, it pulled the muscles in his lower back and thighs taut, as if trying to peel them into a ball of misery.

Finally, Striker dropped onto his side. Relief flowed through Paul's body in a tingling current that felt wonderful. He looked around. Spotted the Ruger and moved. On all fours, Paul crawled to where his gun lay in the dirt. He picked it up, fingering the dirt out of the barrel as he looked at the melee before him.

Howie, with Mackenzie on his back, was slamming backwards against the cavern wall. Each hit pounded against Mackenzie's back. Though she hadn't released his brother, she was definitely showing signs of weakness. Any moment now she would fall off his back.

The Bigfoot had palmed Bubba's head and was pushing him back. Bubba's arms flapped. The hand gripping his .45 pulled the trigger, firing rapidly, as if hoping one of the bullets would catch the beast. None did. The bullets skidded off the walls, whipping through the tight area with whistling zips.

One bounced off a jut of rock beside Paul's head. He felt bits of rock and the heat of the spark the bullet caused before it was thrown in another direction.

"Shit!"

Paul dived forward, landing on his front.

Bubba's going to kill us all!

Bigfoot swatted the gun away, forced the big man to his knees, and kept pushing. Sounds like cracking wood came from Bubba's back.

Raising the gun, Paul almost started firing wildly. But he steeled himself, made himself steady the shot.

Bubba's body crumpled and burst like a balloon with too much air. Innards exploded from his front, his ribcage popped wide through his chest like an opening boney hand.

Paul fired four shots.

Spats of red appeared in the beast's arm, side, and two in his leg. Roaring, the beast whipped around. His eyes locked on Paul, and he felt the gun become much too heavy in his hand.

"Oh, shit on me..."

Another roar and Paul felt what was left of his courage drain from him. Crouching, the Bigfoot spread its arms as if wanting a hug. Then it stepped forward to charge.

Caine's arms wrapped around the beast's leg as if it was heading for work and the mayor didn't want it to go. The Bigfoot stopped, looked down.

Caine lifted his nodding head. Patches of crispy bubbles had spread over his cheeks from the fire. Some of his hair had been burnt away, leaving melted streaks of coagulated flesh and hardened ridges. Curls of smoke rose from his scalp.

"You were supposed...to help us!" screamed Caine.

The Bigfoot tilted its head as if confused.

Caine took in a phlegmy breath and screamed, "You were supposed to...save this town!"

Paul didn't know if a Bigfoot could smile. But he swore this one did—a cocky smirk that reeked of arrogance. It jerked its foot away from Caine's pathetic grasp and lifted it above Caine's head.

Paul saw what was coming. "No!"

The massive foot stomped down on Caine's head, flattening it with a juicy crunch. When the foot lifted off, Caine's skull was a trodden bloody ruin. The beast slid a little to the side, as if stepping in loose mud, and started for Paul.

"Oh, shit on me..." Paul muttered.

The beast was sprinting at Paul, bent forward, arms pumping.

Shoot it, Paul! You've got the shot!

He glanced down at his limp hand, the fingers that barely curled around the Ruger's handle. It felt too heavy to lift, as if it were a car that he needed to pull above his head.

In his peripheral vision, Paul was vaguely aware of Howie flinging Mackenzie forward, flipping her over his shoulder. Styles's loaned shirt flew wide, showing Mackenzie's bare rump, the backs of her thighs and bottoms of her feet on her way down. Her back pounded the ground. Air puffed from her mouth. She lay on the muddy sand with her arms splayed wide on either side of her.

Paul shook the fog that was slowly covering him from his head, thinning the cloud that had been shutting his body down to shock and his looming demise. Somewhere in his mind, he knew it would be easier to let the void take hold, to dumb him to what was happening.

His head cleared, his vision became steady, his hearing, which had turned muffled and bubbly and seemed to squeal from the gunshots, became crisp again. He felt the gun in his hand. Now the familiar weight was no longer a handicap, it soothed him. It gave him courage, power. It gave him hope.

He raised the Ruger.

And was too late.

The Bigfoot was right on top of him, reaching down, still running. Any moment now, Paul would feel those beefy hands clamp down on his head and rip it from his body. Now he wished he would've let the shock take him.

Howie slammed into the Bigfoot's side, intercepting him as if Paul was a quarterback about to be sacked. Howie speared him at an angle. His shoulder pounded the beast's side. The Bigfoot, bent slightly toward Howie, stumbled away from Paul.

Pulling back, Howie stood up and started throwing punches into the beast, quick repeated jabs in its side and stomach. Paul saw Howie's fists pounding where the Ruger's bullets had nailed it.

Growling in pain, the Bigfoot twirled and threw back its long hairy arm. Howie ducked the swing and landed four more quick raps to its wounded side.

Paul aimed the Ruger. If he fired now, he might hit Howie.

"Howie! Move!"

Ignoring Paul, Howie kept hitting. Blood squirted in red ribbons from the bullet wound, splashing Howie, darkening the front of his uniform.

Paul wanted to shoot. There was a good chance he wouldn't hit Howie, but he wasn't completely sure. He was tempted to put one in Howie's leg to get him out of the way, but he didn't want to hurt his brother, the man who'd just saved his life.

"Howie *move!*"

Howie was about to throw another jab into the Bigfoot's side, but suddenly stopped. He looked at Paul, panting, his face dripping with the beast's blood.

Then Howie's face switched to one of surprise and he was hoisted off the ground. The Bigfoot, an arm gripping Howie's crotch and the other the nape of his neck, held him up. Howie's back was above the Bigfoot's head, arms flapping, legs kicking as he squirmed to get free.

"No!" screamed Paul, aiming the gun. His finger started to pull the trigger, but Howie suddenly blocked his shot.

For a brief moment, Paul wasn't sure how this had happened. Then he realized Howie was being hurled down.

The Bigfoot brought its knee up.

Howie's back folded over the beast's thick thigh. His shirt bulged in the stomach, then a crooked hunk of spine burst through the tanned fabric, tearing the shirt into shards around Howie's navel.

Paul didn't realize he was screaming until he felt something in the back of his throat come loose, killing his cries. He watched Howie slump off the Bigfoot's leg. He fell onto his side, facing Paul. Blood was already trickling from the corner of his mouth, forming a dark blob in the squishy sand.

Paul's eyes landed on the protruding tip of spine. Saw the blood spilling from his brother's stomach. Saw the Bigfoot bent at the waist, a hand to its side. Saw its long gnarly fingers pressed to the bullet wound, the dingy hair matted with crimson splashes. It was winded, taking in heavy breaths that rattled in its chest like soft snores.

Paul shook his head. He wouldn't accept what had just happened. No way had his brother just—no this didn't happen.

"Puh…Paul…" Howie coughed up blood.

236

The shock began to dissipate, shoved aside by rage that made Paul's skin feel as if he'd been in the sun too long. Paul gave a roar of his own.

And pointed the gun at the Bigfoot.

His finger started tugging at the trigger. The gun kicked in his hand. Blasts deafened his ears. The rotten egg odor of gun smoke filled the air. He didn't know how many bullets actually hit the beast. But he was still pulling the trigger well after the gun had stopped jerking. There were no more blasts that sounded like explosions, only hollow *clicks* of an empty pipe.

Then something heavy minced the back of his head.

Paul dropped.

In his dimming vision, he glimpsed Howie, wincing and struggling to breathe. He caught a quick glance of the Bigfoot on its knees, and Mackenzie going to its aid. She dropped the coconut-sized rock that was dark and wet with Paul's blood, and began to assist the beast to its feet.

Darkness swarmed through Paul, taking away his sight. His last thought before a black emptiness filled him was of his kids.

CHAPTER 31

Becky had no idea where they were. Blake seemed just as disordered, though he kept going, sweeping his flashlight this way and that. In his other hand was his handgun. Becky didn't know what kind it was, but it had a long barrel and a cylinder. She had no clue what had happened to her own flashlight. Probably dropped it during the commotion back in the cave.

God...

The attack replayed in her mind in a series of jarring images. She couldn't even begin to fathom them all. Maybe someday, if she lived, she could process everything that had happened. But right now it seemed impossible. Too much madness and things she'd been told all her life that weren't real, actually were. And Mackenzie...God, what had happened to her? She'd somehow grown to worship the creature. *Loved* it. Killed for it. What kind of lunacy had she experienced for all her reason to abandon her like that?

Stockholm Syndrome with a Bigfoot.

It had been several minutes since any hollow reverberations of gunfire had drifted through the caverns. And that worried Becky. Hopefully it meant the Bigfoot had been killed, but for some reason she doubted it.

Please let them all *be okay.*

Remembering what happened to Lillard, she doubted he was okay.

Poor Lillard...

Blake's head bopped and turned as he looked around. Groaning, he turned back, pointing the light behind him. It cut a narrow funnel through the thick darkness and ended as if smashed by the black. He suddenly turned to the side, pointing the flashlight ahead of him.

Winded, sweat drenched Blake's face. His shirt was dark with stains.

The light pointed into a narrow corridor. It was much too short and skinny than any they'd come through on their way in.

"We didn't come that way," she said. Her lungs felt tight and achy as she tried to catch her breath.

"I don't think we were…in here at…all…" Blake could hardly finish the sentence through his pants.

He's about to keel over. Is he going to be able to go much further?

He'd been a deputy for as long as she could remember, and knew he had to be pushing fifty in age. Plus he was out of shape, and not just by a little. His gut towered over his crotch like an awning of fat. Becky didn't know what she'd do if he couldn't carry on.

Blake pointed the light back into the narrow chasm as if considering going inside.

There was no way he'll fit in there. He might be able to go in a little ways, but he'll probably get stuck.

And even if he didn't somehow lodge himself inside, they would have to crawl to get through. Since there was no way of knowing how deep the tunnel was she didn't want to risk him not being able to handle the exertion.

"Don't think about it," she said. "We're not going in there."

Blake nodded, as if he'd needed to hear her state the obvious. "Right."

"Let's keep moving forward," she said.

"We've been going this way for a long time," he said. He took a deep breath and let it out with a soft wheeze. "I'm afraid we might be doing circles."

"There has to be some damn way out of this place."

"Right. The way we came in."

There had to be other ways. No way was there only one way in and out.

"Let's go," said Blake.

Walking slightly at an angle from Blake, Becky stayed close. She followed the funnel the flashlight made through the darkness before them. It turned every which way as they moved slowly.

Several minutes later, Blake jerked to a stop. He flung the disc of light onto the wall.

"There!" he said.

Becky saw it. The orange X. One of the many Striker had drawn on the cave walls on their way through.

"We're going the right way!" said Becky.

"Damn right. Come on."

They walked to the X and saw where the tunnel led to the right. Following it, they had to move single file to go through. This time, Blake had Becky take the front.

"I'll cover you," he said.

Becky was aware of how often the flashlight seemed to linger on her backside. All she saw in front of her was a dark Becky-sized shape thrown against the soggy sand floor. Blake was probably enjoying how her buttocks moved in her shorts. She regretted wearing them now, knowing Blake was getting a good view. But she liked how they didn't restrict her, how her legs moved freely in them. It was the same shorts she wore when she would go hiking with her sister.

Becky saw another X.

"There," she said.

The light wavered across the gaudy marker.

They kept walking.

A little ways longer and another X appeared.

Blake moved up beside her as the space around them widened.

"I think we're almost there," he said.

Becky thought so, too. Though this area looked the same as all the others they'd been through, she thought it seemed more familiar.

"Our footprints," said Blake.

She looked down and saw in the wash of light many sets of footprints. She recognized her petite pair among the many other larger ones.

Blake took the front again, and Becky was glad to have the light off her ass.

More minutes passed and a toothed portal of light appeared ahead of them in the distance. A chasm of brightness bore through the dark cave, pushing the shadows against the bumpy walls.

Blake laughed. Becky cheered. Both started running. This corridor was wide enough that they didn't have to worry about bumping against the blunt edges of the walls. As they closed in on their exit, it seemed to grow, opening like a wide bright mouth eager to swallow them.

More like a large ass spreading to shit us out.

Becky started laughing. Blake, having no idea why she was, decided to join in.

The sunlight was blinding when Becky dashed from the cave. Glaring white filled her vision, triggering tears and hurting her eyes. A dark shape stepped in front of her and caused her to gasp.

"We have to get to the cars and call for support." Blake's voice.

Relieved, Becky nodded. "Okay. I can't see shit."

"Me either, but I know the way. Come on."

She felt his pudgy hand take hers. It was slick with sweat as he guided her to the edge. Below them, rocks slanted down, their tops pointing up like spikes. Her stomach cramped, imagining those serrated tips piercing her.

If we fall…

She blinked away tears the sunlight had caused and could see a little better, though it still appeared as if she was looking through liquid contacts.

Blake took her to a small footpath that etched through the rocks. It was very skinny and would be hard to maneuver. But if they were careful, neither of them should get hurt.

"Shouldn't be as strenuous going down," said Blake.

"Yeah, especially if we fall."

Blake frowned. "Let's hope that we don't."

"Already hoping."

Blake gave her a single nod. "You want to go first?"

She figured she might make it down quicker if she was in the lead. But if she started to fall, nobody would be in front of her to stop her.

And if Blake falls, there's no way I could catch him. He'd take us both down.

It would be safer with him in the front. Hopefully he wouldn't trip, since *nobody* would be there to catch him.

Though Becky didn't like it, she said, "You go..."

Nodding, Blake holstered his firearm and started forward. He sidled down the path, prancing as if moving over hot coals. Both arms out, he used them for balance.

Following, Becky simulated his posture. She was surprised how much it helped. With such a steep slope, it took no time to pick up speed. Soon, the salty wind was whipping her. It threw strands of hair across her face, rocked her ponytail behind her. She felt the tips of her hair slapping the nape of her neck.

The ridge started to level out as it neared the bottom. This threw off her momentum and she dropped forward.

Blake caught her before she landed on the rocks.

"Careful," he said, helping her back up.

Bent at the waist and panting, Becky nodded. She had a hand pressed flat on Blake's flabby chest. She could feel his heart sledging behind the shirt. The fabric felt soaked, as if he'd gone swimming in his uniform.

"Almost there," he managed to say between huffs.

Standing up straight, Becky took a deep breath. Her throat was dry and her lungs felt as if they were being slowly crushed between two bricks.

Blake's face had turned crimson under the sheen of sweat. "We can take it slower the rest of the way," Blake added.

Not quite jogging, Becky followed Blake onto the sand. The padded ground felt great on her feet after the hard surface of the ridge. It was tricky to walk on from how much it slipped under her shoes. She stumbled her way around bigger rocks to her left. Waves crashed against the shore behind her. She felt moisture in the air, adhering to her already slick body. Her tank top was glued to her back. Reaching behind her, she tugged it from her skin.

The cars came into view beyond the chain cordon that shaped out the old parking area. Far off in the distance, Mayor Caine's large house was a blocky dark shape against the bright blue of the sky. The peak of the tower stabbed into the sky as white clouds grazed in fluffy plumes behind it.

They passed a few vehicles until reaching Blake's. He opened the passenger door for her. "Get in," he said.

Becky dropped into the seat, pulling her legs in just as Blake shut the door. Inside was stifling, making it hard to breathe. The seat was hot against the backs of her legs. But she left the door closed.

She saw Blake through the window on the other side, hobbling to the driver's door. It opened and he climbed in. With a groan, he settled down in the seat, then grabbed the door and pulled. It banged shut. The interior filled with the odors of sweat and stale breath like a puppy's.

Blake had a hard time catching his breath. Head leaned back, he took several breaths. His arm below the short sleeve of his shirt was soaked and dripping. Sweat clung to his mustache, making it sag on his lip.

"Okay," he whispered. "Okay. Okay, okay, okay."

He closed his mouth, breathed in through his nose and exhaled a heavy breath that rattled his cheeks. Sitting up, he looked at her. And nodded.

She supposed he was affirming to her that he was better now. He was going to be fine. So, she nodded back.

Something flitted past the window. Becky saw the elongated hairy arms an instant before the door behind Blake was wrenched away from the car in a groaning crumple of metal. The Bigfoot filled the open space, flinging the door behind him. Becky watched it spin through the air.

Blake, screaming, didn't even attempt to grab for his gun. A big brown hand with pruned skin and raggedy fingernails slapped down over Blake's face. Fingers slipped into his wide screaming mouth. The other hand reached around his throat, fingers gripping Blake's chin.

In a simultaneous yank, the head was snapped back and the jaw pulled down. A deep crunch overpowered Blake's cries. His jaw hung in front of his throat, dangling by webby threads of flesh. His tongue darted, lapping at the air, poking his upper teeth.

The gnarled hand gave the jaw another pull and tore it all the way down his throat, ripping open two deep ruts in the skin. Blood poured through the gaps, streaming down his collar, drenching his shirt.

Then he was plucked out of the car and tossed aside.

Becky, too, had been screaming. Frozen, with her back to the door, her hands slapped the air in front of her as if fighting a swarm of flies.

The Bigfoot leaned into the car, arms out. It began to roar, but its rage quickly diminished when it saw her. The roar petered off to an almost coo. The deep pitch of its growls rose to a squeaky whine. Tilting its head, the snarling expression dropped away and it seemed to attempt something like a smile. Big bulging teeth appeared.

And this caused Becky to scream even more.

Using its hands, the beast patted the air, like an adult trying to comfort a sobbing child. It reached for her.

Becky pressed herself even tighter against the door. Her screams turned to gasping groans as she moved her face away from the pawing fingers. Her right hand swatted along the door, found the handle and pulled.

She dropped backwards out of the car and landed on her shoulder. It raked across the sand-sprinkled concrete of the parking area. Pulling her legs out, she rolled onto her stomach and crawled away from the car. The hard ground hurt her knees as she put distance between her and the car.

Looking over her shoulder, she saw the Bigfoot's giant head appear above the car. He let out a single grunt as if asking her what her problem was.

Another scream building in her throat, she turned away from the beast and her eyes landed on a pair of abraded shins. There were ruddy rings around the scratches. Becky, leaning back on her knees, looked up.

Mackenzie's wild hair blocked the sun, making her face a twisting grimace of shadow. She raised the jagged rock.

"Your turn, bitch," Mackenzie said.

Becky closed her eyes, preparing for the blow.

The Bigfoot growled.

"What?" asked Mackenzie. A few quick stern grunts and Mackenzie sighed. "Why? She's one of *them*. She came here to hurt you." More grunts. "Baby, please...we don't need her. Remember? It's already been done."

Becky slowly opened her eyes. Mackenzie still stood above her, the rock poised to strike in one hand and the other hand was rubbing her naked belly exposed between the lapels of Styles's shirt. She was no longer looking at Becky, staring over the top of her head.

What's already been done?

Becky realized both of them were distracted by their little spat, and briefly contemplated making a run for it. But when she heard the heavy pads of the beast's footsteps behind her, she knew her short moment of opportunity had already passed.

Looking over her shoulder, Becky saw the Bigfoot standing just a couple short steps away. He was slightly hunched over, caressing his side. Blood trickled between the cracks of his fingers.

He's wounded. Looks kind of bad.

She wondered who'd been the one to hurt it and hoped it was Paul.

The Bigfoot grunted a few more times, and pointed at Becky. She turned to face Mackenzie and saw the wild woman's upper lip curl, baring teeth.

Mackenzie trembled with anger. "You should just let me kill her now!"

A short, angry grunt.

Mackenzie's scowl fell away to worry. She shook her head. "No, baby, no. Don't say that. I didn't mean it. I'm sorry."

How in the hell does she understand him?

Becky felt dizzy from the insanity on either side of her.

Mackenzie's bottom lip puckered out. "You're hurt, baby. We have to get you patched up."

The beast released a soft groan of despair. For a moment, Becky felt bad for it. Then she remembered what it had just done to Blake, what it had done to Lillard and probably everyone else, and was glad it was hurting.

"There," said Mackenzie. "We'll head over there. Looks big enough, we can hold up there for a little bit. Surely they have first-aid supplies."

Where?

Becky turned to see where Mackenzie's gaze was focused.

"Oh...God..." Becky muttered.

Mackenzie was looking at the mayor's house.

CHAPTER 32

"You let me win, didn't you?"

Megan, standing with the cue beside her like a spear, feigned a gasp. "How could you accuse me of throwing the game?"

Laughing, Gunner shook his head. "Because I'm not any good at pool. And somehow I annihilated you."

"Maybe you just have beginner's luck?"

"Highly doubtful," said Gunner.

Laughing, Megan leaned her cue against the pool table. All that remained on top were a few solid color balls. She turned around, facing him. The light from the machines blinked across her dusky skin, making her bikini top look like white-painted triangles on the tips of her breasts. The matching shorts were a pale wedge that sprouted a pair of gorgeous legs.

Gunner put his cue with hers. "Or maybe I had somebody take pity on me because I'm so terrible."

Megan laughed. "That's probably it."

"Thought so."

"Either way, you won. And what does the winner choose as his prize?"

Gunner turned to Megan. She stood with a hand on her jutting hip, leg pushed out and foot tapping the floor. He felt a tremor of excitement.

"My prize?" he asked.

Megan nodded. "Yep. The winner gets to select a prize, his choice. Whatever he wants."

Whatever I want.

Words flowed through Gunner's head, so many things he wanted to say. What if he told her he wanted to see her bedroom? Would she think badly of him?

She said whatever I want.

And if he did say something like that, and she agreed, what would he think of her afterward?

I'd think she's really damn cool!

But if this was some kind of test…a way for her to judge his character. What he said next could make or break it for their relationship.

What relationship? We're not even dating yet. Or are we?

Gunner took a trembling breath. "I'll take another kiss, if that's one of the prizes."

Megan looked relieved. A smile parted her mouth. "Good choice."

She walked to him, her breasts slightly jiggling with each step. Pressing against him, her skin felt slick through his shirt. She hugged his neck and pulled him down. His hands slid over her back. Their mouths connected. Her lips were soft and cold, quickly warming as they kissed. She sucked in his bottom lip, ran her tongue over it. Then she was kissing him faster, more eager, as if she couldn't get the amount of his lips she desired.

Gunner's hand slipped down her back, over her rump. And squeezed.

She gasped in his mouth. He tasted her breaths.

Walking backward, Megan guided Gunner to the pool table. He put his hands together to form a sling and hoisted her off the floor. Megan let out a small squeal as she swung around. He set her on the rim of the table.

Her thigh bumped Gunner's pool cue, sending it against the other and both onto the floor. Laughing, Megan put her hands on his shoulders. "That was fun," she said. Then she pulled him between her legs. Thighs rubbed him on both sides. They felt soft and velvety against him.

Gripping the bottom of his shirt, Megan raised it over his face. The shirt blocked his view of her for a moment, then it was gone.

Megan slid it down his arms, tossing it over her shoulder. Gunner didn't see where it landed. He didn't care, either.

Oh, wow. This is it!

Her fingers slipped into the front of his trunks, behind the knotted tie, and pulled him closer. The tips of her fingernails lightly tickled the shaft of his penis. It sent a tingling surge through his hips.

As Megan kissed him, she reached behind her with the other hand and flung the billiard balls back. Some rolled to the other side, one hit the pocket and fell in, and others didn't go very far. But she managed to clear a space on the plushy green surface.

Megan scooted back, dropping over the rise onto the green. Gunner climbed up, following her as she crawled backward.

We're going to do it! We're really going to!

Gunner couldn't believe it. He'd never gone this far with a girl before. He'd never had one want to, either. Megan was a completely new experience for him and he was excited and ready to see how far this moment would go.

Lying on top of her, Gunner kissed her some more. If felt different kissing her in this position, as if he might be crushing her. His wallet felt big and hard in the tight pocket of his trunks. He dug his elbows into the plush top and raised his torso off of her some. He felt the silky material of her bikini rubbing his chest. Her legs were spread and he settled his jutting crotch between them.

Megan moaned as he pressed against her. She unbuttoned her shorts and pushed down the zipper. Then she lifted her rump enough to run her shorts down her thighs. They seemed to catch there and Gunner helped her pull them all the way down her legs. At her ankles, he pulled them off and tossed them over the table.

As he studied her smooth pubic mound, she reached behind her neck and untied the strings of her bikini. The patches went limp on her breasts. She slid them off.

Gunner could hardly swallow. It was hard to breathe as he gazed at her perfect body. Her breasts were large and plump, slightly flattened from lying on her back. Her nipples were like tiny dots on the tips of her breasts.

"Like what you see?" she asked in a breathless voice.

Gunner didn't trust himself to speak, so he nodded.

Smiling, Megan sat up, widening her legs and reaching through them. Her hand found the string holding his trunks up. His erection poked the netting inside.

She worked at the knot. Finally, she got it to come undone, then shoved his trunks down his legs. The wallet bounced against him. His penis fell out, bobbing in the air. Megan's mouth dropped open.

"Wow," she said. She looked nervous.

"What's wrong?"

"It's…big."

Gunner smiled. "Really?"

Megan laughed. "Don't tell me you had no idea."

"I didn't."

"It is…wait…" She looked up at him with those huge sapphire eyes. "Is this…your first time?"

Gunner wanted to lie and say it wasn't, but he imagined his performance would give him away. Though what few friends he had back home had been having sex since they were fourteen, Gunner had never gotten the opportunity. When his dad's popularity was at its peak, there were many girls he could have gotten with, but they were usually the kind he knew to steer clear of. And if they weren't in that category, it wasn't Gunner who made them want him, it was his dad.

Instead of lying to her, Gunner nodded.

Megan's smile dropped away. "Really?"

"Really."

Her eyes twitched. Filled with moisture. Her jaw trembled.

Is she going to cry?

"Maybe we shouldn't," she said.

"I have a condom, if that's what you're worried about."

Gunner regretted the words the moment he spoke them. She looked at him from one eye, her eyebrow arched. "You do, huh?"

"Yeah, I mean…" He shrugged. "I've had it since I was fifteen, but…"

Megan laughed. "Doubt it's any good by now." Her lip trembled. She bit down on it to hold it still. "I'm sorry…I'm making it move too fast. Your first time…we should…I don't know."

Though disappointment streaked through him, Gunner nodded. "If that's what you want, we can wait."

"Obviously, it's *not* what I want. Look at me."

Gunner did. He'd never seen somebody so beautiful. Even more so than Trish and that was saying a lot.

"I *more* than want to," she said. "I don't want you to think I'm a slut. I want you to talk to me again afterward."

"I will," he said.

"Oh, sure," said Megan, shaking her head. She smiled, though it was without merit.

No! Don't upset her, for the love of God!

Gunner could feel his erection softening, sliding down his thigh.

He looked her in the eyes. "I've never met anyone like you before," he said. "You'd probably get sick of me way before I even thought about getting sick of you."

Her eyebrows lifted, mouth contorting into a goofy grin. "I like you, Gunner."

"I like you, too."

"And I'm serious when I say that I've never liked anybody as quickly as I did with you. I don't know what it is...but you just..." She shook her head.

"I feel the same way. It was instant for me. The first time I heard you speak, you had me forever."

She looked up at him with her earthy eyes, said "Come here," and laid back.

"Are you sure?" he asked.

"Very sure. Just don't hate me when it's over..."

There was no teasing in her voice. She really seemed to worry Gunner was just using her.

"I promise I won't."

Gunner crawled over her, felt her legs hug around his back. Reaching down, he found his penis and held it as he aimed it between her legs. Megan tensed up, preparing herself. "Should I put on the condom..."

She shook her head. "Just put it in me...now."

Gunner started to push in. He felt her spread around him, the walls of her heat tight and slippery.

Bells chimed through the house.

Gunner sat up in a flash, banging the back of his head on something hard. Gasping, Megan reached out to him, trying to grab him as he started to tilt. Light danced across her naked body, glinting off the smudges of sweat on her skin. He let out a *Yaaah!* before toppling over the edge of the pool table.

He seemed to fall for a long time before his shoulders slammed the floor. His legs swung over and came down next. They hit in front of him, extended, feet out. Rolling onto his back, he gazed up. A bar light, hanging from a bronze-colored chain, trembled and swayed above the pool table.

Was that there this whole time?

Megan's head appeared over the lip of the pool table. Lemon-colored hair hung in her face. She looked concerned. "Are you okay?" she asked.

"Sure," he muttered.

She started to laugh, but quickly stopped. "Sorry...I don't mean to laugh." Apparently admitting this was even funnier to her, for she exploded with laughter. Shaking her head, she put a hand over her mouth. She held up a finger. "Hold on..."

"Yuck it up..."

Still laughing, Megan swung her legs around and let them dangle from the pool table. Her breasts shook with her laughter.

Gunner groaned. "What was that noise?"

His question seemed to kill her amusement. "Oh, shit...I almost forgot. That was the doorbell."

Fear seized Gunner's insides. He felt the solidity vacate his penis. "It was?"

The chimes clamored throughout the house again, a melody of bells in different pitches.

"Damn," said Megan. She began to look around.

Sitting up, Gunner felt pain in his shoulders. As he rubbed the left one, he spotted Megan's shorts on the floor by his feet. He assumed that was what she was looking for.

He grabbed them, held them up to her. "Here."

"Thank you," she said. "Just when it was getting good." She smiled coyly.

"Yeah," he said, feeling a smile of his own.

"Maybe we can get back to it in a few. See who's here."

"Expecting anyone?" He grabbed his shorts and pulled them to him. Spreading them wide, he stuck his feet in.

"Nobody. Other than you. My brothers are working at the restaurant all day, and Dad is off on some excursion, said he'd be home late. But none of them would ring the doorbell…"

A hint of dread began to build in Gunner's chest. He didn't know why, but he didn't want her answering the door.

"Maybe you should ignore it," he said.

Sticking her head through the hoop of her bikini, she paused before tying it behind her back. She seemed to consider Gunner's suggestion. Then she shook her head. "I can't. Could be somebody dropping off something for Dad. If I don't answer it, I'll catch hell." She tied the top.

Gunner grabbed his shirt and stood up. He rolled it up and pulled it over his head. When he got his arms through, Megan was already heading for the door.

"Wait," he said.

She looked at him over his shoulder. "Maybe you should hang out right here. Don't want one of Dad's cronies seeing you here when he's not home."

Gunner understood. He nodded. "Sure thing."

"Be right back." She blew him a kiss, then pranced out of the room, her blonde hair swooshing behind her back like yellow water.

Gunner smiled. He couldn't believe how much he already cared about this girl. He didn't know if that was good or bad. Probably a little of both. Good if things worked out, but very bad if she suddenly stopped wanting to see him.

He walked to the doorway, leaned against it, and put his ear to the open space.

I'm being nosey.

Ashamed of himself, he was about to head back into the room. He heard the clacking of locks being undone and paused. That bad feeling squirmed through him like a cold slug.

It's none of my business who's at the door.

But he wanted to be close, just in case.

Of what?

He had no idea.

"Yes?" he heard Megan say.

There was a pause that seemed to last forever. Then a voice spoke. Female.

"Is Gunner Thompson here?"

253

And Gunner knew why he was so worried.

He mouthed, *Oh, shit.*

He said, "Trish."

There was another pause before Megan said, "Um…"

"We know he's here." Natalie's voice. "Where is *he?*"

Trish laughed. "Natalie, quit being so bossy. Sorry. I just wanted to see if he's here."

"You're Sheriff Thompson's wife, right?"

"That's right."

Though he didn't need the confirmation, hearing her say it weakened his knees.

"Yes, he's here," said Megan. "I was going to make him lunch in a few."

"Ah."

"Please, come in."

"Thanks," said Trish.

There was a squeak that Gunner recognized as the door being opened. Footsteps followed.

"Where is *my* brother?" said Natalie in a demanding voice.

"Natalie," said Trish. "Knock it off."

Megan laughed. "It's all right. He's in the game room."

They're coming in here!

Gunner pushed himself away from the wall, hurrying over to the pool table. He turned, put his back against the rim and tried to look casual.

Then he saw the cues lying in an X on the floor.

"Damn," he muttered.

He quickly picked them up and was trying to lean them against the table when Megan entered.

"You've got some visitors," she said.

Gunner jumped. Trying to catch the cues, his hands swatted them to the floor. They clattered when they landed.

He froze, arms out, trying to hide his cringe. Turned his head. Saw Megan standing off to the side of Trish, who had her arms on the shoulders of his younger sister. All of them looked as if they'd caught him fondling himself.

"Hi, Trish," he said.

"Gunner," she said.

Megan cleared her throat. "I'll leave you all alone. I'm going to get started in the kitchen."

She walked to the doorway and glanced back at Gunner, giving him a sympathetic look. Then she left the room.

Trish stepped closer, and kept her voice low when she said, "What are you doing here?"

Gunner leaned back against the pool table, crossed his arms. "Nothing." His voice rose when he spoke, turning high. He knew Trish wouldn't believe him.

"Nothing?" said Trish, imitating his tone. She sniffed the air. "Really? Then what do I smell?"

"I don't know. Popcorn?"

He pointed to the popcorn machine.

Natalie gasped. "Popcorn!" Then she ran over to the machine, putting her face against the glass.

Trish didn't take her eyes away from Gunner. "That's not what I'm talking about."

Gunner was getting annoyed. He had no idea what she was talking about. Shaking his head, he turned around. His eyes landed on a stain on the pool table that had turned a small blot of green dark. Eyes widening, Gunner's throat felt tight.

Must have come from Megan...

Probably when she sat up, she accidentally rubbed herself across the green.

Gunner gulped.

Trish can smell it.

And though they didn't get to go through with it, Gunner could smell it too. He knew the sex smell well. During the peak of Dad's popularity and before Mom's breakdown, Mom would hoist Dad away to the bedroom to *talk*. Whenever they were finished *talking*, the same smell would drift through the house afterward, as if it had clung to their bodies. Gunner began to despise the odor, but now found it quite pleasant.

Because it came from Megan.

If Trish sees that stain...

Gunner turned around, hoping to block her view of it.

Trish stood before him, arms folded under her breasts. She had all her weight on one foot, the other hip seemed to point up. "Are you going to tell me what this is all about?" she asked.

"It's not about anything," said Gunner. "I don't see why you're so mad. You know, you could've just texted me instead of coming out here and embarrassing me like this."

Trish shook her head. "I thought about it, but figured this way was best."

"Embarrassing me was the only conclusion you came up with?"

Trish held her breath, closed her eyes. When she opened them again, she said, "Yes. I figured a little bit of embarrassment was better than you trying to lie your way out of it and causing more trouble for yourself."

"Whatever," said Gunner, though he understood her point.

"Gunner, you know how upset your dad's going to be."

"So what?"

"So what? Really, Gunner? You're going to be like that?"

Gunner sighed, lowering his gaze to the floor. Trish had on flip flops, the tips of her toes dusted with sand. He shook his head. "No. I'm not going to be like that."

"You told me you were meeting a friend at the beach…"

"You knew it was a girl…"

"Maybe I did. But I thought you would be hanging out on the beach. Within earshot, or something. Maybe taking strolls, or swimming, or going to get ice cream. I had no idea you would be here alone with her, doing…other things."

She does know.

Cold dripped down Gunner's back. "I didn't know we were going to come over here. She texted me after we got to the beach…"

"But you still came over, knowing I would have said no, knowing your dad would have said no."

Gunner didn't respond. He continued to stare at Trish's feet.

"What kind of girl invites a boy over to her house when she's home alone?"

"Hey, come on," he said. "Like you've never done it."

Trish's mouth slowly hung open. Gunner regretted what he'd said right away.

"Sorry," he said. "I didn't mean it like that. I just meant…" Gunner crossed his arms, bumped his shoulders up and down. "I don't know what I meant."

He gave his sister a glance and saw she was moving around the room, admiring the game machines. Her eyes were wide, as if she was experiencing something her mind couldn't comprehend. Wanting to smile at her reaction, he didn't have the energy to lift his mouth. He was going to be in deep trouble when Dad found out, no doubt about it. He'd probably get grounded until school started, and that would damper his social life, kill any chance he had with Megan.

This probably already has.

And the thought of that made him feel weak.

Trish sighed. "Gunner, we have to go."

"Thought so…" His mouth trembled. His throat felt as if it was squeezing his words. "I'll tell Megan bye."

Trish's eyes looked sad and pitiful. She nodded. "Okay. And I'll tell her sorry for dropping in like this."

"And you can tell me sorry for ruining my life," said Gunner.

"Gunner!"

He walked past her, making sure his shoulder gave her a little nudge.

"Damn it, Gunner. I didn't do anything wrong."

Her voice, coming from behind, sounded muffled through the blood in his ears. Never had he been so humiliated. And for it to have been caused by Trish made it feel even worse. Out of everyone, he trusted her the most.

She had no choice. Dad would be mad at her.

But she didn't have to come here. There were other ways. She could have texted him and told him to leave.

Would he have left? Probably not. And Trish knew that, she'd said so.

Gunner walked up the hall on wobbly legs. His vision was slightly blurry and his head a little dizzy. He had tears in his eyes.

Don't cry in front of her, jeez!

Using a knuckle, he wiped his eyes. That helped.

He walked through the doorway to the kitchen.

"Megan, I have to go. I'm sorry for all this…"

His words died in his throat.

She stood on the other side of the island, her back to the door. Slabs of meat that looked like steaks were on the counter. He saw bottles of spices beside a bowl of dark fluid that he assumed was the marinating sauce.

257

The woman in the kitchen was *not* Megan. The island blocked her to the waist. Her hair was dark and frizzy, tangled into a wild ball that hung over her shoulders. She wore a tan shirt.

Hearing his voice, the woman slowly turned around. Megan was in front of her, screaming into the filthy hand covering her mouth. A weapon that looked like a sharp rock was pressed to her throat. For a moment, Gunner thought Megan had been stabbed from how her skin dented in. There was no blood and the tip didn't seem to be penetrating.

Seeing him, the woman smiled. "Wow, aren't you a hotty?"

Megan's eyes were round and full of tears that spilled down her face and the wild woman's fingers. Squirming in her hold, Megan's attempts to free herself were feeble.

"But not as hot as my big cuddly..." she added. Her head turned.

Gunner followed the path of her eyes to the corner of the kitchen, near the long table that Megan said her dad used for parties. First, he saw a woman, on her knees, shoulders slouching, head low. She wore a dirty tank top and shorts. Her dusky legs were streaked and filthy.

Next, he saw what was behind her.

Had to be a costume. No way was it real. *No way!*

Hunched over, a hand flat on the table was a monster. Its fur looked dingy and dry around the infected bald spots on its chest and neck. Oozing callouses were spread all over like bad acne. It had a brick-shaped forehead, tiny eyes that were nearly hidden by the shade the bulging brow provided. Its face was apelike, wide nostrils that seemed to curl down above its mouth.

And it was bleeding all over the table, dripping onto a spreading puddle on the floor.

Gunner's back felt as if it was being scraped raw by icy claws. His penis retracted, as if trying to imbed itself inside his body. His bladder filled and threatened to empty in his swimming trunks.

He heard screams behind him. Two sets. He figured the deeper of the two was Trish.

The monster stood up straight. It roared.

Gunner felt his hair stir, smelled the putrid stench of its breath.

It stalked toward him. The weight of its footsteps trembled through the floor.

It's only a costume. It's only a costume.
But Gunner knew it wasn't.
He was looking at Bigfoot.

CHAPTER 33

Paul! Paul!

Paul heard his name being called, knew he should acknowledge, but couldn't bring himself to do so. Sitting cross-legged, he cradled Howie's head in his lap. He'd closed his eyes a few moments ago, and his fingers still rested on his brother's face.

My dead brother...

Howie was dead.

No! Please, don't let him be dead!

He was. And Paul knew there was no mistaking it. He'd died in his arms.

"Tell Trish...and the boys...I love them..." Howie had said through a mouthful of blood. It trickled down his cheeks from the corners of his mouth.

Paul had tried to speak, but could only sob. He'd wanted to tell Howie so many things, but the words wouldn't come. So he nodded.

Howie reached up with a palsied hand. Paul grabbed it, held it tightly.

"It's...not your fault..." Howie had said.

Paul sniffled, started to sob.

"I mean it..." Howie took a bubbly breath. "Alisha's problems...you didn't cause them. She was a crazy bitch from the start. Tuh...take care of your...kids. They...need you."

Again, Paul nodded. Tears streamed down his cheeks.

"You're...a good man...Paul...I love you, baby brother."

Paul moaned. His chest felt like it was being slowly crushed by cold weights. "I love you, Howie! Please...don't die..."

Howie's grip had tightened on Paul's hand, jerked Paul down close. "And...kill...that son of a bitch..."

Paul had opened his eyes. His brother's face was a teary blur, but he'd seen the conviction. "I promise," Paul had managed to say.

Howie then released a gurgling breath and never took in another.

He'd been holding his brother ever since.

"Paul. We have to get moving."

Finally, Paul turned his head. It sent streaks of pain through his skull and down the back of his neck. The bleeding had stopped, but the pain was immense. Mackenzie had bashed him with a rock. Though he couldn't see how bad the wound was, he figured it must look pretty nasty if she'd left him afterward. Probably thought the blow had killed him.

Striker stood a few feet away, holding his assault rifle by the grip. The barrel pointed at the ground. "It's up to us to stop it now."

"Becky—she's with Blake."

Striker shook his head. "Who knows if they're even still alive?"

Paul didn't want to think something might've happened to Becky or Blake. Carefully, he slid Howie off of his lap, putting him on the ground. He made sure to keep his eyes away from the gore of his brother's stomach. Turning his head, he saw where Caine laid. From this vantage point, he couldn't see over his back. He was thankful for that, knowing his skull had been crushed. Styles lay on her back, arms out to her sides, motionless. He turned away. His eyes landed on Lillard, whose head looked to be sitting on a pair of shoulders without a neck. Bubba was in a bloody pile of body parts, innards, and blood like the leftovers of a slaughterhouse.

It is just us. Jesus Christ, we're all that's left.

He hoped Blake and Becky made it to the cars, called in some help. He wasn't sure how much Seashell Cove had left to offer for reinforcements. But anything was better than the two of them.

Paul got to his feet.

"Here," said Striker, leaning over. He picked up Howie's rifle and tossed it. Paul caught it. "Figured you'd want it."

Paul nodded. He looked down at his brother, saw the strip of extra magazines strapped to his thigh, and removed it. He put the gun on the ground, leaning the barrel across his thigh as he fastened the strip to his own thigh. Then he snatched his empty Ruger from the ground. It felt slightly damp from the oatmeal-like sand adhered to the steel body. He thumbed the clip release, watched the empty magazine drop out, and reached behind his back where a full one was attached to his belt. He snapped it off and put it to the chamber.

Then he slammed his hand against the bottom, shoving it into place with a rachet-like snap.

"Ready?" asked Striker.

Paul nodded, holstering the Ruger. "Let's move," he said.

The two men began their long trek through the caves.

CHAPTER 34

Becky dug the pliers into the Bigfoot's side, sloshing around the blood to find the bullet. His growls of pain shook the walls. A few photos fell and shattered on the floor.

"You're hurting him!" Mackenzie cried, covering her ears.

"You do it!" snapped Becky, offering her the pliers.

Shaking her head, Mackenzie said, "I can't! I already told you I'm too squeamish."

The image of Mackenzie stripping the dog's skin from its corpse replayed in her mind.

She can do that, *but not this?*

Becky went back to work.

Mackenzie had forced Gunner to drag in two mattresses from the guest bedrooms and put them together to form one large bed for the beast to rest on. She only knew his name because Trish had said it when Mackenzie took him away.

Even before she'd asked Trish to be sure, Becky had already guessed he was Paul's son. He looked just like his dad, and though Natalie didn't have all of Paul's features, there were enough semblances to identify her as Paul's daughter.

After making everybody hand over their cell phones, Mackenzie had cut the landlines. Then she'd forced Megan Caine to escort her around the house. When they'd returned, Megan was carrying a stock of first-aid supplies and tools to perform the makeshift operation of extracting the bullets from the Bigfoot. So far, Becky had removed a total of four slugs from its stomach, leg and arm. The one in its side had been giving her the most trouble. It was bleeding all over Becky's hands, coating them in sticky warmth and spreading a dark wet patch on the mattress.

The pliers' mouth clamped down on something hard.

The Bigfoot growled again. He flinched back, making Becky pull the pliers out from the bleeding hole. His colossal fist pounded the floor, cracking the hardwood and causing Natalie to start crying again.

Mackenzie spun around. "Shut that kid up! She can't concentrate with that kid's racket!"

Sitting in Gunner's lap, Natalie trembled in her brother's arms. Megan sat beside him, pressed close, a head on his shoulder. And Trish sat behind them all, an arm around Megan, the other around Gunner and folded across Natalie's back to form a petrified huddle.

Becky smacked her hand across the back of Mackenzie's bare leg. She turned, glaring down at Becky. She still wore Styles's shirt but the buttons had been popped. It hung open over her breasts, covering them except for the sides. She thrust the jagged rock at Becky. "You *slapped* me, bitch!?!"

"*They're* not the problem," said Becky. "The only one being loud enough to distract me is *you!* Now shut the hell up! The bullet's in deep. I need you to entertain him as much as possible so I can pull it out. He won't quit jerking away and if he doesn't be still I'm going to keep jabbing him."

The anger seemed to drain from Mackenzie. Nodding, she sunk to a crouch near the Bigfoot's head. He turned to her, looking up, mouth moving as if whispering to her. She continued to nod, stroking his face, running a hand through the shaggy hair of his head, saying soothing things to him. It really seemed to help calm him down.

She couldn't help watching with a vague interest inside the repulsion. Mackenzie really seemed to care for the monster, and it looked as if it cared about her.

And it wants me for a grotesque threesome.

Frowning, Becky grabbed the bottle of vodka and poured some more on the wound. The beast groaned, but not very loud. Mackenzie quietly shushed him, continuing to talk to him in a sweet voice.

Before setting the bottle down, Becky took a quick sip. The vodka burned a path down her throat, spreading warmth into her belly. It was much needed and helped to settle the shakes ravishing her insides.

The pliers plunged again, searching for the hard piece once more. It didn't take long to find it this time. She squeezed the pliers. She twisted her wrist this way and that. There was some hesitation as a squelching sound like raw meat being torn apart came from the wound.

Gritting her teeth, Becky wrenched back her arm. The Bigfoot roared the loudest yet, shaking Becky's lungs, jostling her insides. Mackenzie leaned over and hugged him, patted his sore-spotted chest.

When Becky lifted her hand, a flattened bloody nub of lead was clamped between the pliers' rutted mouth.

The Bigfoot's roars subsided to a groan. Huffing, its chest rose and dropped. It lifted its head, flat nostrils flaring as it seemed to try to sniff the bullet. Becky turned it so the beast could see it, then angled it at Mackenzie.

It was a large bullet. No doubt it had damaged some vital organs inside. Plus all the blood the beast was losing...

"I'm not sure if he's going to..."

Mackenzie shoved the rock in Becky's face. "Shut up. Don't even say it. Stitch him up."

"Mackenzie, listen to me...he needs real medical attention...and I'm not any kind of doctor."

Mackenzie coldly laughed. "Sure. I'll rush him to the ER. No problem. You stitched the other wounds, stitch this one..."

Becky glanced down at the thread and the blood-crusted needle. She sighed. "Mackenzie...he's lost a lot of blood..." When she looked up at Mackenzie, she saw the woman had tears streaming from her eyes. Somewhere she felt pity for the crazy woman, even knowing what she'd done. "Okay. I'll stitch him up."

"You do that. We'll all hang out here for a little while, let him rest. We can work as a team to wait on him. And when he's feeling better, we'll get out of here." She turned to the others. "And if you all help, just play along like we need you to, we'll leave you be. I see no need to kill any of you, especially since so many people know my boo exists now."

Becky noticed how Mackenzie kept referring to things in a plural sense. Meaning, she had all intentions of taking Becky with her.

Because the beast has my scent...

Wasn't that what Striker said?

A cold feeling squirmed inside Becky. She grabbed the needle and thread with shaky hands. The blood had dried on her fingers, leaving a filmy dark layer over her skin. It made soft crinkling sounds whenever her fingers flexed.

It took her a few tries to get the thread through the eye of the needle, but finally she managed. All those years of working in a library repairing books were paying off with her stitching abilities. The other lacerations had been smaller than this last one, though, and easier to sew. She looked at the large cavity in the beast's side. It wasn't bleeding as badly as it had been. Becky wasn't sure if that was good or bad.

One thing was certain, she realized. Once the beast was asleep, she was going to kill Mackenzie. And if she could kill the Bigfoot as well, even better. There was little doubt they would kill the boy, but she would bet the beast would want to take the women with them. Kind of a bizarre bestiality version of *Charlie's Angels*.

No. That's not going to happen.

She looked at the little girl, saw her shaking in her brother's arms. Her face was pressed into the nook of his neck and shoulder. Becky hoped Paul wasn't dead. Not just for her sake, but for his children's sake. They wouldn't be able to move on without him. They were a tight-knit trio that desperately needed each other. And Becky had to wonder if things would be different, could she somehow fit in with them? She liked to think so.

As she stabbed the needle through the lips of the hole and pulled the thread through, she hoped Paul was okay.

****

Paul threw a blanket he'd found in the trunk of a cruiser over Blake's battered remains, avoiding looking at the ruin of his face and throat. It resembled a peeled banana—the jaw ripped down the front and left hanging by a curve of skin in front of a pulpy band of red.

There was no sign of Becky anywhere. No indication that she'd been hurt or killed by the beast or Mackenzie. Striker told him they'd probably taken her with them. Paul hoped so. That meant she was alive, at least for now.

The cars had been vandalized—slashed tires, busted windows, and smashed radios. There was no way they could drive any of the vehicles out of here, and no way to call for help. Striker's cell phone was still in storage at the station, and Paul had left his in Howie's Suburban. He hadn't been able to find it.

"Why'd they do this?" Paul asked Striker, standing up.

Striker, standing beside Howie's SUV, dropped the mouthpiece of the radio on the ground. He walked around the side, and stepped to where Paul stood at the rear by Blake's body. "I guess they're just covering their asses."

"But if they thought we were dead, there wouldn't have been any need to do this."

"Well...they thought we were dead. Because if they hadn't thought so, we really would be."

Paul nodded. He knew it, too. "So nothing works?"

Striker shook his head. "Even my handheld radios are destroyed. Found them busted on the ground. Five hundred bucks a piece..." He shook his head again, the words turning to angry mutters that Paul couldn't understand.

"Where'd they go?"

Striker turned to Paul. "Good question. There's blood over here, a lot of it. Followed the trail to the car."

"Blake's car?"

"Yeah. It's wounded pretty bad, so we might be able to find the blood and just follow it."

"Maybe we'll get lucky and the bastard'll bleed to death."

"I doubt he's wounded *that* bad. But he's definitely weakened. And that works in our favor."

What was it going to take to kill this thing? Paul must have pegged the beast point blank several times. One bullet from a Ruger like his would easily drop a big man. But the Bigfoot was able to walk all the way through the caves, kill Blake, and smash all these cars before moving on.

And it has two women with it, one of them being Becky. He wanted to get to her as soon as possible. Thoughts of what it might want to do to her tried to invade his mind but he wouldn't allow them to enter.

Striker walked to where the sand of the beach met the parking area. A cool breeze came from the ocean, stirring his short hair. The scar under his eye was a pale line that reflected the sunlight twinkling off the water.

Somewhere in the distance a seagull squawked over the crashing sounds of waves. The sounds were something Paul would have found soothing in other circumstances.

"No blood over here, but I found a print."

Paul joined Striker. He saw the large footprint that definitely belonged to the Bigfoot. The toes pointed toward Caine's house.

"There's another one," said Paul, pointing to one further up. "How are they spaced so far apart?"

"That's its gait."

"Jesus..."

"It sprints when it runs. With a stride like that, it's able to cross distances pretty quickly. Probably just scooped the women up and carried them over his shoulders."

"I thought you said it's weakened..."

"It is."

"Jesus."

"We're still in for a hell of a fight when we catch up to it."

"Where do you think it went?"

As soon as the question left his mouth, Paul seemed to have the answer already waiting. In a synchronized motion, Paul and Striker's heads turned.

Mayor Caine's house sat like a sinister dwelling with the possibility of horrors inside. Somehow, Paul knew the possibility was accurate.

CHAPTER 35

"Do I really have to use this on her?" asked Becky.

Mackenzie scowled. "Yes."

Becky looked down at Natalie. She sat in the chair, eyes staring at her feet. Her face was wet, eyes puffy and raw. She didn't want to use the duct tape to bind her to the chair, but she was afraid if she didn't, Mackenzie would. And Becky figured the crazed bitch wouldn't be anywhere as delicate as she would be.

Crouching, Becky looked up at the little girl. "I'm sorry," she said.

Natalie acted as if she hadn't heard her.

Becky looked at the others, arms and legs wrapped to the chairs, sitting around the table as if about to eat. But that would be impossible, since a strip of gleaming silver had been placed over their mouths. Sets of wide eyes watched her as she began using the tape on Natalie.

She did the little girl's legs first, rolling the tape around her ankles. She tried to keep the bondage as loose as possible. Next, Becky did her wrists. Palms flat on the arms of the chair, she taped her wrists around the narrow posts.

Becky stood, tearing off one last strip for the little girl's mouth. She dropped the roll onto the floor, then held the piece up to Natalie's mouth between her thumbs and forefingers. Natalie lifted her head, shook her hair out of her eyes. The look on her face was blank, eyes looking past Becky as if she didn't notice her.

Right before Becky pressed the tape to her lips, Natalie started to say something, but it was cut short. The tape silenced the words.

"Wha…?" asked Becky.

She wanted to tear the tape back off and ask her if she heard the little girl correctly.

To Becky, it had sounded as if she was about to say: *Look out.*

Look out for what?

Becky felt somebody was right behind her. Looking back, she glimpsed Mackenzie as she lunged at Becky. A large kitchen knife swung down.

Becky tried to spin around, but her feet tangled together and she fell against the table, just missing landing on top of Natalie. Mackenzie slammed against her, grunting, bringing the knife down.

Becky managed to get her arm up. The blade skidded off Becky's forearm, slitting a path of fire across her skin. The sharp point flew at her face. Ducking to the side, she felt the blade part the hair that was falling out of her ponytail.

Mackenzie kept pushing, all her weight throwing Becky onto the table. Leaning over her, Mackenzie hefted the knife up and slammed it down. Becky caught the wild woman's wrist to stop the blade's plunge a hair before it punched into her chest. She held her there, trying to shove her back, but Mackenzie's strength was impressive and surprising.

"He's mine…" said Mackenzie through gritted teeth. She brought her weight up on the tips of her toes and slammed it down.

Becky shoved back, keeping the knife poised a breadth above her. "You…can have him!"

The muffled cries of the others filled the room.

"He wants you to come with us…" Mackenzie strained. A vein bulged in her forehead. Spittle hung from her bottom lip. "He'll want all the girls…I know he will…But he's not getting you…or them…"

Becky realized what was going to happen, why Mackenzie had made her tape the others. She was going to kill them all. Starting with Becky, she'd easily make her way through the rest of them.

"Don't you think he'll be pissed if you kill us?" Becky tried to kick Mackenzie, but her foot only bounced off the woman's side, hardly affecting her.

"He'll forgive me…I'm carrying his child!"

The strength tried to drain from Becky's arms, but she managed to snatch it back. She shoved with all she had, throwing Mackenzie back. The table's legs groaned across the hardwood floor.

Becky stood up. Saw Mackenzie charging, the knife above her head. The shirt flowed behind her like a cape, opening up the front and showing her swinging breasts. She brought the knife down.

Becky rolled to the side. As she fell off the table, she glimpsed the blade stabbing into the wood where she had been. Deep. By the time she landed on the floor, Mackenzie was struggling to dislodge it from the wood.

Mackenzie's announcement reverberated in her mind. She was pregnant. How was this even possible? It didn't make sense. Maybe she really wasn't. Maybe she was just crazy enough to think so.

But for some reason, Becky believed her. She knew it was true.

And the beast must know it, too. That was why he was so protective of her.

Jesus Christ this is some sick shit!

Mackenzie tore the knife from the table. She turned, spotted Becky on the floor, then twirled around to face Natalie.

Ignoring Becky, she swung the knife at the girl's throat.

"No!" cried Becky.

Becky wasn't quick enough to stop her.

Glass shattered. A noise like a hammer striking raw meat followed, then came the recoil of a gunshot. Red burst high on Mackenzie's chest, spinning her like a top. The knife flew from her hand.

Mackenzie's back struck the island, throwing her legs forward. Her back came down, legs swung high and over. Her feet brought her all the way around. She vanished on the other side.

Becky, on the floor, looked up at Natalie. She expected to find the girl's throat had been slit, blood pouring from the wide gash.

There was no blood. No wound. Just a crying little girl, eyes screwed shut.

She was fine.

Not fine...but alive.

Getting to her knees, Becky hobbled to Natalie and wrapped her arms around the little girl. Becky stared over the top of her head, down the table to where a set of tall windows were. One of the panes was broken. A few jagged pieces of glass still hung inside the frame. A man stood outside the window, a rifle lifted to his shoulder.

"Paul!" Becky shouted.

Heads turned. Seeing him, they started calling out through their gags.

Then an explosive roar overpowered their excitement. Becky felt the floor tremble under her knees. She looked back.

The Bigfoot stood in the doorway. His gauze bandages looked bright white compared to the darkness of his dingy fur. He looked at the kitchen island, head lowering. Becky couldn't see Mackenzie, but she knew the beast could.

Head titled back, the Bigfoot roared at the ceiling. Pots and pans hanging above the stove fell from their hooks, clattering when they hit the floor.

More glass shattered. More gun blasts rung out. Becky saw three pops of red appear across the beast's chest. It turned away, running out of the room as holes punched into the wall after it.

"It's going to the front!" she heard Paul shout.

"Got it!" Striker's voice.

A loud crash came from deeper in the house. More gunshots. A roar. Then even more gunshots.

The door in the dining room was kicked inward. Becky screamed until she saw it was Paul who'd entered. Relief gushed through her. She tried to stand up, but her legs shook too much to allow it. He looked rough, beaten. He had a swollen eye that was already turning black, and blood caked the front of his shirt. Specks of red covered his face like freckles of blood. His hair was clumpy on top and looked sticky with blood.

He looked around the room. He nodded, as if affirming to himself that his family was fine.

"Help me get them loose," he said to Becky.

Nodding, she pulled away from Natalie. She started on her while Paul went to Gunner. He got his son loose a lot sooner than Becky did Natalie. The little girl winced when Becky peeled the tape from her mouth. When she was free, Natalie pushed past Becky and ran around the table.

"Daddy!"

"Hey baby," he said, dropping down to one knee. He pulled his daughter into his arms and held her. His other hand, reaching up, grabbed Gunner's leg and pulled down. Gunner dropped, falling against his father and into his arms.

Becky glimpsed the disheveled hair at the back of Paul's head. She saw blood through his curls, the pink pulp of a wound underneath. He'd been hurt.

That's okay. Hurt can be dealt with...at least he's alive.

And so was Striker. She wondered if there was anybody else.

Seeing Trish and Megan were still tied up, Becky ran around the other side of the table and freed Megan. Together, they worked on Trish.

Once Trish's mouth was uncovered, her first words were: "Howie? Where is he?"

Paul held his children closer, eyes pinching tighter.

"Paul?" said Trish. "Paul! Where's...?" Her words faded away.

Paul pulled away from his children. Becky stepped over to them and took his place. Megan crouched behind Gunner and hugged him from behind, crying.

"I'm so sorry Trish...he..." Paul started to cry.

Trish's lips trembled. Eyes closed. Her face crumpled into furrows of agony. "No...no...no, no, no..."

"I'm sorry..." said Paul.

Crying, Trish slid out of the chair, sinking to the floor. Paul crawled to her and pulled her against him. She fought his hold at first, slamming his chest with her fists. Her hits didn't look hard enough to hurt him. He kept holding her as she bawled, screamed, and kept telling herself it wasn't true. Paul never let go. Eventually she succumbed to his embrace. Though she didn't hug him back, she allowed him to hold her.

Becky pulled Paul's children closer to her. Gunner didn't seem to be reacting to the news of his uncle's death, but Natalie was bawling. Becky could feel her tears seeping through her shirt. Once she heard the little girl ask God for Uncle Howie to be alive.

Megan raised her head off Gunner's shoulder. She turned to Paul. "My dad was with you all, wasn't he?"

Paul nodded without looking back.

"Is he...?" Megan said, letting the silence finish her question.

Paul's lack of response was all that was needed.

Oh, God...the poor girl...

Becky watched Megan's struggle. A range of emotions washed over her face. She looked as if she wanted to cry but was determined not to do so. She nodded. "Are you sure?"

Again, Paul didn't react to the question.

But it was all the answer Megan seemed to need. She nodded again. Her eyes turned shiny with tears and she quickly lowered her head to Gunner's shoulder. He pulled her against him, then she hugged his neck.

Becky realized Paul and Striker were the only survivors. She knew she should feel bad for so many deaths, and deep down she really did. But seeing Paul was alive had somewhat numbed her to the shock of everything else. She knew one day she would spend a lot of time living with the remorse of so many casualties, but right now she couldn't bring herself to start.

Heavy footsteps resounded from the living room. Becky's first thought was the Bigfoot had returned and her chest turned to ice.

"Paul!" Striker. He was in the house.

Becky hoped he was coming to tell them he'd killed the monster.

When Paul didn't respond, Striker called for him again. Paul still didn't react to Striker's call and held his sobbing sister-in-law to his chest.

"In here," said Becky.

The footsteps grew in volume as they neared the kitchen. Striker's bulky form filled the doorway.

"Is everybody okay?" he asked.

Becky shook her head.

Striker looked over her shoulder to Paul. A look of sorrow hardened his face but it was quickly gone. "Paul, we have to get moving. It already has a head start. It'll disappear soon. If we don't get it now, we'll miss our chance."

Paul started to pull away from Trish. She quickly grabbed his arms, pulling them to her. "No," she said. "Not you, too...no..."

"I have to go," he said. "I promised Howie..."

That seemed to do it. She released him, though it looked as if any moment she might grab him again.

"Does anybody know if there's a car here?" asked Striker. "Preferably something that can handle sand?"

Megan raised her head again. "Not any cars that'll work..."

"Are you a Caine?"

Megan nodded. "Megan. Mayor Caine was—is my father."

Striker's lips pressed tightly together. "Nothing we can take on the sand?"

"No cars..."

"Damn," he said through gritted teeth.

"But we have some four-wheelers," Megan said.

Striker nodded. "That'll do just fine."

CHAPTER 36

Megan led them to a massive detached garage with five large bay doors that resembled an airplane hangar more than a garage. They stopped at a narrow side door. She tapped a code into the keypad with one hand, the other clamped in Gunner's hand.

Paul wanted to know how Gunner, Natalie and Trish had ended up at the Caine house. But now wasn't the time to ask.

"That killed the alarm, but I forgot to get the key," Megan said. She ran a hand through her hair. "Shit."

"No problem," said Striker. He gripped his rifle high and smashed the stock end against the door, close to the frame. It took three tries to bash the door in.

They entered the building. It was air conditioned and felt wonderful to Paul. He scanned the collectible cars that probably hadn't been driven since parked in here. More money than Paul would ever know was inside this building.

"Down there," said Megan. She pointed past an old Corvette at the end of the line. Parked in a configuration of four were the ATVs. All were the same yellow color, the same size, make, and model.

"Perfect," said Striker, then ran toward them.

Paul rushed to catch up. The sounds their feet made on the concrete floor made tinny echoes all around. By the time he reached the ATVs, Striker was already mounting one.

"Are they gassed up?" Striker asked.

"They're supposed to be," she said, approaching. "It was Malcolm's turn to do it."

As Paul straddled the one beside Striker, Megan and Gunner walked to the bay door. She thumbed the top of two buttons on a keypad. A machine clicked on, raising the door with a low hum. Sunlight poured in, pushing back the dimness and hurting Paul's eyes.

Paul couldn't find anywhere to put the rifle, so he put the stock against his crotch, pushing the barrel under the bar that connected to the throttle. He shook it to see if it would stay. Seemed to be fine.

"Do you want the helmets?" asked Megan.

"No," said Striker.

"You at least need to wear goggles or the sand will kill your eyes."

Striker considered this. He nodded. "Make it quick."

"Come on, Gunner," she said, grabbing his hand.

Gunner looked pale, even with the sunlight coming inside highlighting his body. He nodded when Megan took his hand, then ran with her to the wall behind the ATVs. Helmets sat in a row on a table. She ignored those and reached up to the pegs above them where several pairs of goggles hung like bats. She grabbed two, handing a pair to Gunner.

Then they ran back. Megan gave Striker a pair.

Gunner stepped over to Paul, looking at the floor as he held out the last pair. Paul took it from him.

"Are you okay?" Paul asked.

Gunner shook his head without looking up.

"Me either," said Paul. He reached out, stroked his son's face.

Finally, Gunner looked at him. "You're coming back, right?"

Seeing the fear and pain in his son's eyes made Paul's chest go tight. A tingling ache seemed to spread from his heart. He briefly considered telling Striker he was on his own. His kids needed him more than he did. The big guy could do this without him. But he didn't say anything of the sort. Nodding, he said, "Yes."

"I would ask you to promise, but…"

"Yeah," said Paul. "*But* I will."

Gunner rushed forward so quickly, Paul flinched. His arms wrapped around Paul's back, squeezing hard. Paul hugged him back. Tears spilled down his cheeks. It was the first they'd hugged since Gunner was little.

"I love you, Gunner."

"I love you, too, Dad."

Gunner squeezed him even harder. It triggered pain in all of Paul's sore spots, but he didn't dare stop this moment.

Striker even allowed their emotional grip to last longer than they could spare before he finally said, "Paul..."

"I know," said Paul. He eased Gunner back, put a hand on each shoulder. He was surprised by the muscle he felt on his son. "Watch after everyone. You're the man while I'm gone."

The corner of Gunner's mouth arched. "I will." He stepped back.

Paul gave his son one more smile, then turned to the ATV. He wasn't exactly sure how to operate one, but he figured it was similar to other bikes he'd been on in the past. He turned the key. Flipped the killswitch on. Held the brake. Then he pressed the ignition button.

The ATV brattled to life.

The noise was nearly unbearable as it reverberated off the tinny walls around them, filling the hollow space with deep roars. Megan, shoulders high, cupped her hands over her ears. Paul looked at Gunner, shot him a thumbs-up, then popped the clutch. Gunner gave him one back.

Striker peeled out, the backend fishtailing as he launched from the garage.

Paul wound back the throttle. The engine raised and steadied. Then he released the brake. The ATV hurled forward, throwing Paul back on the seat. It felt like he'd just crossed over the dip of a rollercoaster. Air buffeted him, threw his clothes against his body as he shot out of the garage. When the tires hit the sand, he nearly lost control of the ATV. Quickly, he turned the front wheels into the slide and corrected himself, throwing sand out beside him in a gritty arc.

Now that he was going straight, he pulled the throttle back and really started to fly. He surprised himself by loosing a loud hoot into the air.

Striker was already a short distance ahead. The tracker glanced over his shoulder, saw Paul and threw a fist in the air. He gave a hoot in response, then pointed at the sand to his right. When Paul passed the spot, he saw large footprints in the sand. The rising tide had nearly washed them away. All that was left were some bulbous depressions of toes and a curve of the foot.

His mind tried to distract him from the pursuit with thoughts of his brother. With the regret of how he'd allowed their relationship to sour over the years. He thought back to his reserves about coming here. And the main reason that had nearly kept him away was Howie.

Howie would still be alive if I'd stayed away.

Paul wasn't sure how true that was. The Bigfoot would've still been here and Paul would have missed out on Howie's last moments. They never would've erased the tension between them. How he wished he would've never become so bitter to those who cared about him the most. Because of Alisha, he'd turned into a hermit that just wanted to shut himself off from everyone except for his kids. And even they were growing tired of his bullshit.

A body was sprawled in the sand. A man. Flat on his back, his head was canted far to the side. A bulging ripple of flesh protruded from the side of his neck that suggested it had been snapped.

Damn.

Poor guy was probably just jogging on the beach.

How could he have possibly known what was heading his way?

CHAPTER 37

The bells above the door jangled and Malcolm Caine checked to see if it was Mrs. Thompson and her sweet little girl. He sighed. Just another pair of regulars. The seats were filling up with the lunch rush, and so far, they hadn't come in. He was beginning to think they weren't going to.

Malcolm looked at the empty table he was saving for them. He couldn't keep it reserved forever. And if a paying customer was to come in, and he had nowhere to seat them, he'd have to give up the table.

I tried to be fair.

Standing behind the counter, he leaned down to the register book and drew a line through the name of an older couple who'd just taken a seat at the bar. They didn't look familiar to him, so he assumed they were lingering tourists, not ready to go home yet. The bar filled up fast during lunch and dinner hours, so they had a number system to keep it fair.

He watched the servers dash back and forth as the volume of chatter steadily rose inside the restaurant. He looked at the empty table with the best view in the whole place and sighed. If he gave that table away, Mrs. Thompson would stroll in right after wondering why he didn't hold it like he'd promised.

She probably wouldn't be mad. I'd explain how long I tried to keep it open. Put them somewhere else and keep the food free of charge.

He figured Mrs. Thompson would be okay with that. She didn't seem like the kind of person to make a big fuss about anything. Hopefully, she wouldn't tell the sheriff or his dad about what happened earlier.

Stupid idea. Why would Dad want somebody running around dressed like a monster anyway? I don't see how that's supposed to bring in business.

Malcolm was getting quite fed up with all this Bigfoot bullshit. He couldn't wait until he graduated. He'd live on campus or near it, so long as it was far away from his asinine father and this fatuous town.

From outside came a sudden tumult of shrieks and cries.

The various conversations inside petered down to silence. The servers stopped where they were, some holding trays balanced on their arms. One held two empty cups in her hand as she neared the soda fountain. Others were empty-handed with their ears pointed in the air.

The chatter started back up again, but this time they were all talking about the same thing.

Did you hear that?

What was it?

Sounded like somebody screaming...

It was. I heard it.

Did you hear that growling? Something growled. Heard it with my own two ears.

Ronald, there wasn't any damn growling.

Don't tell me there wasn't when there was!

Malcolm stepped out from behind the counter, preparing to address the customers. He needed to calm them down before they got too worked up. That was Malcolm's special talent. He could smooth out anyone once they got riled up. He'd gotten that trait from his father, who was a natural at it.

Then a woman who sat at a table with two children pointed at the large window and screamed. Heads jerked in the direction of her trembling finger.

Malcolm traced the path to the empty table reserved for Mrs. Thompson. Right outside, on the wraparound porch, he spotted a hairy beast peering inside. With its hands flat on the window, its face was squished against the screen, bowing it inward. The mouth snarled, showing a set of big teeth that were shaped like Domino chips. Small yellow eyes seemed to glow from the bar of shadow underneath its bulging, curdled forehead. From where Malcom stood, he could see bald areas spread across its hair, inside the pink islands were open sores that secreted yellow ooze.

Malcolm smirked.

"Calm down, everyone," he said. "Looks like my father's up to his old tricks again."

Customers faced him as he started across the main floor, passing the line at the hot dog bar.

Turning around, he walked backwards and held out his arms. "This is just a really bad joke."

"A joke?" said a man sitting with a woman who looked young enough to be his daughter in college. For some reason, Malcolm didn't think they were related. How the woman's long bare leg extended under the table, the heel of her foot resting on the wedge of chair between the man's legs, toes rubbing his crotch, suggested she was his trophy wife.

"Yes," said Malcolm. "My brother has already terrified some poor customers in this costume, and although I told him to knock it off, it looks like he's trying to have some fun with you."

Malcolm heard some quiet laughter mixed with the hushed tones of whispers. The parties in attendance seemed to be talking to each other rather than watching him.

At the window, he noticed the smell right away—an acrid stench that drifted in through the screen, making Malcolm's nose run. "Jeez, Max, what did you do to yourself?"

"What?" his brother said.

The Bigfoot stared at Malcolm through the screen. Its breaths rattled in its throat, choppy like a boat motor, with a quiet growling underneath. Malcolm imagined a sleeping pig might sound similar.

He realized the voice hadn't come from in front of him.

Looking over his shoulder, he saw Max standing by the hot dog buffet. He had changed out of the costume and was now wearing his uniform. He stared at Malcolm with a confused grimace on his face.

"Max? How long have you been standing there?"

"Just a couple minutes."

Malcolm nodded once, then turned back to the window. The big face furrowed into a downward arc that showed snarling anger.

"Oh…shit…"

Hands tore through the screen and grabbed the front of Malcolm's shirt.

Behind him, he heard screams. Chairs knocked over. Dishes crashed on the floor.

Then he was jerked through the window.

****

A young man crashed through the wooden railing that ran along the porch and down the ramp. He tumbled over the edge and dropped onto the sand.

Before Paul could react to what he'd just witnessed, a panicked crowd tore out of Quincy's, screaming and trampling each other to get away.

A poor woman dropped onto her stomach among the crowd. Nobody paused to help her, instead, they stomped her motionless as they fled.

Paul, still several yards away, wound the throttle back all the way. He felt his body pull as the speed whipped faster. The sand yanked the ATV this way and that as he struggled with the steering bar.

Suddenly Striker cut in front of him, heading for Quincy's.

Paul eased up on the throttle for the tracker to take the lead, then he followed him toward the restaurant, where a swarm of terrified customers piled out of the building.

He scanned the mob for the beast. As the crowd thinned, he spotted its dark fur, the clumps of bald spots like islands of infected flesh among an ocean of dingy hair. Arms raised high as if reaching for something, it roared at a man passing in front of it. Then it caught the man's arm and pulled. The man kept running as the arm tore from the socket as easily as the ants' legs did when Paul was a kid. He used to torture ants as a boy, finding it funny how simple it was to tear their legs off. Now, holding the arm above its head and roaring, Paul detected the same kind of twisted glee coming from the beast.

Screaming, the man stomped around in circles as blood sprayed from the ragged stump below his shoulder. A stick of bone protruded a couple inches from the spout of mushy tendons. People were splashed in crimson as they ran by.

"Get out of there!" Paul tried to shout above the pandemonium and twin rumbles of the ATVs' engines.

The beast, holding the arm like a baseball bat by the wrist, swung at the man's head. The chunky tip that had once been connected to a shoulder bashed the man's head back. It landed between his shoulder blades, making his back look as if it had sprouted an inverted face with a large gash stretched across the brow.

The man dropped.

Bigfoot turned. It saw the ATVs approaching and roared. With both hands, it held the severed arm out and spun around. When it faced Paul again, it released the arm. Propelling circles, the arm soared through the air straight for Paul. There was no time to dodge it.

The young man who'd been thrown through the window stood up. Dazed, he saw Paul and was opening his mouth to say something when the arm burst through his chest. Somehow, the guy's heart was clutched in the hand protruding from the chest as if being offered to Paul.

Paul squeezed the brake handle. The ATV bounced and rocked to a halt.

The kid's bright blond hair fell into his eyes as he slowly looked down. He saw his heart on the flat of the hand. He watched it offer a couple lethargic beats before going still. When he looked back at Paul, his eyes looked confused. Mouth moving, he tried to speak. Then he dropped to his knees.

Poor kid.

"Sorry," muttered Paul. He raised his gun.

The beast was gone. But the scattering crowd remained, screaming and crying.

Striker dismounted his ATV, bringing his rifle up and letting the base drop into the flat of his hand. He looked around, dodging fleeing screamers.

Paul wiggled back on the seat and threw his legs over the side. He hopped down. On the sand, his eyes scanned the area, searching for Striker. The patrons of Quincy's had all but fled the

287

establishment. Only a few lagged behind, looking confused as they sidestepped the prostrate bodies dispersed about.

"Striker!"

The big man appeared at the main entrance. He stepped up to the broken railing the boy had crashed through. "Gone," he said.

Paul nodded. "I have to use the phone, call all this in, get in reinforcements up here fast."

"No. We have to keep after it. This is exactly what he wants."

Paul stared at the tracker. The harsh ultraviolet rays that threw glowing daggers off Striker's rifle hurt Paul's eyes. "What he wants?" Nose wrinkled, he shook his head. "You're saying he *planned* this?"

"To keep us distracted, yes. This was a diversion."

"For what?" asked Paul.

"So he could get away." Striker punched a tilted post, the broken section of railing bobbed from the impact. "And we fell for it. But that's okay. We're not finished with him yet." Striker took a step back and threw his leg up. The sole of his boot hit the tilted post and knocked over. It broke away from the porch with a splintery crack and crashed on the sand. Then he leaped from the top, landing in a squat. Slowly, he stood up.

As the big guy approached his ATV, Paul said, "I'm the acting authority figure in this town at the moment."

"Who gave you that right?"

"I did. When everybody else was slaughtered by your Bigfoot. And we have to call this in."

"It's being handled," he said, pointing behind Paul.

Turning around, Paul saw a small congregation of spectators. All of them had cell phones. A couple of them held them out, the tiny lenses documenting this pointless disagreement. Those who weren't recording were shouting for ambulances and police assistance to be dispensed from whoever they were talking to.

Striker was right. It was handled.

"If we wait for them to get here," said Striker, "the beast will be long gone. Who knows how long it'll take us to find it again? The plan hasn't changed. We stay in pursuit."

Paul nodded. "All right. Where?" He gulped. His spit tasted like sand and he could feel grits sprinkled down the back of his throat.

Striker mounted his ATV. "Hell if I know. We'll keep following his trail. He's bleeding like a stuck pig, he's weak, and all he wants is to find some place to rest. Some place quiet, some place where there aren't any people."

Paul nodded. "All right."

"Let's go," said Striker.

His ATV brattled to life.

CHAPTER 38

Becky had an arm around Trish's waist, helping her walk. The poor woman's legs couldn't stop shaking as they made their way through the kitchen. She kept Trish angled away from Mackenzie's sprawled body and the blood spreading red around her on the linoleum.

Blubbering and sniffling, Trish moaned as if in pain. And Becky knew that she really was. She wasn't hurt in a physical sense, but beaten by her emotions. The pain had started in her broken heart and spread through her entire body.

Megan appeared in the living room's doorway. "Here," she said. "I'll take her."

Nodding, Becky slipped out of Trish's hold and helped Megan take her position of support. When Becky was sure Megan had her, she stepped back, rubbing her lower back. There was dull pain that made it hard to stand up straight.

"Come on, Mrs. Thompson," said Megan. "Let's get you in here."

Trish sniffled, tried to breathe. She made some jerky moans and shambled alongside Megan into the living room.

Following them, Becky watched as Megan struggled to remain strong. Most might be convinced Megan was doing a good job of it, but Becky could tell the poor girl wanted to join Trish in her misery. But she wouldn't allow herself to submit to her sentimentalities. She knew Gunner needed her help, and not only did she *want* to be there for him, she was probably glad to have the distraction. Anything to keep her mind off her father's...death, she'd gladly welcome.

Megan helped Trish down to the couch, where she fell onto her side and hugged the pillow.

Natalie, clinging to her brother's leg while he sat in a chair with Megan's laptop on his knees, squirmed away from him and ran to her aunt. She climbed onto the couch and settled into the space between Trish's arms. Watching this, Becky put her fingers to her mouth to hold back her emotions. Her chin trembled.

Trish pulled Natalie close and bawled harder as Natalie softly patted Trish's head.

Becky looked away, tears filling her eyes. Her eyes locked on Megan's. They shared the same sorrow. Becky gave a terse nod. Megan returned the gesture and turned around.

Gunner sat in the chair, his fingers paused above the laptop's keys. He watched Trish and Natalie. His eyes were grim. Frowning, he looked back down at the computer. Becky could tell how much he wanted to be with them, but he was busy trying to find a way to reach the outside for help.

"I found some Wi-Fi," he said, smiling slightly. "No password required."

Megan, cramming herself into the chair with Gunner, hugged him.

"It's working?" Becky asked. Hands on her hips, she stepped closer.

"Sort of," Gunner said. "We only have one bar, but I'm connecting to it."

"Thank God," said Megan.

Becky smiled, though she felt no different inside. She was worried about Paul now, just as she imagined Gunner, Natalie, and even Trish probably were. He was out there with Striker, trying to bring an end to this. She wouldn't feel relieved about anything until she knew it was over. She supposed everybody else felt the same way—offering a false sense of hope for the others' benefit, but surrendering to defeat on the inside.

"I'm in," he said.

Megan squeezed him harder, whispered, "Good job," in his ear.

"Great," said Becky. "Go to Seashell Cove Sheriff's Department dot com, there should be a link for emergency contact."

"It's loading slowly," he said. "But I see it."

Becky looked around the room. Though she wasn't expecting to find much in here, she at least thought she might find a poker for the fireplace. Anything that could be used as weapon in case they needed it. She found nothing.

"Be right back," she said.

"Where're you going?" asked Megan.

"Grabbing a knife from the kitchen. We need something, in case..."

Gunner pursed his lips. Nodded. "I'll go with you," he said. "Nobody should go anywhere alone...just in case..."

"Right," said Megan. She wiggled her way onto the arm of the chair, draping her tawny legs over the edge. "But you keep trying to contact the police. I'll go with Becky."

Gunner turned in the seat. They shared an uneasy look. Becky saw in his worried gaze that he didn't want her to go. She was tempted to tell Megan to stay, but knew it would be a good idea to have somebody with her if she needed help.

"I'll be fine," Megan said, leaning forward. She gave him a quick kiss, then stood up and walked over to Becky.

"Be careful," said Trish through her sniffles.

Though she sounded pitiful, Becky was glad to know her mind was back in the room with them. "Will you be okay with Natalie?" Becky asked.

Trish sniffled again, rubbed her nose with the back of her hand, and sat up. She pulled Natalie's back against her side, hugging her from behind. "I'll guard her with my life."

Becky's throat tightened. She turned to Gunner. Thin layers of moisture glittered in his eyes.

"I know you will," he said. He looked at Becky, huffing out a breath that rattled his cheeks. "Do it quickly. By the time you get back, the page should've loaded."

"Okay," she said. She grabbed Megan's hand. "Come on."

Becky turned, gave another glance at Trish and Natalie, and left the room with Megan. They followed the short hallway to the kitchen, and entered.

With a gasp, Becky jerked to a halt. She gazed inside.

How? There's no way...

Becky stared at the vacant spot Mackenzie was lying in earlier. Left behind was a crimson puddle. She quickly swiveled her head, looking all over. Though there was evidence of her hasty retreat, she didn't see Mackenzie anywhere.

"Oh no," whispered Megan. "Where'd she go?"

"She's gone," said Becky.

"How can you be sure?"

Becky pointed at the floor. A trail of bloody footprints started behind the counter and carried to the back door. It had been left open, slowly swaying from the breeze outside.

Mackenzie was alive.

And she'd escaped.

Becky ran through the kitchen, made a wide step over the footprints, and stopped at the door. She stuck her head out. She looked in all directions and saw no sign of Mackenzie anywhere. Surely there would have been some blood or something. Pulling her head inside, she slammed the door and locked it. Megan watched her, her hands clutched together at her chest. Her arms squished her breasts. On her way back to Megan, Becky jerked a knife from the block on the island. She noted one was already missing.

"Let's check on Gunner," she said.

Hearing the boy's name seemed to be what Megan needed to pull her back from the shock trying to grip her. She blinked. "Gunner."

Together, they hurried into the hall. Their feet hammered the hardwood, shook the walls. Becky entered the living room first, Megan second. Becky felt the girl slam into her back when she jerked rigid.

Gunner looked pale. His hands, no longer on the computer, were flat on the arms of the chair. His fingers dug into the front padding, picking at loose threads. When they'd left him, his hair had been only slightly damp. Now it was soaked, his bangs clinging to his forehead by sweat. His eyes jerked toward them, wild and dancing between the lids. Then they shot back to the couch.

Becky followed his panicked leer to the couch.

On her knees, Trish was on the floor, braced on straight arms. Tears glazed her face, dripping from her jawline. Natalie stood beside her, arms rigid by her sides. A bare leg reached out on either side of the girl's thin waste, Natalie leaning between them. The shins were sprinkled with nicks and cuts, the knees pale and smooth. A third arm reached around Natalie's chest, a hand flat on her torso, holding her back. A knife's sharp tip was pressed against the side of her neck, denting the skin. A hand with calloused knuckles gripped the handle so tightly the scabs were splitting and making fresh blood. The arm was covered by a khaki sleeve.

Mackenzie's evil face appeared from behind Natalie, her hair a wild bushel crown. Spatters of blood left dark markings on her face.

"My God," muttered Becky.

Mackenzie smiled. "Hello again."

CHAPTER 39

The old Comet Crash Putt-Putt Hut was an abandoned stretch of displays and obstacles on the other side of a rusted chain-link fence. The condition of the parking area alone showed Paul that it hadn't been used in years. A casualty of Seashell Cove's financial crisis that had begun closing down businesses left and right. Part of the disease that led to them embracing the Bigfoot prospect as if a Godsend that would save them from ruin. He hadn't truly grasped how desperate people like Caine must've been to even consider such foolishness. Now he understood. Fraught mentalities lead to dumb things, and being the mayor, Caine had taken great risks to ensure his town's survival.

If only he wasn't such an idiot...

They'd left the ATVs in the sand. Crossing the parking lot, their boots made scraping sounds on the sand that carpeted the blacktop. Through the gritty layers, the faded yellow lines of parking spaces looked pale and old.

From the course obstacles Paul could see, he thought it resembled a miniature golf course more than putt-putt. A faded volcano jutted from the center, filled with cracks and fissures that showed the gray of the mold underneath. That one must be the final hole, he thought, as he followed Striker. Get a hole in one and the volcano probably erupted.

Striker pointed at a dark wet spot on that had turned the sand scattered on the parking lot dark and wet. Blood. A lot of it. How this creature was still walking on its own accord was a mystery to Paul. How much blood did the damn thing have to lose before it finally ran out?

The tracker reached the ticket booth first at the end of the parking lot. A turnstile blocked immediate entrance. He paused and turned back, the rifle sweeping this way and that.

Paul did the same, shouldering Howie's semi-auto. His finger slipped behind the trigger guard, the skin brushing the sleek bowed metal.

Howie.

Paul couldn't fathom his brother was dead, nor could he allow himself to focus on it. If he let his brother's demise haunt him now, he'd be useless to Striker. And more importantly, useless to his family and Becky. They needed him now. Too many people were relying on Paul Thompson for him to let his grief cripple him.

Sorry, Howie. I'll mourn later. I promise.

He figured once he began, he'd never be able to stop.

Paul gave a quick scan of the parking lot. It was flat and empty, the asphalt a sunbaked ash color under the tan shade of sand. Weeds had sprouted from the cracks in the blacktop like parasitic growths that trembled in the balmy breeze.

"Are we going to stand here all day?" asked Paul. "Or are we going in?"

Striker smirked. "Fine, tough guy. Let's move out." He spun around and hopped over the bar of the turnstile in one smooth motion. His feet slapped the ground, the extra cargo on his uniform making a loud padded sound as it shifted. Standing straight, he turned around and waited for Paul.

"Show off," said Paul.

He needed to brace his hand on the banister as he leaped, swinging his legs over. The unyielding ground jolted him when his feet smacked down.

They hurried through the foyer area. Two stands had been placed on either side for payment and refreshments. Their shutters were down. A rusted latch kept them closed with an old padlock. Weeds protruded here and there. Some places were overgrown with grass. Vine-choked flower beds were all around. To Paul, it resembled how the world would look during a zombie apocalypse—desolate and wild.

Striker paused at the first hole of the eighteen-hole course.

"Where to?" asked Paul.

Striker held out his hand, finger pointing up. Paul gave an involuntary glance up. All he saw was blue sky.

"Smell that?" asked Striker.

Paul hadn't noticed anything at first, but now he began to detect a foul stench that reminded him of the deck of a fishing boat after the day's catch had been gutted and cleaned. He nodded.

A corner of Striker's mouth arced. "He's in here. Look for more blood."

Nodding, Paul walked in one direction while Striker took the other. Paul gave quick glances to the ground, the balconies above him that ran over top of the course, and the shadowy recesses between small sheds and other buildings. So many areas for the beast to hide behind. He saw clusters of fake palm trees at the bottom of metal stairs that led up to where the course began. He paused at the bottom rung, turned and looked behind him. If he bypassed the stairs, he'd go toward a row of PolyJohns in front of a cinderblock barrier. It was doubtful the beast could squeeze into one of those cramped edifices. He turned to the left, where he'd left Striker and didn't see him.

Cold dripped down his spine. The big guy should've been easy to spot. He wanted to call out for him, but so far, they'd managed to be quiet. Shouting would give them away.

Damn it. Where are you at?

There wasn't much back that way for Striker to search, so he couldn't have gotten lost.

It got him.

Paul shook his head. He didn't think so. Striker wouldn't have gone down without a fight. He must be looking somewhere Paul couldn't see.

Paul turned around, faced the stairs. His eyes landed on a dark streak three rungs up. Blood. It dribbled over the edge, draining through the holes in the metal treads. He spotted a thicker smear on the railing that probably came when its body slid across.

Another arctic tendril wormed through him.

It's up there.

Paul looked up. The stairs led to a landing. He couldn't see beyond the top step. For all he knew, the beast was sitting just out of sight. He might stumble right on it. Checking behind him again, he still saw no sign of Striker.

Paul took a deep breath. His lungs felt like cold tubes inside his chest. This was it. There would be no more chances to kill this bastard. If they didn't succeed this time, it would be because they were dead. Paul's arms suddenly felt filled with cold lead. They could no longer hold the rifle. His legs weakened. He wanted to sit on the stairs, hug his knees, and wait for Striker to come back.

What if he doesn't come back?

Surely, he would. He wasn't dead.

"Nope," Paul muttered. His throat was dry, so the word came out a quiet rasp.

Come on, Paul. It's up to you. Kill this thing.

"For Howie," he whispered.

And so many others the beast had slaughtered. Look what it had done to Mackenzie Dalton. Poor girl was so bonkers she thought she was in love. He felt terrible for her parents. How would they react when they learned everything she'd done?

An image of Styles's throat being gouged with the rock tried to manifest. He shook his head to keep it away. He couldn't let anything distract him now—not his fear, not his love for his family, not his grief.

Nothing.

His arms felt strong enough to hold the rifle. Lifting it with one hand, the other swung up and slapped the base of the barrel. His fingers curled around the handguard. Finally, he felt ready.

Paul brought a foot up, setting it flat on the step.

Then the putt-putt course exploded to life in a tumult of carnival-like music and tinny bursts. Whistling sounds like launched rockets and fireworks surrounded him.

CHAPTER 40

"Hey, cutie," said Mackenzie.

Gunner looked at her and felt as if his wind had been punched out. Those eyes, so cruel and insane, leered at him. "Wha-what?" he said.

She titled her head, winking. "That computer there?"

At first, Gunner had no idea what she was talking about. When he looked down, he saw the opened notebook, the screen darkening more and more. The Seashell Cove Sherriff's Department emergency page was up. A small box was open. He could see what he'd typed of his message waiting to be finished, the cursor blinking beside the last word. If he could just click send...

Would it be enough?

Probably. An unfinished emergency message might make them move even quicker.

But he hadn't typed the address.

Trace it through the I.P.

His hand shot for the computer.

"Hey!"

Gunner froze, looked up. Mackenzie pressed the knife to Natalie's throat with a palsied hand. He saw blood streaming down her fingers and felt his stomach pinch. It took him a moment to grasp that the blade was clear, so the blood was not his sister's, but Mackenzie's. Her jaw jutted out, gnashing the bottom row of teeth.

"Keep your damn fingers away from the keys," she said through a growl. "Smash it."

"Smash...?"

Gunner turned. Becky and Megan watched him from the floor. Mackenzie had made them get on their knees after they came into

301

the room. They weren't gone five seconds when Mackenzie seemed to appear out of the air, brandished a knife, and snatched Natalie from Trish's lap.

"Yes," said Mackenzie. "Can't be beauty and brains, can you?" She snickered. "The computer. Smash it on the floor. Now."

His hands trembled above the keys. Fingers so close to the machine, it would only take a short thrust to hit enter and send the message.

But Mackenzie...she'd kill Natalie for sure.

Gunner saw the knife shove into his little sister's throat. The image would become reality if he didn't listen.

"Do it," said Trish. "Please, Gunner!"

He gave Megan a fleeting glance, saw her nod, and grabbed the laptop. The bottom was hot from where his legs had blocked its air flow. Holding it above his head, he turned to Mackenzie.

"Good boy," she said. "Good boy might get a kiss for his obeying."

Ignoring her comment, Gunner threw the laptop down. The plastic casing exploded when it hit the hard floor. The screen blacked out before cracking up the middle. Its impact was loud in the quiet room, but Mackenzie's hoots were even louder.

Gunner looked at his sister. Her eyes were closed as she quietly sobbed. Mackenzie shook her. "Did you see that? Huh? Your big brother loves you a lot, doesn't he? Wow! He actually did it. I had my doubts, but he came through for you. What a good guy. Maybe if I would've met him sooner, none of this would've happened. I could easily see a guy like him by my side."

Gunner felt no pride for smashing the computer. He felt as if he'd damned them all.

Mackenzie pressed her lips against Natalie's cheek so hard it seemed to mush her face sideways.

"Don't touch her!" Trish shrieked.

Mackenzie kicked the back of her head, making her cry out and stumble forward. Her lips tore away from Natalie's cheek with a wet smack. "Shut up!"

Trish, on her elbows, ran her hand along the back of her head. The kick hadn't been very hard, but Gunner bet it still hurt a lot. His hands gripped his swimming trunks, making the wispy fabric crinkle. His body felt hot and cold all at once as rage flowed through his insides like lava.

Mackenzie turned Natalie so she faced her. "You've got a good big brother, right?" She shook Natalie. "Right?"

Natalie cried. Nodded. "Right!"

"Right," said Mackenzie. "He listens well. Let's see if his friend is as good of a listener." Mackenzie brought her feral gaze onto Megan. "Blondie."

Megan's mouth pressed together tightly. She stared at Mackenzie.

The Bigfoot bride smiled. "Pick up the knife."

Gunner's anger quickly thinned as a sick feeling hardened his muscles. He watched Megan struggle with her emotions as she stared down at the knife. It was on the floor, not far from her hands. He hadn't once questioned why Mackenzie hadn't made her toss it away.

She'd had plans for it this whole time.

Megan was hesitant as her hand moved toward the knife.

"Come on, Blondie, we don't have all day." She turned to Gunner. "I don't know what you see in that girl, she seems too spacey to me."

Megan grabbed the knife. She brought it back and let it settle on her thighs. It looked very clean and bright against her tawny skin.

"There you go," said Mackenzie. "Now do me a favor and stab the woman beside you."

Gunner's skin crawled. She wants Megan to…

Oh my God.

"What'd you say?" asked Megan. Her voice sounded hoarse.

Trish folded her arms on the floor, lowered her face on them, and sobbed.

Becky looked to be in a daze.

Mackenzie only smiled as she repeated the order. Then she said, "I don't want that bitch hanging around me and my boo. She's got to go. So, I *want* you to *stab* her. Just keep at it until she's dead. Our little sweet stuff here will go with me and I'll use her to coax your father into giving me back my boo. Then we'll be out of your hair forever. But if you don't use that knife…" Mackenzie shook her head.

Megan looked at Becky, then Gunner, and back to Becky. "I-I-I can't. I won't…"

"You will or I'll stab this little girl in the throat, then I'll put the knife to the worthless basket case down here." She nudged Trish's rump with the heel of her foot. "If you still don't, I'll slit *her* fucking throat and before the blood has even started to pour out, I'll plant the knife in our cutie's heart."

Megan turned to Gunner. Her mouth hung open, trembling. "No…"

Mackenzie smirked. "Then stab the cunt and be done with it."

Gunner felt a hollow chasm open deep inside his heart. He knew if Megan didn't kill Becky, then his sister was going to die. And even if he felt that trying to intervene would somehow work in their favor, he didn't trust his weak legs to move him from the chair.

Megan lifted the knife from her sleek thighs. The blade shook in her hands. She moved on her knees, hobbling sideways to face Becky. The woman looked at Megan, closed her eyes, and nodded, giving Megan the signal that it was okay to do what had to be done.

"I'm…" Megan choked on her words. She took a deep, shaky breath. "I'm so sorry, Becky…"

"Don't be," she said.

"So sweet," whispered Mackenzie as if watching a romantic movie on TV.

Megan turned the knife in her hand. Now she held the weapon above her, in a stance that reminded Gunner of nearly every horror movie poster he'd ever seen. He didn't want Megan to do this, but he didn't want his sister to die.

Becky moved so that she was directly facing Megan. She spread her arms, fluffed out her chest, so Megan wouldn't miss. "Do it," she said.

From where Gunner sat, he could only see Megan from the side. But it was enough to see the torment on her face. Tears flooded from her eyes, spilling over her trembling lips. Her throat clucked as she tried to breathe.

"Times ticking, Blondie," said Mackenzie.

Natalie gasped. When Gunner turned, he saw the tip of the knife had vanished in Natalie's neck. A ribbon of blood trickled down. There was no mistaking it this time. The blood belonged to his sister.

"No," said Gunner.

304

"I'm going to keep pushing," said Mackenzie.

"Okay!" cried Megan. She reeled back, raising the knife. "I'm sorry!"

Becky closed her eyes, waiting.

The knife shot down.

Natalie screamed.

CHAPTER 41

Paul spun around. The blaring music came from all around as the displays spread throughout the course came to life. Lights flashed. Some bulbs popped from age, but others stayed alive as they flashed garish colors all over.

Somehow the putt-putt course had been resurrected.

Paul clutched the rifle close as he back-stepped away from the stairs. Looking around, he saw no signs of the beast. Briefly, he considered the beast had been the one to trigger the power, but quickly shoved that aside.

Striker.

The tracker was alive.

And he saw him rounding the corner of a concession stand. His vest shook on his massive torso as he ran toward Paul, the rifle held out before him like a soldier in a march. His biceps bulged and flexed as his arms pumped.

He stopped in front of Paul. "Found a generator, fully gassed up."

"I see that," said Paul. "Damn-near gave me a heart attack."

The big guy smiled. "Whoops."

"Let me guess, using this to cover our asses?"

"Yep. Hopefully all the ruckus will distract it long enough for us to sneak up on it."

"Or it'll draw it out into the open."

"We could only be so lucky. Let's just pray that it doesn't prevent *us* from hearing it sneak up on us."

Paul hadn't thought of that and wished Striker would have kept that possibility to himself. "Blood over here," said Paul, pointing at the stairs.

"Already saw it."

"So what's the plan?"

"Well," said Striker, not even attempting to hide the smile on his face. "Let's pretend we're here to enjoy the course. We'll start with the first one here." He nodded toward the stairs that led to the first hole. "And work our way through."

"Wonderful," Paul muttered.

Striker took the lead. He climbed the stairs, two at time, to the top. Paul rushed to keep up as they dashed through the obstacles, spinning around, throwing their rifles ahead of them. Sometimes they put their backs together to cover all angles. But there was no sign of the beast as they moved from hole to hole, bypassing playful putt-putt challenges, one after another.

They paused at the halfway point. A large plaster spaceship jutted from the side of a rubber mountain. Alien carcasses were scattered along the frizzy green meant to be grass. Green paint, representing alien blood, coated the flooring in faded flakes and smears. Plenty of areas for Bigfoot to hide.

The fake mountain was taller than Paul and he had to climb to the top to look behind the plastic trees. Nothing was hiding back there. He turned, found Striker walking around the wide brim of the saucer. It looked as if the hole for the golf ball was in one of the windows of the disc-shaped spaceship. Paul doubted many people were able to sink the hole into such a ridiculously complicated challenge.

Reaching the other side, Striker stopped and shook his head. "Clear," he said.

Within seconds, they were moving again. On the tenth hole, Striker found some spatters of blood along the rim of a dried out pool where a chinking porcelain shark head jutted from the blue-stained concrete. Other than the fresh drippings, there were no other signs Bigfoot had come this way.

Though Paul couldn't see the beast, he could *feel* it nearby. Could feel the malicious gaze of its eyes all over him, making his skin go crawly as it watched them. Each time he turned to look, he saw nothing. But it was somewhere, waiting for the right moment to lash out.

They reached the final hole, the ultimate end to a quite impressive course run. Paul had been right when he'd first spotted the top of the volcano distended like a smokestack from the parking area. Go out with a bang, Paul thought, as he studied the tall structure. It was even larger than Spaceship Mountain, and much bulkier, like the size of two manholes put together. He rubbed the side of the volcano, expecting it to be hard, but to his surprise it was very soft, like foam. Through the gauze-like wall, he felt a steady draft of air. Behind the padding, he heard a loud hum that sounded industrial.

In the corner of his eye, he saw movement and quickly spun around.

Striker stepped around from the other side of the volcano, scratching the back of his neck. "Nothing."

Paul held out his arms. "Where the hell could it be? Think it got out and we've been wasting our time here?"

Striker seemed to consider it for a moment before shaking his head. "Doubtful."

"Then where?"

Striker's shoulders rose and dropped with an exasperated sigh. Then his eyes locked on something and widened. He pointed. "Look."

Paul turned. He spotted a gate at the far side of the bordering wall. It was probably knee-high to Paul. *Access* was spray-painted in white on the front. Sprinkles of blood dotted the gate like bullet holes. Beyond the gate was a set of stairs that led up to a platform above them.

Paul looked up. A catwalk was above them. Attached under the narrow walkway was high-dollar stage lights angled down, the bulbs pointing at the course. For night playing, he assumed.

"I'll be damned," muttered Paul.

"It's above us," said Striker.

CHAPTER 42

Becky waited for the sharp puncture of the knife, but Natalie's screams stopped it from coming. Another scream followed, but it was deeper, older. Sounded like Trish.

Opening one eye first, Becky saw that Megan was frozen before her, head turned to the couch. The knife had stopped less than an inch from Becky's breast.

My God, so close...

Something like growls came from beside her and Becky turned sideways, becoming confused by what she saw. Natalie was now facing away from her and looked as if she was fighting to hug Mackenzie. Her little arms flapped as she worked to nestle against the feral bitch, while making sounds like a tiny zombie.

Trish, on her knees, leaned back. Her fingers were pressed to her lips as she cried. "Natalie, stop!"

Mackenzie's mouth was open in a silent scream, eyes gazing upward to show only her whites as her head trembled. Her arm was straight out, the quivering knife pointing at the ceiling. Mackenzie's body quaked and jerked as her throat made quaking sounds.

Natalie pulled away from Mackenzie and spun around. Her chin dribbled blood as she ran toward Gunner. On her way, she turned and spat out a red pulpy wad that splatted on the floor. Gunner dropped out of the chair, landing on his knees. Opening his arms, Natalie slammed against him. They fell back, Gunner holding her tightly.

Becky was even more confused. But when she looked at Mackenzie and saw the dark jagged cavity in the side of her neck, spurting blood in thick lashes, it all made sense.

Natalie bit her throat...

"Holy shit," Becky whispered.

Mackenzie stumbled to her feet, pawing at the deep wound on her throat. She pressed her hand against it. Blood shot between her fingers. Opening her mouth to either scream or talk, blood coughed out, killing any attempts of communication. She shuffled along, leaving a trail of blood on the floor on her way to where Gunner and Natalie laid in front of the chair.

"No!" cried Trish, pushing herself to her feet. She ran at Mackenzie. "Stay away from her!"

Mackenzie turned, saw her coming. Her hand clutching the knife made a quick whip outward. Trish's back blocked Becky's view. She heard the sound of tearing fabric mixed with a wet rip. Trish spun around, arms held out. Her shirt was sliced open around her midriff. Between the gaps was a wide arc of blood that split her naval and poured a curtain of red down her stomach. Her legs folded. She landed on her knees, caressing the wound.

Seeing this, Gunner screamed. Natalie joined him.

No more!

On all fours, Becky prepared to lurch forward. She was knocked aside by Megan as she jumped to her feet.

Becky landed on her side.

Saw Megan charging, holding the knife out with both hands.

Mackenzie grinned wildly as she primed a slash of her own.

Becky could already tell that Megan wasn't going to make it. Her fate would be similar to Trish's. So Becky got to her knees, straightened her back. Readied herself to run.

And Natalie hopped between the two women, clung to Mackenzie's leg, arms hugging her shins, legs wrapping her ankles. She opened her mouth wide, sinking her teeth into the meaty jut of Mackenzie's calf.

The disheveled woman threw back her head and screamed. The knife just missed Megan's side as it shot high.

And Megan rammed her knife straight through Mackenzie's exposed throat with a sound like a melon being split. The tip of the blade tore through the nape of Mackenzie's neck, parting the bushel of hair behind her.

Either on reflex or pure luck, Mackenzie's arm gave a quick thrust outward.

Punching the knife into Megan's stomach.

Megan stumbled back, arms held out, mouth yawning as she gasped. The knife protruded from her stomach like a lever. It was in fairly deep.

"God, no!" Gunner cried as he rolled onto his stomach. His eyes shot from Megan to Trish and back.

Mackenzie and Megan faced each other, one with a knife in the throat, the other in the stomach. Staring at Megan with evil determination, Mackenzie reached up and curled her fingers around the handle poking out from under her chin. She slowly pulled. The knife made juicy crinkling sounds as a tent of skin rose around the blade when it slid out. The blade came loose, and blood squirted.

Mackenzie made slurping sounds as she tried to speak. Through the groans and wet gurgles, Becky could make out what she was saying: *Bitch.*

Then she stumbled and dropped. Her back hit the coffee table and crushed it. She fell to the floor, the thin wood exploding under her. With her arms splayed wide and legs parted, she looked like somebody ready for a nap that had simply collapsed onto the bed.

As if waiting on the crazed woman to drop first, Megan suddenly pitched back. Holding out his arms, Gunner caught her before she pounded the floor.

Becky looked around. Blood and madness surrounded her.

Trish started to crawl forward, using one arm as a brace and the other bent and pressed to her stomach. Natalie met her halfway, hugging her. She heard the little girl ask if she was okay.

"Fine," said Trish. "Looks worse than it is…"

"You're bleeding," said Natalie through her sobs. The little girl bawled the hardest yet, nearly screaming as Trish pulled her close.

Hell of a kid, Becky told herself. To go through so much and not break down until it was over. Trish's eyes rose above Natalie's head, a mournful expression on her face. Becky offered something that she hoped was a smile. Trish couldn't return the gesture. She lowered her face onto Natalie's head and they cried together.

"Don't close your eyes," said Gunner. "Megan! Stay awake!"

Becky turned. Gunner, on his knees, held Megan in his arms. Her back swathed the bends in his elbows, her arm draping the floor. Long hair spread across the floor in a puddle of bright tangles. Wincing, Gunner looked Megan over, saw the knife, contorted his face, and looked at the ceiling. Becky could tell he didn't know what to do, whether he should pull the knife out or leave it in. Whether he should lay her flat on the floor or keep holding her.

Gazing above him, Gunner started to cry.

Megan's hand slowly rose in front of his chest, moving past his neck. Her fingers shook as she stroked his chin. Gunner gasped and looked down at her.

"I'm not sleeping," said Megan. "Kind of hard to when a knife's lodged in your stomach."

Laughter broke through Gunner's sobs. He shook his head, tried to speak and only laughed again.

Relief sapped Becky's strength. She dropped onto her rump. The floor was hard and uncomfortable underneath her, but she didn't care. Pulling her legs to her breasts, she hugged her shins, resting her chin on her knees. She took a deep breath and let it out slowly, flapping her lips.

Thank God.

Though none of them were unscathed, they were alive. She felt something like honor for all of them, especially Natalie, who'd turned into a warrior to protect her family. The bond the Thompsons had formed over the years was unbreakable and Becky smiled knowing true unconditional love was what had kept them together.

Kept them alive.

But her newfound elation was short-lived.

Paul was still out there. And so far as she knew, so was the Bigfoot.

CHAPTER 43

Paul hated heights. Hated hiking in the mountains. And even more, hated being inside tall buildings and driving over bridges. But trying to maneuver along this skinny rafter was worse than all of those others combined. He felt the floor sag under his feet, felt it tremble as it strained to support his and Striker's combined weight. He hated peering over the edges of the noodle-thin railing, but Striker had told him to check all over. Each time he gave a quick glance over the side, his legs wobbled. His knees felt like sand that couldn't keep his legs straight. His vision turned wavy, ears buzzed.

Coming up here to look for a monster and I'm worried about how high up I am.

Paul shook his head, regretting the vertigo it caused. His hand slapped the railing. Fingers gripped. And he felt it waggle in his hold. Not secure at all. If he were to put any of his weight against it, the bar would break without much effort.

So don't lean against it, dumbass.

Paul took a deep breath that felt cold when it entered his lungs.

Striker stopped in front of him, leaned over the railing, and aimed the rifle down. He looked like a sniper, ready to fire the killing shot.

Paul stepped beside him, took another deep breath, and turned. Looking down, he saw they were just now above the volcano. It felt as if they'd been shuffling along the shuddering platform for hours.

Thick tube-like casing of the stage lights stuck out a few inches beyond the footbridge. In the quick glimpse he managed to get of the volcano, he saw tattered streamers reaching up and flailing in the gust of wind caused by the fan. He supposed at one time it was meant to replicate fire or erupting lava. Now the flimsy bands were

315

too old and torn up to do much other than make rattling sounds. The hole for the volcano was wide and round, like an oil drum. It looked fairly deep. Dark until the swirling winks of the fan blowing air upward to operate the plastic flames.

He was about to turn away so he couldn't see how far down it was but movement arrested his attention. Straining his eyes, he stared down.

A hand reached up from the other side of the volcano's mouth.

Paul's skin went tight.

Elongated fingers curled over the rim. The haggard nails were nearly black.

A matching hand slapped down beside it.

"Oh, shit," said Paul.

Striker looked at him. "What?"

Paul slowly lifted his chin toward the volcano. Striker turned. He felt the big guy's body tense as the beast pulled its gargantuan body up, hoisting with its arms as if climbing out of a swimming pool. Its huge feet landed on the rim, making the rubber slump and expand, molding around its soles. The beast didn't straighten up, remained in a squat, gazing up at them through its beady yellow eyes. Its bulging forehead broke in the middle, forming two downward slants that flashed with rage.

It roared.

We're out in the open with nowhere to run.

Paul gulped. He understood they'd been led into another trap right before the beast sprung. Its body launched, soaring high, arms reaching up. Striker loosed cusswords as he started firing. Paul watched the bullets zip past the beast, watched one dig a runnel across its collar bone. The beast roared again, this time with some pain. Though the bullet left no real damage, it did make the Bigfoot slightly turn midair.

Now it was off course.

Instead of landing on the platform like it had probably intended, it was a few inches short. Paul watched its face change from seething rage to regret. Its roar lowered to a confused moan before it fell out of sight.

Paul felt a moment of triumph before the floor rocked under his feet, throwing him against the railing on the other side. Just as he'd expected, the bar snapped like a twig and he kept going. He released the rifle and reached out for the dangling metal bars.

And missed.

His hands closed on nothing but air. He dropped.

In his tilting point of view, he saw Striker lurch at him. Felt fingers brush the front of his shirt, latch on. Buttons popped and flew.

He saw the deepening blue of the sky washed in a yellow-orange glaze, showing it was nearing evening. Saw his foot appear in his line of sight as he performed a backwards flip.

Then he was falling, head down, the speed of his plunge increasing. A wall of dingy fur filled his vision. He glimpsed a beefy hand make a grab.

His leg was yanked, jerking his plummet to a jarring halt. The contents of his pockets rained down. Chewing gum sprinkled past his arms. His wallet smacked his chest, tumbled down his neck, and dropped into the volcano. He heard it get minced in the fan. Its flakey remains sprayed out.

His shirt hung around him like useless wings while his arms pawed the air. Looking up, he saw his body extending high. One leg kicked out. The other was straight and stiff, caught at the ankle by the Bigfoot that hung by its other arm from the light rack as if it were a large branch.

"Shit!" screamed Paul. "Striker!"

"Paul!"

The big man's head appeared above the railing. He looked down and, for the first time, Paul saw something that could've been fear on the man's scarred face.

"Get me up!" cried Paul.

"I…" Striker shook his head, looked around.

"Hurry! It's not going to hold us much long—"

The tinny rafter's high-pitched wail cut Paul off. It dropped like a drawbridge below Striker. The tracker flew back. Paul saw his arms flapping as they vanished above the rafters.

Sparks exploded and sprinkled down like twinkling snow. The light rack broke, bursting into a loud pop of blue sparks and fire. The platform continued to swing back.

Paul felt his foot come free. He began to plummet again.

The section of platform crashed against the volcano's rim and stopped. The sharp tips of metal stabbed into the cushiony rubber, transforming the falling bridge into a ramp. Paul's back hit the metal and he began to slide down.

Twisting, he looked above him. The volcano's hole was only inches from the top of his head. If he went over the edge, he'd go headfirst into a spinning fan.

NO!

Paul slapped the platform's slick surface. His fingernails scraped metal as he struggled to find purchase. Realizing this wasn't working, he looked up. His eyes landed on his boots. He spread his legs, digging his toes into the inch-high section of wall on the skinny bridge. It didn't stop him, but he felt his speed decrease immensely. Slapping his hands flat on either side of him, he came to a lethargic halt at the end of the platform. His head drooped over the edge. Hot air buffeted his face, threw his hair wildly.

Huffing, Paul swallowed the lump of fear that had formed in his throat. "Shit...shit..." He took a deep breath, unable to comprehend how close to a horrible death he'd come.

A roar from above pulled him away from the shock he felt trying to numb him. Paul forced his hands to move from the platform and grip the raised rim that had saved his life. Holding onto the edges, keeping his toes dug into the sides, he performed a painful sit-up. Then he swung his legs around, felt them dangle over the edge briefly, felt his pants flap against his ankles, felt the hot air blowing his legs.

His boots slapped the metal behind him.

Now he was on his hands and knees, facing forward. His body trembled as he checked the durability of the slanted rafter. It seemed as if it would hold him, the volcano acting as a brace that supported its bulk.

Paul heard another growl. He looked up. Crawling, the Bigfoot was much closer to the top. It reached for the platform that was still intact where the section dipped down. A few more steps would lead it to higher, albeit unstable, ground.

Smoke billowed from down below, most likely from where the lights had landed. It filled the platform with thick swirling walls. A dark shape appeared between the railings like a gatekeeper preventing access.

Striker.

He recognized the big man's mass right away. He also recognized the gigantic rifle that was leveled at the beast's chest.

"Down to us, huh?" Striker asked.

Paul thought he'd been talking to him, but he quickly understood the question had been directed to the Bigfoot.

The Bigfoot loosed something that was part growl and groan. It dropped down to one knee, as if surrendering.

"Look at me," said Striker. "I want to see your face."

Paul watched the beast's head tilt back. It understood Striker, comprehended the order and followed it. Were all Bigfoots like this one?

"See this face before you die," said Striker. "You killed my Papa and now I'm going to kill you."

Striker lowered his head to the rifle. The beast looked away.

Paul waited for the blast.

Click!

Paul jerked as if a grenade had detonated. Another click resounded, then another.

"Shit," muttered Striker.

Paul felt his mouth go slack. The big guy was out of bullets.

Quickly, Striker swung the gun behind him as if it was baseball bat. He brought it down, but the beast was already rising and easily caught it before it connected. Jerking the gun from Striker's hands, it snapped the weapon in half as effortlessly as a pencil. Then it tossed the halves over the edge.

Striker screamed as he pounded the beast with his fists.

Not again!

Paul jerked his Ruger from the holster and trained the sight on the hostile shadows above. The Bigfoot would be an easy target if it was standing still. But it was busy fighting with Striker. If the beast moved, his bullet would tear through the tracker. Like in the cave, he was in a bad situation. Just the slightest error would kill the wrong person.

Paul put the gun away. He wasn't going to hesitate this time. He started climbing. His brother had tried to square off with the monster and had been killed. He didn't want it to happen again.

Going up, Paul didn't take his eyes away from the fight.

The beast grabbed Striker's vest and jerked him off his feet. Holding him up, the beast roared at the man dangling from his burly hand. Striker pounded the Bigfoot's arms, the top of its head, to no avail. What saved his life this time was the vest's ripping up the middle. Striker's arms slipped through the holes and he fell.

This seemed to annoy the beast even more. It roared at the sky and tossed the vest over its shoulder. The heavy garment smacked Paul's chest hard enough to knock him back. He trundled down the incline but was able to stop himself easier this time. Rolling over, he got to one knee and lifted the vest.

Grenades adorned the lapels, the trembling pins making clinking sounds.

He looked up.

Striker ducked a lashing arm, only to meet another that clamped around his throat. His scream was killed, replaced by a choking sound as he was hoisted high. His legs hung before the beast, kicking at its face and missing. The beast shook him from side to side, like a farmer trying to ring a chicken's neck. Striker's legs flew high on one side, shot back down and out the other way.

Screaming, Paul got to his feet. No longer trying to climb, he ran. As if trying to mount a difficult hill, he leaned forward as he ascended. The platform trembled underneath him with each heavy step.

Holding Striker out before him, the beast looked over its shoulder. It spotted Paul and its eyes widened when Paul jerked a grenade from the vest. The pin remained clipped to the garment.

Grenade armed, Paul threw the vest away and jumped. He crashed into the beast's back. It released Striker. Paul curved an arm around its thick hairy throat, holding on as he squirmed up the dingy wall of nappy hair. The Bigfoot reached over its shoulders, swatting and slapping. Paul felt stings on his face and back as he wiggled higher. His shirt was gripped, but he yanked his arm and tore the sleeve.

Paul's stomach flattened against the thick knob of the beast's shoulder. He curled around the back of its neck like a human scarf, bringing his face close to the Bigfoot's. Their eyes met. Feral rage boiled behind the yellow slits.

Paul winked.

Seeing this filled the beast with fury. Paul felt its undulating muscle through his clothes. It opened its mouth to roar.

And Paul shut it up by shoving the grenade into its mouth.

His arm vanished up to the elbow between its rock-like teeth. The beast shook and twisted, like a wet dog trying to dry itself. Paul watched the front of its neck bulge around the grenade lodging in its throat.

Paul jerked his arm back. It was soaked in saliva. He slithered around the beast's neck and tumbled over its front, landing in a squat. His face was level with the tuft of hair that covered its genitals. Tugging out his Ruger, he shoved the barrel into the wild nest of hair, and pulled the trigger.

Red surged through the matted hair as the bullet ripped through its groin. Muffled, the beast's agonized screams rose above the hisses of the electrical fire below and the constant drone of the fan. Keeping one hand on its throat, the beast reached down to its ruined groin with the other. Its fingers came back stringed with thick blood.

It stepped back, feet tangling together.

And fell.

Paul leaned over the edge, watching it roll like a giant hairy boulder down the ramp. Its feet went over the edge first, sliding into the gaping hole of the volcano. Juicy crunches overpowered the beast's cries as blood showered out.

Paul threw his fist into the air and loosed a celebratory cry.

The fan spun and chewed, eating the beast up to its hips. Then it seemed to act as if it was clogged by the beast's meat and locked up.

The fan whined, the motor rumbled.

Pawing at its throat, the beast's eyes were wide and yellow. Paul saw worry through the scabs and hair, pinching its ugly face with deep creases.

Something cracked. And with a screech of metal, the beast was yanked down, vanishing inside a chunky red fountain.

The grenade detonated.

Then the volcano erupted. An explosion of blood, gore, and sinewy chunks launched from the volcano's spherical maw, ejaculating the mess high in a geyser of destruction.

Paul leaned back, holding out his arms and laughed as he was drenched in the Bigfoot's sloppy remains. Chunks splattered around him with sounds like a beef being pounded by a giant hammer. Paul didn't care. To him, he'd been trapped in a prolonged drought, and the beast's blood and innards were the rain to quench his thirst.

A gap of time passed before the last bits of the Bigfoot came down. Still laughing, Paul lowered his head. Blood streamed down his face, sliding under his shirt. He felt more seeping between his buttocks, tickling his anus. Somehow, the spongy mess had even gotten into his shoes. Using two fingers pinched together, he dug mush out of his eyes. He blinked until he could see again.

Then he remembered Striker, and his laughter died.

Paul looked beside him, where he expected to find Striker's dead body.

The spot was empty.

Hobbling around on his knees, he stared down the catwalk. The bars extended outward, vanishing inside the smoke. The platform extended like a long aluminum tongue. Standing where the rafter parted the smoke was Striker. He held a hand to his stomach. His face was streaked in red soppy bits, making his exhausted eyes look very white. His clinging tank top was ripped around a large pectoral muscle.

They stared at each other for several long moments before Striker gave him a terse nod.

Paul returned the gesture.

Then Striker turned around and started walking. The smoke closed behind him like curtains. Paul could no longer see him.

Hopefully you can finally find some peace, Big Guy.

Paul took a deep breath and started coughing when he sucked blood into his nostrils.

A YEAR LATER

Crouching, Paul put the flowers beside the fresh set that was already on the grave. He figured Trish had come into town recently, maybe with the boys, and put them there. Paul felt sad knowing she'd come back and hadn't contacted him. But for her sake, it might be best to keep communication scarce. He probably reminded her too much of Howie, especially now that he wore the sheriff's badge.

"Hey, Howie," said Paul.

He hadn't been here since the funeral and, now, he couldn't help feeling silly for the two words he'd just said. Sighing, he looked up. Tall trees blocked most of the sun. The leaves trembled, making sounds like a baby's rattle as a heavy breeze pushed through them. He shook his head.

You came here to talk, so do it.

Paul saw a blade of grass was taller than the others, so he plucked it out.

"Well, I just got back from helping Gunner move into his apartment. Not surprisingly, I noticed a lot of Megan Caine's belongings were already there. Guess she's going to be a frequent houseguest at Gunner's place. I'm pulling for them, Howie. Really, I am. Seems to be going great now, but around Christmas I thought they were going to call it quits. Guess the shock of everything was fading and neither of them knew how to deal with it."

Paul plopped down on his rump. The grass felt warm through his pants. He removed his ball cap and ran a hand through his sweat-damp hair. He wasn't looking forward to his vacation ending and having to put on that dopey campaign hat again. But it had been Howie's, so really, he didn't mind. It was a little big on his head and sagged over his ears, making them dip out like tiny wings.

"Now they seem to be even closer. I even found some jewelry store pamphlets, with engagement rings circled. So I imagine before long I'll have a daughter-in-law. That'll tickle Natalie. She loves Megan. We all do, really. She's tough, that's for sure. Losing her father and a brother…" Paul's voice suddenly strained. He cleared his throat. "Well…I know what she's been dealing with, what her *and* Max Caine have been dealing with. And it helps to have somebody by your side through dark times who understands. Gunner understands, so they're lucky to have each other. Max is going to marry one of the waitresses from Quincy's. They're opening up a pancake house in town. He has his father's knack for business, that's for sure. And he has somebody too, to help him through the adjusting phase."

He looked over his shoulder. "And so do I."

Becky stood underneath another tree filled with pink blossoms. Pedals fluttered down, landing on the pink carpet around her feet. If she stood there much longer, she might be buried in the lavish flowers. Paul smiled. She looked like an angel as she smiled back at him. She held out her hand and made a shooing gesture. Paul understood she was telling him to keep talking and to stop using her as a distraction not to.

Paul waved, then turned around.

"To be honest, I was the one who brought home those pamphlets. Though I assumed it was Gunner who found them and confiscated them for his own use. Maybe we can have a double-wedding?"

Paul laughed. He liked how it made him feel inside, how it eased the tension making his muscles feel so tight. His vision turned splotchy, and when he rubbed a finger across his eye, he felt moisture.

"Shit," said Paul. "Sorry, Howie. Not meaning to get choked up." Paul took a deep breath to settle his nerves. When he felt like talking again, he said, "The town's doing much better. The new mayor's busting his ass to get things back to normal. The Bigfoot ordeal brought people in from all over. When Becky's book came out last spring, things really boomed. It's not like we're celebrating the Bigfoot, at least not in Caine's way, but we are *embracing* it. The beach will never be Bigfoot Beach, but they are changing the name. To Howie Beach."

Paul laughed.

"I can see you rolling your eyes right now and I have to agree. Goofiest name I've ever heard. But the mayor insisted, so I obliged. Trish was even okay with it. We have a memorial being built to honor the victims and their families. People flock to it, although it's not even close to being finished. Becky has become a hometown celebrity thanks to her book. It was a good read. Even I was amazed by how well-written it was. She was on the morning show last week and made the announcement about the movie they're going to make. I see Matthew McConaughey playing you. Knowing my luck, somebody like Ben Stiller or Vince Vaughn will play me. I bet Striker will be played by Stallone. Speaking of, nobody knows where our Bigfoot expert has disappeared to, but I'm sure he's getting bored. Maybe he's out on another monster hunt somewhere."

Paul's chest felt tingly and hot. His voice had turned thick, as if a bubble had formed in his throat.

"But, Howie, we miss you. And...I'm sorry...you know? For everything. I know I wasn't always the easiest to handle, but you loved me anyway. You are the best brother a guy like me could have and I'm sorry I never told you how much I appreciated everything you did for me. But I'm telling you now."

Paul gave a quick glance back at Becky. She smiled, nodded. Then he looked at his brother's headstone through tear-blurred eyes. He saw Howie's full name, the years of his life below.

"I love you, Howie."

Sitting on the ground above his brother's grave, Paul felt the direction of the wind shift. The grass that had been swaying lazily to the right leaned to the other side as the wind came back and curled around Paul in a delicate swath. Warmth swirled through him as if he'd just swallowed coffee.

Smiling, Paul nodded. Then the wind returned to normal, its direction flowing away from him instead of toward him.

"Thanks, Howie."

Paul approached Becky. Hands in the pockets of her shorts, she smiled. The tree shaded her, but left nets of bouncing light scattered across her smooth skin.

"Say everything you needed to say?" she asked.

"No."

Becky frowned. "Paul."

"If I did, then what would I say when I come back?"

She looked into his eyes and must've seen that he wasn't lying. Her frown smoothed into a pleased expression. "Good. I'm glad to hear it."

"Ready to go?"

She nodded. "Sure. Hungry?"

Paul was and told her so.

"Great," she said. "Let's head over to Quincy's."

"Think our table will be open?"

"Max promised nobody but us would be allowed to sit in it."

"Yeah, but you know Max."

Laughing, Becky threw her hip against him. "Be nice."

"I am. I could've said—"

Becky made a sound like a buzzer. "Don't. Can't say anything nice, don't say anything at all."

Smiling, Paul stayed quiet until they reached Becky's car. She'd replaced the beater with a Mustang. It suited her personality much better.

"But," said Paul, "we better pick up Natalie first."

"Day Camp doesn't stop until five."

"Yeah, I know. But if we get hot dogs without her she'll pound our heads."

Becky laughed. "True."

Inside the car, Becky cranked the A/C on full blast. The air blowing from the vents was hot but quickly cooled.

On their way into town, Paul stared out the window.

Though so much had changed, and his life had been plagued with more misery than he cared to reflect on, he was happy in this moment. For the first time in a year, he almost felt free. Maybe he would sleep through the night for once.

Doubt it.

Though he did feel better, he knew nothing would keep the nightmares away. Nothing would stop him from being shocked awake. Finding himself drenched in gelid sweat, unable to drift back to sleep unless Becky held him tightly and whispered over and over in his ear that it was over.

Holding his breath, Paul fought the cold shakes that were trying to come on. He wanted this good moment to last. They seldom came, and he didn't want it to end.

ABOUT THE AUTHOR

Kristopher Rufty is the author of *The Skin Show, The Lurkers, The Lurking Season, Jagger, Proud Parents,* and many more. He has also written and directed the independent horror films *Psycho Holocaust* and *Rags*. He hosted Diabolical Radio, an internet radio show devoted to horror fiction and film, for five years. But what he's best at is being married to his high school sweetheart and the father of two (soon to be three) crazy children he loves dearly. Together, they reside in North Carolina with their giant dog, Thor, and numerous cats.

For more about Kristopher Rufty, please visit his Website: www.lastkristontheleft.blogspot.com

He can be found on Facebook and Twitter as well.

Printed in Great Britain
by Amazon

83629659R00195